Finding Twigs

Charles Tabb

This is a work of fiction. Names, characters, places, and incidents are either the product of the author's imagination or used fictitiously. Any resemblance to any actual person, living or dead, is entirely coincidental.

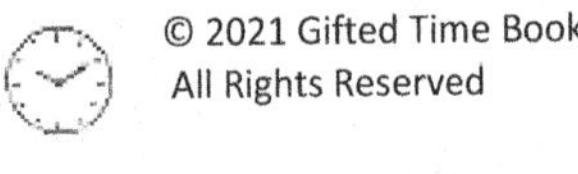

ISBN: 9798746893956

ACKNOWLEDGEMENTS

Thanks are due to my BETA readers, Sue Schorling, Chuck Shelton, Trisha Shelton, Elin Call, and my wife, Dee Tabb. Thanks are also due to my editor, Kristine Elder, who did a phenomenal job. This book would not exist without any of you.

The cover art is by Dane of Ebooklaunch.com.

DEDICATION

For my daughter, Cherisse. May you continue to find your happiness.

OTHER BOOKS BY CHARLES TABB

LITERARY NOVELS:

Floating Twigs
Canaries' Song

THE DETECTIVE TONY PANTERA SERIES:

Hell is Empty
The Purger

COMING IN 2022:

The Whirligig of Time (A Pantera Book)

To arrange personal appearances, often at no charge, go to charlestabb.com and click "CONTACT" in the top banner.

It was the story of how lives are like dominoes in a row. One action has a ripple effect, touching the lives around us, and that thought made me recall the floating twigs of my childhood and the solitary game I had played for the last time in my life during the trial.

–Jack Turner in *Floating Twigs*

"A hero is a man who does what he can."

–Romain Rolland, French Dramatist

1
April 7, 1969

Private First Class Rick Turner trudged through the mud about a hundred kilometers west of Hue, South Vietnam, wishing he was anywhere but there. He'd joined the Marines mostly to get away from a bad home life, leaving his parents and his only brother, Jack, for what he hoped was a life of adventure. While he'd hoped he wouldn't be sent to Vietnam to fight in a war he considered senseless, this is what the U.S. government paid him to do, so he had to do it. Besides, not fighting would lead to certain death. Killing was a matter of self-defense now.

It had rained the night before. March wasn't part of the monsoon season there, but it wasn't as if no rainfall existed outside of the mid-autumn months when rain was nearly constant. Now, he and the platoon of men he fought beside were on their way to a bridge the U.S. military had decided was important enough to sacrifice lives to hold.

Still, he'd been thankful he hadn't arrived during the Tet Offensive, which some of the other Marines said was much worse than what they endured now. The effects from the offensive could be seen everywhere. What remained of many buildings in Hue still dotted the landscape like dinosaur bones. The citizens there had the hollow-eyed look of people used to death and destruction. Rick hoped he would never have that look.

The rain had stopped, and the sun now beat on Rick with the same fierce determination of the Viet Cong during Tet. The muck slowed their progress, so instead of reaching their destination that morning as originally expected, they would arrive sometime in the early afternoon.

What they were doing now was dangerous but necessary. They had come upon a treeless field that stretched a mile in each direction. They would need to cross it, exposed, to reach the bridge six kilometers ahead. Sergeant Lennon, the platoon commander, had chosen this route because of a lack of roads and, presumably, a lack of the Viet Cong. They were strictly on foot, so Lennon chose this middle-of-nowhere route to avoid roads.

Rick was nervous about crossing this emptiness. No trees grew where they marched, just some brush that lay close to the ground. This lack was either from napalm's assault or just the whims of nature, so there would be no cover if they were attacked. A stand of trees several hundred yards wide and about the same distance from where they now slogged through the mud and brush would be the first cover available to them since leaving the cover of the trees, which were now about a hundred yards behind them.

Their position would be easy pickings for a sniper, Rick thought.

As if signaled by that thought, Darwell, one of the young men in front of him, keeled over as if his bones had suddenly been removed, followed almost simultaneously by the distant thunder of the sniper's shot from behind.

"Everyone down!" Lennon shouted, as the men fell face forward into the mud, holding their weapons up to prevent them from being swathed with the thick muck.

Rick swiveled to face the stand of trees they'd left a few moments before and stared at them, hoping to see a flash if the sniper fired again. Minutes dragged by until Sergeant Lennon said, "Alright, we need to belly crawl the rest of the way across this godforsaken field! A to M forward first, N to Z covering."

Rick understood this to mean that everyone whose last name began with A through M would crawl for about twenty yards or so and turn to cover those with last names beginning with N to Z while they moved to a point about twenty yards beyond the A to M's. They would more or less leapfrog each other until they reached the tree line they had been marching toward.

One of the Marines stopped to check on Darwell and called out, "He's dead, Sarge!" They would radio their position to allow a chopper to retrieve the body later.

When the shout of "N to Z's forward!" came, Rick turned to crawl through the mud to a new position beyond the first wave.

A sudden blow to his body felt like a dozen horses had stomped on him. He screamed out in pain and shock. He was hit. His right hip felt as though it had exploded.

"Turner?!" Corporal Rodenberg, or Roddie, one of his buddies, called out from his right. "You hit?"

"Yeah," he managed.

"How bad?"

"Don't know."

"Where were you hit? Body? Legs?"

"My right hip."

Silence followed as the pain radiated out from his lower back until another shot and another scream rang out.

For a moment, Rick wondered if Roddie had been hit, but he heard his buddy shout again. "You still there, Turner?"

"Yeah." Rick said, though no longer able to shout. He wondered vaguely if Roddie could hear him.

"Hang on, Buddy!"

Rick could hear Roddie moving through the muck and the stubby brush toward him. The last thing to cross his mind before losing consciousness was a memory of throwing a football with his little brother, Jack, who had turned thirteen the previous October, and the thought he would never see him again.

2

March 18, 1992

Jack Turner sat in his new office, wondering if the move home to Denton, Florida, from New Orleans was the best decision. He had inherited the house where the man who had been a surrogate father, Hank Moreland, had lived until his death eighteen months ago, and after spending the time since wondering why he wasn't living there, he had decided to return. He had made the move nearly two months ago, in late January, after the calendar turned over to 1992.

Of course, frequent letters from Mrs. Dawson, the eccentric woman who had also helped raise him, had contributed to his decision, but he had left a fairly busy law practice to set up shop here. He wanted clients, but his name was not well-known in legal circles, at least not yet.

His bank balance was still more than healthy, the result of his inheritance and his hard work as a criminal defense attorney in New Orleans, but he was eager to work. His sense of self, like that of most adults, was tied to his view of how his work contributed to the world.

He had become a member of the Florida bar, and he hoped to at least receive some work through the Public Defender's Office.

Looking down at his latest canine companion, he said, “How about you, Brinkley? Been arrested lately?”

Brinkley wagged his tail, raising it from the floor where he lay with his head resting on his paws, letting it thump twice against the thin carpet before he went back to snoozing since his human’s unenthusiastic voice told him that was all that was expected.

Being back in Denton, which had grown from a small village to a bustling tourist town since his childhood, had brought back the memories of that time, just as it had when he’d returned after many years to attend Hank’s funeral.

Now, however, the memories tended to center on his brother, Rick, who had joined the Marines when Jack was twelve and hadn’t been heard from since.

Mostly, he wondered if Rick was alive. Jack knew he’d been sent to Vietnam, but beyond that, he knew nothing. He didn’t know if he died over there, if he’d moved to another country entirely, or if he’d returned to the states and settled somewhere else.

Their parents had not been the best, though certainly not the worst. They had been alcoholics who were more interested in their drinks than their sons, and Rick had decided never to return home after joining the Marines. Jack had received one letter from him when he was shipping off to ’Nam, but nothing since.

The thought had been gnawing at him to search for Rick. Jack wanted to know what had become of him, and if he was now the only survivor from his family. He had no children and had never been married. He was happy with just himself and whichever dog served as his companion, or at least that's what he told himself.

Jack had owned a dog since finding his first dog, Bones, on a deserted stretch of beach. He had mourned Bones's death and hadn't owned another until finishing his undergraduate degree. After graduation he adopted another dog after realizing he didn't feel complete without one.

Brinkley, a hound-shepherd mix, was the third dog he'd owned since Bones had died. Speckles, a hound mix who'd been covered in small spots like freckles, had died of cancer after three years, followed by Rocky, a German shepherd mix that he'd had for eight years. Brinkley had been with him for a little over three years now. Jack adopted all his dogs from shelters, and Brinkley was still a puppy when Jack brought him home, no more than four months old.

His dogs had been one reason Jack never wanted to work for a firm again. Firms rarely allowed their attorneys to bring a dog to work, and Jack would not go to work without his dog.

His first job in New Orleans was with an old firm there. One of the partners, Mr. Rayburn, had stopped in his office one day, supposedly to chat about how things were coming along but really to talk about Speckles.

"It's not a seeing-eye dog. You aren't blind, right?"

"Of course not."

"Didn't think so. If you were, you wouldn't be working here. We don't hire blind lawyers."

"So, you're saying I can't bring my dog to work? She doesn't bother anyone. She's house broken."

"I don't care if she can file and type. I see the dog here again, and I will personally wrap a rope around her neck and toss her carcass in the dumpster."

Jack had resigned on his way out the door that afternoon and opened his own office. A risky thing for a rookie lawyer, but he'd made ends meet by working with the Public Defender's office, taking on indigent clients who couldn't afford attorneys. The state paid him a modest sum as a state-appointed attorney, barely enough to qualify as minimum wage when the hours working on the cases were considered, sometimes not that much, but it was pay, and he took it gladly.

Now, he was in a position to do whatever he wanted. Hank had left him more than comfortable, and because the home he had inherited was paid for, he had little in the way of expenses.

As he sat there, thinking of Rick, he wondered if he might take some time off soon to see if he could find him. He could begin with a Department of Defense inquiry to see if he died or was M.I.A. If he'd survived the war, perhaps Jack could find him.

Of course, he could afford a private detective to search for Rick, but Jack felt the need to invest the time himself. After all, assuming he was still alive, Rick was his only living relative. If he had returned and died later, at least Jack could visit his grave.

Jack made a kissing sound and patted his knee. Brinkley stood, wagging his tail and offering his head for a good scratching behind the ears, closing his eyes at the pleasure of it.

"What d'ya say, boy? Are you up for a trip this summer? Don't know where we might go. Depends on where the trail leads, but I have to find my brother."

Jack took Brinkley's silence as a yes. "Great, boy. It'll be a new adventure."

At that moment, his office phone rang. The new caller ID system on his phone read, "Public Defender."

"Well, maybe I'll have some work to do while we wait to start that adventure, huh, boy?"

He answered, "Jack Turner."

"Mr. Turner, this is Jenny Walton with the Public Defender's Office. How are you today?"

"Looking for work. Do you have some?"

"Yes. Judge Shelton has assigned you to take a case." Jack smiled. Judge Shelton was Trisha Shelton, who had been an attorney for Hank when he was accused of molesting Jack as a boy. The reasons the authorities hadn't believed Jack when he insisted nothing happened ranged from simply not believing a child to downright prejudice. Chuck Shelton, her husband, still practiced law in the county, but his cases were never heard before his wife to avoid any possibility of a conflict of interest. Recusal wasn't required, but Trisha always made sure Chuck did not appear before her in a case.

"What the public doesn't understand is that I'd probably be harder on him, not easier," she had said with a laugh when they had invited Jack to dinner a few weeks after he'd arrived in Denton.

Denton and Wharton, the larger town about six miles to the east of Denton, were large enough to be able to avoid Chuck being on Trisha's docket, but the fact was the judges and lawyers all knew each other, some rather well. It wasn't unusual for an attorney to present a case before a judge all week and go fishing or play golf with the judge after the case was settled.

Still, Trisha set a boundary on family members arguing before her. She was a stickler about appearances.

"Look at you and Hank," she'd said. "You were just spending time with him, talking, and how'd that turn out? Appearances are everything to people. It's reality that gets the short end of the stick."

"Mostly because reality isn't as interesting," Chuck had said.

Jack continued the conversation with Jenny. "What's the case?"

"It's a big one. Armed robbery."

"That's pretty big."

"Yeah. She chose you for the case. I hear the defendant wasn't too happy about it, though."

"Oh? Why not?"

"He must know you."

"What's his name?"

"Thomas Gordon."

Jack sat back in his seat. Tommy Gordon had been Denton's chief bully when Jack was growing up. They had had numerous run-ins, most of them ending badly. Tommy had even committed perjury as a witness at Hank's trial to try to bring a conviction for no other reason than he hated Jack.

"Yeah, he knows me. We grew up together."

"Really? I didn't know you were from here," Jenny said. "I just thought you moved here from somewhere and set up shop to be near the beach."

"Nope. I just decided to move back home."

"Well, I'd like to move to New York or something. The men around here are all air force. Too much machismo for my tastes."

Jack wondered if she might be flirting but decided she probably wasn't. He'd seen her several times before in the Public Defender's office located in the courthouse annex, where she worked as a clerk. He had even considered asking her out. He hadn't because he had never felt comfortable asking out women he thought would never accept a date with him. He thought of her as too pretty for a nerdy guy like him.

Once a nerd, always a nerd, Jack thought to himself. Thinking, what the heck, he said, "Not all of us are loaded with machismo."

She actually giggled. "I guess some guys have more than they think they do."

That cinched it. She was definitely flirting. She was perhaps a few years younger than he was and took care of herself. Maybe he should ask her out.

He glanced down at Brinkley, as if he could provide an answer. Deciding to put off asking for a date until he could consider the situation, he said, "Well, I don't pay attention to guys, so I wouldn't know."

An awkward silence lasted a few seconds before he asked, “Is he in jail or did he make bond?”

“Who?”

“Tommy Gordon.”

“Oh!” She laughed loudly, probably out of embarrassment. “Yes, he’s in jail.” Then composing herself, she asked, “I take it you two weren’t best friends?”

“Anything but.”

“I guess Judge Shelton didn’t know that.”

“Oh, she knew alright. I’m just wondering why she put me on this case knowing what she does.”

“Well, all I know is she assigned you the case.”

“Yeah, well, I guess I should go see him.”

“You want me to fax over the basics from his file?”

“Sure.”

Another silence. “Jack?”

“Yes?”

“The jail’s across the street from here.”

“Yes, I know where the jail is.”

“I was just wondering if maybe after you see him, you might want to grab a bite of lunch somewhere?”

Stunned again, Jack was speechless for a moment. She was asking him out instead.

“Uh, sure. Why not?”

“I take lunch at 12:30. I’ve no plans for today unless you count the ham sandwich and sliced cucumber I brought.”

“Today?”

“Well, you know what they say, ‘no time like

the present.' How about it? I mean, you really should see him today, right?"

Jack glanced at his watch. It was closing on ten. "Yes, I suppose I should, though to be honest, I'm not looking forward to seeing him. See you at 12:30," he said.

"Okay. See you then!" she said and hung up.

He wondered why he felt like a teenager after the call ended, then decided it was because he was not used to asking women out, and he certainly wasn't used to being asked out. Yes, it was only lunch, but she had made it clear she wouldn't mind making it dinner and a movie one day soon.

After taking Brinkley for a quick walk, Jack put him in the small kennel he kept at the office. While Brinkley didn't mind the kennel, he certainly didn't love it, so Jack apologized.

"Sorry, boy. No dogs allowed at the jail, not to mention wherever I'm going for lunch."

His fax machine hummed and began spitting out pages from Tommy's file. When he looked at them, he found Tommy had been in prison before, which didn't surprise him. He'd been convicted on a number of drug charges and assault, as well as burglary. This would result in his third stint if convicted, which seemed likely, based on the facts of the case he read.

As he drove to see his combination old enemy and new client, he wondered if Jenny knew where she wanted to eat, or if he should come up with a place. He decided Perry's, a small bistro near the courthouse, would be okay if it turned out he was expected to decide. He still felt like a kid who was going on his first date ever.

Arriving at the jail, he went inside and stepped up to the counter to check in. His knowledge about the crime was scant. He wasn't sure what he was getting into and decided to ask Trisha Shelton why he'd been handed this case. He wanted to know that more than he wanted lunch with Jenny Walton, which once he considered it, was quite a lot.

3

As Jack entered one of the small rooms reserved for lawyers to talk to their clients, he sat down and waited while the jailer brought Tommy from lockup. The man who entered in the standard issue, thin blue jumpsuit was only a few years older than Jack but looked much older. He'd obviously lived a hard life. Hand-drawn prison tattoos lined his forearms. His hair, once tar black, was lighter and gray-streaked. His face was hard and worn, his skin rough from years of exposure to the sun and etched with lines that accented what appeared to be a permanent frown. The jailer locked Tommy into the manacles that were anchored to the table which, like the chairs, was bolted to the floor.

Tommy's first greeting was a profanity-laced tirade in which he called Jack every bad name he could think of.

"Not a very smart way to greet your public defender, Tommy," Jack said. "Like it or not, I'm the one who's been pegged to represent you, and while I won't enjoy a minute of it, I intend to do my job."

"I don't go by 'Tommy' anymore. I'm just 'Tom' now. Tommy's a kid's name."

Jack pictured the man who sat across from him as he looked when he was sixteen and realized with surprise that he was indeed just a kid back then. When Jack was thirteen, Tommy had seemed more like an adult to him. A mean one, but an adult nonetheless. "I'll try to remember that," Jack said, "but I make no promises. Old habits die hard."

"Whatever."

"You're charged with third-degree armed robbery."

"Yeah, I know what I'm charged with."

"Care to tell me what happened?"

"Not really."

"I can't defend you if you don't assist in your defense. If that's the way it will be, you might as well have pled guilty."

"Don't matter if I'm guilty or not. They'll find me guilty anyway. It ain't like I never been in prison. Jury can take one look at me and decide that much. If I been there before, I must be guilty now, right?"

"The attorney who stood with you at arraignment—did you tell him this?"

"Wasn't a him, it was a her. No need to tell her anything. I just said not guilty because I ain't. They got the wrong guy this time."

Jack did his best not to look skeptical, but didn't do well at it.

"Yeah, I know you don't believe me. I don't care."

"The file says you entered a convenience store at approximately ten o'clock on the evening of Saturday, February 27, while wearing a Halloween mask. You pulled out a small handgun you owned illegally because you're a convicted felon and demanded the clerk give you the money in the cash register as well as put two cartons of cigarettes and a twelve-pack of beer in bags. The clerk complied, you shot your revolver into the ceiling for some insane reason, and you ran out the door. You were subsequently questioned when they found your fingerprints at the scene, and an anonymous tip came in. With suspicion raised because of your past legal problems, a search warrant was issued and resulted in finding your handgun, a .22 caliber. Ballistics matched your gun to the one that you fired into the ceiling."

"Someone musta borrowed my gun without me knowing. That's probably the 'anonymous source.' And I've been in that store plenty of times, so of course my prints were there."

Jack looked at Tommy, now Tom, and said, "I'm going to give you the best defense I can, but I have to tell you it won't be much because of the evidence against you. My main attempt will center around trying to have the charges reduced so you don't spend the maximum amount of time in prison."

Tom leaned forward. "I know you will never believe I didn't rob this place. Oh, I've done a lot of bad things in my life, maybe even robbed some people, but I didn't do this one. I also know you have a problem with me because of what I did when I was a kid, but that judge won't let me change lawyers. I figure she just wants to get back at me for beatin' the snot outa you when we were kids. She was the old guy's lawyer and probably has had it in for me ever since I lied on the stand." Jack sat back when Tom confessed to perjury. "Yeah, I'm admitting I lied. It ain't as if you didn't know it. But it wasn't me who suggested I make up that story. I ain't sayin' who it was cause he's still around and I don't want anyone takin' revenge on him, too."

"I'm not interested in revenge. What happened when we were young is water under the bridge now. Judge Shelton isn't interested in revenge either."

"Whatever you say," Tom sneered. "But I'm still not happy with you as my lawyer. I asked the judge to give me a different one, but she wouldn't do it. So I guess I'm stuck with you."

Jack gathered his papers and returned them to his briefcase. "And I'm stuck with you," he said as he rose and walked to the door.

"Done in here!" he shouted into the hallway, and a jailer came into the room to let Jack leave and to return Thomas Gordon to his cell.

Walking across the street, Jack entered the building that served as the courthouse annex in Denton. Entering the Public Defender's Office where Jenny worked, he stepped over to her desk and said hello.

"Hey, Jack! You're early," she said. "I don't get off for lunch for another fifteen minutes."

"That's fine. Is Judge Shelton around?"

"She'll either be in court or in her chambers."

"Okay. I think I'll step down there to see if I can talk to her for a second. I'll be back in fifteen, okay?"

"Sure."

He looked back at her as he walked away and asked, “Is Perry’s okay for lunch?”

She smiled. “Sure beats that sandwich I brought.”

Jack walked down a hallway to Courtroom B, Trisha’s courtroom. As he entered, he saw only Trisha’s clerk.

“Is Judge Shelton around?”

“She’s in her chambers having lunch. Should I give her a message?”

“Would you tell her Jack is here to see her?”

“Okay. Just ‘Jack’?”

“Yes. She’ll know who it is.”

He stepped through the back door that led to Trisha’s chambers and returned a moment later. “She said you can come in.”

Jack walked behind the bench and entered a narrow hallway that ran behind the courtrooms. Trisha’s chambers were directly across the hall from the door that led into the courtroom.

He knocked lightly and heard Trisha answer. “Come on in, Jack!”

As he entered, she laid the fork she was using to eat her salad aside and stood, holding her arms out for a hug. A handshake would never be good enough for Trisha when it came to Jack. She saw him as an adopted son more than anything else.

“How you been?” she asked, as if they hadn’t seen each other just a few days ago at the Shelton’s home in Wharton.

“Doing okay. I have a question I wanted to ask you.”

“Ask away.”

"Why did you put me on Tom Gordon's case?"

"Well, first I knew you could use the work if not the money."

"And second?"

"Given your past with him, I knew that you would give him the best defense possible to put the lie to any suggestions you didn't."

"Does someone think I might not do my best in a case?"

"No, but we don't want those rumors getting started, either. Anyone in the profession would be able to look at what you do for him and decide you didn't hold a grudge against possibly the worst person you knew as a boy."

Jack sighed, shaking his head.

"You're not going to ask me to remove you, are you? Because the answer's no. It's my job to make sure a public defender is assigned that I know will represent the accused with integrity and a devotion to the job. If I'm asked, I can give a good reason for tapping you for the job instead of someone else."

"Seems to me you'd choose someone else to avoid the scrutiny."

"Sometimes scrutiny is a good thing. It forces us to be as good as we can be and provides proof of our loyalty to a client, regardless of the past."

"He thinks we're both out to get him."

"He thinks a lot of misguided thoughts. I suspect he may say you did a bad job as his attorney one day. Let him. I'm confident your advocacy for him will withstand the tightest scrutiny."

"Well, I guess it's not a big news case. I think he's guilty of the charge."

"That's what makes this interesting. You'll defend him regardless."

"He swears he didn't do it."

"Both the guilty and the innocent say that."

"The weird thing is I think he believes it."

"Maybe he was stoned when he robbed the place and doesn't remember."

"Aren't you supposed to be impartial as well?"

"Yes, but the truth is when the case is pretty well open and shut, even judges aren't stupid. In any case, I will have to make my decisions without prejudice, and I will. Not an easy case for me, either, you know. He was a chief witness in Hank's case, and it's possible some scrutiny will come my way, too. But I can take it. You can, too."

"He admitted to committing perjury against Hank. Surprised me that he admitted it as if he were telling me he'd had two cups of coffee this morning instead of only one."

"Well, we've known that for years."

"Yes, but he said someone else put him up to it. Wouldn't say who because, as he put it, 'he's still around.' He thought we might try to take some sort of revenge on that person."

"Someone put him up to it?" Trisha asked.

"Yeah. I have my suspicions as to who it might be."

"Who?"

"Officer Hicks. He's chief now, even if I have no idea how that could have happened."

"Politics, Jack. Workplace politics. His brother's on the force, too. I know you remember Carl."

Jack stood to leave. "How could I forget?" He shook his head. "Politics. Reminds me why I'm so happy to work in a one-man outfit."

She chuckled, rising again for a goodbye hug. "And this conversation was about you inviting Chuck and me to dinner at your place this Sunday evening. We don't need people thinking we were talking about a case, even though nothing we said is a problem. But as I said, people think the worst."

"You're coming to dinner Sunday?"

"Why thank you for asking, Jack. We'd love to. Say around six? That way we can chat for a bit before sitting down to eat."

A thought occurred to him. "Would it be okay if I have a date there as well?"

"Besides Brinkley? Sure! Is there someone we don't know about?"

"Maybe," he said with a smile. "It depends on how lunch today goes, I guess."

Leaving the chambers, he exited back through the courtroom, thanking the clerk as he left. Walking towards the Public Defender's Office, he wondered what he and Jenny would talk about at lunch. He didn't want to talk about the case—or any case for that matter. He suddenly saw himself at a loss for words, the lunch growing more awkward by the second, and he prayed conversation wouldn't lag.

When he stepped up to her desk, she met him with that same happy smile. He reminded himself that she had asked him out, so the interest was definitely mutual.

"I hear you're a good friend of Judge

Shelton's," she said by way of greeting as she gathered her coat and purse.

"Where did you hear that?"

"Through the grapevine."

"Which grapevine?"

"The most reliable one around. The courthouse grapevine."

"Reliable? I doubt that," he said.

"Sometimes it's dead on," she answered as they left, turning right to walk to Perry's.

"Maybe you're right. Yes, we go back a ways."

"Did you get in trouble and your parents had to hire an attorney?"

"No, nothing like that. She and her husband represented a friend of mine. An older man who more or less raised me."

"What happened to your parents?"

He wasn't sure he wanted to get into that over lunch. Talking about such personal subjects on a first date might make a second one unlikely.

"Disinterested, mostly." He tried to make his tone reveal an effort to dismiss the topic and was happy that it worked, or maybe the fact of his parents' disinterest was something she didn't want to talk about over lunch either.

After ordering their food, she asked, "What did you talk to Judge Shelton about?"

Jack didn't want to lie to her, but he also didn't want to advertise the reason they'd met.

"Nothing special," he said. "As you pointed out, she's been a friend since I was thirteen."

"Okay. Point taken. One thing about you attorneys, you don't share much information."

"Well, it's sort of part of the job, you know. That attorney-client privilege thing is important. Breaking it can lead to disbarment in some cases." He paused as he remembered he had mentioned he might have a date for dinner Sunday.

"One thing we talked about was having them for dinner this Sunday. Would you care to join us?"

Her smile widened. "A second date? You work fast, Jack Turner."

"Well, it's just dinner with friends."

She giggled. "No need to be embarrassed. I'd be happy to come. I just need to know where you live and what time to be there."

"428 Kelly Avenue. Six o'clock would be fine."

Taking a sip of her iced tea, she said, "Don't be surprised if I'm a little early."

Changing the subject, he said, "So what about you? Where did you grow up?"

"Mostly everywhere. My dad was in the navy. We were stationed in Pensacola when I became a teenager and I loved it here. The area's so beautiful. When I grew up, I decided to live in the area. I chose Denton because it has a small town feel."

"Where's your dad now?"

"Up in Washington. He's civil service now, still working for the military."

"Washington?"

"Yep. Veteran's Affairs."

Jack thought of his brother. "My brother, Rick, was in the Marines. Vietnam."

"Oh? Where is he now?" He could tell by her tone she was hoping Rick hadn't died in the war.

"Actually, I have no idea. I was thinking just today that I needed to see if I could find him."

"Maybe my dad could help with that."

"That would be nice," he said just as the waiter brought their lunch. The aromas made his mouth water.

They continued chatting as they ate, and by the time he had escorted Jenny back to work, he was glad they'd spent the time together. He liked her and found he was looking forward to Sunday.

4

That afternoon, Jack went over the complete file on Tom Gordon that Jenny had given him after their lunch. The file added little to what she'd called the basics that she'd faxed him. He'd been convicted twice before, and his next conviction would likely lead to additional time, giving him habitual offender status. If Jack had been told this would happen in Tom's life when they were kids, he wouldn't have been surprised at all.

The next day on his way to work, Jack stopped at the jail again to speak with him about his case. When they were seated with Tom handcuffed to the table, he told his new client how this charge would likely turn out.

"Because this would be your third conviction, that will probably add some time to your stretch."

"What for?"

"You'll be sentenced under the category of habitual offender. That tends to happen when you are a third time offender."

"How much time?"

"Can't say. Maybe two years. Maybe more. Robbing a store with a handgun and firing a round into the ceiling is a big deal."

"Yeah, yeah. That's one problem with having

you as my lawyer. Our past keeps you from believing me when I say I didn't do it."

"Tom, they found the gun that shot the bullet into the roof in the trailer where you live. If you had a roommate, maybe you could cast some doubt as to whether you or the roommate is guilty, but you don't."

"I have friends over all the time. Maybe one of them borrowed my gun and returned it a day or two after holding up the store."

Jack thought of Trisha's confidence that he would do his best because of their past to avoid anyone being able to prove otherwise. "Okay. Tell me who else might have done this."

"This guy named Phillip who comes over sometimes looks a lot like me. Same hair color, same kind of beard. I wouldn't put it past him to do this. He's—what do you call it?—an opportunist. If he saw my gun, he'd think about doing that."

"Sounds like good friends you have there."

"He's just someone I know."

Jack checked the paperwork in the file, specifically the arrest report, which contained Tom's statement. He wanted to make sure his memory of what he'd read was correct. "You told the same thing to the police, and they checked it out. Your friend Phillip couldn't have done it. He was locked up for drunk and disorderly that night."

"Maybe it was someone else."

"How many people knew you had the gun?"

"I dunno. Maybe ten."

"How many of those ten might have taken your gun and replaced it?"

"All of 'em."

"How many of those ten are women?"

"Why would that matter? Women rob stores too, you know."

"Because the person who robbed the store was obviously a man. Beard, man's voice. Couldn't be a woman."

"Oh. Yeah. Well, I know three women who come over on a regular type basis."

"So that leaves six if you don't count Phillip. How many of those would not have done this?"

"Zero."

"So everyone you hang out with is capable of armed robbery? Again, what nice friends you have. Be thinking about it until I see you again tomorrow. Try to narrow it down to just three at the most."

"Are you here to judge my choice of friends or get me outa here?"

"If you mean getting you out of jail until your trial, that's not going to happen unless you have enough to make bail, which is $50,000. That would cost you $5,000 for a bondsman since I'm pretty sure you don't have the full fifty grand stuffed in a mattress somewhere."

"I mean outa this problem."

"I'll do what I can, but there's not much hope in getting you off completely. The best I can probably do is get the sentence reduced and maybe avoid having you sentenced under the habitual offender statute. As for judging who you choose for friends, I apologize. It isn't your fault you were raised with a different interpretation as to what a friend is."

Tom's face grew hard. "You saying my parents didn't raise me right?"

Jack stood to leave, knowing they would get no further today. As he put his paperwork in his briefcase and closed the latches, he asked, "Are you saying they did? Look around you, Tom, and ask yourself how much of this is because you were never taught to make better decisions."

Jack watched as Tom's eyes changed from menacing to surprised, possibly even hurt, before flashing to anger. As Jack left the room, angry, profanity-laced shouts followed him down the hall. Jack knew he had hit a nerve with his old enemy. As some might say, the truth hurts. Jack had seen the recognition in Tom of how right Jack was a split second before the anger took over.

Because of their history, Jack felt that Tom Gordon belonged in the category of those people who were jealous of how other people lived. They would see people they considered happier than they were and want that life. The problem was they lacked the emotional tools necessary to make the change. That involved recognizing where they were wrong in their thinking. Given their belief they had been wronged by society rather than having an understanding they were responsible for their lot in life, these sad souls were almost never able to make that leap from unhappy to contented.

A life of walking in and out of prison wasn't the case every time for people like Tom, of course. Some people recognized their own part in making the bad decisions they made, often as a result of getting therapy or having something happen that changed their thinking. This usually led to becoming capable of changing their lives.

Those in the category where Jack placed Tom continued believing that if they could get the money or force love from someone or be looked up to by others without having to change themselves, they would find the happiness others seemed to have and enjoy. But Jack knew that money derived by illegal means was a reminder of how bad a person was and, of course, could never buy happiness anyway. Besides, love and admiration could never be forced from someone, only subjugation, resulting in hatred instead.

For those like Tom, it was a sad way to live, and down deep, Jack was pained at the incapacity for real happiness, which ultimately lay in people's feelings about themselves. Those feelings were always not as good as they pretended when around others. Down deep, they all knew they would never be happy, but were unable to understand exactly why or how to change that. It was the definition of a vicious cycle, the most vicious of all.

Arriving back at his office, Jack was greeted by Brinkley, who could not contain his excitement after being left alone for over an hour. Jack felt that people could learn a lot from dogs. Their love was always total and required nothing from their owners. It wasn't really love, it was adoration and total devotion. They were the creatures that Jack felt God had placed in their care so humans could understand what adoration truly was. Jack knew that when he was away from Brinkley, his dog's thoughts never strayed from waiting for the moment

Jack arrived back in Brinkley's presence. Of course, there were momentary distractions, but his entire being was focused on Jack's return. If people could feel that way about each other, starvation and wars would end. The fact that dog was God spelled backwards seemed appropriate, though the word's origins had nothing to do with that. It was just a lucky happenstance.

"Hey, boy! Ready to go for a walk?"

Brinkley knew the word and reacted as Jack expected.

Grabbing the leash from the hook near the door, Jack snapped it on Brinkley's collar, locked the door, and walked down the street, his dog strolling beside him and matching Jack's pace despite Brinkley's obvious desire to move faster.

They arrived at a beachside park, and Jack took him for a walk down the beach and back. When they arrived back at his office, he was surprised to see Chuck Shelton waiting outside.

Brinkley greeted Chuck by wagging his entire back half, as if his tail weighed a hundred pounds and, when wagged, would pull his hips along with it. Chuck squatted beside the dog and accepted the dog kisses that would continue for as long as Chuck allowed them.

"Hey, Brinkley, boy! Miss me?"

"Of course he did, but don't let it go to your head. He misses me if I'm away from him for five minutes," Jack said in greeting, offering his hand for Chuck to shake. "So what brings you to the distinctive offices of Turner and Brinkley?"

"Just wanted to chat a bit. I was in town on

some business and figured I'd stop in. Busy?"

"No more than usual, which means not at all."

"Well, then, let's step inside and have a cup of java."

Jack opened the door and after unhooking the leash from Brinkley's collar, signaled Chuck to follow into his office. Brinkley went straight for his water dish and began to slurp.

Chuck laughed. "He looks thirstier than I am after a bike ride." Chuck liked to ride his expensive bike on journeys that sometimes went as far as fifty miles round trip.

Jack started a pot of coffee as Chuck relaxed into one of the two chairs that faced Jack's desk. Jack chose to sit in the other client chair to keep the conversation informal.

"Well, I made a decision," Chuck said.

"Which decision is that?"

"Going to run for state senate."

"You're already president of the Florida Bar Association. That's not good enough for you?"

"A mere stepping stone."

"Why would you want that hassle? Seems the politicians are just a target for people who want to blame someone for bad things that happen."

"Well, as a state senator, I might be able to make a real difference. Help the district as we struggle toward the 21st century."

The pot finished brewing, and Jack poured two cups, handing one to Chuck.

"Is Reed running for re-election?" Jack asked. Bobby Reed had been the district's state senator for the past ten years, having taken over in the middle of the former state senator's term when he had to resign.

"Nope. Wide open field. I'm going to campaign on how it's time for a change."

"What, exactly, would you do that's different?"

"Listen to people for one. Bobby hasn't really listened to his constituents for the past six years, at least."

"Well, good luck. You have my vote." Jack raised his cup in a silent toast, and Chuck did the same.

"Thank you. I'll be filing the paperwork on Monday."

"Does Trisha know?"

"What makes you think I'd make this decision without her input? Do I look like a fool?"

Jack laughed. "Just checking to make sure you hadn't suddenly become mentally incapacitated. Couldn't vote for you if you had."

"Why would I want to make the world's most amazing woman mad at me? It took enough to get her to say 'I do.' I don't want to mess that up."

"I envy you for that."

"Everyone does," Chuck said and sipped his coffee. "Speaking of amazing women, Trisha tells me you invited us for dinner Sunday and you might have a date there."

"News does travel fast."

"Especially when you live with the person sharing the news."

"Yes, as a matter of fact, I will have a date there. She accepted my invitation yesterday at lunch."

"Could this be something serious brewing?" Chuck asked with a smile.

"It's a second date, Chuck, not an engagement party. And the first date was just lunch, not dinner and a movie with drinks after."

"Sunday will be the dinner with drinks after. Maybe you could do the movie for the third date."

"If there is a third date," Jack said.

"Don't be cynical. She could actually like you."

"I think she does, considering she accepted the dinner invitation. Things can change quickly though. What if she doesn't like dogs?"

"Then run from her as fast as you can. No woman could ever be happy around you if she doesn't like dogs."

"True dat," Jack replied, using an expression popular in New Orleans. "Not to mention I don't trust anyone who doesn't like dogs."

"Why don't you invite Ms. Dawson to the dinner, too? She could get a take on your date and advise you."

"I'd rather hold off on that. As I said, it's not anyone special, just a date. I'm sure Mrs. Dawson will give me advice on this eventually. I may even ask for it."

"She's more your mother than your natural mother was. You have to give her the right to advise you. It's the law of Nature."

"True, but not for a while, yet. As I said, it's just a second date."

"About time you settled down with a good woman. I've had nothing but wonderful times with Trisha."

"You two have argued. I've seen it."

"All couples argue. It's part of living under the same roof. You know that. The secret is to love someone, not just like them a lot. I love her more than breathing."

"Yeah. I know."

"And you know what makes our relationship work?"

"What?"

"She loves me more than breathing too."

Brinkley wandered into the office and lay at Jack's feet. Jack reached down to scratch him behind the ears while Brinkley raised his head to try to keep the hand there.

"Brinkley loves me more than breathing."

"Of course he does. He's a dog."

They sat sipping their coffee, refilling once. Finally, Jack asked Chuck, "You remember I have a brother?"

"Yeah, I remember."

"At least I hope I have a brother. It could be 'had' instead."

"What about him?"

"I'm thinking about looking for him. See if he's still alive. Meet him if he is."

"Seeing as how he's never come home, what makes you think he wants to be found?"

"Maybe he doesn't, but I want to find him anyway."

"That's fine," Chuck said, "but don't be surprised if he's not as thrilled at being found as you will be at finding him. If he doesn't appreciate your efforts, his reaction could hurt, you know."

"I'll keep that in mind."

Chuck stood and stretched. "Well, I have to be going. I have some work to finish at the office before I can head home."

"Before you go, you never answered my question."

"What question?"

"Is Trisha okay with this whole running for state senate thing?"

"You think I'd do it if she weren't?"

"I guess not."

Chuck lifted a hand for a small wave. "See you Sunday, Jack."

"Yeah, see you then."

Jack watched as Chuck left his office. Jack raised his cup in salute to him. Brinkley placed a paw on Jack's knee, wanting to be petted. Jack scratched his head and thought about what Chuck had said. What if Rick didn't want to be found? What then?

5

That Sunday, Jenny arrived at Jack's at 5:15. She carried a bottle of wine and was dressed in blue jeans and an attractive sweater top. Jack gave her a brief tour of the downstairs, avoiding the upstairs where the bedrooms were. She was impressed with the beautiful home Hank had purchased not long before Jack and his first dog, Bones, moved in with him.

Brinkley greeted her with a wagging backside, his tongue lolling outside his mouth in obvious glee at having another set of hands to pet him.

"What a beautiful dog!" she said, bending to scratch his head, ears, and cheeks. "Yes, you are," she added.

"You're a dog person?" he asked, pleased.

"Absolutely, but I can't have one in the apartment where I live." She grinned down at Brinkley. "I'll just have to come over here and get my doggie fix, eh, boy?"

"He would certainly love it."

"Where did you get him?"

"He's a pound puppy. I always find dogs there to adopt rather than buy one from a pet store or breeder."

She grinned up at him from where she was bent over petting Brinkley. "Typical defense attorney, I guess. Gotta spring 'em from jail."

"Well, can't seem to get any of my clients sprung, so I'll settle for dogs."

"I heard you inherited this house from the man who more or less raised you," she asked, standing back up.

"Where did you hear that?"

"Oh, around."

"Have you been checking up on me?"

"Hey, a girl can't be too careful, you know. You could be the next Ted Bundy."

"I assure you, I'm nothing like that."

"That's what I'm hearing, anyway, so don't sweat it."

"I'm not."

"So, what about it? Did you inherit this place? It's fabulous."

"Yes. Hank took me in when my parents died in a car accident."

"How did you two meet?"

Jack decided she would continue asking that question, along with related ones, if he declined to answer, so he decided to tell her, figuring it was part of her little investigation into who he was. In a way, he was flattered.

"When I was nearly thirteen, I found a starving dog on Sugar Isle. I talked my dad into letting me keep him, but I had to earn the money to pay for everything, including the vet bills. Hank was the first person to hire me."

"Did he hire you to take care of this place?"

"No, in fact he lived in a broken down school bus at the time. He hired me to help take care of that place instead."

"Wait! I've heard about him. Wasn't he accused of molesting a boy?"

Her tone suggested she thought Hank was guilty. "Accused is the operative term there. And he wasn't accused of molesting a boy. He was accused of molesting me."

Her shock was evident in her face. "Oh. Wow. I'm sorry if I said something wrong. So he didn't molest you, then?"

"Far from it. He was kind to me. In fact, he was the best thing that ever happened to me, along with finding Bones."

"Bones?"

"The starving dog I found. Hank was tried and found not guilty. In fact, that's how I know Chuck and Trisha Shelton. They were his attorneys."

"So, how is it he went to trial if you told people he didn't molest you?"

Jack breathed an involuntary sigh. This was getting more involved than he'd wanted. "Sign of the times, I guess. I was poor, the son of two people whose only claim to fame was being known as the town drunks. Nobody would believe me, saying I was protecting Hank."

"I'm sorry that happened to you."

"I've moved on. Hank and I were more like father and son. My own father loved me, and so did my mother. They just lacked an ability to love me more than their alcohol of choice. Hank made me forget the pain of that life."

Jenny glanced at the counter where the bottle of wine sat. "Is it okay that I brought wine?"

Jack chuckled. "Yes, it's fine. I don't mind a drink now and then, especially a good wine. I just watch how much I consume. Moderation is the key in everything we do. Overindulgence in anything is what's bad. When an obsession that hinders your well-being takes over, life turns sour."

Jenny seemed to breathe again. "Wise words. So, when will the Sheltons be here?"

"Around six. They aren't early birds."

"I warned you I might come earlier."

"I'm glad you did. Gave you time to learn a few things about me. Let's open that wine, okay?"

"Sounds good to me," she said.

Inspecting the bottle for the first time, he said, "Cabernet Sauvignon. One of my favorites."

"It's not a very expensive one, I'm afraid."

"Many expensive wines are overpriced. This is fine." He uncorked the bottle and half-filled a pair of wine glasses. "Let's go sit in the living room and enjoy our wine while we wait for Chuck and Trish."

She laughed suddenly.

"What is it?"

"I just realized I've always referred to her as Judge Shelton and him as Mr. Shelton. I don't know if I can ever call them 'Chuck' and 'Trish' without feeling embarrassed, as if I'm overstepping a boundary or something."

"Nonsense. You can call her Judge Shelton at work, but while in my house, they're just Chuck and Trish, or Trisha."

As they sat down to drink their wine, he

decided to ask her about herself since she knew a lot about him now.

"So what about you? You mentioned you fell in love with the area when your dad was stationed in Pensacola and he works in Washington. What are your plans for the future? How did you become the person you are now?"

"Wow. My plans for the future aren't much, really. I'm happy with where I am now, at least for the time being. I wouldn't mind working up to a better job with better pay. As far as how I became the person I am now, I guess you're asking about my history, right?"

"Well, you know mine."

"Not all, I bet."

"No, but a lot of the main story."

"Was it hard to tell me all that?"

"I have to admit it was, sort of."

"Sorry. I can be kind of pushy sometimes. My dad says it's my biggest fault."

"I can see why he would say that."

"Don't let it push you away, though. I'm basically harmless. It's just that I have three older brothers and if I wanted anything as a kid, I had to push to get it."

"What do you do in your spare time?"

"I volunteer to teach an art class in Wharton every other Sunday at a rec center."

"Is this your Sunday off?"

"Yeah. Lucky you, eh?"

"I'll say. What kind of art do you teach?"

"Just visual art. You know, drawing, painting. That sort of thing."

"You teach adults?"

"No, strictly disadvantaged kids. I won't even teach the kids who come from families with money."

"Why not?"

"First, because they can afford to take classes they pay for. Second, because so many people think disadvantaged people are just the janitorial staff of life, as if they have no real talents to sharpen."

"Are most of your students black?"

"Sadly, yes. I say 'sadly' because that's where most of the disadvantaged kids come from—minority families, not because I wish I had more white kids. I do have some, though. Poverty is colorblind."

"That's really nice of you to volunteer to do that. So, you're also an amateur artist?"

"I've actually sold a few paintings, so I guess that makes me a professional."

"Sorry. So you're a professional artist, then."

"I do my best," she said with a grin.

"What else about your life should I know? Like have you ever been arrested? Are you the female Ted Bundy? That sort of thing."

"Well, I was arrested once. At a protest in college."

"You're not old enough to have gone to college in the sixties."

"Hey, college kids can still protest things that are wrong."

"What were you protesting?"

"Nothing earth-shattering. One of the professors was fired for his political views."

"What were his views?"

"He was a card-carrying Communist."

"You mean, you're a Communist?"

"No. Far from it, in fact."

"So you were protesting because he was fired for his views, not because you agreed with them?"

"Yep. We're all entitled to our views, whether or not we agree with them."

"Good for you. I take it you're not a female Ted Bundy, then?"

She laughed. "Afraid not."

"Seriously, though, what else should I know about you? There has to be something negative."

She took a deep breath as if steeling herself to break bad news, her demeanor instantly changing. "I was married once. It—well—it didn't work out."

Hoping to ease the tension, Jack said, "Well, that beats still being married and coming over for dinner at my place without your husband."

Her laugh told him his comment worked. "Some men wonder how much I had to do with what went wrong. They don't mind a casual fling with a divorced woman, but anything more permanent is out of the question. It's more than looking at divorced women as damaged goods. It's more about 'if one guy got rid of her, what's wrong with her?' The fact that most men think I'm pretty doesn't help, actually. Then it becomes 'she's so pretty but her ex threw her back.' As if I'm a fish or something."

Jack could tell this reaction to her being divorced bothered her more than a little. He supposed he couldn't blame her. Divorced men were usually seen as a target by a lot of women. It was a double-standard, and Jack hated double-standards.

He said, “First, I can tell you aren’t a fish. No dorsal fin.” She giggled. “Second, it’s not always the man who ‘threw her back’ to use the phrase you did. Sometimes, the woman throws the man back. I suspect that’s what happened with you.”

“Actually, you’d be wrong. He just came home from work one day and announced he wanted a divorce. He was involved with another woman. So, yes, he ‘threw me back,’ as it turns out.”

Jack wasn’t sure what to say to all this. If he suggested he wouldn’t leave her or stop asking her out, that could turn out to be a lie. He liked her, but it was certainly too early to start making plans. He suspected she knew that, but he hoped he wasn’t getting someone on the rebound. That was almost never a good thing.

“Well, you should move on. His loss, if you ask me. This is only our first date, but—”

“Second,” she said. “You’re forgetting lunch.”

“Okay, second. At this point, I am open to a third, but who’s to say one of us will decide that’s not a good idea by the time you leave this evening. Life’s a crap shoot. Sometimes you get snake-eyes, and sometimes you hit the jackpot.”

“I’m sorry. I must sound like a real loser.”

“No, just a woman who had the rug pulled out from under her. You didn’t suspect anything?”

“No. I was blind to the whole thing. He handled the finances, so I didn’t know he was wining and dining her behind my back.”

"How long ago did this happen?"

"A little over two years."

"I wouldn't worry about it." He raised his glass of wine in a toast, "Here's to you finding the fish of your dreams."

She smiled and raised her glass in return. "To finding the fish of my dreams!"

As they drank, the doorbell chimed.

"Ah, Chuck and Trish are here."

After the Sheltons had come inside and presented their own two bottles of wine to share, Jack poured them some of Jenny's wine and topped off his and Jenny's glasses to finish off that bottle. They all sat in the living room and Chuck gave his usual toast, "To those who are at sea!"

Jenny's look of confusion, which he expected, brought the explanation from Chuck. "It's actually a Russian toast. My father worked on some large fishing boats and sailed with some Russian sailors. Loosely translated, the toast is to those who could not be present for whatever reason, from death to being at sea."

"Interesting toast," Jenny said.

"It's a traditional toast among us Sheltons," Chuck said before asking, "You work at the courthouse annex here in Denton, don't you?"

"Yes. I'm part of the clerical staff at the Public Defender's."

"Thought I'd seen you before. You like working there?"

"It's a job. I wouldn't mind moving up one day, maybe be in office management somewhere. I might even go to law school."

"If that's what you want, then go for it," Chuck said.

"Well, we'll see where life leads."

Chuck turned back to Jack. "So, how's that search for your brother going? Started yet?"

"Not yet. I've been considering what you said about whether he wants to be found or not. I've pretty well decided he doesn't want that. If he did, he'd have at least come back to Denton to see if I'm still around."

"Maybe he did and you were in New Orleans," Trisha said. "It's not as if he knew someone who might know where you were. Town's grown a lot since you were a kid. More people have no idea who you are than remember you as a child."

"I guess that's true, but he wouldn't have needed to look too far to find someone who remembered that time. He could have gone down to Moreland docks and asked around."

"Be that as it may," Chuck said, "forget about what I said. He's your brother. You should find him."

"I could get my dad to look for his service records," Jenny offered. "That would at least give you a starting point. You could find out where he was when he got out of the service."

"Or if he died in 'Nam and I don't need to go looking for him."

"Well, yes, but let's hope for good news, okay?" Jenny said.

Jack smiled at her optimism. "I guess it couldn't hurt. How much would a records search cost?"

"Usually, there's a nominal fee for that, but I'm sure my dad would help out for nothing."

"No, I'll do it the right way. What your father can do is get the ball rolling instead of having my request sit on someone's desk for two months."

"I'll call him tomorrow."

When the stove alarm sounded, Jack removed the roast and baked potatoes from the oven. He put the rolls in to cook while carving the roast. He took the salad he'd prepared earlier that day out of the refrigerator, and told everyone to serve themselves, buffet style.

"This looks delicious!" Jenny said. "I didn't know you could cook!"

Trisha said, "Oh, honey, Jack Turner is the best cook in the county."

Jack said, "And all his friends overstate his talents."

After the meal, they listened to soft classical music that seemed to melt from the built-in speakers that surrounded them.

"Great meal, as always," Chuck said, patting his full stomach.

"It was delicious," Jenny said. "Your friends' praise is not overstated."

Later, as the Sheltons were leaving, Chuck was saying goodbye to Jenny while Trisha pulled Jack aside. "She seems to like you," she said.

"It's only a first date, Trish. Well, a second date. I keep forgetting to count the lunch we had the other day."

"Well, if I were you, I'd make sure there's a third date. I absolutely guarantee she'll say yes."

"Thank you, but I don't need advice on my love life."

"You're thirty-six and you've never married. Someone has to offer advice. You're too good a man not to have someone in your life. Kids, too."

"Thank you. I'll keep my advancing age in mind."

Trisha smiled and hugged him goodbye before moving to say goodbye to Jenny. Jack overheard her call Trisha 'Judge Shelton' and be reminded by Trisha that when not at work, she was just Trisha.

Chuck stepped over to say goodbye to Jack. Apparently, he had the same ideas Trisha did. "Better latch on to that one. It's plain as the nose on your face she likes you."

Jack sighed. "You and Trisha need to stop worrying about my love life. It is what it is and will be what it will be."

Chuck laughed. "She said the same thing?"

"Yes."

"Well, we can't both be wrong!"

"I'll take it under advisement," Jack said, and ushered him toward Trisha and Jenny.

"Well, goodnight, y'all," Trisha said. Turning to Chuck, she said, "Let's go, so we can give them some time alone for Jack to arrange for their next date."

Jack and Jenny both blushed, and Trisha and Chuck laughed.

"Thanks for putting the pressure on," Jack said.

"Think nothing of it," Chuck said as they left.

Jack turned to Jenny and sighed heavily. "They're just trying to help."

"I know."

They stood silent for a moment before Jenny said, "So, are you going to do the asking out this time, or is it my turn?"

Jack looked at her, bent over, and kissed her lightly on the lips. Leaning back, he asked, "Would you like to go to a movie or something?"

She grinned back at him. "Took you long enough," she said and laughed. "How about Friday night?"

"Sounds good. Maybe we could grab lunch one day this week as well."

The kiss she gave him was not as light.

As he lay in bed that night, he hoped he wasn't getting into a relationship he would later regret. She had obviously been waiting to be asked to stay, despite the fact she would have to leave early in the morning to prepare for work, but he wasn't ready for that.

He patted the bed and Brinkley jumped up, always polite enough to wait to be invited. "I bet you're glad she didn't stay. Otherwise, it would be the dog bed for you."

Brinkley licked his face as if thanking him. Turning off the light, Jack turned onto his side and tried to sleep, which didn't happen for hours.

He listened to the storm that had arrived about a half hour after Jenny left. He thought back to his childhood and his game of floating twigs in the road wash. He was too old for that now, but the memory was a nice one. He remembered taking Bones with him and wondered what Brinkley would do if he tried to take him out into the rain for a silly game.

6
April 9, 1969

The sounds of quiet conversation drifted into Rick's mind. He could hear the words, but his brain was too foggy to make sense of them. Struggling to both hear the words and understand, he forced himself to swim up to consciousness. As he did, pain seared along his side, and for a moment, he wondered what had happened to him to cause such pain.

The words now became language. He recognized Vietnamese and remembered. He'd been crossing a field and they were ambushed. Without opening his eyes, he struggled to remember everything he could, but most of the memories were still tucked away in his mind. His brain was somehow connecting being shot with a football, but that didn't make sense.

He wondered if he had been captured and was now in a North Vietnamese hospital. He'd heard horror stories about what they did to POW's, and he prayed he would survive the ordeal that was to come.

When he heard someone say, "Private Turner?" in an accent that sounded very much like someone from Alabama, he eased his eyes open a bit. A pretty woman was bent over him, smiling. "I thought you were coming around. Hey! Welcome to the land of the living."

He took in the woman's face, its softness and full smile that showed her white teeth. He saw her blond hair was pulled back in a ponytail that was gathered up and pinned on top of her head. She wore a white, tri-peaked hat with a red cross on it. She was a nurse, or something similar. And she was undoubtedly American. He breathed a sigh of relief.

Glancing behind the woman, he saw an older Vietnamese man speaking to a young Vietnamese man in the bed beside him. That was what he'd heard that had frightened him. He was in a U.S. military hospital, or maybe a MASH unit, though the ward looked bigger than what he would expect from one of those. This ward stretched for at least a hundred feet from one end to the other, and dozens of soldiers were in the beds that lined both sides of the ward.

"Where am I?"

"You're in the U.S. military hospital in Hue. You were shot in the hip and they medevacked you out. You were in surgery for a long time, but you'll be okay now. Can I get you something?"

"Where's Roddie?"

"I don't know a Roddie. Is he a friend of yours? Was he in your platoon?"

"Yeah. Last thing I remember was shouting back and forth with him. He was asking how bad I was hurt."

"Well, he's not here that I know of, but I can ask around."

He tried to move and winced from the pain.

"You have anything for pain?"

"I'll talk to the doctor and see what he wants to give you since you're awake. I suppose what we gave you before is wearing off. You rest up, okay?"

She hurried away, presumably to find his doctor. Rick lay there, doing his best to ignore the pain and listening to the old Vietnamese man talking to what Rick figured was his son or some other relative.

When the nurse returned, she said, "We're gonna give you a shot of morphine. It'll make you sleepy, but that's a good thing. It'll also take away the pain."

For the first time, he noticed he had an IV tube running from a bottle of dripping liquid into his right arm. He'd always hated needles and wondered how it was he had not noticed this one embedded in his flesh then figured it must be the pain in his hip taking all his attention.

The nurse pushed a needle into the rubber-capped end of one of the tubes and forced the syringe's plunger to its seat, giving him an injection of the drug that would control his life for years to come, his dislike of needles dissipating with each fix.

Rick lay back in his bed, and in a few minutes he could feel the drowsy euphoria the drug supplied. Soon, his side was no more than a distant ache and his brain once again grew foggy. Sleep took him soon after that, and by the time he woke, it was time for more of the morphine.

7

Monday, March 23, 1992

Monday morning came before Jack was prepared for it. He'd lain awake the night before and hadn't slept well once he was asleep. He'd dreamed many things but couldn't remember any of them. The covers on his bed were almost knotted, evidence of his sleepless night.

Once he and Brinkley had arrived at his office, he again looked over the folder on his single case. He wouldn't be paid much by the state, but he was determined to do his best to represent a man he still loathed. Not only had Tom committed perjury to try to convict Hank, but he also had poisoned Bones, nearly causing his death. To say he hated Tom would not cover the feelings Jack had for his client.

However, Trisha had been right. Despite all that, or maybe because of it, he would do the best he could to defend him, though seeing him get away with this crime was more than unlikely. Jack wouldn't turn down the money the state paid him to represent Tom, but he should have pled guilty, though even the most obviously guilty people rarely did that, especially when they didn't have to pay the attorney themselves.

He would have to stop by the jail again this

morning so Tom could give him a list of possible friends who might have stolen the handgun. Jack knew nobody had stolen it, but searching for a non-existent scapegoat was part of doing what he was paid to do.

He microwaved the cup of coffee that had sat untouched since he'd begun looking at Tom's file and finished it before giving Brinkley a goodbye scratch on the belly and heading to the jail.

When the jailer brought Tom into the room and cuffed him to the table, Jack noticed his left eye was swollen and a shocking shade of purple.

"Rough weekend?" Jack asked.

"Nothin' I can't handle."

Jack moved on, not wishing to know the details of the fight as much as Tom didn't want to share them. "You said the other day that one of your so-called friends might have taken your handgun and replaced it after robbing the store."

"Yeah. What about it? You believe me all of a sudden?"

"I'm here to defend you, despite my personal feelings. Part of doing that is investigating what you tell me might have happened, provided what you say is plausible. Do I think you're lying? Yes. Will I work to find out if you're not? Absolutely."

"Yeah, right," Tom said, picking at his grubby fingernails.

"I asked Judge Shelton why she picked me to defend you. Want to know what she said?"

"Not really, but you're gonna tell me anyway."

"She said that because of our past, she knew I would do the absolute best job I could defending you. She knows that I would want to avoid any possibility that you or anyone else could claim you weren't represented to the best of my ability."

"That so?"

"Yes, that's so. I might not be the best attorney available in Denton, but I'm the best attorney who works with the Public Defender's Office. I will do what I can to prove you didn't rob this store. I think you did. In fact, I'm rather sure of it, but that's beside the point. I'm paid to defend you, and that's what I plan to do unless you decide to change your plea, which, if you are as guilty as it looks, you might want to consider."

Tom leaned forward, folding his hands into a single, tight fist, and said, "I've done a lot of bad stuff in my life. Most of it I got away with. You know that yourself. I stole that rod and reel when you were working for Moreland. I lied on the stand to try to convict that old guy Hank who took you in. I poisoned your dog, but he lived. Gotta be honest, I was disappointed he didn't die. But I didn't rob that store. This is one I really didn't do."

Jack knew Tom was a good liar, and this could be a case of showing that skill, but part of Jack wondered if he was telling the truth. If he was convicted for this and ended up spending a long time in prison, he would be where he likely belonged. The probability that Tom was being honest was similar to the likelihood that lightning would strike him when he left the building. Still, the tiny possibility still existed that Tom didn't do this. He considered what Tom had said before thinking to himself, *and I'll win the lottery this week.*

But still….

"I need the names and addresses of anyone you suspect of taking the handgun you weren't allowed to own in the first place."

"Let me think," Tom said, tipping his head back to look at the ceiling as if the names might be printed there. "I told you about Phillip, but you say he couldn't have done it because he was in lockup himself." He continued looking at the ceiling. "Lonnie's another guy who mighta taken it. Lonnie Gilchrist. In fact, he was over a couple days before the robbery. I didn't have enough beer to share, so he told me he'd pay for it if I went to get it. He's a trucker and doesn't like to be in a car or anything if he doesn't have to. He was alone at my place for maybe a half hour."

"Okay, anyone else?"

"There's Kyle, but I don't recall leaving him alone at my place. Still, he mighta done it."

"Does Kyle have a last name?"

"Jackson."

"Anyone else?"

"One of my ladies mighta taken it when I was asleep."

Jack ignored the suggestion Tom owned the women. "It was definitely a man who robbed the store."

"Hey, I got more than one lady. I wouldn't be surprised if they had other guys. Maybe one of 'em got her to take my gun so he could use it to rob the place."

"Not likely, but did they know you had a gun?"

"Marti definitely did," he said, chuckling.

"What's funny about that?"

"I pulled it on her once as a joke. She freaked." He continued chuckling as if it truly was amusing. Jack only thought of how Tom thought pulling a gun on someone, loaded or not, was somehow a funny joke. His cruelty had grown worse since childhood.

"Anyone else?"

"Maybe, but after thinking about it, I don't think my other friends would be the kind of person to take my gun and use it in a robbery."

Because Jack considered this a wild goose chase, he didn't press him to remember anyone else. The more people Tom thought might have stolen his gun, the more people Jack would have to investigate.

"Okay," Jack said, "can you think of anything else that might help me?"

"Nope."

"Okay, do you know Lonnie's and Kyle's addresses and phone numbers?"

Tom gave him the addresses. Kyle lived in Denton, but Lonnie lived in Wharton. He could visit Kyle first. Tom didn't have phone numbers for either of them. He said Lonnie had a phone but it was unlisted and he didn't remember the number. He didn't know if Kyle had one.

"You say Lonnie is a trucker. What about Kyle? Where does he work?"

"He's a deckhand for your buddy Jerry Moreland. Works on one of the big party boats."

"Okay, do you know what Lonnie's driving schedule is?"

"Nope. Either he's in town or he ain't."

"Okay. I'll check them out. In the meantime, here's my card," Jack said, fishing one from his briefcase. "If you need to reach me, leave a message at that number."

"You gonna check out my ladies?"

Jack couldn't ignore his use of the possessive any longer. "First, they don't belong to you, and second, I'll only do that if evidence shows up they might have done that."

"Yeah, well, whatever."

Before he rose to leave, Jack said, "I'm not going to tell you I believe you, but I don't necessarily not believe you either. I'm going to check out these guys and see if they have an alibi for the night of the robbery because that's my job. Right now, there's not much else I can do."

Tom looked at him, shrugged, and said nothing, and Jack went to the door and called for the jailer.

When he left the jail and stepped into the sunshine, he took in a deep breath of the salt air that flowed from over the Gulf. Air near the sea always smelled different, fresher somehow. After being in the small room with Tom Gordon, the fresh air was invigorating. He inhaled deeply again before setting off across the street to see Jenny.

When she saw him approaching her desk, she grinned. "Hey, handsome!"

The thought that she was this happy to see him made him realize he was wearing his own grin because he was happy to see her as well. He reminded himself to slow down and wondered if he would take that advice. A serious relationship seemed to be blooming rather quickly, and he knew that a romance that caught fire too soon would usually burn out. Still, he couldn't deny how happy he was to see her.

"Hello, sunshine. What are you doing for lunch?"

"Well, I was hoping this guy I'm seeing would come by and ask me to go to lunch with him, but I guess I can settle for you instead," she replied, giggling.

"Well, I wouldn't want to trespass on another guy's relationship."

"Nah, you can trespass. I'll handle him." Her phone rang and she answered it, speaking for a few minutes with the caller before hanging up and turning to him.

"So, where do you want to take me?"

"Where would you like to go?"

"I'd like to go to Nassau and soak in some sun with a drink in my hand, but I don't have a week for lunch."

"Then would you settle for The Captain's Dock?" Jack asked, referring to a popular restaurant on Sugar Isle that was built on a pier over the water.

"I accept," she said.

He suddenly yawned and she said, "Bored already?"

He smiled. "No, sorry. I didn't sleep that well last night."

She smiled knowingly. "Yeah, me neither."

"See you at 12:30?" he asked, suddenly worried about that smile.

"See you then, handsome."

Jack arrived back at his office and took Brinkley for a short walk. He had too many things he needed to do, so he couldn't go far. When they turned to go back to the office, Brinkley seemed to look up at him to see if anything was wrong.

"Sorry, boy. Busy day. I promise to take you for a long walk tomorrow, Wednesday at the latest."

When he was seated at his desk once again, he typed a letter requesting information on his brother. He included all the information he could even though it didn't seem to be much, but it was all he knew. Other than his name, of course, he included when and where he went to basic training, his place and date of birth, and the approximate time when he shipped off to Vietnam.

He printed the address to the National Personnel Records Center in St. Louis on the envelope. Jenny had told him to give her the letter so she could send it to her father. Jack still didn't know if Jenny's father could or would help.

Sealing the letter in the envelope, he left to take Jenny to lunch. He just thought of it as lunch, but she would surely see it as a third date. The dates were beginning to pile up quickly. He wondered on the way to the courthouse annex if they should talk about slowing down a little bit. He liked her and was worrying that one or both of them might be moving too fast toward something more serious.

Arriving, he decided to hold off on that talk for now. He was afraid such a conversation might serve to bring their budding relationship to a screeching halt, and he didn't want that, just a slowing down.

When they were in his car for the ride to The

Captain's Dock, he asked, "Did you talk to your dad about helping me out?"

"Yes. I called him last night when I got home. Woke him up in fact. I'd forgotten how late it was."

"He wasn't mad, was he?"

"Are you kidding? I could call at three AM and he'd be okay with it. I'm his little girl, even if I am thirty-one." She paused for a second. "By the way, don't tell anyone that."

"My lips are sealed. So, what did he say? Will he help?"

"Yes. He said to send the letter to him and he'll make sure it gets priority."

"Your dad sounds like a nice guy."

"He is, and when I told him about you, he was more than eager to help out."

"What did you tell him about me?"

"Not that much really, except that we'd had two dates already, and you'd asked me out for a third, though this lunch will make that the fourth."

"So he's not one of those 'I have to meet the man who's dating my daughter before I let him live' kind of dads?"

She giggled. Her laughter could have been annoying to some people, he supposed, but he found it to be the exact opposite. He felt his brain pushing the brakes. They wouldn't have the 'where is this going?' talk today. But it had to be soon. Very soon. He just had to figure out exactly what he would say. He didn't want to mess things up. He just wanted some clarity.

"No, he's not one of those dads," she said. "He's as nice as you think he is."

"What about your mom?"

"She's great, too. Maybe you'll meet them one day."

Her intent was clear. He'd meet them if they became serious. Apparently, the thought they might become serious had occurred to her as well. The problem was she didn't seem to be disturbed by it in the least.

When they were seated for lunch, she asked about Tom Gordon's case.

"Well, I can't really say much about it, attorney-client privilege being what it is."

"Do you think he did it?"

"What I think doesn't matter. It's what the jury thinks."

"Doesn't it bother you that you might be setting a criminal free?" she asked.

"Everyone deserves an attorney, but to be honest, I don't think I've managed to set many of them free. The guilty ones usually end up where they belong. Tom's not a killer, but he's not a model citizen either. My guess is that he'll end up being found guilty. As he said to me when we first met at the jail, he clearly looks like an ex-con, and juries usually assume an ex-con is guilty as charged. It's just the nature of the beast."

"Even if you spruce him up a bit?"

"There's no way to turn that sow's ear into a silk purse. Who he is comes off him in waves. I'm looking into the possibility that someone took the gun he illegally had, robbed the store, and returned it." She looked at him as if he'd lost his mind.

"I didn't say I thought that's what happened,"

he said, "but I have to investigate the possibility in order to do my job the way it should be done."

"I've seen him on the streets. He looks dangerous."

"See? Now, imagine a jury looking at him in court. He's dead on arrival, but that can't stop me from doing my job to the best of my ability. I couldn't look myself in the mirror if I didn't do the best job of defending him that I could."

Their lunches arrived and they ate, chatting between bites about other matters of no importance.

Dropping Jenny off at the courthouse annex, Jack gave her the letter requesting information on his brother, which she would put in a larger envelope and send to her father. Then he drove back to the office and planned his afternoon around going to see Tom's friends Kyle and Lonnie.

8

The first thing Jack did was call Jerry Moreland. Kyle worked for him, and Jack wanted to get some information from Jerry before questioning Kyle.

"Moreland docks," one of the employees said as he answered. Jack had once had the same job working in Jerry's bait and tackle shop.

"Is Jerry around?" Jack asked.

"Who's calling?"

"This is Jack Turner."

"Hang on. I'll see if he can talk to you now."

The employee put the phone down and Jack could hear his voice in the distance talking to Jerry. A moment later, Jerry was on the line.

"Hey, Jack! What's up?"

"Jerry, I have some questions about one of your employees. Kyle Jackson."

"Whatcha need to know?"

"Do you think he's honest?"

"Well, he works on my boats. A deckhand. I've never suspected him of anything. Honest enough, I suppose. Not the friendliest guy, though. Doesn't talk much, just goes about his business."

"Do you think he's capable of being tempted to

take someone else's handgun and commit a robbery and then return it without the owner knowing?"

"Kyle?"

"Yes."

"I guess anyone can be tempted, but I don't see Kyle Jackson doing anything like that. You know, following through on the temptation."

"Do you know about his personal life? What he does in his free time?"

"Not really. He just doesn't seem like the kind of guy who'd do something like that. What's this about?"

"A case I caught the other day from the Public Defender's Office."

"Which case is that?"

"Tom Gordon."

"Tommy Gordon?! That Tommy Gordon?" Jack could hear the shock that he would end up defending Tom Gordon in court. Jerry was very aware of Jack's history with Tom.

"The very same. But he goes by Tom now."

"He'll always be Tommy to me. How in the world did that happen?"

"Judge Shelton picked me for the case."

"Why in the world would she do that?"

Jack explained Trisha's logic for putting him on the case.

"Well, I guess that's so," Jerry said. "Still, I have to bet you aren't enjoying it much."

"You're right about that, but it's my job. And she's right. I'm making sure I do everything I can, though I'm ninety-nine percent sure he's guilty."

"Only ninety-nine percent?"

"I always reserve one percent of doubt."

"Well, I'd say good luck, but I wouldn't really mean it. Tommy Gordon's been a bad one since—well I guess you know that."

"All too well."

"Keep in mind that people don't change. As they say, a leopard can't change its spots."

Jack didn't believe that about people. If they couldn't change, what was the use of rehabilitation? Why offer to help anyone? He used an old stand-by response for when he disagreed but didn't want to continue that thread of a conversation before changing the subject.

"That might be so," he said. "So, Jerry, about Kyle Jackson. Is he working today?"

"Yep. He's on the Miss Delia," Jerry said, referring to one of his larger party boats. "They'll be back at five."

"When will he be through with his duties?"

"At six."

"Do you mind if I use your office to talk to him?"

"No problem. Just be sure you're here by six. I can't hold him here."

"Will do. See you then," Jack said.

"Sure thing."

After he'd jotted notes about the call, Jack took Brinkley and drove to the address in Wharton where Lonnie Gilchrist lived. The unit number in the address turned out to be a single-wide trailer, not an apartment.

He climbed out of the car, taking Brinkley with him, and knocked on the door. A bleary-eyed young woman answered. She looked as if she'd been asleep five minutes ago. She was still wearing a thin cotton nightgown and shabby robe.

"Yeah?" she asked.

"Is Lonnie around?"

"He's on the road." She looked down at Brinkley. "He bite?"

"Not unless you give him a reason to. Do you know when Lonnie will be back?"

"Friday night. He left this mornin' on a run to Chicago and back."

"What trucking line does he work for?"

"Pyland Trucking. Why the questions? You a cop?"

"Nope. A defense attorney." Jack included the word defense to keep her from believing he was from the state prosecutor's office. People like Lonnie might get spooked if he'd been visited by a prosecuting attorney.

"Did Lonnie do something?"

"Not that I'm aware of. I'm representing a friend of his and wanted to discuss my client's character with him."

"Oh, you mean like as a character witness?"

"Yes. Like that."

"Who's your client?"

Jack ignored the question. "Does Lonnie ever call when he's on the road?"

"Sometimes from a motel if he wants to talk."

"If I give you my card, would you ask him to call me? He can call collect."

"I can give it to him, but can't make him call."

"Do you know if he'll be home Saturday?"

"He always sits at home the day after a trip. Says he's too tired to go anywhere." She chuckled. "That's why I tend to have my fun when he's gone."

He ignored what he thought might be a come-on. "Thank you for your help on this."

"You never told me who your client is."

"To be honest, I can't say. Attorney-client privilege." The fact was the privilege did not extend that far, but he didn't want to share Tom's name. If Lonnie was involved, he might try to dodge meeting or talking to him about the case.

Giving Brinkley's leash a gentle tug, he said, "Let's go, boy."

"Pretty dog," the woman said as he walked toward the car. "What's his name?

"Thank you. His name's Brinkley." Jack replied. "And thank you for giving my number to Lonnie, either when he calls or when he gets back."

As he drove back to the office, he considered his next move and found he didn't really have one. He'd studied the file on Tom's case, and knew there was little he could do if the case went to trial unless the impossible happened and someone else confessed to robbing the store. Someone like Lonnie or Kyle. Jack knew things like that only happened in movies or on TV shows. As he'd said to Jenny, Tom Gordon was dead on arrival. It was nearing 4:15, and he had little to do until six o'clock when he'd interview Kyle Jackson, so he decided to stop in and see Mrs. Dawson.

Mary Jane Castor Dawson had been more like a mother to Jack as he grew up than his own mother had. He had met her when he'd become her gardener. She had loved him like a son from the beginning. It had taken him a bit longer to love her like a mother, but that had eventually happened. He still sought her advice about his personal life, and talking to her about Jenny might help him deal with what was beginning to frighten him. He'd never fallen for anyone this quickly. It felt like being in an earthquake. The ground beneath him felt unstable, and he hoped everything would remain intact once the shaking ended.

As he arrived at her house, he pulled in and took Brinkley with him to the front door. She opened it before he could ring the doorbell. She was holding her latest dog, Goose, in the crook of her arm. It was an odd name for a dog, but Goose wasn't named for the breed of bird, but for one of her favorite baseball players, Goose Gossage. It was her habit to name her dogs for favorite players on her favorite team, the New York Yankees. Jack, on the other hand, would suddenly know the names of his dogs at first look. The names would pop into his head, as if whispered by some deity that was in charge of the canine population of the world.

"Jack! Come in!" She looked down at Brinkley. "You too, Brinkley! Goose has missed you!"

Brinkley strolled in as if understanding the invitation, and for all Jack knew, he did. Mrs. Dawson closed the door and set Goose down. He yapped at Brinkley, who was considerably larger than Goose, and they both went to the back door to be let out into the fenced yard.

"I guess you boys want to go outside and play,"

Mrs. Dawson said and let them out. They began to run around and wrestle, Brinkley seeming to be careful not to hurt his smaller companion.

Turning to Jack, Mrs. Dawson asked, "Well, what brings you here? I was wondering when you'd stop by for a chat and a cup of coffee or something."

"I found I had some time on my hands and figured I'd stop by to say hello."

"Well, I'm glad you did. Coffee?" She headed into her kitchen to brew some, whether he wanted any or not.

"I wouldn't turn down a cup," Jack answered.

"Have a seat at the table and we can chat while I get some brewing."

He sat down and looked around her kitchen. As always, it was the cleanest, most orderly kitchen he had ever been in.

"How's work coming?" she asked. "You have any new clients?"

"One."

"Oh? Who?"

"You won't believe this."

"Try me."

"Tommy Gordon."

She froze with the coffee grounds scoop poised halfway to the coffee maker and turned to him. "Who?"

"Told you that you wouldn't believe it."

"Why would you take a case defending him?"

"First, I had no choice. Trisha Shelton tapped me for the job."

"Trisha?! Why would she do that? She knows

your history with him. Heck, she's even got a history of her own with him. He nearly wrecked Hank's trial." She continued making the coffee.

Jack explained Trisha's reasoning, but Mrs. Dawson didn't look convinced. Her brow furrowed the entire time he was explaining.

"Well, I know you'll do your best for him because it's who you are, but it's like she put two mean dogs in a room with one bowl of dog food."

"It's not like that, really. I've moved on. I still don't like him, but that's all in the past now."

"I admire you for that. I don't like him either, and I've moved on too, but she still could have picked someone else for the job. You may have moved on, but you don't have to be forced to be in his company."

"It's fine, Mrs. Dawson. I really don't mind. I need the work."

"Well, if you say so, but be careful of him. As my mama would say, the truth isn't in him."

Jack smiled. "I'll keep that in mind." He smiled at how much like Jerry she was when it came to dealing with people, and it made him a bit sad for people like Tom. He realized Tom was right—he was convicted before ever appearing in court.

Mrs. Dawson sat at the table with Jack while the coffee brewed.

"So what else is happening in your life?"

"Funny you should ask because that's one thing I wanted to talk to you about."

"Oh?"

"Yes. You see, I've sort of started dating a young lady."

Her eyes widened. "Really?"

"Yes."

"Not too young, I take it. It always looks sleazy when an older man is dating a woman obviously too young for him."

"No, not too young. She's only a few years younger than I am."

"Do I know her?"

"I don't know. Her name is Jenny Walton. She works in the Public Defender's Office at the courthouse annex."

"I don't do my socializing at the courts, especially at the Public Defender's. I have no business with them. If I were charged with a crime, I'd just call you."

"I'll be waiting for your call," he teased.

"I wouldn't hold my breath if I were you. So, tell me about this young lady. Do you like her more than just a little?"

"Well, we've only had a couple of lunches together and I invited her to have dinner with me yesterday."

"Where did you take her?"

"For dinner?"

"Yes."

"She came to my house."

Mrs. Dawson frowned. She was nearing eighty and was old-fashioned when it came to romantic relationships. A first dinner at his house seemed provocative to her.

"Your first dinner date was at your place?"

"Yes, but we weren't alone. The Sheltons were there as well."

She visibly relaxed. “Oh, okay.”

“But I do have a concern.”

“And what’s that?”

“I’m finding I like her more than I thought I would. I’ve found myself thinking of her all the time. And she seems to like me a lot as well.”

Mrs. Dawson sat back, frowning. “I must be missing the problem. You like her. She likes you. Isn’t that the reason you’re dating each other?”

“Of course, but I didn’t expect to be, well, falling for her. It’s weird. I’m a good attorney, able to make split-second decisions in that regard, but personal relationships are like trying to read Japanese.”

“Ahh. I see. You’re afraid you’re falling in love.” It was a statement, not a question.

“I guess so, yes.”

“How old are you, Jack?”

“Thirty-six.”

“You’ve spent your entire adult life mostly alone. Don’t you think it’s time to start looking to settle down a bit? Maybe even get married one day?”

“I didn’t mention anything about the two of us getting married. It’s much too soon to be thinking about that.”

“Yes, it’s too soon to be seriously considering marrying this lady, but it’s never too soon to realize that it’s possible. Love creeps up on you. It doesn’t announce itself. Something small happens and you meet someone as a result. You hit it off and suddenly you find you like that someone more than you expected to. It begins as a fling or a ‘let’s enjoy each other's company' kind of thing. Next thing you know, you find you can't imagine your life without that person. It usually happens at a much younger age, but then your upbringing didn't exactly prepare you for trusting long-term relationships. Your parents were not good examples of that, forcing you to become self-reliant at a much earlier age than usual."

"So, what should I do?"

"What do you want to do?"

"I'm not sure. That's why I'm asking you."

"Well, you know me better than to think I'm going to tell you what to do. I can just ask questions to help you make that decision."

"So, ask the questions because I'm at a loss."

"You've already said you enjoy her company. Not in so many words, but it's obvious you do. And I suppose she enjoys your company as well."

"She seems to."

"Do you have another date already planned?"

"We're going out Friday night."

"What is your plan for the evening?"

"Nothing special. Just dinner and a movie."

"At a restaurant and theater, or your house?" she asked, frowning.

"A restaurant and theater."

"Good. Does she seem to be looking forward to this, or does she act as if she's doing it as a favor?"

"She's looking forward to it. Maybe even more than I am."

"Well, here's my advice. You can do what you want. I'd say go on this date, and if you want to go on another, do so. Eventually, the relationship will grow or it won't. If it does, follow where it leads. If not, your questions will be answered for you."

"What if I fall in love with her?"

"Then you fall in love. It can be amazing, you know."

"What if she doesn't love me back?"

"Then you have your heart broken. It won't be the first time, nor the last, though the previous heartbreaks didn't involve a romantic relationship. You'll pick up the pieces and move on. That's what life is about, you know."

"So I should accept how I'm feeling and see where it goes?"

"I always did say you were smart." She grinned at him and stood to fix them coffee.

"Now, let's go sit in the living room. These chairs aren't that comfortable for my old body," she said.

When he left Mrs. Dawson's forty minutes later, he drove to the Moreland docks. He arrived just before six o'clock and said hello to Jerry, who pointed Kyle out.

Jack looked him over before stepping up to him. He had a wiry build and went about his business like an insect scurrying about to prepare its home for a storm. He was sure of each step on the boat and dropped down to the dock precisely at six.

Jack stepped up to him. "Kyle Jackson?"

He looked up at Jack. "Who wants to know?"

"My name is Jack Turner. I'm Tom Gordon's attorney."

Kyle visibly relaxed. "Oh, okay. Whatcha need?"

"What can you tell me about Tom?"

"What do you want to know?"

"Are the two of you good friends?"

"I guess you could say that."

"When did the two of you last see each other?"

He thought for a moment. "Don't know the exact day, but it was about a week before he got arrested."

"Where did you see him?"

"Up at Kirby's," he said. It was the bar where Jack's father had worked years ago. It had been sold years before, but the new owner kept the name.

"When was the last time you were at his home?"

"I don't know. Maybe a few days before that."

"Were you with him the night of the robbery that he's accused of?"

"No. I was in Orlando. My aunt had died and they were burying her that day. I remember because when Tom got arrested for it, I realized I couldn't vouch for him because I was down in Orlando."

"How did you get to Orlando?"

"Drove."

"Which funeral home handled it?"

"Why all the questions?"

"I'm just making sure of some things. Tying up loose ends."

"Did someone say I mighta done it?"

"Well, if they did, wouldn't you want me to help clear you?"

Kyle shrugged. "I guess so."

"So, which funeral home handled your aunt's funeral."

When Kyle provided the information, Jack said, "I'll be in touch if there's anything else." He left, waving to Jerry as he climbed into his car.

Turning to Brinkley, Jack said, "Well, that's one strike. I'll need to call the funeral home to verify it, but I think his story will pan out. He couldn't have made it back in time to rob the store, and even if he did, it's not likely he would have chosen that night to rob anything after a long drive."

Jack drove home and was surprised to find Jenny's car parked in his driveway. When he got to his door, Jenny stood there holding a bucket of fried chicken and a bottle of wine. The incongruity of drinking wine with fried chicken made him laugh.

He was surprised she was there but decided to take Mrs. Dawson's advice and let the relationship take its course. He'd pick up the pieces if his life shattered.

9

The next morning, Jack awoke to the alarm and for the first time in a long time, he didn't want to get out of bed. The night had lasted longer than he thought it would. They had ended up on the couch, making out like a couple of teenagers who had unexpectedly found themselves alone for the evening. They had stopped short of doing more, but that they would eventually end up in bed was as obvious as the sun rising in the east.

He was suddenly overwhelmed with the reality of life regarding adult relationships. Either they would end up realizing they weren't right for each other and stop dating, or they would sleep together. That was the way of life, and the path was clear.

The thought had occurred to him that he could ask her to stay the night last night, and she might have accepted, but he wasn't ready for that yet. Despite Mrs. Dawson's advice, the fact she appeared to be ready for that next step brought back his fears that this might become serious.

He had lived with a woman in New Orleans, Carmen Brandywine, for a while, but he had never seen the situation as permanent. He had originally felt they each recognized they were just using each other to avoid being alone. They were monogamous, but not serious. At least he hadn't been. When they'd parted, though, he'd discovered she had more feelings than he'd thought, but he wasn't in love with her at all. Mostly, he was unable to handle her spoiled nature. She could be almost maniacally insistent that she get what she wanted. He rarely took time to consider that relationship anymore because he didn't like to recall the pain he'd caused Carmen or her almost insane personality.

Still, he'd never felt like this about a woman before, and how quickly his feelings had developed was frightening. Their first lunch date had been Wednesday, followed by dinner Sunday, lunch again Monday, followed by dinner and a steamy make out session last night.

Less than a week had passed, and he was already realizing this was speeding toward becoming his first real relationship with a woman. Part of him wondered what took him so long. Another part knew the answer.

He wasn't a psychologist, but he was aware of how his parents' relationship shaped his beliefs about marriage. Most people learned the value of relationships from their parents. He believed that this was the reason for an exponential increase in divorce rates over the past hundred years. Children saw their parents divorcing, so lifelong commitment became rare. Society had grown to view marriage as being as disposable as an appliance.

He'd watched alcohol become his parents' true commitment. They didn't fight or argue much, mostly because they were each happy with their drinks. The other person—not to mention himself—became another piece of furniture in the house. As long as his mother had her beer and his father had his whiskey, they were content. Jack figured the only reason he was interested in a relationship with any woman was more due to Hank's and Mrs. Dawson's influence on his life. He often wondered what he would have become without them and always concluded that it wouldn't have been much. He would probably have become involved with drugs in his teens. A lifetime of giving thanks for them would never be enough.

Part of him knew that his fear of commitment was really a fear of failure. He panicked at the thought of falling in love only to watch the fires die into cold embers. It had occurred to him long ago that Carmen's childhood had been much like his own, which may have influenced how he ultimately felt about her.

Jenny, though, was different. She had come from a stable childhood. Her father was successful and had shown his love without hesitation. She'd not talked much about her mother, but he knew that one day soon she would, and that her parents' relationship would turn out to be solid.

Jenny had gone through a divorce she hadn't wanted at the time but seemed willing to plunge in again. He lay there thinking about all this and decided it was time for a conversation with her about where this was heading. He needed to know if this was just a casual attraction or if she was wondering, like him, if it could or would go further.

He winced at the thought of talking about this

so soon, but the relationship seemed to have boarded a high-speed train and he needed to know now rather than later if they needed to tap the brakes, if not bring everything to a sudden halt.

Glancing at his bedside clock, he found he'd been lying there thinking for nearly a half hour. Pulling himself up, he reminded himself he was the boss at work and nobody else was expecting him, so being late wasn't a problem unless someone came to his office in search of a criminal lawyer, which wasn't very likely.

He stared at the bedside phone and made up his mind. Lifting the receiver, he dialed Jenny, surprised that he'd already memorized her number.

"Hello?"

"Hey."

"Hi! I was sort of hoping it was you."

"Sorry to call so early."

"Oh, no. I've been up for nearly an hour. Just finishing my breakfast and watching the news."

"That's good." Silence followed, stretching into an uncomfortable range.

"So, did you call just to make sure I didn't oversleep?" she asked.

"Oh, sorry. No, I called to see if you prefer a ham sandwich and cucumber slices or another lunch adventure with me today."

She giggled. "Oh, wow, let me think about that one. Kinda tough to choose."

"I'll wait."

She laughed. "Of course, I can go to lunch with you."

"You sure?" he asked. "It's a difficult choice."

"Not difficult at all really."

"See you at 12:30?"

"Sure thing!"

After hanging up, he sat for a moment, mentally preparing how to begin the conversation about their relationship. He didn't want it to sound desperate or needy, nor did he want it to sound overly serious and frighten her away. The topic of whether or not a relationship was serious or just for fun would have lasting effects. He just needed to see if they were on the same highway and let her know how he'd been feeling about their budding relationship and why it was a problem for him. It would entail giving her all the information he could about his upbringing. She needed to be able to continue their relationship, whatever it might turn out to be, with all the information. Anything else would be unfair to her, not to mention unfair to him as well.

When he and Brinkley arrived at the office that morning, no lines of people were waiting for him. He opened up and began preparing how he would go about keeping Tom Gordon from receiving an extended sentence. That he would be found guilty was more or less a foregone conclusion, despite any efforts to prove he might not have done it. Mostly, whatever he presented in court regarding whether or not someone else might have committed the crime would be viewed as feeble attempts at best, an attempt to create reasonable doubt, but he knew it wouldn't work in the long run, even if it were true.

Just before 12:30, he put Brinkley in his crate, gave him a good scratching, and drove to pick up

Jenny for what he knew was their most important date thus far. As he entered the Public Defender's Office, he steeled himself for what could be a bad response from her.

"Hey!" she said as he approached. "Where do you want to go? My treat this time."

This surprised him. "I don't mind paying for lunch. I invited you, after all."

"And for the first lunch date, I invited you, but you paid. So this one is making up for that one."

He did his best to smile, and she asked, "Are you okay with that? You're not one of those guys who thinks he has to pay for everything all the time, are you?"

"No, I just didn't expect it."

"My dad would say you need to watch out. I'm full of surprises."

He wanted to change the subject, so he asked, "Will your dad call you when he receives the letter?"

"Yeah. We usually talk a couple of times a week anyway."

He gave her an uncomfortable smile. "Okay."

"Are you sure you're okay? You look upset about something."

"No, I'm not upset."

"Okay," she said, sounding unconvinced.

"Since this is making up for my buying lunch the other day, let's go to the same place, Perry's. That sound good to you?"

"Sure."

They chatted about her work as they walked toward Perry's and when they were seated, she asked, "Is this a breakup lunch?" Her face was pinched, as if expecting him to say it was.

"What? No. Nothing like it. I just, well, I have something I need to talk to you about, and I'm not looking forward to it."

She sat motionless for a moment, her eyes broadcasting her worry. "Okay," she finally said. "What do you need to talk to me about?"

He sighed heavily. "Our relationship."

"Oh?"

"Yes. You see I'm starting to like you a lot. I really enjoy being with you. And I wanted to sort of discuss where you think this all might lead."

"Oh." Her look made him brace himself. "Am I scaring you away? I sort of wondered last night if I was going too far just showing up with dinner without even calling first. I just wanted to surprise you."

"I understand. It was a surprise. A good one. I just feel myself growing closer to you than I thought I would, and I need to know how you feel about where we are right now."

"Let's just say the feelings are mutual. I don't know where this is going, but I want to find out."

"It doesn't frighten you that it could get serious?"

"A little. Mostly, I'm scared I'll get serious but you won't."

"Okay, then the feelings are extremely mutual," he said, chuckling to dispel the tension he felt.

She appeared to start breathing again. "Then you're scared of the same thing?"

"Yes."

She smiled and he could see her brown eyes tear up slightly. “Then I think we’re on the right track. I do enjoy being with you, and if things continue down this path, perhaps I will fall in love with you. But do me a favor, okay?”

“What?”

“If at any point you realize this isn’t going anywhere for you, let me know. Like right then.”

“I will if you will.”

She grinned. “Deal.”

He held out his right hand as if to shake on the agreement, but she brushed it aside. “Oh, that ain’t gonna do it, buster!” She leaned across the table and kissed him, a gesture that made him smile.

“There is one other thing you should know about me,” he said.

“What? You’re actually a bank robber on the run?”

“No, my life growing up was nothing like yours. As I told you, my parents loved me, but they had no idea how to show it. As a result, I can be distant. I’m really not sure how to have a long-term relationship with a woman.”

“You’ve never dated before?”

“I’ve dated. I just haven’t felt anything like this before. I lived with a woman in New Orleans for a while, but it was a case of better than being alone for both of us. We didn’t have a mutual, romantic relationship, just a sort of roommates having sex kind of thing.” He decided to avoid talking about how he’d hurt her. Telling the small lie stung him, but he knew it was for the better in the long run.

“Yeah, I’ve heard about the roommates with

benefits kind of thing. That must have felt weird."

"Not really. We were both raised by parents who didn't show love. I guess I was lucky to have met Hank and Mrs. Dawson. They say a child's first university is the home and family. I didn't really have a family until I met them. They showed me what love was, but I never really experienced watching parents love each other. My parents were more in love with their alcohol of choice."

She reached across the table and took his hand. "I'm sorry your life was like that."

"Well, as I said, at least I met two people who showed what parental love was."

She smiled. "If this grows into anything more serious, maybe I can be the one to teach you what romantic love is about."

Her words made him push the memory of Carmen aside.

The waiter brought their food and they ate, moving on to other topics. The mood was relaxed and when Jack walked her back to work, he said, "Are you planning another surprise dinner?"

"If I tell you, it won't be a surprise, will it?"

"I guess not." As she sat at her desk, he said, "See you tonight."

She laughed. "I apparently can't keep a secret with you."

10

The next morning, Jack woke at 5:04, according to his bedside clock. He lay there, wide awake, running the night before over in his head to try to understand it. Jenny had stopped at the grocery store for food and arrived with two bags. She'd bought ribeye steaks, potatoes, fresh asparagus, and a lemon tart pastry for dessert. The night played in his head as he lay there, wondering what was wrong with him.

"I have food, you know," he'd said.

"I know, but we didn't discuss what we'd be having, and I didn't want to put that on you."

"Nice of you."

"So, what would we be having if I hadn't stopped for steaks?"

He considered for a moment. "Let's just say it's a good thing you stopped for something. I hadn't actually thought about it."

They'd had dinner and retired to the den for wine and, as she'd put it, "getting better acquainted." They'd ended up impersonating teenagers again, and she'd finally said, "Do you want me to stay?"

He couldn't get over how she could take charge of a situation, such as asking him out for the first lunch date and now, suggesting she spend the night. He didn't think of her as forward, but as bold. He admired it, yet it also scared him. Part of him realized that the world had moved on to this equality in relationships, but another part feared the consequences of her suggestion—good or bad—for himself and his life.

She had immediately seen the fear in his eyes and he could see in her eyes that she instantly regretted asking the question.

The moment had ended their evening.

"I'm sorry. You must think I'm awful to ask that," she said.

"No. I'm just not ready for that yet."

"I don't just hop into bed with guys."

"I know." He thought about what to say next. "What about your work? Wouldn't you have to leave early enough to get ready?"

"Oh, Lord! This is not how I saw this happening," she said, blushing deeply. "I packed an overnight bag just in case."

"You did?"

"Yes. I'm not weird or anything. It's just that I figured we were getting pretty worked up the other night, and you might want me to stay this time. I didn't want to have to say no because of having to get ready for work tomorrow."

He'd not known how to respond to that as he came to terms with how prepared she'd been to stay the night.

She'd left soon after that, and he was miserable the entire night, getting to sleep well after midnight and waking so early this morning.

Glancing at the clock again, he found nearly ninety minutes had elapsed since he woke up thinking of her and what he would do about it.

He knew she'd be up and getting ready for the day—she'd mentioned she woke up every morning at six to enjoy leisurely mornings before getting to work at eight—and considered phoning her.

Still unsure what he'd say, he lifted the receiver and dialed her number.

"Hello?"

"I'm sorry about last night."

She paused. "I was hoping it was you. I'm sorry I rushed you. Here we'd just talked about where things were going, and I had to slam the accelerator. It's just that—" She paused and he waited for her to continue. "I don't want to lose you." Another pause. "I'm falling in love with you, Jack. I'm sorry if that scares you, but I can't go on with this the way it is. You're the most amazing man I've ever met."

"We've only been dating a week."

"I'm like my mother, I guess. The day she met my father, she knew he was the man she wanted to marry. I suppose it's like that for some people. Her mother was the same way."

He was silent for a moment, processing what she'd said and uncertain of her meaning. Had she decided she wanted to marry him? Is that what she was saying?

"Jack, do you want to keep seeing me?"

"Absolutely." He didn't need to think about it.

"May I come over again tonight?"

"If you want."

"I want. What's for dinner?" she asked.

"Baked chicken sound okay?"

"Sounds great. I'll see you at six."

"I have a question," he said. "When will you invite me to your place?"

"Well, it's this tiny one-bedroom apartment. There's barely enough room to turn around."

"I don't mind." Her silence suggested she was looking around at a mess that needed cleaning.

"How about this weekend? You can come over for lunch or something."

"That'll work," he said.

After hanging up, he sat thinking about the conversation and the fact that tonight would be a big step in the relationship. Reconsidering, he corrected himself. This wasn't a relationship. It was a romance.

"Jack Turner," he said aloud to himself. "I think you're falling in love." He wasn't sure what he thought about that, but the smile that greeted him in the mirror spoke volumes. Maybe he was more ready to fall in love than he thought. He chuckled, wondering what Mrs. Dawson would say.

After going to his office and dropping Brinkley off, he drove to the jail. On the way, he noticed a roadside stand that sold flowers and considered how his reaction to Jenny's offer last night must have made her feel. He pulled in and purchased a colorful bouquet along with a small glass vase to hold them. Before going to see Tom, he went into the courthouse annex with the flowers and vase, went to the men's room to fill the vase with water, and stepped over to the Public Defender's Office.

Jenny was busy jotting notes while on the phone when he entered, so she didn't see him until she hung up. Looking up, she gasped, placing her hand at her open mouth. "Not even my ex-husband ever bought me flowers, not even for our anniversary."

She stood and walked around her desk and hugged him. One of her co-workers called out, "Go, Jenny!"

Jenny turned to the woman, smiled, then laughed.

She kissed him lightly, saying, "See you tonight."

It was his cue to leave. Turning, he walked out of the office and crossed the street to the jail, where another surprise awaited him.

When Tom Gordon entered the room and was cuffed to the table, he asked, "So, how did it go with Kyle and Lonnie?"

"Kyle has an alibi. He wasn't in town the night of the robbery. He was in Orlando at his aunt's funeral."

"What about Lonnie?"

"I haven't talked to him yet. He was on the road."

"When will you talk to him?"

"Either Friday evening or Saturday, I hope. I left a message with his girlfriend."

"What did she look like?"

"Thin. Brunette. Kind of tall."

"That would be Elyse. Good. She'll give him the message."

"I pretended I needed a character witness. I

didn't want him thinking you had suggested he might have taken your gun and used it in a robbery."

Tom nodded. "Yeah, he would definitely not get back to you if he thought he was a suspect."

Jack considered *suspect* to be too strong a word, but it would do for now. *Person of interest* would be more accurate.

"I'm going to put in for a reduction of bail. We'll see how that goes."

"Okay, but I doubt I could make bail anyway. I ain't got much."

"I think I can get Judge Shelton to agree to something you can afford, but if you skip bail, I'll hunt you down myself."

"I ain't gonna skip. That's stupid. Never heard of anyone yet who managed to skip bail and not get caught. Bail bondsmen don't like that, and it's cheaper for them if they can get you back, and they can be pretty violent about doing it. They're awfully good at tracking people down."

"Maybe I could hire one to find my brother," Jack joked.

"You don't know where he is?"

"Nope. I haven't seen him since he left for the Marines. All I know is he ended up going to Vietnam. I don't even know if he came back alive."

"Oh, he's alive. At least he was three years ago."

Jack stared at Tom in shock. "How would you know that?"

"I was in prison with him. I mean, we didn't hang out together or anything. I barely knew him when he lived here, but he was there. In for burglary and drug possession."

Jack had a difficult time processing this unexpected news. "What prison?"

"Raiford," he said, naming Florida's most notorious prison.

"When was this?"

"Back in '89. I was there when Bundy was executed." He said it proudly, as if this were some sort of accomplishment or a brush with fame.

Jack jotted down this information. He would get in touch with the office of prison records, as well as search the court records of the time prior to Bundy's execution.

"Do you know where he was when he committed the burglary?"

"Nope. We never talked that much. The longest talk we had lasted only a few minutes. You know, whatcha in for, that kind of thing."

"What else can you tell me about him?"

"He walked with a bad limp. I asked him why and he just said, 'Vietam.' He didn't tell me anything else about it, but I guess he was shot over there."

Jack didn't know what to say. It felt odd that he'd been defending someone who had seen Rick just three years ago.

"Did he get out while you were there?"

"Naw, but he was supposed to get out not long after I did. That's about all I know."

He stared for a moment at Tom Gordon, unable to speak. After gathering his thoughts about the impact of this news, he was able to move on to the case, but his mind was still distracted by what he'd just learned. He ended their meeting by telling him he would see him the next day to discuss his appearance before Judge Shelton when they asked for a bond reduction. Jack had planned on doing that today, but his mind couldn't focus enough on that with the thought nagging him that his brother might be much easier to find than he'd thought.

"Maybe we could get you out on house arrest. Are you willing to wear an ankle bracelet to keep track of where you are at all times?"

"I heard about them. They track where I am?"

"Yes. You can't remove it, but if you manage to, a warrant is put out for your arrest and bail would be a pipedream after that."

Tom touched his bruised face and said, "That sure beats bein' in here."

As Jack was packing his briefcase to leave, Tom said, "You really think she might let me out on house arrest?"

"As long as the prosecution doesn't mind much, I think so." Jack was thinking about what Trisha had said about not wanting to appear biased herself. "Maybe you could offer to tell her who put you up to commit perjury against Hank." It was a joke, but Tom's reaction was violent.

"Ain't no way I'm telling anyone about that!"

"I was just kidding." Jack said, wondering why the suggestion riled Tom up that much.

Returning to his office, Jack wrote the motion requesting that Tom be released on house arrest after posting a small bond. Once that was finished, he wrote a letter to the warden at Raiford Prison.

11
June 8, 1969

Rick stared out the window at the sundrenched street below. He had arrived in Honolulu in early April and was rehabbing his hip. He'd been told he would be reassigned soon. All he was waiting for were the orders to ship out.

The doctors had decided the injury was now as good as it would get, and rehabbing was to strengthen the muscles. Rick didn't like the news, but he hoped to be able to get morphine once he was back in the lower forty-eight. Drugs were plentiful around military bases because a lot of young men and women were around to keep the dealers in business.

Rick walked with a noticeable limp now, which was better than needing to wheel himself around in a chair. He kept reminding himself it could have been worse, but he often didn't care. It was bad enough, and he wondered how bad life would get when he became an old man in forty or fifty years, assuming he lived that long. Would he end up in a wheelchair anyway?

Honolulu was nice and warm, and he'd visited the Hawaiian beaches on the south shore as often as he could. It reminded him of home, though the waves here dwarfed the ones back in Denton. Great surf back home consisted of waves that rose to heights of six to eight feet at their crests, and that usually only happened when a hurricane was in the Gulf, its eye to the west of Denton. Here, they sometimes towered over the surface, fifteen or twenty feet high along the south shore in the summer, and he'd heard the north shore's waves could be dangerous in the winter months.

Of course, surfing was now something he would never be able to do again. The sniper in 'Nam had seen to that. As if to underscore this reality, he knew he would ride a desk in his new assignment.

Dana, one of the nurses on his floor, came strolling along the ward, saying hello to the guys there. Rick had asked her out a dozen times, and she'd declined his advances every time. Of course, nearly every guy on the ward had done the same and been shot down without fail. He'd heard recently that Dana was seeing a doctor, so he figured she was out of everyone's league anyway, but it was no reason not to ask one more time.

"Hey, Dana! I'll be shipping out soon. Last chance to get to know the best Marine in the hospital."

"Thank you for asking, Rick, but I think I'll have to say no. I'm doing my hair that night."

"You don't even know when I was asking you to go out."

"Exactly." She continued along the floor, speaking to the men and torturing them with her smile.

The next day, June ninth, his orders arrived,

sending him to Camp Pendleton in San Diego. Rick figured he was going to be stationed there to keep from having to ship him farther than they already had to. The military always seemed to do everything for its own convenience.

He would be assigned to the military personnel office there, shuffling paperwork as one of the clerks. He could barely type, which said a lot about how efficient the military could be when utilizing the strengths of the people at their command. It was part of the "save pennies, blow billions" method of spending the military seemed to embrace.

He would be shipping out in three days on the twelfth.

When the day arrived, he said goodbye to all the people he'd met while there, including Dana, who took him to an out-of-view spot and gave him a kiss he wouldn't soon forget.

"See you again, maybe," she said, though they both knew that would never happen. Her smile made promises he knew she'd never keep.

On the commercial flight to San Diego, he had to get up every half hour and walk around. He couldn't stay seated for long, or his hip would start bothering him more than usual. By the time they were coming into San Diego, he was in a near panic about having to stay in his seat for the descent, which could last well over thirty minutes. The discomfort of the flight had increased over time. The worst would be during their descent when he had to remain seated with the seatbelt securely fastened around his hips.

He longed for some morphine to get him

through this, but of course, it wasn't on the flight's *a la carte* menu. He'd have bought some booze on the flight, but he had little cash on him and no credit card, so he would just have to suffer through it. He managed to do this without screaming by reminding himself how difficult boot camp had been and how he had lived through those miserable months.

He finally limped off the plane like a man four times his age and caught the bus that was waiting to take him, along with other Marines who had arrived on various flights, to Pendleton. While he rode and looked at the passing San Diego scenery, he thought of his little brother, Jack, and considered whether to write him or not. He finally decided not to bother him, figuring he had enough worries having to deal with their drunk parents.

Hobbling down from the bus at Pendleton, he limped into processing, where he would eventually work himself, and began his new life, even though he felt like an old man ready for retirement.

After three days on the job, he met Lance Corporal Gary Higgins. Gary was what some of the enlisted men called a "specialty supply officer." The title was bestowed because he was able to get drugs, especially narcotics, for those willing to pay the price for them. Scuttlebutt was that he had an inside line to people who worked in various pharmacies who were willing to falsify records to skim some of the drugs from shipments.

Rick had no idea how Higgins obtained the drugs and didn't care. He just wanted to buy some morphine or a derivative to feed his craving.

It wasn't long after arriving at Pendleton that

he'd spent most of the money that awaited him in his bank account when he arrived in the states. His expenditures over the time he was in 'Nam and Hono were next to nothing, so most of his pay was still in his account when he arrived at Pendleton. Drugs had eaten the savings in no time.

The first time Higgins had met Rick one-on-one, he'd told him, "Just so you know, if word gets out that I sold you anything illegal, you might want to arrange for your funeral. I wouldn't do it, but the people who supply me would have no problem with it."

Rick had understood and assured Higgins he would say nothing.

Rick had been mildly hooked before arriving at Pendleton. Now, he was totally dependent on the drug. The morphine wasn't just a supplier of a good, relaxed feeling. It was a cruel slave owner. Failure to get the drug he needed would result in intense agony as his body cried out for the pain suppressor that had turned into a pain creator. Once he'd taken the drug, all was fine, but without it, he could not function.

His need pushed all other activities aside, rendering him no longer interested in anything beyond his next high. He was arrested for breaking and entering four months into his stint at Pendleton. He'd managed to escape prison time since it was his first offense, being given probation instead.

The second arrest came two months after that, and his discharge from the USMC was dishonorable.

His drug-fueled life of crime had begun.

12

Wednesday, March 25, 1992

As Jenny entered the house that evening, Jack greeted her by saying, "You're not going to believe this."

"What?" She could see that whatever news he had was extraordinary. His exuberance seemed to make him glow.

"I found out my brother Rick was alive as recently as three years ago! He didn't die in Vietnam."

She blinked, her mouth dropping open. "How do you know?"

"An unlikely source. It turns out that Tom Gordon was in prison with him in '89. Rick was in Raiford back then."

She laughed. "I don't know that I've ever seen someone so happy to find out his brother went to prison."

"It means he's alive."

"Do you know if he's still there?"

"Tom said Rick was scheduled to be released soon after he got out. Rick was in on burglary and drug charges."

"What are you going to do?" she asked.

"I wrote a letter to the warden at Raiford. I

hope to find out where he was living when he committed the crimes that landed him there. Maybe he went back there and is living there now."

Jack sat down as if the excitement was too much for his legs to continue holding him up.

"Do you still need to know what my father found out when I hear back from him? I don't want him to go to the trouble if you don't need the information."

"No, I still need it. I figure knowing whatever I can find out will make the search easier."

When she sat beside him, she said, "Jack, I don't want to be negative. I know you're excited to hear this, but think about it. Your brother is into drugs. Drugs kill. He might have been alive three years ago, but not today." He looked at her, the truth dawning. "I don't want you to be too disappointed if you find out he died of an overdose or something."

"Sorry. I didn't think about that. I was just so excited to find out he was alive and in Florida so recently."

"I know, honey, and I hope I'm so wrong you get mad at me later for worrying you, but you have to keep all options open."

"You're right. Still, this is good news, isn't it?"

"Oh, yes. Of course it is. I don't mean to suggest it isn't. I just—I don't want to see you hurt."

He smiled at that. It felt good for her to feel that way, looking out for his feelings.

"So, what about that baked chicken?" she asked.

"Oh, wow. I completely forgot we had to eat!" He was embarrassed at the odd failure. "I can forget about things like food when I'm excited."

"Lucky you!" she said. "I never forget about food unless I'm sick. Gotta watch my figure because of that."

"Are you up to going out? It could be a sort of celebration of lots of things."

"Other than finding out your brother was alive and in Florida three years ago, what else are we celebrating?"

He gave her a half shrug. "Us."

She smiled. "You want to celebrate us?"

"Why not? I'm not that big on tiny anniversaries, but we did go to lunch together for the first time one week ago today, despite the fact it seems as though I've known you forever. I think our relationship is going very well."

"You do?"

"Of course. Don't you?"

"Yes. So, I didn't frighten you talking about falling in love with you?"

"At first you did, but then I realized my feelings are heading in the same direction. I've been more worried about my own feelings than yours. When a woman says she's falling in love with a guy, it usually only bothers guys who aren't starting to fall in love as well. If you didn't fall in love with me, I'd be left stuck in the muck in the road wash."

"Huh?" she said.

Jack told her about his childhood game of floating twigs along the road wash after—and sometimes during—a storm and imagining that the twigs were capable of making decisions about their lives, so he would leave the twigs that became mired in the debris there because he felt they chose to stay there.

By the time he was finished explaining his childhood game, surprise colored her expression. “Oh, my God! You, too?”

“You mean you floated twigs? Thought of them as alive?”

“Yes, except I didn’t leave them in the muck.”

He sat back. “Wow. Small world, huh?”

“I suppose a lot of kids did that and still do, but I think it’s appropriate that we both did it.”

He kissed her and asked, “Ready for dinner? Now that I’m thinking of food, I’m starved.”

“Sure. Where ya taking me?”

“How about Antonio’s in Wharton?”

“Great! I love Italian!”

When they were seated at their table a half hour later, Jack asked, “When do you think you’ll hear from your father?”

“Probably tomorrow. I sent it on Monday, so he should get it by tomorrow. My guess is he’ll call and let me know it arrived.”

“Thank you for doing this,” he said. “You really didn’t have to, you know.”

“Hey, all I did was mail a letter to my dad. He and somebody in St. Louis will be doing the work.”

“Thanks, anyway. I couldn’t have called your dad and asked him to speed things up.”

“You have a point, there,” she said, laughing. “He probably would have hung up on you.”

When dinner arrived, she asked, “So, what are

you going to do once you have all the information about your brother?"

"Find him."

"Okay, but what does that mean? Are you going to leave town and search? Phone people? Hire a private detective? What?"

"I guess I could hire someone to do it, but that doesn't feel right. He's my only brother, and I don't feel right paying someone to do the grunt work. I probably will have to leave town for a while at some point. That's what I was planning, anyway. It will be easier to talk to people that way. If he was into drugs, I might need to speak to some people who knew him but are reluctant to talk. I'll need to prove I'm his brother and not a cop."

"How will you do that?"

"Well, first I have a driver's license with the same last name."

"Turner. Yeah, that's not a very common name," she said, smiling.

"It's a start. We also look alike, or we did when I last saw him. That will help along with the last name being the same."

"Unless drugs have altered his appearance over the years. Some drugs can make you look like a walking corpse."

"Yeah, meth is especially bad about that," he said, "but Tom recognized him, so any physical changes shouldn't be too drastic."

"Are you sure Tom is telling you the truth? He could be leading you on for his own reasons."

"I guess he could, but what reason would he have?"

"Just because he doesn't like you would probably be enough for him."

"Maybe, but the truth is that he seems to sort of like me now. I think he's surprised I'm going to the effort of checking out his story that his gun was stolen."

"You do know how unlikely that is, right?"

"Yes."

"Okay, just checking. Some defense attorneys are kind of gullible when it comes to believing their clients. Those types often want to see everyone's good side so badly they'll believe anything."

"That's a prejudicial statement."

"Sorry, but it's true of many defense attorneys I've dealt with."

"Not this one," Jack said. "Especially not where Tom Gordon is concerned. I've seen his bad side up close. But I need to check it out, mostly in case he comes up later saying he didn't have adequate representation because of our past problems with each other."

"So this is more of a CYA maneuver?"

"You could say that."

When they arrived back at Jack's house, she went inside with him, but not before stopping at her car that was parked in the driveway and taking out the overnight bag. She smiled shyly at him as she did. He could have told her to put it back in the car, but he didn't want her to do that.

He quelled the panic that rose in him as he realized their relationship would be taken to the next step. It was as inevitable as the rising sun. He wanted to move on from the lone person he had been all his life, save for the times with Hank and Mrs. Dawson. They'd been among the few people he'd trusted as a child, along with his friends Lee and Roger, who had both moved away years ago, and the Sheltons. It was time to trust someone else. As Mrs. Dawson had said, he needed to follow this where it led for his own peace of mind.

As they entered the house and she took her overnight bag to the bedroom, he realized he wasn't falling in love with her. He'd already fallen and was beginning to fear what his life would be like without her, and deep inside he knew he'd never had a chance from their first lunch together.

13

When the alarm went off the next morning, Jack roused and moved to shut it off to find Jenny was between him and the alarm clock. She pressed the button on top of the clock radio and the silence made Jack wish for the alarm. He wondered if last night was a mistake. The next few minutes would provide the answer.

She lay back, stretching. Seeing him, she smiled. He could see the same question in her eyes. Was this alright? Had they moved too quickly after all? A timid fear stared back at him, her gaze wanting answers to questions she seemed as afraid to ask as he was.

"How you feeling?" he asked finally. The simple question held a thousand more. He knew she would know that, too.

"Fine. You?" Her eyebrows rose, punctuating her question with import.

He smiled, grinned actually. "Great."

Her grin matched his and they kissed briefly. "Gotta brush my teeth," she said, climbing out from under the covers and padding into the attached bathroom where she had put her toiletries the night before.

Jack lay there wondering now just how permanent their relationship was. Would they move in together? Perhaps marry one day? This was his first serious romance, and he was at a loss as to what to do next.

When she came out of the bathroom, she wore a small robe. “I have to get ready for work,” she said. “What about you?”

“Same here, but I’m not under the time constraints you are. Brinkley’s my only co-worker, and he doesn’t care when we get there. You go ahead and do what you need to. I’m going to go make some coffee. What do you usually do for breakfast?”

“Not much, really. Just coffee and something light, like a bagel, but toast would be fine if you don’t have bagels.”

“Maybe I can take you to Joe’s in Wharton one Saturday morning. Best breakfast in the state.”

She smiled at him. “Are you suggesting I stay over again some Friday night?”

“Only if you want to,” he said.

She placed a finger on her chin as if considering. “Hmm. I’ll have to think about that.” After a second’s pause, she said, “Okay, I thought about it. How does tomorrow night sound?”

“Peachy,” he said, grinning.

He left to allow her time to get ready and popped some bread into the toaster while he brewed coffee. While the drip coffee maker worked, he pulled butter, jam, and peanut butter out to let her choose her topping. He noticed he needed to go to the store soon. He could buy some bagels as well.

As they ate breakfast and chatted, he wondered in the back of his mind if she had decided she loved him or if her feelings were still in the "I could love you" stage.

She left for work and he sat on his sofa, thinking about where his life was going. After considering it, he found he was happy with the current direction. He knew his brother had been alive three years ago, and his personal life was definitely looking up.

That left his professional life, and he needed to see Tom this morning to prepare him for the hearing, which was tomorrow. He knew Trisha had made sure it was set for the first possible time available on her calendar, especially with the weekend coming. She, too, didn't want any scrutiny coming her way about this case, though it was certainly not one that had a lot of interest from the press or anyone else beyond those involved. Taking steps not to delay a bail reduction hearing was part of her efforts.

Arriving at the jail, he sat waiting for the jailer to bring Tom into the room. When Tom walked in, Jack nearly gasped. This time his face was a mask of bruises and cuts. His nose was bandaged and looked broken.

"What happened?" he asked.

Tom glanced at the officer before replying. "Nothing I can't handle."

Jack could see he didn't want to discuss anything in front of the deputy and said nothing. When the deputy left the room, Jack said, "Who did this to you, Tom?"

"I mighta made a few people mad at me."

"Like who?"

"Listen, I know you want to know, but that won't help anything. The black eye and stuff was a warning. I guess they felt I needed a bigger warning."

"A warning? From whom? About what?"

Tom heaved a sigh as if he was not being understood by a feeble-minded person. "Look, the truth is if I say anything, it will be worse next time, so drop it. I ain't saying nothin' to you about this. Just drop it." He finished by asking, "What do you have for me?"

"Anything you say to me is privileged."

Tom just sat there, silent, but Jack noticed a slight movement of his eyes to glance over his right shoulder, as if indicating perhaps their conversations weren't so private after all. With the glance, he said, "I said I ain't saying nothing."

Jack was shaken by this. Had something been said in here that had resulted in the attack on Tom? Attorney-client privilege was sacrosanct in the American legal system. All of the presumption of innocence was based on that privilege. It was the bedrock of the legal system.

Finally, he decided to do what Tom wanted and drop it, at least for now. Apparently, further talk could be detrimental to Tom's health. He still didn't like his client, but he was his attorney nevertheless. While he could look at this beating as some sort of comeuppance for all the times Tommy Gordon had beaten the snot out of kids younger than he was, like Jack himself, or for attempting to poison his first dog, Bones, his sense of right and wrong prevented him from doing that. Jack wasn't interested in revenge, especially after so many years had passed. Tom Gordon was still not a good person, but Jack didn't like that he was being used as a punching bag by some of the inmates.

"Well, we need to prepare what you plan to say in front of Judge Shelton tomorrow. I think we have an excellent chance of getting you out on house arrest. I may have to guarantee your appearance for trial, and if I do that and you run, the bail bondsman won't be the only person looking for you."

"I ain't skippin' out. It's not as if I ain't been in prison before. Not so bad really, as long as there aren't people who want to kill you or something."

This admission caused Jack to consider again the added circumstance of the label of habitual offender that was part of the charges. If he was as comfortable in prison as he was in society, the term was an apt one. Still, Jack could see Tom didn't want to go to prison. He just didn't see prison as the worst thing that could happen.

Jack moved on with the reason he'd come there in the first place. "You have to convince Judge Shelton that you won't leave or commit any other crimes while you're out. One reason bail is set so high is to keep you in here where you aren't a danger to society. You'll have to convince her you won't be that danger."

"Okay." He tried to smile beneath the bruises. "I always had a way with the ladies."

"Well, I can tell you that won't work in this case. It's not as if Judge Shelton hasn't been faced with a criminal trying to schmooze her. She'll see right through that. You have to be sincere."

"Okay."

"So, let's pretend I'm the judge. Convince me."

"What?"

"It's called practicing what you're going to say."

"Oh. Okay. Um—" he sat thinking for a moment.

Jack prompted him to get him going. "Mr. Gordon, why should you be allowed to wait for trial at your home instead of in the jail, where you'll be prevented from possibly committing another crime?"

After staring at Jack for a moment, Tom said, "Well, Judge, I'm a little too beat up to do much."

"Let me handle your physical condition," Jack said. "You concentrate on what you plan to do while you're out."

"I need to be out so I can make money to pay my bills. I swear I won't run and I won't do nothin' I shouldn't. I just want to be able to live my life until the trial. Have a few friends over."

"Don't include that, Tom. She doesn't care a whit about your social life, and your friends could be a bad influence. In fact, she's sure to see it that way."

"Okay," Tom said. "How's this? I don't mind wearin' one of those ankle bracelets. Everyone will know where I am all the time. I just want to go to work and eat what I fix myself instead of jail food. I swear I won't do nothin' that'll put me back in this jail."

"Okay, she'll probably ask you a few questions and warn you what will happen if you violate any of the conditions of your release. Again, I'll probably vouch to the court that I will ensure your presence at the trial. That will go a long way."

Tom stared at him for a moment. "Why you doin' this for me?"

"What do you mean?"

"You're willin' to guarantee I'll show up for the trial? You're actually lookin' into whether someone else mighta committed this robbery?" He phrased these as questions he wanted answers to.

"It's my job, Tom. Our past doesn't mean anything when it comes to doing my job. I'm paid to be your advocate in court. I take that job seriously, even if the pay barely covers my expenses, if that. If I didn't do my best, I couldn't be an attorney."

"How often have you represented someone you don't like?"

"More than I care to think about."

Tom sighed. "I'm sorry I did all that to you when we was kids."

Jack ignored the apology and said, "You mentioned before that someone else put you up to saying you saw Hank molest me. Who was that? I really want to know."

Tom's expression changed. Jack would not have been surprised if it was a look of anger, but this was a look of fear.

And with that look, Jack figured out the rest of the puzzle beyond previously having a hunch. He knew the answer to his question as well as why

Tom had been beaten so badly. He wasn't sure what Tom had said or done to receive this latest beating. Perhaps he'd said something to another inmate, something that contained more information than just "someone" had put him up to committing perjury when he was young. Tom knew where that someone's skeletons were buried, and that someone, most likely Chief Hicks, was getting nervous that Tom might open up that hidden grave.

Then he remembered. He himself had suggested jokingly that Tom reveal to Judge Shelton who put him up to perjuring himself in Hank's trial to get on her good side. This latest beating was his fault and showed how nervous those involved were that Tom would say something if he thought it would help him in his current situation.

Jack suddenly said, "Never mind. I don't want to know after all. It's water under the bridge, and I think you should just keep it a secret the rest of your life. Just talk to the judge about how you promise not to do anything to get you put back in here and your total willingness to wear a monitoring bracelet."

"Got it," Tom said, looking relieved. "When we going to see the judge?"

"Tomorrow."

"If she lets me out, tonight will be my last night in here?"

Jack began putting away his legal pad and pen, closing the briefcase and standing. "That's the plan."

As he went to the door and knocked, saying loudly, "We're finished in here," Tom spoke.

"Jack?"

"Yeah?"

"Thanks."

Jack wasn't sure whether he was thanking him for the work he was putting in, the fact he would vouch for him in court, or for dropping the subject of who put him up to committing perjury as well as suggesting it remain a secret forever that had prompted the thanks. Perhaps it was all of them.

The officer came in and led Tom back to his cell, and Jack returned to his office to prepare an addendum to his motion to allow Tom to be let out of jail pending his trial. The addendum concerned the apparent danger Tom was in while in the local jail and requested he be immediately transferred to the jail in Wharton if not allowed to go home. His motion requested that the addendum be kept sealed for the safety of his client, at least until his safety in Wharton was clear. The prosecution wouldn't care where Tom was locked up if he wasn't let out to await trial, so that would at least take place if their motion for release was turned down.

14

That evening as Jack sat eating a frozen dinner for supper, he realized how lonely he was. Prior to beginning a relationship with Jenny, loneliness never seemed to be a problem. Now, it was smothering him. He'd become used to seeing her every day. They hadn't seen or talked to each other since she'd left for work that morning.

Finishing his sad meal, he decided to call her. At least he'd find out if she was feeling the same way he was. As he reached for the phone, it rang. Because his hand was already on the receiver, he lifted it from its cradle before the first ring ended.

"Hello?"

For a moment only silence greeted him. Then he heard the familiar giggle. "Were you, like, sitting there with your hand on the phone waiting for it to ring? I didn't even hear the burring sound on my end."

He laughed with Jenny. "No, I was actually reaching for the phone to call you."

"Oh, okay. How nice of us to call each other."

More silence ensued. Finally, he broke it by asking, "So, why were you calling?"

She didn't respond immediately, and he

suspected she was thinking of how to phrase what she wanted to say. He understood this mostly because if she had asked him the same question, he would have to consider his response. Neither of them wanted to sound desperate.

"I just wanted to find out about your day and make sure everything was alright."

"I thought about calling you a hundred times, but I thought maybe you wanted some space. I don't want to smother you."

"Jack?"

"Yes?"

"I love being smothered if it's by the right person."

"Okay. I'll remember that."

"Have you, um, felt smothered?"

"No."

"Okay." She paused and changed the subject. "So, how was your day?"

"Fine until tonight."

"What happened tonight?"

"I found out how much I miss you when you're not here."

"Good. Because I miss you, too. It's crazy, isn't it? I feel like we're a couple of fifteen-year-olds or something."

"I guess love can make you do silly things."

Silence. Then, "Love?"

Jack decided it was time to admit to her and himself what he was feeling.

"Yes, love. I love you, okay?"

"You do?" she asked, nearly a whisper.

"Yes. I didn't expect it, but yes. I'm in love

with you. I hope that doesn't scare you or make you feel I'm taking this way beyond where you thought it would go this soon. It's an odd feeling for me. I've never been in love before."

"No, it doesn't scare me or make me think or feel anything other than I'm relieved. I love you, too. I've known that since Sunday."

"Then I guess I'm a little slow then, huh?"

She laughed. He could hear the tension being released in the laughter.

They spent a half hour discussing their feelings. Finally, she said, "So, you going to ask me to come over?"

"Is your overnight bag packed?"

"Of course."

"How long will it take you to get here?"

"Ten minutes?"

"See you in ten minutes, then."

Later that night as they lay in bed, she said, "So, you never told me about your day."

"You didn't tell me about yours either."

"My days are always boring. Yours aren't. You don't do the same thing day after day."

"I see your point. As a matter of fact, it was a very interesting day."

"What happened?"

He told her about Tom and his injuries, along with his odd reactions to some of his questions. "He acted like the walls had ears. That bothered me. Still does."

"Do you think it's possible the room is bugged or something? Isn't that illegal?"

"Very. Attorney-client privilege is the bedrock

of the rule of law when it comes to defending someone. In fact, I have to be careful what I say to you about the case."

"How can you find out if they are listening in?"

"That's just it. I can't. It's not as if I can walk in there with some people to check the room for bugs. That takes a search warrant. I could see if I could get one, but if Chief Hicks finds out I'm the one who did it, he'd make my life as miserable as he could, especially if nothing was found, and it's probably more likely than not that would be the case."

"Who would do the search? Not Chief Hicks or the locals, right?"

"It would probably be the state bureau of investigation."

"Couldn't you get a search warrant from Judge Shelton?"

"Maybe, but then again, what if nothing's found?"

"If they discovered the room was bugged, what would happen?"

"Chief Hicks would have to resign at the very least, along with anyone else with knowledge of the bug."

"He's a terrible person," she said. He was surprised at the venom in her voice.

"I don't disagree, but why do you think that?"

"Let's just say I'll never be alone in a room with him again."

Jack felt his heart pound. "Did he rape you?"

"No. He just—put his hands where they weren't welcome."

"That son of a—"

"Let's just concentrate on your problem for now, okay?" she said, interrupting. "I know what he is and have avoided him ever since."

He looked at her and she smiled tenderly. "It's nice you are so angry, though."

"Chief Hicks and I have a history, too."

"Oh?"

He told her about how then Officer Hicks had testified for the prosecution against Hank. "He didn't say he had witnessed anything, but I'm pretty sure he was the one who put Tom Gordon up to lying on the stand to say he did. Chief Hicks' brother Carl was supposed to testify to the same lie. That's what makes me wonder about a bug. On an early visit with Tom, he told me he was put up to lie on the stand by someone that he wouldn't identify because that person was still around. Tom thought I might cause the person problems if I knew who it was. It was after that the jailhouse beatings started."

"You don't know that was what caused it."

"No, but coupled with the looks Tom gave me when I tried to talk about it again, it's a good bet that's what triggered them."

"So, what are you going to do?"

"Not sure yet. First thing I'm going to do is try to get Tom out of there, if not released, then at least moved to the Wharton jail."

As she settled back onto her pillow, she said, "See? I told you."

"You told me what?"

"That compared to your days, mine are utterly boring."

The next morning, Jenny reminded Jack that they had a dinner and movie date that night.

"What do you want to see?" he asked.

"*My Cousin Vinny*. It's a romantic comedy that just came out about a lawyer."

He smiled. "Sounds perfect."

He was due in court at ten o'clock, and arrived fifteen minutes early. Tom was already waiting in a courtroom holding cell. Approaching the cell, Jack looked Tom over and did not find any new bruises. However, he looked as though he hadn't slept, and Jack wondered if that was true. He had mentioned how it would be his last night in the Denton jail if he was allowed release until the trial, and it had probably been a sleepless night while he waited for a final beating.

This area, Jack knew, was not bugged, but it also wasn't very private, so he kept his comments to what would happen in court. "You ready?" Jack asked.

"Ready to get out of here. Yeah."

"I've requested that if you remain in custody, you be transferred to Wharton's jail. It's safer, and besides, I hear the food is better there."

"The baloney sandwiches are fresher?"

Jack smiled. "Yeah, and they use the thick slices of baloney," he joked.

When Tom was brought into the courtroom, he sat beside Jack and waited for Judge Shelton to enter.

Finally, a bailiff entered the courtroom from the judge's chambers and told everyone to rise and that court was now in session.

Trisha glanced at some papers and looked down from the bench and said, “First thing on the docket today is a motion from Thomas Gordon requesting his bail be reduced or he be allowed release on his own recognizance. Mr. Turner, are you prepared to argue your motion?”

Jack stood and said, “I am, Your Honor.”

Turning to the prosecution, she said, “Mr. Herndon, are you prepared?”

“I am, Your Honor.”

“Then let’s proceed. Mr. Turner?”

“Your Honor, while we admit that my client has previously been convicted for two felonies, he is anxious to address these charges for the crime he is accused of, and which he swears he did not commit. I am willing to personally guarantee Mr. Gordon’s attendance at trial.”

“Mr. Herndon?” Trisha said.

Lawrence “Larry” Herndon, the assistant DA assigned to the case, stood and said, “Your Honor, even the defense recognizes that Mr. Gordon has served time in prison twice before on felony charges. We consider him a flight risk and do not wish to see his bail reduced, much less allow him to walk the streets as if he never did anything wrong. Mr. Turner’s faith in his client is considerably larger than the state’s.”

Trisha turned back to Jack. “Mr. Turner, how do you propose to put the prosecution’s mind at ease?”

“Your Honor, Mr. Gordon is willing to wear an ankle bracelet monitoring his whereabouts at all times. He will go only to work and home, with occasional stops at the grocery store. He won't even leave Denton."

"Mr. Turner," Trisha said, "I am not inclined to give Mr. Gordon his wish without bail of some kind being posted. He should offer some guarantee that he won't flee beyond simply promising he won't leave town."

She turned to Tom. "Mr. Gordon, please rise." Tom stood. "What do you have to offer to this conversation?"

"Judge, I didn't commit this crime. My attorney is looking into that already. I don't mind wearing the ankle thing. As you can see, I've had a bit of a rough time in jail."

"Yes, I couldn't help but notice. Have you received medical treatment for these injuries?"

"Yes, Your Honor."

"And what did you do to antagonize someone enough to do this to you?"

"Nothin', Your Honor."

"You mean someone beat the tar out of you for no reason?"

"I'm sure he had a reason. I just don't know what it was. Maybe he didn't like my looks or somethin'."

Moving on, she said, "Mr. Gordon, are you aware that an alarm goes off if you even attempt to remove the ankle bracelet? The police would be at your door, or whatever your location might be, within minutes?"

"No, ma'am. I didn't know that, but it don't matter. I wouldn't be tryin' to take it off. I just want to be able to make money to keep my rent current and not have to eat the food at the jail. No offense, but it's awful."

Trisha smiled at that. "No offense taken. After all, if the jail served filet mignon, people would be committing crimes just to get in there if they were hungry enough. Mr. Gordon, what do you plan to do to make money?"

"I have a job working a fishin' boat. I'm pretty sure the captain will hire me back."

"Do you understand that if I lower your bail and you can afford it that any violation of your house arrest orders will result in your return to jail?"

"What are the orders?" Tom asked.

"You may not leave the town limits of Denton without approval from this court. You cannot get into any trouble, not even for jaywalking. Finally, you're not allowed to consume alcohol or any drugs, other than those prescribed by a doctor. Do you understand and agree to abide by these limits?"

"Yes, Judge."

Jack spoke up. "Assuming Your Honor is considering a reduction in bail, what kind of bail were you thinking?"

Trisha thought for a minute. "I'm willing to drop it to $10,000, provided he also wears the ankle monitor."

Jack turned to Tom and spoke softly. "You have a thousand dollars available?"

Tom considered the question. "I have it. It was supposed to go for somethin' else, but I guess this is as good a deal as I'm gonna get," he murmured back.

"It's better than I expected," Jack said before turning back to Trisha. "Thank you, Your Honor," Jack said. "Mr. Gordon can raise enough to pay the bondsman's fee."

Trisha turned to Mr. Herndon. "Mr. Herndon? Do you have anything to add?"

"Not beyond what we've already said," Herndon answered.

"Fine," Trisha said. "Bail is reduced to $10,000. Is there anything else, Mr. Turner?"

Jack put the request to move Tom to the jail in Wharton back in his briefcase. "No, Your Honor. Thank you."

"You're welcome, Mr. Turner."

Trisha turned to the bailiff. "Next case, Brad."

Two hours later, Jack was at the jail to give Tom a ride home.

"Tom," he said. "I'll be coming by later to talk about what we couldn't talk about in the jail."

"I don't want to talk about that."

"We'll have to talk about it whether you want to or not. I have some valid interest in what you were implying the other day, and we need to discuss what you couldn't say in jail."

"I'm not going to tell you who got me to lie on the stand."

"You don't have to. I think I already know."

Tom stared at Jack. "How would you know?"

"As Sherlock Holmes would say, 'Elementary.'"

That evening when he arrived home, Jenny was waiting for him.

"I got a call from my dad," she said in greeting.

"What did he say?"

"He's called someone in St. Louis and told him to expect your letter to arrive in an official envelope from his office. He opened your letter and gave him the preliminary information. My dad says they will probably have the information on your brother before the letter even arrives."

"That's great!"

"There was one other thing."

"What's that?"

"He called me this morning around six-thirty to tell me."

"That's a bit early."

"He calls me then because he knows I'll be home. He knows I'm up by then and have my coffee before beginning my day, and he knows that's the best time to catch me. He leaves a message if I don't answer for some reason, like I'm in the shower, and I always call him back before I go to work."

"Okay," Jack said, not comprehending.

"Yeah. He called me at work—something he never does—and asked where I was."

"You're a big girl now."

"Yes, but it was still embarrassing to tell my dad I had spent the night with you."

"You said he wasn't the kind of dad who got upset about things like that."

"He wasn't upset. It's just, well, I had to tell him a few things about our relationship."

"Like?"

"We're in love."

"And that's bad?"

"No, it's not bad. It's just, well, something that leads to other questions."

"Like what?"

"If I'm moving in with you."

"Okay, that's a shock."

"I'm not going to push you on that. I'm not ready to go there myself. I don't know what the future will bring. I suppose if I remain in love with you that I'll want to do at least that much. I miss you when we're not together."

"That's a big step."

"You told me about that girl you lived with in New Orleans."

"Yes, but we weren't in love."

"How do you know she didn't love you and you just weren't aware of her feelings?"

"Because we told each other we didn't love each other. Not like that, anyway." Jack didn't tell Jenny that he was the one who said that because he didn't want her knowing how much he'd hurt Carmen. He'd only assumed she felt the same way until she told him she didn't.

"Okay, but be aware my parents will expect us to move in with each other at the least if this keeps going."

"You have some rather liberal-minded parents."

"My parents were hippies before being a hippy was cool."

He smiled at her. "Jenny Walton, you're just full of surprises. So, did your parents live together before marriage?"

"Not that I know of because their parents

would have had a cow. But they're liberal with a capital 'L.' Anyway, isn't it the way of the world now, though? Living together first? How many people do you know who don't live together before getting married?

"Good question."

She smiled back. "Am I at least staying the night?"

"Did you bring your overnight bag?"

"It's become a staple of my existence."

"Then you're definitely staying if you want to. Then maybe tomorrow you can have me over to your place so I can finally see it."

"It's a deal."

The movie was better than either of them thought it would be. As they drove back to Jack's, they laughed about various scenes.

As they prepared for bed, one word occurred to Jack to describe their relationship: *comfortable.* He'd never known such comfort with a woman. They could talk about any topic, and he didn't wonder if he might say the wrong thing or if he would be at a loss for words. Their romance was quick to ignite, but seemed to be burning steadily with no hint of going out. The fire wasn't blazing with an unsustainable heat, just small, steady, constant flames.

As he fell asleep that night, he realized with some surprise that he was amazingly happy.

Now, if only he could find his brother and help him return to good health if that was needed. He'd promised himself he would do all he could.

He prayed that would be enough.

15

December 17, 1969

Rick left the Camp Pendleton Military Personnel Office for the last time and caught a bus into San Diego. From there he had no idea what he would do. He'd just signed the paperwork separating him from the Marines. That didn't bother him nearly as much as knowing he'd become just a different version of his father. His father craved liquor. Rick had chosen something stronger—morphine. The illegality of procuring the drug was just an added bonus in the way a burn was an added bonus for a toddler's curiosity about fire.

Rick only felt the fire when he was without his drug for any length of time. That's how he would describe the pain he felt when he was sober, like a constant fire that burned from the inside out. Only the morphine would put the fire out, and he would need to buy more soon.

While still in the Marines, he had worked out a plan with Higgins. Rick would sell for him in exchange for enough dope to keep the fire from raging. Now, he had enough in his duffel for a couple of days and knew he'd have little trouble finding more in the city, which was why he'd headed downtown after leaving Pendleton and the Marines behind.

He'd also managed to find out who Higgins got all that dope from and knew where they could be found. Maybe he could swing the same deal with them that he'd had with Higgins. If they wouldn't supply him voluntarily, he might be able to skim enough from what they gave him to sell for his own use. They weighed what each of their runners received with precision, but Rick could skim some after getting what they wanted to sell on the street and replace what he skimmed with a filler, maybe ground up aspirin or something.

Of course, Higgins would always pay for the stuff up front and keep the profits. However, Rick didn't have enough money for that but would offer his services as a small-time dealer, selling small amounts and returning to them with the money. He'd be able to make a tidy profit in addition to what he could successfully skim.

He arrived at the small auto body shop where Higgins' suppliers did their business in a back room. He'd met them a couple of times when he was with Higgins, and they'd checked him out enough to know he was no danger to them.

He entered the small shop, walked up to the guy behind the counter, and said, "My name's Rick Turner. I'm here to see Rod." Rod was short for Rodriguez, who was the mastermind behind this criminal enterprise. He owned the body shop. Rick figured it was probably used more for stripping stolen cars or changing their appearance than doing legitimate auto body repair. He didn't care. He just needed enough work to keep him high enough to ward off the scorching pain.

Rick didn't know Rod's first name. Everyone just called him Rod. It was best if he didn't know.

The guy behind the counter said, "What do you need to see him about?"

"Higgins is a friend of mine. I've met Rod a few times and need to talk to him."

The mention of Higgins' name brought a spark of recognition to the guy's eyes. "You know Higgins?"

"Yeah. We're both stationed at Pendleton." He said nothing about his discharge. It wasn't important enough and wouldn't look good on any resume, even one for a job like this.

"Wait here. I'll see if Rod wants to see you."

The guy stepped through a door that led to the offices. A moment later, he returned and said, "Rod says to come back tomorrow."

Rick didn't argue. What use would that do? "What time?"

"He didn't say, but make it in the afternoon. He's usually busy in the mornings."

Rick couldn't help but reply, "It's afternoon now. He can't see me?"

The man narrowed his eyes. "Come back tomorrow." Menace dripped from his voice, as if any further argument could result in a severe beating.

"Okay. No prob, man. I'll be back around noon tomorrow."

"No. Later. He has lunch at noon."

"Okay. How does one sound?"

The guy nodded. "A lot better than noon."

"See you then."

Rick left and limped a few blocks to a cheap hotel in the area. He checked in, paying for his room with cash, and went up the creaking stairs to his room on the fourth floor.

Once inside, he conducted a brief inspection while hoping there were no bedbugs in the mattresses. The bathroom held a small sink with a funnel of orange stains leading into the drain, a toilet with the same rust color marring the bowl, and a shower badly in need of new grout.

Dropping his duffel on the double bed, he opened it and retrieved his stash. Ten minutes later, he was on his way to what he thought of as a combination Heaven and Hell.

The next day he arrived at the auto body shop promptly at one. The same guy was behind the counter.

"Wait here," he said and disappeared through the door as he had the day before. A few minutes later, he came back out.

"Rod says to come back tomorrow," he said, as if he hadn't said the same thing the day before.

"Wait. What? You told me yesterday he said to come back today at one. It's one and I'm here."

"He can't see you today. Come back tomorrow."

When Rick returned the next day at one, he was told the same thing, and it finally dawned on him that Rod was never going to see him. He couldn't very well force himself in to see the man. Even if he succeeded, busting in on the guy who had no desire to talk to him was no way to convince the man to hire him.

He left the shop and limped down the street, looking for a likely business to break into that night to steal what he could to hock for money to buy drugs. Maybe he'd even get lucky and find some money in a cash register, but he doubted it. This wasn't the type of neighborhood where the merchants trusted anyone. The cash would either be locked in a safe, taken to the bank, or taken home with the manager or owner.

Rick came upon a shop that sold stereos and other sound equipment. He hobbled around to the back door and saw he could probably break it open that night with a crowbar. He could shoplift a crowbar in a hardware store that afternoon. He wore a loose-fitting jacket and could slip it up one sleeve.

Rick returned that night with the stolen crowbar. Breaking the lock proved to be harder than he'd thought it would be, but he finally managed to get inside. Once there, he took enough merchandise to fence the following day to get enough money for another night at the fleabag hotel and a couple of fixes. He worked quickly and left just in time to avoid the cops that arrived because of the alarm.

Three days later, Rick decided it was time to move on. He thumbed a ride east, saying goodbye to San Diego forever.

16

Saturday, March 28, 1992

Because it was Saturday, Jack chose to spend some time with Jenny before heading to see Tom at his home, where they could talk without worrying about eavesdroppers.

He and Jenny had a leisurely breakfast with Café Du Monde coffee. Jack had arranged to have the coffee with chicory sent to him by the famous Café Du Monde in New Orleans. It had been his favorite place to sit on Saturday mornings when he had lived there, and when he moved, he made arrangements for three pounds of the famous freshly ground coffee to be mailed to him each month. He always gave Mrs. Dawson one pound and kept the other two for himself.

As they chatted at the breakfast table that sat in a glassed-in alcove off the kitchen, the topic turned to their budding relationship.

"I've been wondering something," Jack said.

"What's that?"

"Why did you decide to ask me out instead of waiting for me to ask you?"

"First, we're almost in the twenty-first century, and that whole 'only a man can approach a woman for a date, not vice versa' thing is as archaic as TV antennas on houses. Second, I had waited for you to ask, mostly out of politeness and to see if you would, but when you didn't, I decided if it was going to happen, I'd have to do it."

"How long did you wait?"

"Since the first time you walked into the Public Defender's Office."

"You wanted me to ask you out the first time you saw me?"

"Yep."

"How did you know we would get along?"

"I didn't. That's why I wanted to go out with you. To find out."

"And you've known since Sunday that you love me?"

"Yes."

"Didn't that frighten you? Didn't you worry I wouldn't fall in love with you?"

"Of course. I was petrified. You don't know the sleep I lost thinking about it."

Jack considered what she was saying. "Yeah, I've been a bit of a nutcase myself." Looking at her, he wondered something. "What did you find so attractive about me?"

"You care," she said. "I'd heard about you before you ever walked in the door. When Leah Crandall saw you were on the list of attorneys willing to take on indigent cases, she said you were a good attorney. I asked how she knew and she said she'd heard from reliable sources you really cared about the people you represent. Caring is a big thing with me. Then when I saw you—well, I had to find out after that."

"So you were attracted to me because I care?"

"That was the first attraction, sure." Jack started to ask another question when she stopped him. "Not so fast. It's my turn."

"I wasn't aware we were taking turns." He smiled at her.

"Well, we are. Why didn't you ask me out?"

"Good question."

"What's the answer?"

"I've never been much of a ladies' man. I knew of you and found you attractive."

"Found? Past tense?"

"Well, no. Find is more accurate. Anyway, I think I was afraid you might say no."

"There's something else I find attractive about you. You don't think you're God's gift to women."

He shrugged. "I'm not sure I'm God's gift to anyone," he said, "except maybe Brinkley."

"Dogs are God's gift to us," Jenny said, reaching down to stroke Brinkley's head, which he'd been offering for several minutes.

"I agree."

"When did you realize you were in love with me?"

"We're acting like teenagers again," he said.

"So? Beats growing old in your heart and mind."

"I guess you're right."

"Then answer my question."

"Remember when we were at lunch on Monday and you made a fuss over that little girl? Going on about how cute she was?"

"Yeah."

"I watched you interact with her and her mother. You were great with her. Kind. Love just oozed from your every pore. I thought it must be great to have that much love in you. Then there was the tip."

"The tip?"

"Yes. When we were leaving, you said to be sure to leave a nice tip. I always do, but again, that shows how much you care about people. Then there's the fact you volunteer to teach art to disadvantaged children and you protested the firing of that professor even though you didn't agree with his politics."

"Thanks," she said. "But there's something I need to tell you about the little girl."

He smiled. "She was a plant? You hired some mother to bring her child to Perry's that day so you could show how much love you have for others?"

"No." She wasn't smiling, and he wondered if he had gone too far.

"I'm only joking, you know."

"Yes, I know. But there is something you should know before we get any further in our relationship."

"What's that?"

"I can't have children. I have what is known as polycystic ovaries. They're full of cysts." Her eyes teared up. "I will never be a mother."

"Oh. I'm sorry."

"Me, too. I didn't want you to start making plans for us or something and not know that."

"That must be awful to love children and not be able to have one of your own," he said.

She used a napkin to wipe her tears. "I'm sorry. I never intended for this to go there. It's just you were talking about how I was with that little girl, and I figured I should tell you."

"I'm glad you did."

"The tip thing, though. That's different," she said, doing her best to move on. "I've waited tables, and it's always hard to do. Bad tips are sometimes caused by stuff out of your control, like the kitchen getting behind or someone not showing up for work, which happens all the time in the food service industry. It's so hard to have a job that barely pays you anything and have to depend on the tips just to get by, and then people stiff you or leave like ten cents."

"Someone left you a ten-cent tip?"

"Yes. It was awful. The kitchen staff was shorthanded by three people, and we were having to take over doing things people in the kitchen usually did. That led to slow service. This guy was with a party of five, which included a toddler in a high chair, and he wrote on my ticket that it was the worst service he'd ever received at a restaurant, and he left a nickel and five pennies for the tip."

"You must have felt awful about that."

"I did. I wanted to cry, but it was too busy. I broke down when I got home, and my ex just said, 'Hey, you give bad service, that's what you should expect.' He wasn't understanding at all."

"Where did you meet him?"

She rolled her eyes. "High school. Big mistake."

"Well, I'm glad he's out of your life now."

"Me, too." She looked at him. "And I'm glad you're in my life now."

"Love's kinda weird sometimes."

"What do you mean?"

"I mean, I've met caring women in my adult life. I've met women who I should have been attracted to, but I wasn't. It's like there really is this divine spark that happens when you meet someone who's special. It's like, men meet you all the time. They come and go and pass the time of day with you, but you don't want to go out with them. It's like something special happens and before you know it, you're in love.

"And that spark," he continued. "It becomes dormant for some people once they're in love. They stop reacting to it, so they stop looking for people to fall in love with. Others, not so much. They keep trying to find the spark again, even after they've married. It's a big part of why people cheat."

"What about you? Are you a dormant spark or a seeking-the-spark kind of person?"

"Definitely dormant."

"How do you know that? You said yourself you've never been in love before."

"Because I know myself. I've always valued faithfulness in others. It's probably one reason I love dogs so much. They're faithful almost to a fault. What about you? Which one are you?"

"Oh, I'm a dormant spark person. I value faithfulness, too, and couldn't look myself in the mirror if I went against that." She paused. "My ex? He must have been a spark seeker."

He raised his coffee mug in a toast. "Well, Ms.

Walton, it seems as dormant sparkers, we are made for each other." He sipped his coffee and almost spit it back into the mug. "Ugh. It's cold. Want a warm-up?"

"No thanks. I have some errands to run. What will you be doing today?"

"First, I need to run over to talk to Tom about what he couldn't talk about in the jail."

"Can you tell me later what he says?"

"No. Not unless he says I can. That's part of being faithful, you know."

"Sorry. I've not been close to an attorney before."

"No problem."

"You said, 'first.' What's second?"

"I need to go see Lonnie Gilchrist."

"Good luck with that."

As they cleaned up, he asked. "Have you ever thought about adopting?"

"It's crossed my mind."

"After all, Hank wasn't my real father and Mrs. Dawson isn't my real mother, but I love them more than I loved my natural parents, even when my father and mother were still alive."

"I'll think about that," she said.

After he was dressed and about to leave, she came up to him and said, "Does it bother you that I can't have children?"

"No."

"Are you sure?"

"Of course I am. I mean, I'm not happy you can't have children because I can tell you want them."

"But does it change how you feel about me?"

"No."

"Okay," she said and kissed him. "I love you."

"I love you, too." Saying the words and hearing them brought him a peace he'd not experienced in years, not since he'd moved in with Hank after his parents died in the car wreck.

Before he left, he thought of something and took out his keys. Removing the spare key to his house, he handed it to Jenny. "Your key. I figure you shouldn't have to wait outside for me to get home on the days you're staying. Besides, you need it to lock the deadbolt when you leave to run your errands."

She took the key and smiled at him. "Thank you. You have a nice front stoop, but there's nowhere to sit except on the steps."

He kissed her again and left.

Arriving at Tom's small trailer, he climbed out of his car and went to knock on the door. When Tom opened it, he was holding a beer in one hand.

"You know you're not supposed to be drinking, right?"

"Hey, one beer. What's the harm in one beer?"

"That it leads to a second beer, which ultimately leads to a fourth."

"I can handle it."

Jack looked him in the eye and made sure he had his attention. "It's not about handling it, Tom. It's about staying out of jail. If you're caught breaking your agreement with the court, they'll throw you back in there and you'll get out only to attend your trial before going back in at the end of the day."

"I said I can handle it."

"I've seen my parents say they could handle it. They couldn't. It ended up killing them."

"Yeah, well, they ain't me."

"Tom, if I come by again and you're having a drink of any alcoholic beverage, I'll be forced to turn you in myself."

"Are you crazy?"

"No. I'm an officer of the court."

"But they're payin' you to defend me."

"That doesn't change my obligations. If I know you're breaking the agreement, I have to tell the judge. I'm willing to let it go this time."

Tom stared at him for a moment then walked to the kitchen sink and poured what little remained of what was probably his third or fourth beer down the drain. "Satisfied?" Tom asked with a sneer.

"Where's the rest?"

"You ain't takin' that, are you?"

"Yep."

"What am I gonna do if I get thirsty?"

"Drink water. Or soda. Tea, even. But no more booze of any kind."

"Dang. Spend time in jail and I can't even celebrate gettin' out."

"You can celebrate, just not with booze or drugs of any kind."

"You owe me whatever you take when I'm found not guilty."

"If you're found not guilty, I'll buy you double what I take with me. Do you have any drugs stashed anywhere?"

"No."

"If you do, get rid of them."

"Whatever. What're you here for?"

"We need to discuss a few things we couldn't talk about when you were in jail."

"I'd rather we didn't."

"Your objection has been noted, and we'll talk about what I need to know anyway."

"Maybe you will, but I don't have to. Right to remain silent and all that."

"First, I'm not arresting you, so that doesn't apply, though you can refuse to discuss your case with your attorney, but then I'd have to go before Judge Shelton and inform her you aren't cooperating with your defense. That won't look good."

Tom sat looking at Jack, working his jaw back and forth as though trying to loosen it after being punched. "Okay. Maybe I'll talk, but let's hear what you have to say first."

"The interview room is bugged, correct?"

After a pause, Tom nodded.

"How do you know that?" Jack asked.

Tom said, "Because someone knew what I said in there when I didn't say it anywhere else."

"What was it you said that someone knew about?"

"That someone put me up to committing perjury in that guy's trial—Hank's."

"Why would that matter to anyone at the jail?"

"Let's just say it matters. You say you know who put us up to it anyway," Tom said, a smirk on his face showing he doubted Jack knew anything certain.

"Chief Hicks put you up to perjuring yourself."

Tom's bored expression changed to one of utter shock. "How'd you know that?"

"It was easy, actually. Hicks hated me, still does, I imagine. He's a vindictive person—not the kind of guy who should have worked his way up through the ranks the way he did—and since you and his younger brother Carl were the ones scheduled to testify to a lie, I just knew. I hadn't really thought about it before, but meeting you again and your surprising confession made me consider who would do that, and basically it was a choice of only one. What I don't understand so much is why it matters now. Statute of limitations is long gone for prosecuting it, and since the attempt didn't work anyway, I doubt anyone would pursue it even if they could. So, I'm led back to the same question. Why is it so important now, all these years later?"

"I guess it wouldn't exactly look good for the police chief to have done that when he was a new officer on the force."

"That's true, but the beatings you received seem to indicate more. I would think just a warning would have done the trick." Tom was silent. "Wouldn't you agree? Would a simple warning not to say anything more about that have been enough to keep your mouth shut?"

Tom nodded. "Yeah. I wouldn't have said anything anyway. I made that clear that day in the interview room."

"Tell me about how Hicks went about putting

you two up to it."

"Well, Carl and me was out at Helmer's Creek and saw you and that guy there. Then we saw you shuck your clothes and go swimmin'. Carl and me watched, thinking maybe the old guy might try somethin' with you. When you just came out and got dressed again, we went on our way. Later, Carl was tellin' his brother about it, and his brother suggested after the old guy got arrested that we make a statement that somethin' happened. He told us to come down to the station and claim we saw somethin' that would prove the old guy was messin' with you."

After hearing the story, Jack sat back in thought. The story sounded plausible, even likely. He'd always thought Tommy and Carl had just seen what really happened and had come up with the plan on their own because Jack was their number one enemy.

"Who beat you up?"

"Couple of officers who're close to Hicks. The first time it wasn't much, just a few punches."

"Why the second beating?"

"The chief told me he didn't trust me after you suggested telling the judge to get in good with her."

Jack felt a moment of regret. "The chief was there for the beatings?"

"No. He left the room before they started in on me."

"We can't just let this slide," Jack said.

"If you say or do anything, he'll do something to get back at me—and you."

"Tom, he's listening in on legally privileged

conversations. He's intimidating a potential witness. That's not small potatoes. Those are felonies. Serious ones, in fact."

"Well, the more serious the crime, the more someone like Chief Hicks would do to keep people from finding out."

Jack looked at Tom for so long without saying anything Tom began to squirm in his chair. Jack knew he would have to do something, but he would need to be sure Tom was taken somewhere safe until the chief of police was behind bars himself.

"Have you heard back from Lonnie?" Tom finally asked, an obvious effort to change the subject.

"Not yet. I'll be going out to see him today, but I need to do something else first."

"What?"

"I'm going to see if I can involve the state bureau of investigation in this. It won't take more than a search warrant to verify that the room is bugged."

"You do that, and he'll know it's because of me."

"That's why I'm going to make sure you're in a location nobody can find you."

"You mean like witness protection?"

"Not exactly, but I think we can put you up in a hotel under another name before the interview rooms are searched. You'd not be allowed to leave, but we'd make sure you didn't need to."

"How long will that last? I don't want to be stuck in a hotel room. It'd be just like bein' in jail."

"It'll only be for a couple of days. Besides, you

could order room service."

Tom blew his breath out in a steady hiss between pursed lips. "Great. Trustin' my lawyer was the worst decision I ever made."

"Or the best," Jack said, and packed his briefcase before transferring the beer to the trunk of his car and driving off to see Trisha and Chuck.

17

Arriving at the Sheltons', Jack hoped it wasn't too early to be dropping by unannounced on a Saturday. It was nearing eleven o'clock, and while he knew they wouldn't be in bed—Chuck rose even before the chickens—he didn't want to impose on their morning.

Chuck answered the doorbell. "Well, to what do we owe this honor? Come on in!"

"I apologize for stopping by without calling first, but I have to discuss something with you and Trisha."

"Nonsense. You're welcome whenever you need to see us. You look a little rattled. Is everything okay?"

"I'm not sure. I mean everything is fine with me, personally, but I can't say that everything is okay."

Chuck's brow furrowed. "Then come have a seat and let's talk."

At that moment Trish walked into the room. "I thought I heard your voice," she said to Jack, giving him a small greeting hug. "Let's have a seat. You want any coffee or anything?"

Chuck said, "He looks like he could use a stiff drink."

"No, nothing, thank you. I just need to get your advice about something."

Trisha sat in her chair, concern showing on her face. "What is it?"

"Chief Hicks is bugging the attorney-client interview rooms—well one of them, at least." For the first time, Jack realized he had always been taken to the same interview room. The jail had three of them.

Chuck said, "That's a strong accusation. What proof do you have?"

"He had Tom beaten up because of something he said to me in a meeting."

"Was that what happened to him?" Trisha asked. "I was wondering yesterday when y'all were in court. He looked like he was run over with a truck."

"Two of the officers did it."

Chuck asked, "Are you sure Tom is telling the truth?"

"Mostly sure. I don't see Tom as being smart enough to come up with some kind of lie like this. He really didn't want to talk about it at all. He had real fear on his face in the interview room when I wanted to talk to him about who beat him up. That's when I suspected he'd been beaten because of something he'd said. He flicked his gaze over his shoulder as if indicating someone was listening."

Trisha asked, "Why was he beaten?"

"He told me he'd been coerced into lying on the stand in Hank's trial, but he wouldn't say who did that. It wasn't hard to figure out Hicks had done it, and I figure the chief realized that as well."

Chuck sat back a bit in his chair in shock. “That’s right.” He leaned forward again. “Jack, you need to be careful here. If he’d have officers beat Tom up just because he said something to you, he’d do something to you if he got the chance.”

“I can’t ignore that he’s eavesdropping on privileged conversations.”

“We need to involve the state bureau of investigation,” Trisha said. “They can find a bug if it’s there.”

“And what if he removes the bug because he suspects we’re onto him?” Jack said.

Trisha shook her head in disappointment. “An investigation would still be able to continue because of what Tom is saying.”

“I’m not sure Tom would say anything to anyone. If the bug’s not there, we don’t have anything but an accusation.”

Chuck said, “An accusation that could lead to some bad results for you and Tom.”

Trisha said, “We can’t just let it slide.”

“I don’t know,” Chuck said, “I’m sure this happens more than we know.”

“Well, I’ll do my best to make sure it never happens again in Denton, Florida,” Trisha responded.

“Maybe he removed the bug. If he did, and he’s decided not to chance putting it back in, we’ve taken care of the problem moving forward,” Chuck said.

“But we can’t be sure he did,” Trisha said. “I’m going to have to involve the state bureau in any case.”

Jack looked at Trisha. "If we go in with a search warrant and find nothing, it could get even uglier than it already is."

Trisha said, "What choice do we have? Let me make a few phone calls and see what can be done."

She looked at Jack and somehow smiled despite the problem he'd come to tell them about. "Let's talk about something else. How are you and Jenny getting along?"

"Fine." He preferred to hold off on telling them they were in love. He had too many other things to do that day and didn't have the time it would take once they began asking more questions.

"I heard you brought her flowers the other day."

Jack chuckled. "Yes. Where did you hear that?"

"The grapevine, dear. Because so many of us working at the courthouse are unable to talk about so many things that happen there, when something does happen that someone can tell, it spreads far and wide."

"I'll keep that in mind."

"She's a nice young lady," Chuck said.

"I agree," said Jack as he stood. "Well, I've taken enough of your time. I have several things to accomplish today and need to get started."

"Well, watch your back. Dagwood Hicks is nobody to be messing with," Chuck said.

As Jack was saying his goodbyes at the door, Trisha asked, "How's Mrs. Dawson doing?"

"She was fine when I last saw her a couple days ago. I need to drop by with Jenny so they can meet."

Chuck laughed. "So, already introducing her to your mom, eh?"

Jack was used to the ribbing he received from Chuck and smiled. "I guess so."

Jack stopped at his office and checked for phone messages. There was one from a woman whose daughter had been arrested for cocaine possession, but none from Lonnie Gilchrist. He returned the woman's call to set up an appointment for Tuesday. The woman had not balked at his full rate of $175 an hour. It would be nice to earn that on a case instead of the barely minimum wages paid by the Public Defender's Office. A cocaine possession case would garner him at least ten hours of work, more if it ended up going to trial.

Arriving home for some lunch before heading to Wharton to see Lonnie Gilchrist, Jack was pleasantly surprised to see Jenny's car in the driveway. When he walked through the door, he was greeted by an excited Brinkley, who seemed to be telling him that Jenny was there. He would have known she was there even without seeing her car in the driveway and Brinkley's attempts to tell him. The house smelled of something delicious cooking, and vacuum cleaner lines seemed painted in the carpet.

As he passed the half bath that was just off the entry foyer, he smelled disinfectant.

Entering the kitchen, he found her chopping fresh celery. "Thank you for cleaning my house and cooking something that smells incredible, but you didn't have to do this, you know."

"I know. I wanted to." She looked around. "It's

not that it wasn't clean before, but I just wanted to do that for you. Cleaning my place takes, like, twenty minutes."

"Okay. I just don't want you to feel obligated or something."

"I don't." She continued chopping the celery.

"So, what's for dinner?" he asked.

She answered without looking up from her chopping. "Leg of lamb."

"They must be paying you too much at the Public Defender's Office."

"It's not something I make often. In fact, I've not made it in a couple of years because, well, it's a lot to make for one person. But now, I thought it would be nice to fix one of my specialties for you."

"Mmmm. Cleans the house and can cook, too."

She smiled at him over her shoulder. "I wouldn't get too used to it."

"Oh?"

"Yeah. I'm one of those share-the-labor kind of ladies. This was just me being super nice."

"Well, you succeeded."

His phone rang, so he stepped over to answer it.

"Hello?"

"Is this Jack Turner?" a man's voice asked.

"Yes."

"Jack, this is Louis Walton. I'm Jenny's father."

For a brief moment, he wondered how Mr. Walton had found his home number, which was unlisted, then remembered he'd included it in the letter about his brother.

"Hello, Mr. Walton," he said, including his

name to signal Jenny it was her father calling. She smiled at him.

"I just received a preliminary report on your inquiry about your brother."

"Thank you for helping out, sir. You didn't need to do that."

"Apparently, you don't know my daughter very well. When she insists on something, saying no isn't an option."

This was news to Jack. She had led him to believe her father had offered to help. "Well, thank you anyway."

"Your brother's separation from the Marine Corps was not, well, a good one."

"Oh?"

"Yes. He received a dishonorable discharge. It seems he was arrested twice for breaking and entering and drug possession while stationed at Camp Pendleton in San Diego."

Jack considered confessing he already knew his brother's life had likely been a life of crime for the most part, including the problem with drugs, but decided against it.

"Is there any indication of where he went from there?"

"I'm afraid not. He was wounded in Vietnam in April 1969. Treated in Hue before being transferred to Honolulu for rehab of his injuries. He was shot in the right hip, and if he's still alive, he'd walk with a noticeable limp. He was working in military personnel at Pendleton, a desk job, and could have finished his time there and received an honorable discharge, but he apparently became involved with drugs. One note suggests he may have developed a dependence on morphine after being wounded. Unfortunately, it happened a lot back then. I'm sorry. I wish the news could be better."

"That's no problem, sir. Thank you, again."

Mr. Walton's next question surprised him. "Is my daughter there?"

After a short pause, he said, "Umm, yes, sir. Would you like to speak to her?"

"Yes, if you don't mind."

Jack held the phone out to Jenny. "He wants to speak to you."

Wiping her hands, she stepped over and took the phone. "Hi, Daddy!"

Jack watched her in conversation with her father. Her replies did not hint at what the questions might be beyond how she'd been doing. After talking to her father, she said, "Sure. Put her on."

A conversation with her mother ensued, and Jack decided to take Brinkley for a walk. He silently signaled his intentions, and she nodded, waving at him as if to say, "Have fun!"

When he and Brinkley returned from their walk, she was sitting at the small table where they'd shared breakfast.

"Your dad was nice."

"Yes, he's a great guy."

"You talked to your mom, too?"

"Uh-huh. She wanted to talk to you, but you'd left. She said to tell you hello and she looks forward to meeting you."

"It surprised me when your dad asked if you were here."

"They know we're in love."

"Oh?" This surprised him, but then she was obviously an open person who wouldn't keep her life a secret from her parents.

"Yes. And don't worry. They're thrilled."

"That's good."

She smiled and leaned in to kiss him.

"I stopped in just to grab a bite of lunch."

"I thought we were going by my place for that."

"Oh, yes. I forgot."

"Do you still want to go?"

"What about the leg of lamb?"

"That's for supper."

"Won't it get cold?"

"Don't worry. I warm it up first and I also make a gravy to go with it."

"When will it be done?"

"In about five minutes."

"Fine, then. We can go to your place for lunch when the lamb's done."

When they arrived at Jenny's apartment, he could see what she meant by how small it was. It may have been only seven-hundred square feet, if that. A tiny, cluttered living room led to an even smaller kitchen. The bathroom was the only door beyond the kitchen other than the door at the end of what could be called a hallway that led to the one bedroom. The term shotgun apartment was giving it more credit than it deserved.

"This is small," he said. "But I do have room enough to turn around." He demonstrated. "Barely," he added and grinned. "Don't worry. It's fine."

"At least now you know why I prefer being at your house."

"That, I do." He stepped the few feet into the kitchen. "So, what do you have for lunch?"

"I have some lunch meat."

"That'll do just fine."

They sat at the small table in the living room and ate. When they were done, he asked, "Can I ask why you're living in such a small apartment?"

"Finances. I can't afford much else. At least it's a waterfront complex. That comes in handy in the summer. Just a hop, skip, and a jump to the Gulf, and the view outside my bedroom window is fabulous."

"Oh? May I see?"

"Sure."

A half hour later they dressed and drove back to Jack's house.

After saying goodbye to Jenny until later, Jack drove to Wharton to see Lonnie. When he arrived, he was met at the door by Lonnie himself. He was dressed in blue jeans and no shirt. Jack noticed he had tat sleeves on both arms. Each ended with a star on the back of each wrist. Jack wondered how people sat still long enough while someone used a device similar to a sewing machine to inject ink beneath their skin. He imagined the pain would be considerable.

"Yeah, Elyse told me you'd dropped by," Lonnie said when Jack introduced himself. "This is about Tom?"

"Yes, do you mind if I come inside to talk to you?"

"Guess so," he said, backing up to allow Jack to enter the rundown trailer.

The inside was surprisingly clean, and Jack sat down at the small kitchen table, prepared to ask questions that were typical of those he'd ask a character witness before moving on to the other, less friendly ones. Lonnie sat across from him, but not before grabbing a can of beer out of the refrigerator. "Want one?" he asked, as he popped the top.

"No, thank you." As Lonnie settled himself in at the table, Jack asked, "What can you tell me about Tom?"

"What do you want to know?"

"How long have you known each other?"

He thought for a second. "I don't know. Maybe four years."

"Do you consider him a good friend?"

"I guess. I mean, I don't consider him a foxhole buddy or anything."

"A foxhole buddy?" Jack asked, not understanding the reference.

"Yeah, you know, someone you'd consider a good enough friend that you'd defend each other to the death, like a couple of soldiers pinned down in a foxhole during a battle."

"I see. Do you consider him a really good friend?"

"I consider him a friend. I don't consider him what the kids call a BFF. We're just, you know, regular friends."

"What could you tell me that would qualify as vouching for his character?"

"You want me to vouch for his character?"

"Yes, that's why I wanted to see you. Tom said you were friends and that you might appear as a character witness."

"Wait a minute. I don't want to go into court for no reason."

"Okay, that's your choice. May I ask you a few more questions, though?"

Elyse entered from somewhere in the back of the trailer. Jack was surprised to see she wore only a bra and a pair of shorts. Lonnie seemed not to notice. Jack didn't know if her display had been designed to make him uncomfortable and want to leave as quickly as he could, but if it were, it was doing its job.

"Sure," Lonnie said. "You can ask all you want. I just don't have to answer all of them if I don't want to."

"Is it true that you were at Tom's trailer a few nights before the robbery?"

"I don't remember."

"He said that he didn't have any beer and you said you'd buy it if he went to the store to get it."

Lonnie thought for a few seconds before answering. "Oh, yeah. I remember that. He musta drunk all he had before I got there or something. Why? Is that important or something? I don't know what his going to the store for beer has to do with what he's charged with. He didn't rob anything that night."

"Do you remember noticing if his gun was there?"

Lonnie's expression changed for a split second

before returning to something more casual. "I didn't know he had a gun. He's an ex-con. Owning a gun's illegal."

"Yes, I understand that, but he thinks it might have been taken and returned later after the store was robbed."

"I don't know nothin' about no gun," Lonnie said, his tone a warning.

"Were you in town the night he allegedly robbed the store?"

"I don't remember."

"It was a Saturday night. February 27."

"Man, I don't keep up with where I've been like that."

"I was just wondering if you remembered hearing about the robbery or that Tom was arrested for it."

"I remember when Tom was arrested, but not the night of the robbery."

"Are you usually in town weekends?"

Lonnie glanced at Elyse, still ignoring her scanty attire. Looking back at Jack, he said, "Sometimes yes, sometimes no."

"Would the company you work for know?"

"Yeah." He leaned back. "What's this all about anyway? Is Tom saying I took his gun and robbed that store?"

"He's not accusing you of anything. I'm just trying to get some information."

"Well, you won't be gettin' any more from me. You need to leave."

"Very well," Jack said, anxious to get out of the trailer. "Thank you for your time."

He rose and Lonnie reached out and put a hand on his shoulder. “And don’t come back.” Menace echoed in his tone. “You won’t like what happens if you do.”

18

When Jack arrived home, he mixed himself a drink and went outside to sit on the patio and listen to the surf beyond the dunes. Jenny, noticing his darker mood, joined him, hoping to dispel whatever had upset him.

"How'd it go?" she asked, her tentative tone revealing her cautious approach to the topic.

As he turned to her, he wondered if he wanted to tell her. He didn't know if what had happened would upset her or not. Was she the jealous type who would become upset that another woman had walked into the room wearing only a bra and shorts? Would she worry that perhaps Lonnie might be dangerous? For the first time, it troubled him that he had fallen in love with her without knowing such basic things about her, which made him wonder if this was more of an infatuation. This was the first time he ever felt as if he was in love, so the emotions could be confusing.

He considered shrugging the episode at Lonnie's off but decided if she was either the jealous type or the kind of woman who couldn't handle the inherent risks of being a criminal defense attorney, he should find out now rather than later.

"Not as well as I'd hoped," he said, knowing she would push for details.

"You mean he didn't confess to robbing the store?" she asked, a hint of teasing in her voice.

He supposed she was attempting to calm him, make whatever had happened less troubling.

"No. He didn't take my questions well at all. He was cooperative enough at first, but that changed."

"Did he realize you might think he had committed the robbery?"

"Yes, and I expected that. The truth is he more or less threatened me if I ever came back to speak to him. Actually, more or less is not true. He did threaten me."

Her expression changed. "What did he say?"

"He told me that if I ever came back that I won't like what happens."

"Do you think he would actually do something to you?"

"I wouldn't put it past him. He sort of oozes a threat of violence."

"What are you going to do?"

"My job. I'm going to check if he was in town that night, at least as far as his job is concerned. I may see if I can find out who he hangs around with besides Tom. The truth is he acted more guilty of the crime than Tom did. It makes me wonder if Tom might actually be telling the truth."

Jack looked at Jenny and didn't like the fear he saw there. "Don't worry. I will make sure I don't have any encounters with him again. Besides, his girlfriend sort of freaked me out, too."

"What did she do?"

He looked at her to gauge her non-verbal reaction. "She came into the room wearing only a bra and shorts."

Her eyes widened. "With him sitting right there?"

He nodded.

"Was it one of those padded bras that have more material than a bikini top, or was it—skimpy?"

"Skimpy. Lacy. Practically see-through."

She pulled her lower lip behind her front teeth and frowned.

"Does that bother you?"

Her brow furrowed. "You mean, am I jealous?"

He nodded again.

"I'm not sure jealous is the right word. I'm upset that someone would walk into a room wearing almost nothing with her boyfriend sitting right there, but that's more of a belief in decorum than anything else. Did he seem upset she that did that?"

"No. He barely noticed her."

"Maybe that's what she was doing—seeing if he'd say something."

"You mean she wanted him to get upset at her?"

"It's been known to happen. Some people get almost nothing but negative attention. If that's what she's used to, she'll do things to get that attention. Either that or she'll do anything to get any attention at all, good or bad."

"It's a crazy world."

"A sad one."

"But the truth is he barely noticed. I wondered if he'd have said or done anything if she'd come into the room naked."

"He may have said something after you were gone. Or done something."

"You mean like hit her?"

"As I said, it's been known to happen."

"Or maybe he doesn't really care."

"That would be sad, too."

"I'm glad you're not the jealous type. I wondered since your ex fooled around behind your back."

"Well, I wouldn't go so far as to say I'm not the jealous type. A little jealousy is a healthy thing. I mean if she had openly flirted with you, I'd want to pay her a visit myself."

He laughed for the first time since dropping Jenny back at his house before driving to Wharton. "What if I had flirted back?"

She gave him a faux stern look. "Then we'd have a problem."

The leg of lamb was delicious and for the first time since they'd become intimate, they went to bed and did nothing but sleep.

The next evening, Sunday, Jack lay alone in bed, thinking how empty the bed felt. Jenny had come over briefly before heading to teach her art class in Wharton, but they had decided that Jenny should sleep at her apartment because, as she had said, "Otherwise, I might as well move in." It wasn't the first time the idea had come up—her father had asked her about it and her parents seemed to expect it to happen one day—and for the first time, Jack wondered how soon that might occur. He missed having her there and sleep was slow in coming that night. Part of him wondered if his life spent more or less alone had become a sour note, leading to his desire to never be alone again. That could explain how quickly he had fallen in love. He'd grown tired of the single life and was ready to settle down with someone who loved him in return.

He called her the next morning around the time he knew she would be reading her paper and having her scant breakfast, avoiding the subject of how empty the bed had seemed.

"How was class yesterday?" he asked when she answered.

"Great, as usual. I have this one student, Jamal, who is really talented. Most of the kids just enjoy the class, but this kid is the real deal. It's so much fun working with him."

"How old is he?"

"Fifteen. And I mean this guy has so much talent. He's creating his own comic book, complete with story, pictures in frames, super heroes, villains—the whole thing. He's already good enough he could be the next Stan Lee."

"Who's Stan Lee?" he asked.

Jenny's stunned silence lasted several seconds. When she spoke, she sounded flabbergasted that he didn't know the name. "Who's Stan Lee?! Are you kidding? He's like the combination Shakespeare and Rembrandt of comic books."

"Okay, sorry. I never heard of him. I didn't have a bunch of comic books as a kid."

"Well, you missed out on a lot. I had a comic

book collection many people would kill for. My dad still has some of the first edition stuff I collected. They're probably worth some money today."

"I've heard they can be quite valuable."

"Some are worth hundreds of thousands of dollars, maybe more."

"So this Jamal is good at this?"

"Jack, he could get a job right now with Marvel or DC Comics. He's literally that good. The problem is he doesn't think he's that good. I keep telling him he is, but he won't listen."

"He's only fifteen. He'll figure it out one day."

"I hope so."

"Will you be over tonight?" he asked, trying to sound casual as if the question wasn't important.

"Of course. I can't go more than one night sleeping alone now."

He smiled. "Neither can I, it seems."

"I woke up several times last night. Not having you beside me in bed was like waking to find out there were no sheets or pillows on the bed. You can sleep without sheets or pillows, but it's not the same."

"So, I'll see you this evening, then?" he said.

"Count on it."

That evening when he arrived home, he found a letter in his mailbox from the warden at the Florida State Prison in Raiford. Opening it, he read it, hoping for helpful information.

Dear Mr. Turner:

I received your letter and looked at your

brother's file from when he was here and made a few phone calls on your behalf. It is admirable that you are trying to find your brother to help him straighten out his life.

Your brother, Richard Gray Turner, was incarcerated here from March 1987 through June 1989. He was a model prisoner while here, according to our records. His conviction stemmed from an incident in Jacksonville. He was arrested, tried, and convicted of breaking and entering, burglary, and illegal possession of Vicodin. As I'm sure you're aware, Vicodin has become a very popular drug among those addicted to opioids. His arrest date was December 4, 1986.

You asked where he might be now, but I am unable to help you there. He was released from reporting to his parole officer in March 1990, which finished his full sentence of thirty-six months. We have no record of his whereabouts after he completed his parole. His parole was served in Jacksonville, and his last known address was at 4207 West 29th Street in Jacksonville. That is the extent of what we know.

You may contact his parole officer for possible further details, but I spoke with him, and he has no information about his current whereabouts either. Still, there might be other questions he can answer. His name is Edward Miller, and he can be reached at 904-555-4823.

I wish you good luck in finding your brother.

Jack stared at the letter for a moment. He spent some time beating himself up for not seeking to know what happened to Rick earlier. If he'd started looking just two years ago, he would have been able to find him with ease. In late March that year, he was still seeing his parole officer.

Still, the idea he might be living in Jacksonville, just a day's drive east, excited him. If Rick was still living at that address, Jack could be there tomorrow. He was fairly certain Rick had moved away from there long ago, but it was possible he hadn't.

He dialed the 904 area code and the number for information—555-1212.

The operator answered with the question, "What city?"

"Jacksonville."

"How may I help you?"

"Do you have a number for Richard Turner, or Richard Gray Turner?"

"One moment, please."

A moment later, the operator said, "I see no listing for a Richard Gray Turner, but I have three for a possible Richard Turner. There are two listings for a Richard Turner and one for R. Turner. Do you know an address?"

"Is there one for 4207 West 29th Street?"

"I'm sorry, no."

"Okay, can you just give me the three you have?"

After Jack had the numbers, he called the first on the list. A woman answered.

"Yes, hello," Jack began. "I am searching for my brother, Richard Turner, and directory assistance gave me this number for someone with that name."

"I know my husband's brothers, and none of them would be searching for him," the woman said.

"Thank you," Jack said, and hung up.

The next Richard did not answer. The voice on the message said simply, "Hey, leave a message. I'll get back to you." The voice sounded as though it could be Rick's, but Jack was completely uncertain. He decided against leaving a message for the same reason he had avoided telling Lonnie Gilchrist he might be a suspect in the robbery. If this Richard Turner turned out to be his brother, he might leave town if he knew Jack was searching for him.

The person who was listed as R. Turner answered, but the R was for Rhonda. Jack had suspected it might be a woman since single women who listed their numbers often used only an initial to prevent being identified as a woman by the creeps out there. It was a sad statement about the world that they needed to do that.

He pinned his hopes on the one call that had gone to the answering machine.

When Jenny arrived, they had dinner and watched some TV before going to bed. Jack noted how much better the bed felt now that she was there. The warmth from her made him feel less alone.

The next morning, he tried the phone number again with the same result. This time, he almost left a message, but decided against it. He would try again a couple of times before doing that.

19

When he arrived for work, a courier was waiting for him to open his office.

"I have a delivery for Mr. Jack Turner," the man said.

"I'm Jack Turner."

Handing Jack a sealed box, the man said, "You need to sign for this."

Jack knew what the box contained. It was the discovery file on Tom's case. The state was required to share all material that would be used in evidence against Tom. He had expected a slim envelope and was surprised he'd been sent a box. Was there that much evidence against Tom? He knew it would be a difficult case to win, and if he were being honest with himself, he had no belief he would win. The amount necessary to send a box full of evidence was a bit of a shock, and he casually wondered if he could get Tom to take a plea bargain, assuming he could somehow swing one.

After he signed the papers to prove he'd received the box, he went inside, sat at his desk, and opened it.

The usual items were there of course—the arrest report, witness statements, the ballistics information about the illegal handgun Tom had stupidly used and fired, whether or not the shot was on purpose—along with the search warrant and information regarding where the gun had been found.

The thing he hadn't expected, though, was the video tape. A tape, obviously a copy of the original since the state would never allow the original to leave their offices, sat on top of the various sheets of paper like some kind of odd paperweight.

Lifting it from the box, Jack inspected it. It was marked as video from the store's security camera. The date matched the date of the robbery. He didn't have a video player in his office, so he would have to watch it that evening at home. He knew he need not hurry with it since it would likely lead to his client's conviction. Still, he was required to watch it. Maybe he and Jenny could pop some popcorn and make a movie night of it. She would probably get a kick out of doing that.

As he pored over the paperwork sent from the prosecutor, he heard the door open and someone enter his receptionist's office, though he had no receptionist and currently didn't need one. He'd put a secretary's desk in the small area to make it look less bare. He was fairly certain who it was, and when he heard a woman call out, "Hello?" he was sure of it.

This would be Danielle Wolford, the mother of the girl arrested for cocaine possession, almost certainly with the girl in tow.

Rising from his chair, he stepped into the reception area.

"Good morning. You're Ms. Wolford?"

"Yes. Are you Jack Turner?"

She was an attractive woman in her forties with striking blue eyes and red hair that reminded him of Mrs. Dawson years ago, but as it turned out, that was where the similarities ended. She wore an expensive suit and a coat that looked to have a fur collar that looked like real mink. Jack approached, holding out his hand to shake hands with the woman. "Yes, glad to meet you. Won't you come into my office?"

The girl looked shy and uncomfortable as they walked into his office. Jack indicated two padded chairs with a small wave. "Please, have a seat." When they'd seated themselves and Jack had taken out a legal pad to take notes, he said, "Now, tell me about your case. It's cocaine possession, right?"

"Yes," Ms. Wolford said. "Tiffany has managed to get herself into real trouble now."

The mother's sarcastic tone made Jack inwardly wince. Such attitudes wouldn't be helpful.

To try to make the conversation more between himself and the girl, Jack turned his body toward her and said, "How old are you, Tiffany?"

"Seventeen. I'll be eighteen next month."

Jack jotted this information onto a legal pad. "Could you tell me what happened?"

Ms. Wolford said, "She was out with—"

"I'd prefer your daughter tell me," Jack said, doing his best to be polite. "I need to get to know how she handles herself in a conversation if I'm to represent her."

"Don't we need to sign some sort of paperwork first?" Mrs. Wolford said.

"This initial consultation is free. It's meant to decide if we will be able to work together. Once that decision is made, then we can start charging for my time." Jack did his best to smile pleasantly. He wasn't sure he would be taking the case. He already had a bad impression of the mother, and he felt she would be leading each meeting. She seemed like someone who didn't enjoy not being in charge.

The woman looked at her daughter. "Go ahead, then, Tiffany. Tell Mr. Turner what happened."

Tiffany seemed to hesitate for a moment, glancing from downcast eyes at her mother. Jack could already see that the girl was completely cowed in her mother's presence. "Well, you see, I was out with some friends, and this guy asked if we wanted to party. So Shelly says, 'sure' and he took us to his place. We were thinking maybe he had some booze or some pot or something like that, but he brings out a baggie with white powder in it."

"It was cocaine," the mother accused.

Jack glanced at Ms. Wolford then looked back at Tiffany, doing his best to ignore the unnecessary comment. "Is Shelly a friend of yours?"

"Yeah. She and Pamela were with me."

"Okay, go on," Jack said.

"Well, the next thing we know, he got a mirror out and he's lining up the powder for us to snort. Pamela says 'what is that?' and he says, 'coke, baby' and slides over next to her and puts his arm around her."

Jack interrupted her "Okay, hang on a second. This guy invites you girls over and he serves you some cocaine? That stuff's not cheap, you know."

"Yeah, I know," Tiffany said.

"So you knew this guy?"

"No. We'd never seen him before."

"What else happened?"

"I'd never done coke before, so I said no. Shelly and Pamela did. When we left, he gave me a small baggy and said, 'In case you change your mind. If you like it, you know where to come get more.' On the way home, we got stopped. The officer didn't believe me when I told him a guy gave me the coke."

Jack didn't blame the officer. He watched Tiffany for a moment and could see in her eyes that she could tell that he knew she was lying. The girl flicked her eyes in the direction of her mother, doing her best to hide it. Jack was reminded of Tom flicking his eyes to glance over his shoulder to indicate the walls had ears. There was utter distrust in the girl's quick glance. She seemed to be saying, 'Yeah, I'm lying, but I won't tell the truth while she's in here.'

Her story, though possible, was ridiculous. Guys would not blow hundreds of dollars on three girls they didn't expect to get repayment from in some form, most likely sex. Still, even that was hard to believe given the cost of enough cocaine to get the girls high enough to make getting sex easier. The guy could hire three hookers for less.

Jack had soundproofed his office so that anyone sitting in the reception area would be unable to hear anything said in a conference, even if voices were raised. He had to speak with the girl without her mother there.

He considered how to handle this. The mother evidently believed this story, but there was something her daughter clearly did not want to say in front of her. He could ask the mother to wait in the waiting area with the daughter sitting here, or he could talk to the mother privately to talk her into waiting. Jack figured the woman would not go willingly to allow him to speak alone with her daughter without being coerced into doing that. Being asked to wait in the other room in front of her daughter would make the mother feel weakened in her position of authority.

"Tiffany, could you wait in the reception area?" he asked, nodding toward the door to his office. "I need to talk alone with your mother for a moment."

Tiffany rose from her seat and walked out of the room. As she left, he said, "Would you close the door, please, until you hear the latch?" She did so and Jack turned to Ms. Wolford.

"Ms. Wolford, I will need to speak to your daughter alone if you want me to take this case."

"What for? I'm her mother!"

"Yes, ma'am. And that's precisely why I need to talk to her alone. There's something she's not telling me, and I need to know what that is."

"Then you'll tell me?"

"Actually, no. Not unless she says I can."

"But I'm the one paying the attorney's fee."

"Yes, ma'am, but you're not the client. I wouldn't be defending you. I'd be defending your daughter. What she tells me in confidence would have to stay that way."

"Well, I've never heard of such a thing! If I'm

paying your salary, I should be told everything that is said!"

"You probably will find out eventually, but the fact is, I won't be the one to tell you."

"You mean she will?"

"Not exactly, but she might. I will do my best to get her to take you into her confidence. You'd probably find out anyway once this goes to trial, if it does."

"Why wouldn't it?"

"She might take a plea bargain."

Her expression hardened. "I can tell you that that's not going to happen." Thinking for a moment, she said, "You're certain you can't share with me what she tells you?"

"Absolutely. Look, Ms. Wolford, I have another client that the state is paying me to represent. Not even they can ask me to tell them what is said in a confidential meeting with my client. If I did, I'd be aiding the prosecutors, which is the State of Florida, the very entity that is paying me. If I told you what she says to me, it would be just like having this person she says supplied her with the cocaine stepping in and offering me twice what you pay me to allow him to be paying for her defense and claiming that I needed to tell him what she said against him."

She considered his request. "Never mind. We'll find another attorney." She gathered her purse and stood. "Thank you for your time, anyway."

"Ms. Wolford, I won't try to convince you to hire me, but I will say this. Any attorney worth anything will recognize your daughter is either outright lying or holding something crucial back. He or she will recognize exactly what I have—that she won't talk freely with you in the same room. They will make the same request I have. I can pretty well guarantee you that if the attorney you hire doesn't ask to speak to her without you in the room, all that attorney wants is your money. Your daughter's future means nothing to that person."

She stood still, even the nervous fidgeting that had dominated her presence gone. Jack could see she was considering what he'd said. He could also see she knew he was right. It wasn't that Jack needed the money she could pay him. In fact, he wasn't looking forward to having to deal with the woman over the course of this case. But he felt her daughter Tiffany needed someone who would hear what she had to say. She obviously couldn't trust her mother.

"I need to speak with her alone first before you talk to her," she finally said.

"That's fine. This room is soundproof. If you close the door and talk to her out there, I won't be able to hear anything said, if that's important to you."

She didn't answer but strolled to the door and opened it. He heard a tiny shriek of shock from the room and knew the swiftly opening door had startled Tiffany. The door closed.

Enough time went by that he wondered if they had left to seek a different attorney after all. He was about to check when the door opened and Ms. Wolford more or less pushed Tiffany into the room. "She'll speak to you now," Ms. Wolford said and closed the door, leaving a rather subdued Tiffany standing there, looking like an orphan. As Jack considered this image, he found himself feeling she probably felt like one, too.

"Have a seat," he told her, then added, "please."

She sat in the same chair and folded her hands, her fingers seeming at war with each other.

"Tiffany, I could tell you were either lying outright or leaving something crucial out of your story. I think you know I could see that."

She nodded.

"So, are you ready to tell me the truth? I can't help you, and neither can any other attorney, if you aren't honest with me. If there are some extenuating circumstances, now is the time to let me know."

"Did my mother hire you yet?"

"Not yet."

"Then can't you tell what I say?"

"No. Because you are here for my legal advice, whatever you tell me will remain with me. The thing you can't do is tell me one thing and then lie about it later under oath. I cannot knowingly allow you to perjure yourself." The thought of Tom perjuring himself years ago at the behest of the current police chief struck him, and he quelled the anger that wanted to rise in him.

"Okay. I can tell you. My mom just says not to go into anything involving my family."

"Do they have anything to do with the charges against you?"

"Not exactly."

Jack wasn't sure why the answer was vague,

but he ignored it for now. “Then I see no reason for you to bring anyone in your family into this.”

“The person who gave me the cocaine wanted me to sell it.”

“Now, we’re getting somewhere. Why wouldn’t you want your mother to know about this?”

“It’s the guy she’s dating. Well, living with, actually.”

20

May 7, 1970

Rick limped through the narrow belt of woods toward the clearing. He knew these woods well. Pine trees and scrub formed the woods that were no more than thirty yards wide and lay between Wharton High School, where he had gone from grades nine through twelve, and the backyards of houses on the next street over. As he stumbled to the edge of the woods that faced the school, he stood staring at the field used by the physical education classes for their outdoor activities.

He knew that May was the time when the boys' PE classes played baseball. The girls played softball in the field to Rick's left as he stood beside the baseball field. The first class of the day would be coming out soon.

He knew that Jack would be out there at some point during the day. Freshmen and sophomores were required to take PE. If he didn't see Jack, it was because he wasn't in school that day. If that happened, he'd just come back tomorrow and watch again. He wasn't leaving without seeing Jack.

He didn't plan on speaking to him or even letting Jack know he was there. Rick just wanted to see him, watch him as he had fun playing a game he loved.

Once he'd spent the forty-five minutes or so the outdoor portion of class lasted watching his little brother, he would leave and get high. Tomorrow, or whatever day after he managed to see Jack, he would head for New York. He'd always wanted to see that city, and figured this would be as good a time as any to make his way there, hitching rides with anyone who would pick him up.

As he waited, he pulled out his copy of Dalton Trumbo's *Johnny Got His Gun*. It was an anti-war novel that someone he'd met on his journey east had recommended upon learning how Rick acquired his limp. This was Rick's second time reading the amazing novel.

When the third class of the day came outside, Rick saw Jack immediately. His heart swelled, and the tears began. He longed to rush from his hiding place and hug his little brother, and he marveled that Jack seemed to have grown five inches since he'd last seen him.

Rick thought back to that moment. He'd taken Jack fishing off a pier in Wharton the day before he'd left. Much of the conversation was as clear to him as it had been the day of the outing.

"What if they send you to Vietnam, and you're killed or wounded?" Jack had asked.

"I guess it could happen," Rick had said. "But let's not worry about that. Let's just have fun."

At that moment, a Spanish mackerel had hit Jack's line, mercifully moving the conversation away from the war. Rick had known Jack worried about Vietnam from the moment Rick told him he was enlisting. They had spent the rest of the day fishing and talking about everything but the next day and what lay beyond it. Still, the fact he was leaving home hung in the air like the smell of rotting fish. It was bigger than an elephant in the room. It was all-pervasive, yet ignored until Rick was getting on the bus to take him to Parris Island and, as it turned out, Vietnam. When Rick had boarded the bus, Jack had burst into pent-up tears.

Now, Rick watched Jack as he took the field to play shortstop, his favorite position, despite the fact little league coaches always put him at first base because of his length. Jack had always been tall for his age, and had long arms. Rick knew these were important for a first baseman who would have to stretch out as far as possible for a close play at first. Jack's complaint to his coaches that it was important for a short stop as well always fell on deaf ears.

In P.E. games, he was allowed to play whatever his teammates allowed him to play. Jack was a natural athlete, so in P.E. he was given his choice, and Rick was happy for him.

Rick watched Jack stretch for a high ball that blazed just over his glove and headed toward left field, where Rick now sat just inside the line of trees to hide him from view. The left fielder ran up for the ball and threw it to second base as Rick stepped deeper into the trees to avoid being noticed. Jack had looked right at him, and for a moment Rick wondered if he'd been seen, but Jack's gaze followed the ball to the kid playing second.

Rick almost wished Jack had seen him there and come running to him, but he had warned himself not to allow something like that to happen. He wanted to see Jack without being seen himself. He knew that Jack would try to talk him into coming home that afternoon, but he didn't want to do that, and he especially didn't want to put Jack through having to see him leave again. The first time had been difficult enough.

Rick cried throughout the class, wiping tears and snot from his face when his crying turned to sobs he nearly strangled on to keep quiet.

When Jack's class went inside to change out of their gym shorts and t-shirts, Rick took one final look at the school and for the first time missed going there. He'd hated the school when he attended it. Now, he was nostalgic for all the wonderful things it offered beyond an education. His friends had gone there, and some of the teachers were actually nice.

When the field was silent, Rick moved away toward the back yards on the other side of the woods. As he walked down that street, he thought of all the families that lived there. He wondered, too, how many of them had sons in Vietnam, as well as how many might have lost a son there. He didn't think about the possibility that some of the families might have a son who chose never to come home again.

21
April 1, 1992

Jack's eyes narrowed as he tried to figure out whether Tiffany was lying or not. Her look of fear told him she wasn't. She was in absolute terror that her mother would find out.

"Why don't you want your mother to find out about this? Wouldn't she be angry at him for doing this?"

"No. She'd make me move out."

"Why?"

"Her last boyfriend was, well, handsy. I told her he was touching me where he shouldn't, and she accused me of lying because I was jealous."

"She didn't believe you?" Jack knew parents could react to such news in a variety of ways. His own father, when Hank had been falsely accused of molesting Jack, wanted to make money by extorting Hank. Jack had never forgiven his father for basically wanting to pimp his own son.

"Not exactly. She knew he was doing it. In fact, he would reach out and grab me right in front of her, but she ignored it, like he'd touched my shoulder or something. She didn't want to lose her sugar daddy."

Jack decided to move on from these questions.

"So, how did you get arrested for possession?"

"That part was how I told it. I was with my friends and got stopped. We'd been smoking some weed and he could smell it. They called in a lady cop who searched us and found a small amount of coke on me. That led to searching the car, and they found the larger bag in the trunk."

"This was the coke he'd given you to sell?"

"Yeah."

"How much was there?"

"Maybe two ounces."

"Did he know you were skimming?"

"He said I could have two grams for doing it."

Jack recognized the problem with this. Was it possible she had volunteered to sell for her mother's boyfriend in exchange for the two grams? Powdered cocaine sold for about a hundred dollars a gram, a fact all criminal defense attorneys knew. He doubted Tiffany had two hundred dollars lying around to buy such an expensive drug.

Jack also wondered how much Ms. Wolford knew about what her boyfriend was doing. If she turned a blind eye to her daughter being sexually molested by one boyfriend, would ignoring the fact her daughter was being forced to sell coke for another be such a leap? Maybe she was willing to go along with this to keep her sugar daddy well-stocked with the "sugar" she liked to spend.

For a moment, Jack considered telling Ms. Wolford to seek legal help elsewhere but decided against that. As he'd told her, many attorneys wouldn't care about the client at all, just the money. A few were "sugar daddies" in their own lives and needed to keep that "sugar" coming.

Besides that, Jack was hoping to help Tiffany make better decisions for herself. She obviously needed some guidance, and having come from a family that was less than supportive, he felt he had some advice to share—if she would accept it.

"Did the charges include intent to distribute?"

"Yeah."

"What kind of statement did you give the police?"

"I didn't. I clammed up and didn't say a word, like I was a mute or something."

"Wise choice," Jack said, thinking how all too many defendants destroyed their own cases by trying to talk their way out of the mess they found themselves in.

"Have you been arrested before?"

"No. I just heard it on some TV show that the best thing you can do if you're arrested is exercise your right to remain silent." She bit her lower lip. "Can you help me?"

"I will notify the court I have been hired to represent you. I have to tell you, though, that you will have to come clean to your mother about where the coke came from. If she doesn't know, she needs to. If she does, you're only telling her what she already knows."

Tiffany was silent for a moment before she asked, "You think she already knows he wants me to sell for him?"

"I don't know one way or the other. I'm just saying it's possible she does. After all, she ignored the fact you were being molested by her last boyfriend."

Tiffany sat there, nodding as if this made sense to her. "That would explain what she told me in the other room."

"What's that?"

"She said to be sure not to involve either her or Keith in this."

"Keith's the boyfriend?"

She nodded, still thinking about the possibility that her mother knew all about this and did nothing to protect her from such a person.

"I hate Keith," she said, "but I think I hate my mom more."

Part of him couldn't blame her for feeling this way. Her mother was basically pimping her in a manner similar to how his own father had wanted to pimp him.

"Can I ask you a very personal question?"

"As long as I don't have to answer if I don't want to."

"Has Keith become sexual with you?"

She inhaled deeply. "Nothin' I can't handle," she said.

She hadn't answered the question with anything specific, but she had more or less said he did. Her reply reminded him of Tom Gordon when he was getting beaten up in the jail. The truth was they couldn't handle it at all. They simply thought they could.

Jack asked, "Is there anything else you want to tell me that you haven't?"

"No."

"Okay, if you think of something, call me or

stop by. If I'm here, I'll talk to you, but be aware that each time we talk, I will be charging for the time. Your mother will know we spoke."

"Okay."

Rising from his chair, he went to the door and opened it. "Ms. Wolford, you can come in now."

"About time!" she said as she rose. "I was beginning to wonder if you two went for lunch or something."

Jack ignored the remark. "I will represent your daughter in this case."

"Do you think you can get her off?" Ms. Wolford asked.

"I will do my best. Because she doesn't have a record, I might be able to get her probation, especially if I can get the charges reduced to exclude the intent to distribute charge."

"Can you do that?" Ms. Wolford asked.

"I make no promises. All I can do is try my best."

"Well, I guess that's all we got, right?" Ms. Wolford added.

"I suppose so," Jack answered, suddenly wanting this woman who ignored her daughter's real problems out of his office.

"So what do we do next?" she asked.

"After you both sign some paperwork and you pay my retainer, I will notify the court I'm representing your daughter. Again, I need you to understand that I represent her, not you, despite the fact you're paying the bills."

"Yeah, I got it. How much is the retainer?"

"Twenty-one-hundred. That'll cover my first

twelve hours."

"You'll work that many hours on this?"

"More, I'm sure. That's just the up-front money. If it turns out I work less, you get a refund of the balance."

She wrote a check, and he and Mrs. Wolford signed the paperwork that outlined their working relationship, which included information about attorney-client privilege and where that began and ended.

Taking Brinkley, Jack left the office after they'd gone and headed to the dog park. Brinkley needed the exercise, and he needed some time to think about both his cases.

As he watched Brinkley play with the other dogs there, he thought about Tiffany and Tom. They each had become mired in a mess, the way the twigs floating along the roadside in his childhood had become stuck in the debris. Back then, he'd left the twigs there, believing they had chosen this fate. Now he knew sometimes people chose a fate they would prefer they'd moved past.

In a way, his job involved picking people out of the muck they'd become stuck in, helping them move past the problem and give them a better chance of floating in the wide Gulf. This thought cheered him, and he laughed at the antics of a small dog who'd attached himself to Brinkley, as if to a big brother for protection.

Later, when he told Jenny about how he was no longer leaving the twigs to their fate, she said, "I'm glad. That's what helpful people do."

After about thirty minutes of watching Brinkley

and his new buddy, Jack put the lead back on Brinkley and said to him, “I guess you have your own twigs to help move past the muck of life.” He squatted to pet him for a few minutes while telling him how good he was. Brinkley seemed to agree.

He walked Brinkley back to the office, where he gathered the evidence that had been delivered that morning. He decided to go home for lunch and look at the video he’d been given. He wasn’t looking forward to watching it since he was convinced it would be a final nail in Tom’s coffin, but he had to watch it anyway.

After putting Brinkley in the backyard, he plugged the VHS tape into his player and started it. It held only the few minutes involving the robbery.

The first frames told Jack the video wouldn’t provide much in the way of evidence. It was grainy and no clear details could be seen. Jack was grateful for this, since the images, if they were Tom, would be blurred at best, something he could use for reasonable doubt.

As it turned out, he wished the video was clearer.

Watching the screen, he saw a man about Tom’s height and build enter the store wearing a Halloween mask. The intent was obvious, and the man pulled out a handgun, pointing it at the clerk, who raised his hands in the air. Some words were said—there was no audio—and the clerk opened the cash register and stepped back, allowing the man to reach into the till and remove the cash.

Jack sighed, unhappy that the man’s build resembled Tom’s. He watched until the man left the store, raising the gun's muzzle toward the ceiling and firing a shot before running out.

Jack had wondered if the firing of the gun might have been accidental, a result of Tom, or whoever it could be, shooting the gun out of nervousness and the resulting jumpiness that would have occurred with the rush of adrenalin.

However, this was a deliberate act. The person, presumably Tom, had fired the shot on purpose. Jack considered this strange at best. Why leave a slug where it could be retrieved and matched to the gun, especially since there was no reason to fire the gun at all? The noise itself would attract attention if someone were close enough to hear it. It was a dangerous thing for someone robbing a store to do.

With that in mind, he watched the video again, doing his best to note the details. The third time he watched it, he noticed something that looked like a smudge on the back of the robber's hand. It appeared to be dirt, but he couldn't be sure. Maybe it was just a trick of the light, some kind of shadow.

He decided to see if he could get the image made sharper. Other than the man's build, little else could be used to pin this on Tom, so he wanted to find out exactly what that smudge was.

He pulled out his phone book and turned to the yellow pages. Finding an ad for video enhancement, he dialed the number and waited for an answer. After the sixth ring, Jack was about to hang up when a man's voice answered.

"Van's Video."

"Hello, my name is Jack Turner, I'm an attorney in Denton. I have a video that is rather grainy, and I was wondering if you could enhance it to make the images clearer.

"VHS or Beta?"

"VHS."

"Is it the original or a copy?"

"It's a copy."

"I can digitize it and see what I can get, but in all honesty, if you have the original, I might be able to do more with that, since the copy is more or less like trying to draw an outline of your hand. While it's a reasonable facsimile of your hand, it's larger because it's a sort of copy. The original is always better to work with."

"How much do you charge?"

"It really depends on what I have to do and how clear you are hoping to get the image to be."

"There's a smudge on the back of someone's hand that I want to identify. I need to know if it's a shadow, some dirt, or something more identifiable."

"I'd guess somewhere around two-fifty to three hundred."

Jack considered this. It was about half of what he would get for defending Tom, but now he didn't think he would be doing the job he was required to do if he didn't investigate that smudge. He didn't think it was a shadow or dirt. If his suspicions turned out to be accurate, it would mean a lot in this case. Everything, in fact.

"I don't have the original, but I know who does. I'll do my best to get it and be back in touch with you. What are your store hours?"

"I'm open from 8:00 to 4:30. I take lunch from 12:30 to 1:15, sometimes until 1:30 if I'm having lunch with someone."

"One last question—how long would it take?"

"About a week, maybe a few days less, depending on when I can get to it and what I have to do."

"Okay. I'll be in touch," Jack said, and hung up.

He took Brinkley and drove to his office. When he arrived, he began preparing a motion to allow him to have access to the original videotape.

22

When Jack had finished preparing the motion, he went to the courthouse annex to file it. The clerk scheduled the motion for the following Tuesday. Jack decided to hand deliver a copy of the motion to Larry Herndon since the DA's office was across the street, next door to the jail, a location Jack always considered rather convenient for them.

As he stepped through the entrance, he met Larry coming out. "Just the man I was looking for," Jack said.

"What is it?" Larry asked, looking to be in a hurry.

"I have a motion for you. It will be presented to Judge Shelton Tuesday at nine."

Larry took the envelope and skimmed the contents to get a basic idea of what it concerned. "Why do you need the original? We gave you a copy."

"I need to see if it can be enhanced."

"Knock yourself out. It will only give us more ammunition to nail your client."

"Can I just get it now and withdraw the motion?"

"Nope. While I don't mind you paying to get the bad images enhanced, I'll need a motion to turn over the original to you. Zeke would have my head on a platter if I didn't follow the rules."

Zeke was Zeke Ward, the district attorney.

"Then I suppose I'll see you in court at nine Tuesday."

"Jack, you don't think you're going to get him off, do you?"

"Stranger things have happened."

"Don't count on it. This guy's guilty as they come."

"Ordinarily, I'd believe you, and you still might be right, but I'll hold off on my vote to convict until I see that tape once it's cleaned up."

"Suit yourself, but don't say I didn't warn you."

They parted, and Jack returned to the office.

As he drove, he considered trying to find out where Danielle Wolford's boyfriend, Keith, worked, but decided against it since talking to Keith at this point would go against his client's wishes. He would need to talk Tiffany into not worrying about her mother finding out what happened.

Sitting at his desk, he petted Brinkley and picked up the phone. He wanted to try the phone number in Jacksonville again to see if he could get an answer. This time when he called, however, the phone had been disconnected. He called the phone company in Jacksonville and asked when the disconnect service had been requested.

"Tuesday," the man on the line said after looking up the account information.

"Do you have a forwarding address for the last bill?"

"Sir, if I do, I can't share that information with you, I'm afraid."

"I understand. It's just that I'm trying to find my brother. He joined the Marines in '68 and I haven't seen him since."

"I'm sorry. I still can't help you."

"How about this?" Jack asked, hearing the desperation in his voice and hating it. "Do you have information about that person, like their date of birth or something?"

"I can't tell you the customer's date of birth, sir."

"I don't want you to," Jack said. "I just want you to tell me if I'm warm or cold when I tell you my brother's date of birth. You don't even have to tell me I'm exactly right."

"Sir, I could get into a lot of trouble for this."

"Not if you don't tell me anything precise."

There was a pause on the line. Then the phone company employee said, "What was your brother's date of birth?"

"April 15, 1950."

After a moment, the man said, "I cannot tell you if this customer has the same birthdate, sir. However, I would suggest that it's possible you could locate your brother in the Jacksonville area. I guess anything's possible."

Jack was silent. He had just told Jack that the date of birth on the records for that phone number was the same as Jack's brother's.

"Thank you very much," Jack said.

"Sorry I couldn't help you more," the man said. "Good luck finding your brother."

After disconnecting, Jack began to wonder how long he had until Rick left Jacksonville. If he waited too long to go in search of him, he could leave the area entirely. Without anything tying him to a place, he could go anywhere in the country.

Then it hit him. If his brother had left a forwarding address with the phone company, he probably had left a forwarding address for his mail.

He began typing a short letter to his brother.

Dearest brother Rick,

If you get this letter, please let me know where you are. I've thought about you every day since you left home and want desperately to see you again. I don't care what you've done. I only care about seeing you again. I don't even care that you've never come home. Honestly, I understand why you haven't.

Our parents died when I was in high school, so they are no longer a part of my life either.

Contact me, Rick. Please. I love you.

Your brother,

Jack

After printing his home and office phone numbers at the bottom, he addressed the envelope, put a stamp on it, and left the office. Walking to the corner mailbox, he dropped it in.

As he walked back to his office, he prayed the

letter would find Rick and result in their reunion.

Once in his office, he called the Wolford home. He figured Tiffany hadn't returned to school after their meeting. He had been thinking about how to handle the case and wanted to talk to her today because tomorrow she would be in school.

Tiffany answered the phone.

"Hello?"

"Tiffany, this is Jack Turner, your attorney."

"Hi." Her voice had a "what now?" quality.

"I need to speak to Keith. However, doing that will almost certainly let your mother know what you've told me."

"Look, can't you just see what you can do to get the charges reduced or something? I'm under eighteen anyway. Anything I do as a minor won't follow me. Those records are sealed, aren't they?"

A bold truth about this case hit Jack: Keith had her selling the coke because she would have her records sealed when she turned eighteen, which would be next month. He'd convinced Tiffany—and perhaps her mother—that even if she were arrested there would be no real repercussions other than probation or something similarly minor. Keith was probably giving Danielle Wolford the money to pay the attorney's fees.

"Not if the prosecutor decides to try you as an adult," Jack said. It was his job to tell her the truth of her situation, even if it might not happen.

"What?!"

"Tiffany, you're seventeen. Despite being a minor legally, you were fully aware of the illegality and repercussions of what you did. It's entirely possible the prosecutor will move to have you tried as an adult, especially if he thinks this whole arrangement was made to attempt to circumvent any significant punishment for the crime due to your age."

The silence on the other end of the phone turned to quiet weeping. "What are the chances he'll do that?"

"Fairly high, given that you had two ounces in the car, which would be way too much for personal use."

"Maybe I was having a party."

"Tiffany, you know the street value of that much coke. At a reduced rate of a hundred dollars a gram, that's twenty-eight-hundred for just one ounce. Minus the two grams you skimmed, that means you had around fifty-four grams of coke with you, which translates into well over five-thousand dollars' worth of cocaine. I doubt anyone would believe you could afford to invite a bunch of friends over to snort up five thousand dollars in cocaine." He paused to let that sink in.

After the brief silence punctuated by the sound of her crying, he said, "The state is going after the dealers and the people supplying them. They wouldn't hesitate to charge you as an adult in the hopes you'd make a deal and turn in your supplier. That leads to the question of whether you are willing to turn Keith in and see if I can make a deal by hanging that carrot out to the state."

"I don't know."

"Tiffany, once you tell your story of how you were mostly forced to sell coke for your mother's boyfriend, it's likely the DA will make you a good deal. The only real problem we have with that is you were allowed to skim two grams for your own use."

"What about my mom? She'll kill me if I tell them Keith made me do it."

"She might be angry, but she'll get over it. You're nearly an adult now, so you need to take care of yourself." He wanted to tell her that if her mother disowned her, it might end up being the best thing for her, but he didn't. She wasn't ready to hear that, and such a belief on his part was based on very little information. He recognized that he might be making unfair comparisons with his own mother, though he suspected he was right.

"Can I think about it?" she asked.

"Yes, but don't take too long. I can't really do my job if I'm hamstrung by limitations involving your mother's knowledge of our defense strategy. I probably should have realized this when we talked."

"Okay. I'll call you tomorrow, okay?"

"Okay. I'll be at my office all afternoon at least. Call me as soon as you can after you get home from school."

She promised she would and they hung up.

There was nothing to do, so Jack took Brinkley to the dog park again. While there, he thought about Rick and the letter he'd sent.

He was still thinking about that when he arrived home that evening. Soon after he got home, he received a call from Jenny.

"Hey!" she said when he'd answered.

"Hello. What's up," he asked.

"I can't be there tonight, I'm afraid. My cousin is coming in from out of town, and she wants me to show her around. I know you wouldn't want to be a third wheel."

"Your cousin?"

"Yes. She's younger than me and in college. They're on spring break, and she doesn't want to go anywhere the wild crowd will be, like Daytona or Miami Beach. She's not into the party scene much."

"Sounds like a smart girl."

"She is. She's a chemistry major. Me? I'd blow my apartment up if I tried mixing chemicals."

Jack chuckled. "Will I at least be able to meet her?"

"Sure. We can stop by Saturday."

"How long will she be here?"

"Only through the weekend. She has to go home to see her folks after that."

"Okay. I'll miss you."

"I'll miss you, too."

They hung up and Jack began preparing dinner for one, something he was more than used to doing. Tonight's feast would be a small red snapper filet with wild rice and steamed asparagus.

He spent a mostly sleepless night, feeling the emptiness of the bed. Finally, he went to get Brinkley to let him sleep in the bed with him. At least he felt less alone.

This loneliness was something new as well. He'd lived alone most of his life, so losing sleep because the other half of the bed was empty was disturbing.

The next morning, he went to the office and

spent time working on an advertisement for legal services to put in the local paper. He needed more to do than just two cases, both with their own reasons he couldn't do anything until later. That afternoon, he read in his office and waited for the call from Tiffany.

While he waited, Chuck Shelton came by.

"I hear you're representing the Wolford girl."

"Wow. News travels fast. Where did you hear that?"

"From Zeke."

"The DA's talking about me and my cases?"

"He mentioned this one."

"What's so special about this one?"

"Because the DEA is involved with it."

"The DEA is after a seventeen-year-old girl who's not out of high school yet?"

"Nope. They're after Keith Breslin and his girlfriend, Danielle Wolford, who happens to be your client's mother, as I'm sure you know."

"Did the DA send you to talk me out of representing her?"

"No. First, he knows I'd never do anything like that, and second, even if I would, that would be unethical of him. Mostly, he sent me to let you know to watch your back. This Breslin character is a bad one. He's dodged more charges than Al Capone."

"Al Capone died at Alcatraz."

"Yeah, serving time for tax evasion," Chuck said, his tone suggesting how ridiculously minor the charge was considering all the man had done.

"Can I talk to you as a legal advisor on this?"

"Sure." Chuck said, making everything they said about the case confidential. Jack took out a dollar and handed it to Chuck, the usual fee he charged Jack to advise him. Jack knew Chuck charged at least two-hundred an hour to anyone else.

"My client tells me she was more or less forced to sell coke for Breslin."

"Uh-huh." Chuck didn't look surprised. In fact, he looked as though he expected Jack to say that. Jack had expected a little more than the reaction he received.

"You already knew that," Jack stated.

"Well, let's just say it would surprise me if he hadn't done that. One way Breslin has dodged charges is getting minors to be his street vendors, as it were. The fact he had a teenager living in the same house—one that had a liking for cocaine herself—pretty well made forcing her into selling a slam dunk. He threatens the minors and they just take the heat for him."

"You sound fairly informed about my client."

"I read up a little on the facts of the case already."

"You were sure I would want to talk about this?"

Chuck shrugged. "It's my job to know how different people will react to being told certain facts."

"How does he threaten them?"

"I don't know the specifics, but with teenagers, it wouldn't be that hard. He could threaten her mother's life, her own life, or a pet's life. You know how attached people can get to their pets."

"Does Tiffany have a pet?"

"I don't know, but if she does, it's not hard to imagine someone like Breslin telling Tiffany that he'd kill her dog or cat if she told about him."

"It's too late, actually. She already told me."

"That's one thing I was coming by to check. Now that you know, you might want to watch your back."

"So Zeke sent you here to warn me about Breslin?"

"Yep."

Jack laughed, mostly to dispel the dark mood that had taken over the conversation. "I thought DA's hated defense attorneys."

Chuck laughed with him, perhaps for the same reason. "Some do. Zeke's a good guy, though. Or maybe he just doesn't need another murder or missing person to have to prosecute someone for. There's always the possibility his motives are selfish."

At that moment, the phone rang.

"This is probably my client now," Jack said, answering the phone. "Hello, this is Jack Turner, Attorney-at-law."

The voice on the other end surprised Jack since he was expecting to hear Tiffany Wolford's voice. Instead, it was Ms. Wolford. "My daughter told me what she told you. It's not true. Keith hasn't done anything like that. She's just trying to cast blame on him."

"Is Tiffany there? I'd like to speak to her." Jack glanced at Chuck, who was frowning.

"Sure. Here she is, but you can forget barking up that tree. Keith hasn't done anything." Jack could hear her hand the phone to Tiffany.

"Mr. Turner?" Tiffany sounded frightened.

"Hello, Tiffany." He heard Ms. Wolford saying something in the background. He was glad of this because it meant she wasn't listening in on their conversation. "Is your mother telling me the truth? Just answer yes or no."

"No," she said after a brief hesitation.

"Did he threaten you?"

"Yes."

"Do you want me not to go in the direction we discussed?"

"Not really, but yes."

"You can get him arrested and have an injunction placed if you will go to the DEA about this."

"I can't. Just drop it. I need to plead guilty instead."

Jack was at a loss as to how to handle this. Tiffany was obviously terrified of Keith Breslin and maybe even her mother as well. He figured the best thing at the moment was to agree not to pursue Breslin as her supplier and see what could be done.

"Okay, if that's how you want it, but you don't have to plead guilty to the charges. We should try to get a plea deal at the very least. Maybe get you probation."

"Okay." Silence followed, then, "I'm sorry."

"It's okay. We'll talk again when your mother isn't there."

"I can't do that."

"I'll figure out a way. You stay safe."

When he hung up, he looked at Chuck. "That kid's scared out of her mind."

"Should we get CPS involved?" Chuck asked, referring to Child Protection Services.

"No, not yet. She says she can no longer talk to me without her mother there. I need to figure out a way to get around that, though."

"How? You can't very well tell her to run away."

"No. But I can come up with something. Her mother isn't with her every minute of the day." He glanced at Chuck. "That would definitely cramp her style."

"Well, if you come up with something, call me before you do it. That's what the dollar was for."

Jack smiled. "Never fear. I will definitely do that."

They said goodbye and Jack sat brooding at his desk.

Finally, he picked up the phone and called Jenny. She was at home, having taken the day off to be with her cousin. He hoped they hadn't gone somewhere, but the phone rang until it went to her answering machine.

He drove home and waited until that evening to see if they were home yet. He called again and was thankful when she answered. "If you needed to talk to a teenage girl and didn't want her mother around, how would you go about it?" he asked.

"What?"

"I need to talk to a girl who's only seventeen without her mother being there."

"Jack, you sound like a creep."

He chuckled. "Sorry. I didn't think about how that would sound. I have a client who's been arrested for possession of cocaine with intent and I need to talk to her without her mother being there."

"That's no problem."

"How so?"

"Does she go to school?"

"Of course! I can go to her school and talk to her there."

"That's one thing I shouldn't worry about."

"What?"

"You're terrible at figuring out ways to go behind a woman's back." She laughed, obviously enjoying herself.

"Thanks. I'll work on my clandestine meeting notes for the future." Changing the subject, he asked, "How's your cousin?"

"Fine. We went to the beach and sat in the sun today. Water's still too cold for swimming, but lying out there was nice."

"Did you get burned?"

"No. We used tons of sunscreen."

"Good. See you Saturday?"

"Wouldn't miss it!"

That night, Jack again let Brinkley sleep with him in the bed, chuckling at the 'are you sure?' look on Brinkley's face before jumping up on the bed.

"Don't get too used to it, boy. When Jenny sleeps over, it's back to the dog bed for you."

23

The next day Jack drove to Wharton High School and asked if he could talk with Tiffany. When the secretary asked why he needed to see her, he said it was personal because he doubted Tiffany wanted the school secretary to know her business, but the secretary insisted. As a child, Jack had had enough trouble from one school secretary who liked to gossip, and he couldn't trust this one to say nothing if she found out one of their students had been arrested for cocaine possession. Such details about minors were not released in the press. Instead of telling her, he asked, "Then can I speak with the principal?"

"Let me see if he's in his office," she replied, picking up her phone and dialing the extension while asking Jack's name.

"Jack Turner. Just tell him it's in regards to Tiffany Wolford, a student here."

"Are you with the police?" she asked.

"No." He gave no further details.

After a moment, the principal answered the phone, and the secretary said, "Mr. Freeman, there's a gentleman to see you, a Mr. Jack Turner. He says it's regarding Tiffany Wolford." She listened for a moment before replying, "No, sir. He won't tell me what it's in regards to." She listened to his reply and said, "Yes, sir."

Hanging up, she said, "He'll be with you in a moment."

Several minutes later, a short, balding man entered from a back hallway, his hand extended. "Good morning, Mr. Turner. What can I do for you?"

"Can we go to your office?"

"Sure, come on back."

As they walked, Jack said, "The building looks nicer than when I was a student here."

"Oh, you're a Wharton alumnus?"

"Yes, class of '73."

"I'm class of '68 myself. Yes, the building was refurbished four years ago. Definitely needed it. Come in and have a seat."

Mr. Freeman sat down and leaned back in his chair, clasping his hands behind his head. "So, what can I do for you? Ms. Drake says you have some questions about Tiffany Wolford. Are you with the police?"

"No, I'm an attorney."

"Oh? Is she a witness you need to see? If that's the case, I need to notify a parent and get them here before you talk to her."

"No, actually, she's my client."

Mr. Freeman's eyebrows shot up. "Oh?"

"Yes, sir. I take it what I tell you can be considered in confidence? I'm sure Miss Wolford wouldn't want this to get around the school."

"Absolutely."

"Miss Wolford's mother hired me to represent

her. She has been arrested for cocaine possession. Because she is my client and not her mother, I am within my rights to speak to her alone. Her mother understands this to be the case, and in all honesty, I'd prefer her mother not know I was here to speak to Tiffany."

Mr. Freeman frowned. "I'm afraid that will take some explanation before I let you talk to her. We have our own rules here, and I need to know there's a good reason not to let Tiffany's mother know you were here before I comply with that."

"I understand," Jack said. "Tiffany's mother would rather I ignore certain parts of Tiffany's story because they're, well, inconvenient for her."

"Was the coke the mother's?" Jack was surprised by the question. Mr. Freeman evidently saw that and added, "Let's just say I'm familiar with Ms. Wolford and her—shall we say—lifestyle."

Jack's reply was hesitant. "No. It's not hers."

"Her latest boyfriend's?"

"Actually, I'd prefer not to say, if you don't mind. None of what Tiffany told me has been proved, so for now, it's just her side of the story."

Mr. Freeman sat forward, leaning onto his desk. "Tiffany Wolford is a nice girl most of the time, but she's had her share of problems here. She's a senior this year and has been attending since her freshman year. I can't go into details any more than you can, but suffice it to say, we are aware of the fact her home life is less than ideal."

Mr. Freeman sat back again, but this time he did not lean back to fold his hands behind his head.

Jack recognized this as no longer seeing this meeting as casual. "We'll just say what I just told you was in confidence as well."

"Understood," Jack said. "May I talk to Tiffany in private?"

"Yes. I will keep your presence here to myself until I no longer can, should a situation come up in which I must admit you were here to talk to her."

"Fair enough."

"Is Tiffany expecting you to be here?"

"No."

"Okay." Mr. Freeman lifted his phone and dialed an extension. A moment later, he said, "Ms. Drake, would you find Tiffany Wolford and ask her to come to my office?"

A few minutes later, a gentle tapping sounded on the door and Mr. Freeman said, "Come in." Tiffany Wolford stepped in, her eyes widening when she saw Jack.

"What are you doing here?" she asked.

Jack said, "I needed to speak to you without anyone else around. Your mother doesn't know I'm here because I need to discuss our conversation from yesterday with you and only you."

Tiffany looked back and forth between Mr. Freeman and Jack. She started to say something but thought better of it, obviously preferring not to say it in front of her principal.

Jack turned to Mr. Freeman. "Is there somewhere we can talk in private?"

Mr. Freeman stood up. "I need to walk the halls a bit anyway. You can use my office. How long do you think you'll be?"

"I'm not sure."

"Well, then, maybe you should use the conference room," Mr. Freeman said. "I'll show you where it is."

They followed Mr. Freeman down the hallway lined with various offices until coming to a darkened room. Mr. Freeman stepped in and switched on the lights. A large conference table surrounded by eight executive style chairs sat in the middle of the room.

"You can use this room," Mr. Freeman said. "When you're finished, Tiffany, get a pass from Ms. Drake to return to class." He extended his hand to Jack. "Nice to meet you, Mr. Turner. I hope your meeting is productive."

"Thank you," Jack said, shaking Mr. Freeman's hand.

When they were alone, Jack indicated a seat and sat across from Tiffany.

"I apologize for surprising you like this, but I needed to talk to you alone about yesterday's call."

"Did you tell Mr. Freeman that I'd been arrested?"

"Yes, I had to in order to get to see you without your mother present."

"Great!" she said. "I didn't want anyone here to know!"

"He'll keep it a secret," Jack said. "Nobody but the three of us will ever know why I'm meeting you."

"Fine. Forget it. Just tell me what you want to know."

"I need for you to tell me if what you said in

my office was the truth. Your mother says it isn't, but I have to know before I can proceed with planning your defense."

"I answered that question yesterday on the phone."

"Yes, but I need to look into your eyes when you tell me."

Tiffany burst into tears. "I don't know what to do!"

"Tiffany, do you like Keith Breslin?"

"No!"

"Do you want him out of your life?"

"Of course I do! What kind of question is that?"

"Look me in the eyes and tell me the truth. Did he force you to sell cocaine for him? Was that his coke?"

She stared directly into his eyes, pausing to make sure their eyes were locked. "Yes." Jack could not see any sign of deception. She didn't look away. She didn't even blink. He could almost feel the need to be believed.

"Are you willing to testify against him?"

She thought about that for a moment. When he didn't think she would answer, he added, "Tiffany, you have to start living your life. I know your mother is your mother, but I have to tell you, she's not making decisions that are in your best interest."

"What if he threatens me again?"

"I think we can avoid that. He won't need to know at first it was you who talked."

"He'll know anyway."

"Only after he's arrested, and I think I can

guarantee they won't be giving him bail. Too much time and effort has been put into nailing him, but he keeps slipping through the noose. I'll talk to the right people and make sure you won't have to worry about him coming after you."

"They've tried to arrest him before?"

"The DEA is aware of him, and they are doing their best to put him away for a long time."

"How much time could he get?"

"It depends on how much you can tell the DEA agents and the DA. You need to answer questions like, does he have a large stash of drugs somewhere and do you know where it is? Do you know who his supplier is? What other accomplices does he have? That kind of thing. Any information you can provide will make things harder on him and easier on you."

"I'm scared." It was a simple statement and absolutely true. For a moment, she didn't look seventeen but only seven—a scared child in a ruthless adult world.

"I know you are, but if you ever think you're in imminent danger, call me, even if you have to leave the house and get to a pay phone. Call collect if you have to. I will come get you and take you somewhere you'll be safe."

"If he finds out you did something like that—or even something like taking me to the DEA and stuff—he would hurt you, too."

Jack gave a half-shrug. "Then I'll handle that problem if and when it comes up."

"Why are you doing this? You're not being paid enough to put yourself in danger like that?"

Jack reached out and took both of her hands in his and waited for her to look into his eyes. He needed her to believe this as much as she needed him to believe that Keith Breslin forced her to sell cocaine. “I used to be a cast aside child, too. My parents were alcoholics, the Denton town drunks. Two adults stepped up to help me believe in myself. They believed in me when I couldn’t. I guess you could say I’m doing my best to pay them back for giving me love and the kind of direction I needed. That’s all it takes to change a life, really.”

Her tears had mostly subsided. “So what do we do now?”

“Sit tight. I’ll be right back.”

He went out of the room and went to Mr. Freeman’s office. He wasn’t there, but the door was open. Jack figured the man had offered his office originally for the talk with Tiffany, so he decided to help himself to the man’s phone.

Lifting the receiver, Jack phoned Chuck. When he answered, Jack said, “Is it possible for me to bring Tiffany Wolford in to speak to the DEA agent in charge of the Breslin case?”

“I don’t know, but I can find out. Is she wanting to talk?”

“Yes.”

“We’ll have to involve Zeke.”

“No problem there.”

“What kind of deal are you looking for? There’s probably only so much Zeke will do.”

“Probation and a guarantee she won’t be charged as an adult. I’d like all charges dismissed, but I know Zeke won’t go for that. Her records will be sealed soon anyway, provided he takes my offer."

"Does she know if he has more drugs at the home? And if not, does he keep them somewhere else?"

"I can check. She wants to get Breslin out of her life for good. If she knows anything, she'll tell me."

"I'll call Zeke, have him get me in touch with the DEA agent in charge of the Breslin case. I'll set up a meeting. Will tomorrow work?"

"Make it Monday. That way we can all meet here at the school to avoid having a situation where Tiffany can't get away from her mother."

"Okay. In the meantime, find out what you can from her about Breslin's drug dealings."

"No problem."

They hung up and Jack returned to the conference room. When he entered, he saw that Tiffany was sitting in silence, staring at the table as if it held answers to her dilemma. She looked up at him as he sat.

He carried a cassette recorder with him to tape interviews and proceedings when necessary. He took it out now.

"I'm going to record the rest of this interview." She looked frightened, but he assured her. "Nobody else will hear it or even know it exists. This is just to get what you know down for now."

"Okay."

Jack started recording and began by stating the date and time. "Tiffany, what do you know about Keith Breslin's drug business?"

"Like what?"

"Do you know if he has a lot of drugs in the house?"

"No. He keeps them somewhere else. I think they're in a climate-controlled storage."

"What makes you think that?"

"I heard him talking with someone once. He didn't know I was there listening. At the time, I was just curious, you know? Anyway, he said something about how he'd need to go by the storage if the guy wanted that much merchandise. That's what he called it, merchandise. I knew what he meant, though."

"Do you know how much the guy was interested in buying?"

"A key. That's a kilo."

Jack smiled. "Yes. Are you sure it was a storage facility? It seems odd he would store illegal drugs in someplace like that. They're being broken into all the time."

"I don't really know. He just said it was someplace that wasn't hot. That's why I thought it might be climate controlled."

"Or he could mean someplace that was safe, like somewhere that was being guarded in some way," he suggested. He couldn't see someone like Keith Breslin keeping a fortune in illegal drugs in a storage facility.

"Maybe. I don't know."

"Do you know who the other man was?"

"No. He was just a guy."

"Would you recognize him if you saw him again?"

"Probably. I do know he had a scar on his chin."

"That's great. Anything else about him that you can remember?"

She thought for a second. "No." Then she blurted, "Wait! He did say something about the place where Keith keeps the drugs. He said, 'you got the best setup in the whole state.' I remember because that's when they came out of the room and saw me. Keith was real angry and asked if I had heard anything. I pretended I didn't even know they were in there. I acted like I'd been reading a book for school and when I'm reading, I can get kind of lost in the story and not know what's going on around me. Keith even commented on that before, how I get my nose in a book and the world could come to an end and I wouldn't know it."

"Is there a timeframe for when he went to this place? In other words, does he go fairly regularly, like every Sunday or something?"

"No. He does call someone before he goes there, but always on a pay phone. I guess to set it up so he doesn't get shot or something in case it's being watched. And he's paranoid that the phones at the house might be bugged."

"You were with him when he made such a call?"

"Yeah, the time he wanted to get two ounces for me to sell."

"But you didn't go with him to pick the drugs up?"

"No. No way. He always goes there alone."

"Has he ever mentioned any names?"

"No, just nicknames and stuff like that. Like the guy he calls before he goes to pick up drugs he calls Captain. I figure it must be one of the boat captains in Denton."

This made sense. The people who supplied the drug dealers were often meeting their suppliers in the Gulf to avoid being seen. There, large quantities of drugs could be smuggled into the Gulf Coast region.

Jack continued asking questions but didn't manage to find out much more about Keith and his operation. Still, he had something, and it may be enough for the DEA guys to piece together to make more sense of it.

"Okay, I've set it up for you to be interviewed by the DEA and the DA on Monday, right here at the school. You don't say a word to anyone about this. Saying anything could put you in more danger."

"Okay," she said. She had cried through most of the interview, whether from fear or regret, Jack didn't know.

She went to the bathroom to clean up and stopped to get a pass back to class. Jack stuck his head into Mr. Freeman's office to thank him for his help.

"Did you find anything out that will help her?" he asked.

"Maybe. I guess we'll have to see."

When Jack arrived back at his office, he called Chuck to find out what had transpired on his end.

"Whatcha got?" Jack asked when Chuck answered.

"We'll be meeting you and Tiffany at Wharton High Monday at one o'clock."

"Sounds good," Jack said, then relayed what he'd found out in his interview with Tiffany.

Chuck said, "I don't know if they'll be able to figure much out with that."

"Maybe they can put a tail on him to see where he goes after placing a call at a pay phone," Jack offered.

"Maybe. It's not a bad idea," Chuck said.

Jack turned the conversation to more mundane topics until they ended the call. This allowed him to lose some of the stress that was building in him over the case.

When he'd hung up, he took Brinkley to the dog park to let him run off some of the energy he had built up in his pen at the office while Jack had been at the school.

Jack felt he needed the time to decompress as well.

24

The next morning, Jack awoke to the sound of Brinkley barking at the bedroom door. As he worked to clear his mind of the haze of sleep, the bedroom door opened. Jack blinked at Jenny standing in the doorway, grinning.

"Wake up, sleepy-head!" she called. "What happened? Did you tie one on last night or something?"

"No," he answered. "I just decided to shut off the alarm last night and sleep in for a change." He started to climb out of bed but stopped. "Where's your cousin?"

"Making coffee."

He stood and grabbed a pair of jeans from his chest of drawers. "How long have y'all been here?"

"We just got here. I rang the doorbell but you didn't answer, so I let myself in. I thought maybe you were in the shower. I was surprised to hear Brinkley in here barking. Did he sleep with you?"

"Yes."

She reached down and scratched Brinkley behind the ears. "Are you trying to take my place, Brinkley boy?" she asked in a childish voice.

As Jack pulled a shirt on, he said, "He was rather surprised that I let him."

"Why did you let him?" she asked. "Did he sleep with you before I showed up?"

"No."

"So why the change?"

He considered telling her it was because the bed felt so empty without her, but he wasn't ready to confess to that yet, so he shrugged. "Just thought he might like a softer bed."

She looked at him sideways, as if she knew he was lying or at least there was more to the story than he was saying, but she didn't push it.

"Big or small breakfast this morning?" she asked.

"Let's do small. I'm going to take you and your cousin to The Captain's Table for lunch."

"Ooh, that sounds great! I'll go tell Sandi. Bagels sound okay for breakfast?"

"Sure."

She left him to put on his shoes and shave. When he joined them, Jenny introduced them to each other.

"Jack, this is Sandi. Sandi, Jack," she said as she poured three cups of coffee.

"Hi, Sandi," Jack said and took the hand she extended. Her smile was one that prompted one in return. She wore her hair short and no makeup. Because she wore sandals, he noticed her fingernails were all painted different colors. Then he saw that her toenails matched her fingers.

"I've heard a lot about you," Sandi said. Then glancing at Jenny she said, "And I do mean a LOT." She giggled as Jenny shushed her.

"She's exaggerating," Jenny said.

Sandi gave Jack a conspiratorial grin and wink. "No, I'm not."

"We're thinking of lying out on the beach again this morning," Jenny said. "Would you like to join us?"

"Sure," Jack said. "Oh, did I tell you I wrote a letter to my brother?"

"What?! You found him?" Jenny asked.

"Well, sort of."

Jenny said, "How do you 'sort of' find someone?"

"I found his most recent address."

"How'd you do that?"

Jack told them about his conversation with the guy at the phone company in Jacksonville and his decision to write a letter to him. "Maybe it will get to him and he'll contact me."

The rest of breakfast was spent telling Sandi about Rick and what he'd learned about him since beginning his search, and Sandi offered wishes that Jack would be able to find him.

As Jack changed into a swimsuit for sunning on the beach, Sandi and Jenny petted Brinkley while Sandi talked to the dog about how good a boy he was.

They drove to the beach across the Denton bridge, with Jack pointing out the area of Sugar Isle where he found his first dog, Bones. He didn't go into detail about his relationship with him and how finding him had changed his life in profound ways.

After lying on the beach for a couple of hours, they changed into clothes they'd brought along and packed themselves back into Jack's car for the drive to The Captain's Table on Sugar Isle. During lunch, Jack talked about how empty Sugar Isle had been when he was a boy. "There were literally no condos, no houses, nothing out here back then. Just the bare island."

"Wow. I bet it looked different," Sandi said.

"Very," Jack said. "You could drive from one end of Denton to the other in about two minutes. Now, the businesses and condos stretch for a dozen miles or more before you get to undeveloped land, and it takes up to an hour to drive it in the summer."

As lunch ended, Jenny asked Jack if he wanted to go to the movies with them.

"What are you going to see?" he asked.

"*The Prince of Tides*," Jenny answered.

"No thanks," Jack said. "Not my cup of tea."

"Suit yourself," Jenny said.

When they arrived back at Jack's house, Jenny and Sandi took showers to wash off the sand and left for the theater.

After they left, Jack decided to give Brinkley a much-needed bath before taking him to the dog park.

The following evening, Jenny arrived with dinner and a change of clothes. Jack thought about her assumption that she would be staying the night. He didn't mind—he wanted her to—but the idea that they had grown so close that such things were expected surprised him.

"Did you enjoy the rest of your visit with Sandi?"

"Yep. We had a blast."

"She knows we're in love, doesn't she?"

"Of course."

"And you already told me your parents know."

"Yes."

"Do they think it's too fast?"

"Do you think it's too fast?"

"I won't lie to you. Yes, I do, but I guess we can't help how we feel."

"If it helps you deal with it, I thought it was kind of fast, too, but that's how I am. It doesn't take me long to know I love someone."

"You didn't answer my question, though. Do your parents think it's too fast?"

"Probably, but they wouldn't say anything about that. They let me live my life."

"Mine did, too, but they let me live my own life when I was still a child. Not a good thing."

"You got lucky, though. Hank became a father to you and Mrs. Dawson became a mother. It's good they came along."

"Speaking of Mrs. Dawson, you need to meet her, or rather, she needs to meet you."

"I'd love to meet her. In fact, I was waiting for you to mention it."

"Oh?"

"Yes. It will sort of be like meeting your mother for the first time. I hope she likes me."

"She will."

"I hope you're right."

As they ate dinner, Jack said, "I have a big day tomorrow."

"Oh?"

"Yes. I have a meeting with the DEA and Zeke Ward."

"The DEA?"

"Yes, it's about Tiffany Wolford. She might turn state's evidence against her mother's boyfriend."

"Are you hoping for a deal?"

"That would be great, but to be honest, she'd do it even without a deal. Her mom's boyfriend is a bad dude."

"How bad?"

"Very."

"Is he dangerous?"

"Yes, but you don't have to worry. I don't think he'd be after a clerk at the Public Defender's Office."

"It's not me I'm worried about."

He looked at her and her meaning hit him. "Me?" She nodded. Jack said, "I don't think he's too concerned about me either. It's Tiffany I worry about."

"I wouldn't put anything past someone who makes a kid sell cocaine for him."

"Don't worry. I can handle myself, and I'll make sure Tiffany is safe as well."

The next morning he rose early and prepared for the day. He dressed as if he would be appearing in court. He would be meeting the DEA agent, District Attorney Zeke Ward, and Chuck at Wharton High School to interview Tiffany officially as well as to request leniency for Tiffany. After all, she was more or less risking her life to help put Keith Breslin away. He felt certain he could manage to get her probation under the circumstances. Despite the fact Tiffany would tell her story whether or not she could get a deal, he would present it to Zeke as a "no deal, no meeting with Tiffany about Keith" proposition.

Kissing Jenny goodbye as they each climbed into their cars, he drove to Wharton High School. When he walked into the main office, he saw Chuck Shelton there with a man in a dark suit, probably the DEA agent.

Chuck and the man stepped up to him. "Hey, Jack. This is Clyde Harwood with the DEA." Jack shook hands with Agent Harwood and introduced himself. Harwood resembled a Marine with his close-cropped hair and a muscular build. He seemed poised to defend himself in case someone jumped him.

"This girl has information about Keith Breslin that will help us?" Harwood asked.

"I think she does. I've heard her story, and it might help you find out where he gets his merchandise, as he calls it."

"And where would that be?" the agent asked.

"All in good time," Jack said. Looking at Chuck, he said, "Where's Zeke?"

"Should be here any minute," Chuck answered

"Have you spoken with the principal yet?" Jack asked.

"Yes. He knows why we're here and that we'll be using the conference room. He even rescheduled something that was supposed to take place in there to give us access."

"He seems like a good fellow," Jack said. "Very helpful. Appears to want the best for his students, including Tiffany."

At that moment, Mr. Freeman stepped into the main room of the office and strode up to Jack. "Hello, again, Mr. Turner."

"Mr. Freeman," Jack said, extending his hand.

"This is our second meeting. You can call me Ernie," Mr. Freeman said, shaking hands with Jack.

"I've got you all set up in the conference room," Ernie said. "Nobody should disturb you."

"Thank you," Agent Harwood said.

"I can let your secretary know when we're ready for Tiffany to join us," Jack said.

"That's fine. I'll be in my office or as close as my walkie-talkie if you need me," Ernie said, and strolled down the short hallway to his office.

Zeke Ward hurried through the door to the office and greeted Jack, Agent Harwood, and Chuck. Jack had never met Zeke, but the DA acted as if they were old friends.

"Jack, how are you? I'm glad you and your client will be helping us put away one of the state's worst criminals."

"Actually, Zeke," Jack said, continuing the use of first names, "that will all depend on you."

"How so?" Zeke asked, as if he had no idea what Jack was talking about. Looking around, Jack said, "Perhaps that would best be discussed in the conference room."

"Sure," Zeke said, still appearing clueless as to how he might figure into Tiffany's willingness to help.

The four men walked down the hall, Jack leading the way, which he did on purpose to signal he was in charge of the meeting.

Jack started the conversation by saying to Zeke, "What we have here is a teenage girl who was forced by her mother's boyfriend to sell cocaine. She was caught with the two ounces, the amount she'd been given to sell. The DEA was already investigating the boyfriend, Keith Breslin, and he apparently has been known to force kids under eighteen to sell for him since their records are sealed upon reaching adulthood. I will support my client's plea of guilty to possession of the two grams for personal use with the stipulation she not be charged as intending to sell the cocaine, and that she receive probation and education on the dangers of drug use as her sentence. Otherwise, this meeting was arranged for no reason. I mean, come on. She's a minor."

Chuck looked at Zeke. "That sounds fair to me, Zeke. She's willing to literally put her life in danger by testifying against Keith Breslin, who has managed to avoid any substantial jail time because he's as slippery as a fish in an oil slick."

DEA Agent Harwood said to Jack, "She'll testify in court against Breslin?"

"As long as Zeke here agrees to our offer," said Jack. "Otherwise, you might as well pack your tape recorder and go back to the office."

Zeke looked at the expressions of three men and held his hands up, palms out, as if surrendering. "Hey, I think we can go with that. It's her first offense and hopefully her last."

Agent Harwood said, "Then let's get her in here, swear her in, and get her statement."

Jack reached a hand out to Zeke. "Is it a deal?"

"You have a deal," Zeke said, shaking Jack's hand.

"I'll be right back." Rising, Jack smiled at Chuck before leaving the room. Entering the main office, he said to Ms. Drake, the secretary, "Could you get Tiffany Wolford now, please?"

"Certainly," Ms. Drake said and picked up her phone. Jack returned to the conference room.

After a few minutes, Tiffany stepped into the room, already looking ready to bolt.

Jack stood up. "Come in, Tiffany. We've been talking, and in exchange for your testimony against your mother's boyfriend, the DA is willing to drop the charges of possessing the two ounces with intent to distribute and give you probation for the two grams you had for your own use. You will also have to attend drug education classes."

"I won't go to jail?"

"No."

"And the charges are sealed when I turn eighteen?"

"Yes."

She looked at the men seated at the table then turned back to Jack. "What do you think I should do?"

"I highly recommend you take that. It's a generous offer."

She nodded. "Okay, then. What do I do?"

Agent Harwood spoke up. "Tiffany, I'm Agent Harwood with the DEA. I'll be asking you some questions, and you will answer on tape. You will tell us your side of the story and help us convict Keith Breslin by testifying at his trial."

"Does my mom know you're here?"

"No," Jack said. "At this point we're simply getting a statement from you to give the DEA more information to help build a case against him."

Tiffany asked Jack, "Did you tell them what I said before?"

"No. I wanted this to be fresh information for them. I am here to represent your interests. If I tell you not to answer a question, you say nothing until I tell you that you can answer. I don't want you incriminating yourself in any other crimes."

Zeke spoke up. "She's committed more crimes that you're aware of?"

Jack turned to Zeke. "No. Not that I know about. However, I don't want some question to imply she did if she answers it." He looked at Agent Harwood. "No offense, but I've seen federal agents ask such questions in the past."

"None taken."

"Well, shall we get started so we can get this over with?" Zeke said.

"What if he makes bail?" Tiffany asked.

Zeke said, "I will do everything I can to ensure he doesn't get bail."

"But what if he does and comes after me?" Tiffany's fright was palpable.

"We'll get you through this safely," Jack said. "Even if I have to put you up in a hotel in an undisclosed location."

She blinked. "You'd do that?"

"If I have to, yes."

She stared at him for a moment, her mouth hanging open slightly. "Thank you."

After Tiffany told them about the phone call from the payphone, Agent Harwood blinked. "How do you know he always makes these calls from a payphone?"

"He told me. It's like he's training me to be a dealer or something. He said never use your home phone for business because it's too easy to tap it."

"Does he use the same payphone every time?"

"I don't know. That was the only time he ever made a call to his supplier when I was there."

Jack spoke up. "You guys need to tail him. When he makes a phone call on a payphone, he's probably on his way at some point to pick up the drugs."

Harwood said, "There are exactly two men working on this. I'll see if I can get the manpower to tail him, but don't hold your breath." He looked at Tiffany. "And you have no idea where he goes for the drugs?"

"No! Are you crazy? He wouldn't trust me with that!"

"Okay, let's move on then," Agent Harwood said. After almost an hour, Tiffany had told them everything she knew, mostly what she'd told Jack before. Harwood shut down his recording equipment and thanked Tiffany.

When she'd left the room, Zeke said, "You got a sweet deal, Jack. That wasn't exactly worth giving her probation. I'll remember that."

"You know more than you did."

"I don't know if it will result in much, though," Harwood added.

Jack said, "Maybe you can get the man hours

needed to nail him. Otherwise, he'll be selling dope to kids for the next ten years or more."

Chuck and Jack left the building together and stopped at Jack's car.

"That could have gone better," Jack said.

"I don't know," said Chuck. "You got your client a probation on a cocaine possession charge. It seems to be what is deserved, in fact."

"Thanks, but my client also just put herself in danger of reprisal by Keith Breslin if he finds out she ratted on his methods."

"Unless you or she tells him, he'll never know."

"I hope you're right."

They each stepped into their cars and drove off, Jack toward Denton, and Chuck toward his office in Wharton.

25
March 19, 1987

As Rick entered his cell block in the Florida State Prison near Raiford for the first time, he felt his stomach clench. He thought he would vomit and worked to quell the nausea that rose in him. This time the sudden illness wasn't from withdrawals. He had finished those already while in jail awaiting trial because he couldn't afford to pay a bail bondsman. He was clean for the first time since he'd passed out from being wounded in a field in Vietnam, and he immediately wanted to get high again upon entering the state prison typically referred to as Raiford Prison. Perhaps being high could block out the severe reality. This time the clenching and nausea were from fear. To describe the place as inhospitable would be laughable. It was like walking through the gates of Hell only to realize that Hell was worse than anyone had ever said.

He had arrived with six other new prisoners. They'd talked a bit on the bus ride from Jacksonville. One of the men was being transferred from a lower security prison because he had started several fights there and had almost managed to kill one man in a fight. Two of the men had been convicted of murder, which of course the men denied. Rick had pretended to believe they were victims of overzealous prosecution. He didn't want to make any of these men angry at him from the start. He was sentenced to nearly three years on burglary and drug possession, his second conviction in Florida on such charges. The first time, he'd been given time served in the county jail and a year's probation along with state-mandated time in a rehab facility that hadn't done anything to curb his need for opiates.

Raiford, however, might be enough to get him to never touch the stuff again, he thought to himself as he heard the clang of the cell door behind him. No fewer than five men had eyed him upon his entry into the cell block with looks that were designed to scare him.

Those stares had done their work well.

The cell was empty of cellmates for now, but the presence of three more bunks with debris like magazines and other personal items scattered on the beds told him his cellmates were somewhere else right now. He had been sent to his cell to, as the guards had put it, "get used to your new palace."

Still doing his best not to vomit, he sat on the one bare lower bunk and looked around the tiny space where four grown men would live and thought he would never grow used to it. Rick considered that doing so would be similar to getting used to being in Hell.

The buzzer sounded from somewhere, and the men who had been lounging around the cell block formed lines along the bare floor that stretched the length of the block. Rick noticed the men lined up outside his cell were staring at him with the same malevolence he'd already experienced.

Rick did his best to look tough and completely unafraid, hoping he was doing a good enough job of it.

The cell doors opened automatically and the men stepped into their cells. Rick had only two cellmates. One was a skinny, nervous fellow with dark hair who seemed ready to run with every movement. The other, a large man with small boulders for muscles, had taken up both bunks on one side of the cell. He spoke first.

"You see these beds?" he asked, waving his hand at the bunks on that side of the cell like Vanna White. Rick nodded. "They're mine. Don't ever touch my stuff. Got it?"

Rick nodded again. "What would I want with your stuff?" he asked.

"Nothing. That's what I mean."

"Hey, I'm just here to do my time and get out of here. I have no plans to do anything to anyone. I just want out."

"We all want that," the man said. Rick's other cellmate was silent during this exchange, still standing near the cell door as if ready to run though he had nowhere he could run if he'd chosen to. Rick suddenly realized he was tensed to jump out of the way in case the obvious alpha male of the cell decided to beat Rick up just to make a point.

"Hey," Rick said, "I won't give you any problems, and you can just act like I'm not really here."

The man stared at him for a second and sat in the lower bunk. "I'll just call you Ghost, then."

"Whatever, but my name's Rick in case you're wondering."

"Rick the Ghost!" the man said, and laughed. Turning to the other man, he said, "Don? Meet Rick the Ghost."

Don nodded at him and said, "Hey."

Rick stuck out his hand to shake Don's hand but Don recoiled as if Rick had held out a rattlesnake. Rick got the message. No hand shaking in there.

Turning to the large man, Rick said, "Do you have a name you want to share?"

"It's Darrell, but most people call me Hammer because I got fists like hammers." He held up a fist as if to demonstrate the similarity.

"Hi, Hammer," Rick said.

"What you in for, Rick the Ghost?" Hammer asked, laughing as if this world was one big joke.

"Burglary and drugs. Second conviction, so they sent me here."

"What kind of drugs?"

"Opiates. Morphine. That kind of stuff."

"You a junkie?"

Rick sat staring at the floor. "Yeah. Clean now, though. Sitting in county lock up will do that to you."

"You got any on you?" Hammer asked.

Rick looked at him as if he'd asked if he had an extra million dollars to spare. "Of course not. The way they search you here, if I did have some, it would be long gone now."

Hammer shrugged. "Worth askin'." Changing the subject, he asked, "What's the stretch?"

"Thirty months."

"Not bad. I got twelve years for armed robbery. Already served sixty-two months, so I got about seven years to go. It ain't so bad once you get used to it."

Rick turned to Don to try to include him in the conversation. "What are you in for, Don?"

"Same as Hammer. Armed robbery."

"You get twelve years, too?"

"No, just four."

"I guess you must have been lucky," Rick said.

"Luck ain't got nothin' to do with it," Hammer said.

"Why not?" Rick asked him.

"Look at him and look at me. You notice anything different?"

Rick didn't need to look. "You're built like a Mac truck."

"No, man. I wasn't born with these muscles. That takes work and dedication. C'mon. What's different?"

Rick was perplexed as to what Hammer was referring to. Their sizes seemed to be the only thing different about them. Don was thin with straight, dark hair. Hammer looked like a mountain, and his stare was considerably more intimidating than Don's. Then it hit him. "You're black."

Hammer was humorously startled by the answer. "You just now noticin' that?"

"Actually, yeah. I don't pay much attention to that kind of thing."

Hammer chuckled under his breath. "Ghost, you're probably the only person ever who didn't notice that about me before anything else." He laughed hard. "Imagine that! A real, live non-bigot! I'd heard of 'em but never met one!"

"I don't care what color someone's skin is. It's not as if anyone can help it."

Hammer stopped laughing suddenly and his face became serious. "Well, Ghost, there's some of us who've wished we could." He paused before adding, "Not because we're ashamed of our color. No siree. I'm proud to be a descendant of Africans. But sometimes, life sure would have been a lot easier if I'd been born white."

"Are you saying your sentence is longer because you're black?"

"Man, you are livin' in another world. Yeah. That's exactly what I'm sayin'. Ask any two men in here convicted of the exact same crime, one white and one black, and you'll find the black guy has a longer sentence, often by a lot."

"Were you ever convicted of a crime before the armed robbery?"

"Nope. Never even committed one before. I robbed a place because I needed the money to get my little girl an operation to save her life." He squinted at Rick. "I ain't lyin' about that. I had a job in construction. Wasn't rich or anything, but we lived okay. Then my daughter gets sick. She needed an operation on her heart. I had no insurance or anything. So I walked into a large grocery store one night when it was rainin' so bad there weren't a lot of customers in there. I told them to put all the money in the safe and the cash registers in a bag I had. I don't know how much I got but the weight was considerable."

"You never counted it?"

"Never had the chance. I was arrested that night. Seems one of the customers recognized me."

Rick sat there, wondering if this was a lie Hammer told to get sympathy. He'd heard a hundred sympathy lies in his life. Even told a few himself. "How's your daughter?" he finally asked.

Hammer reached into his pocket and pulled out his wallet. He took out a picture and handed it to Rick. "That's my wife and me and my little girl, Jolene, named for that song by Dolly Parton." Rick looked at Hammer. "Yeah, I'm a country music fan. Anyway, that was about two months before we found out she needed to have an operation." He pulled a second photograph. In it Rick saw the same little girl lying in a casket, roses lying along her side. "I don't have to tell you what that is."

Rick shook his head, feeling tears sting his eyes. He swallowed to ease the lump forming in his throat. "You have a beautiful child," he said.

"*Had*, you mean."

"I'm really sorry," Rick said.

"I can see that," said Hammer, reaching out to take back the photograph. "Roses were her favorite flower."

The mood in the cell had gone from threatening to lighthearted to gloomy in a matter of minutes.

"Were you allowed to attend her funeral?"

"Yeah, but it was weird having four guards there with me, and me in chains."

"I'm sorry," Rick said.

"Ghost?" Hammer said, his voice thick.

"Yeah?"

"If anyone bothers you, you tell them we're friends. They'll stop messin' with you. And if they don't you tell me, and I guarantee they won't even speak to you again unless you want them to."

Twenty-seven months after arriving at Raiford, when Rick was paroled. he talked to Hammer before he left and asked him why he'd been so quick to offer his protection and friendship.

"Because," Hammer said. "You were the first white man I ever saw cry over a little black girl he'd never met. That said a lot."

As the months crawled along at Raiford, Rick, aka Ghost, became popular among the inmates he interacted with. Everyone referred to him as Ghost now, and Rick felt it was appropriate. The old Rick had died and this ghost of a person had taken his place.

One day while in the exercise yard, he saw someone he thought he recognized from his hometown of Denton. Tommy Gordon was playing basketball with some other inmates. He looked like an older version of the teenager he'd known, and the scar he wore that ran down his right cheek was the same.

Rick walked up to him. "Aren't you Tommy Gordon from Denton?"

Tommy stopped dribbling the basketball and said, "Yeah, but I go by Tom now." Rick could see Tom working to remember him. Finally, he said, "You're Rick Turner."

"Yep."

"What are you doin' in here?"

"Time. What else?"

"Yeah, but what for?"

"Burglary and drugs, mostly. What about you?"

"Drugs. Caught me dealin'. Wasn't the first time, so here I am."

"Can I ask you something?"

"Sure, as long as I don't have to answer if I don't want to."

"You ever see my brother, Jack?"

Tom sat for a long time, as if remembering something from his past. "Yeah. I ain't seen him since he moved away, but we saw each other around town some."

"So he's doin' okay?"

"Far as I know. You ain't been home to see him?"

"No. It didn't, well, it didn't feel right to go there."

"Your folks died in a car wreck. Been a long time ago now. Your brother was in school still."

"Where did he live?"

Again, Rick could see a memory playing in Tom's mind. "You remember Hank Pittman? That old guy who lived in an old school bus at the docks?"

"Yeah."

"He went to live with him."

"In that old bus?"

"Naw. Hank was a Moreland. I never knew that until, well, later. Turns out he had more money than he knew what to do with. He took Jack in."

They sat in silence for a moment before Rick asked, “You ever hear the old guy was—getting funny—with Jack?”

Tom took a deep breath and let it out. “No. There was rumors, but I can promise you they weren’t true.” Tom looked down at his hands clasped between his knees. “No, he was like a father to Jack. Bought a house—a nice one—and Jack lived there. Hank even sent him to college.”

“What did Jack study?”

“The law. He became a criminal defense lawyer.”

Rick laughed. “Well, I guess if I ever need defending again, I got an ace in the hole.”

“Yeah. Guess it’s good to have an attorney in the family,” Tom said.

26
April 7, 1992

Tuesday morning, Jack began the day going over his arguments for his motion to be given the original recording of the robbery, though he did not expect any objections from Larry Herndon. He'd told him as much when Jack delivered the motion directly to him. It was just a matter of going through the steps to make it all legal.

Jenny prepared for work as well, and they sometimes found themselves in each other's way. He considered he had another bathroom down the hall but wasn't sure how to broach the subject of making that her bathroom so they could prepare for their days when she slept over without bumping into each other.

She had brought enough of her clothes over that she no longer needed to pack an overnight bag, and a number of her toiletries were stored neatly in the main bedroom's bath. Neatly, yes, but it still looked like more than the counter would hold. He didn't want her to think he didn't want her staying over, but he was beginning to feel the first twinges that sometimes she was in his way, especially on mornings like this when he had court. Giving her use of the other bathroom would solve the problem.

He didn't want to discuss it that morning, though, in case it required more than just making the suggestion and her easy acceptance of it without hurt feelings.

They had breakfast and chatted about mundane things, and he wondered if she, too, might have recognized the problem. She appeared preoccupied, which was how he felt as well.

They kissed each other goodbye and she basically followed him to the courthouse in her own car. He waved at her as he raced into the building, feeling rushed.

When his motion was called before the bench, he and Larry took their places at their respective tables.

Trisha looked over her glasses at Jack. "Mr. Turner, we have a motion before the court requesting possession of the original videotape of the robbery your client is accused of in order to have it enhanced for better quality, is that correct?"

"Yes, Your Honor. After viewing the video, which like many store security videos is very grainy from having the tape reused numerous times. I have inquired with a video expert about the possibility of enhancing the video. He explained that the original could produce better results if I had it."

"Mr. Herndon, do you have anything to add?"

"No, Your Honor, other than we need to know which video expert will be working on the tape. Some are better than others."

"I understand, but why wasn't the video already enhanced by the state for purposes of the prosecution?"

"We didn't feel it necessary, Your Honor. The man certainly appears to be the defendant in the video—same height and build. He's wearing a Halloween mask, so it's not as if we could see his face if the tape were enhanced, and such a process is time-consuming and expensive."

Trisha looked at Jack. "Mr. Turner, since the person robbing the store had concealed his face, what do you expect to find in an enhanced tape?"

"I'd rather not say in open court, Your Honor, since that would reveal our defense strategy, but I do believe that enhancing the original tape would be advantageous to the defense."

"Mr. Herndon?"

"We have no objection, Your Honor, but in all honesty, we're a bit puzzled at Mr. Turner's insistence that an enhancement would yield evidence helpful to the defense."

"Well, then, suppose we find out?" Trisha said, "However, it seems to me that the state should be the ones doing this, not the defense. Mr. Turner is being paid by the state to represent Mr. Gordon, so it's not as if he has a pool of money to use for his client's defense. I think it's admirable of Mr. Turner to go to such lengths to represent his client at what is basically his own expense."

Larry's assistant, who was there mostly to handle the paperwork created by the various cases they would be arguing, tapped Larry's shoulder. Jack was surprised she became involved in this case, a simple hearing on a mundane motion.

The two conversed for a moment as Larry held up a finger to indicate he'd only be a few seconds.

However, the whispered conversation continued until Trisha said, “Mr. Herndon, will we be continuing with this hearing soon?”

Ending the conversation, Larry looked back at Trisha and said, “Your Honor, the state would like to conduct the enhancement ourselves.”

Jack knew why he wanted to do this. He wanted the first look at any evidence helpful to the defense before Jack saw it.

Trisha said, “Mr. Turner, do you have any objections to the state handling the enhancement?”

“Actually, Your Honor, I do. Mr. Herndon wants to figure out what is helpful to the defense before I have a chance to see the video after it is enhanced. I’m not sure I trust the prosecution to provide the enhanced tape if it assists the defense.”

“Your Honor!” Larry said, obviously angry at the assertion, but Jack knew that it was often the case that the prosecution would sit on evidence helpful to the defense until the last minute.

“In a moment, Mr. Herndon,” Trisha said, turning back to face Jack. “Mr. Turner, is there a specific reason you doubt Mr. Herndon would share the results with you?”

“Oh, I’m sure he would share it, Your Honor. I’m just not sure when.”

Trisha sat back. “Funny, this looked pretty cut and dried when I first read the motion.” She tapped a pencil against her jaw, something Jack recognized as a habit she had prior to making a decision that she hoped would be in everyone’s favor.

“Mr. Herndon, the state may have the recording enhanced, but we will all view the results together.

How long would such an enhancement take?"

Larry conferred with his assistant again and straightened back up. "About a month, Your Honor. There's likely a backlog of such things."

"Your Honor," Jack interrupted, "my expert can have it for us next week. If it's all the same to the court, I'd prefer to just pay the expense myself and have it sooner. If the defense is right, a dangerous man is still free to rob someone again or worse while the state's video experts take their time with the enhancement. I would be happy to provide the state with the enhanced tape within hours of receiving it."

Trisha looked at Larry and said, "I think that's reasonable, especially since the state could have taken these steps before now in an effort to dot all their I's and cross their T's." Looking back at Jack, she said, "When, exactly, does your expert say he can have the tape ready?"

"He told me it would take about a week."

"Okay. You will have the right to look at it first since you're paying the fee," Trisha said. "You are to inform the prosecution immediately upon seeing that evidence if it exonerates your client or casts suspicion on the viability of the evidence. If it does neither, then you just paid for an expensive fishing expedition that resulted in catching no fish."

"Thank you, Your Honor," Jack said and began putting his briefcase back in order.

"Your Honor," Larry said, "we still need to know who Mr. Turner plans to have conduct the enhancement. We don't need someone destroying the tape accidentally on purpose."

"Mr. Turner?" Trisha said.

"Van's Video in Wharton, Your Honor," Jack responded.

Larry leaned over to his assistant and listened for a moment. "We've used them before, Your Honor. That would be acceptable to the prosecution."

"Okay, then. If it's okay with you two, I need to move on to the next issue before the court today," Trisha said and banged her gavel.

Stepping to Larry, Jack said, "When can I get it?"

Larry reached into his briefcase and took out the VHS cassette and a form for Jack to sign indicating he was taking possession of the tape until such time as it was returned from the video expert. Larry entered a date ten days from then as the deadline for the tape's return and signed the form.

Leaving the courtroom, Jack stopped by to see Jenny to set up a lunch date before leaving. He wanted to discuss some parameters for their occasional overnight stays.

Jack drove home before driving to Wharton and plugged the tape into his player, speed-playing the tape until the part he needed enhanced came up. He stopped the tape at that spot so he didn't have to cue it up after arriving at Van's Video.

Then he placed a call to Mrs. Dawson before leaving the house.

"Hello?"

"Hi, Mrs. Dawson. It's Jack. How are you?"

"I'm doing fine, Jack. How are you?"

"Doing okay."

After a second, she sighed heavily and said, "So, is that all you wanted, to find out how I'm doing?"

"No, I was wondering if I could bring Jenny Walton over this evening to meet you. She wants to meet the woman who was more a mother to me than my real mother."

"Oh, Jack, don't say that. Your mother loved you."

"So you keep saying," Jack said. "Still, she wants to meet you. Would this evening be okay?"

"What time?"

"How does six sound? I can bring some food, even."

"Nonsense. I can fix something. You've not been to dinner here for so long, I can at least do that much. I'd love to meet your girlfriend."

"Great, we'll see you then."

"Can I ask something first?" she said.

"Of course."

"Is this relationship serious?"

He thought for a moment. "Getting there. We love each other, if that's what you mean, but we've not made any permanent plans or anything like that."

"Sounds lovely," Mrs. Dawson said. "I'll see you two at six."

"What's for dinner?"

"Whatever I decide to fix. Now, goodbye, Jack."

"Goodbye, other mother."

After driving to Wharton, he pulled into Van's Video and stepped inside with the VHS tape. When

Van wanted to know what part needed enhancing, Jack told him the tape was cued to the spot where the robbery began and only that segment needed work.

Van required payment in advance, so Jack put the charge on his business credit card and left. Van told him he should have the work done by Tuesday of the following week, April 14.

Jack thanked him and drove back to Denton, parking in front of the courthouse annex and going inside to take Jenny to lunch.

She chose a Red Lobster in town and Jack drove them there. After they were seated, he said, "I made us dinner reservations, too."

"Oh? Where?" Her eyes were alight.

"Mrs. Dawson's."

She looked as though he'd chosen the nicest restaurant in the county. "Really?"

"Yes," he said, confused at her reaction. "Why the 'oh my God' reaction? It will be a simple meal, I assure you."

"I feel like you're taking me to meet your mom," she said, smiling.

"Well, she's not really my mom, and she lives right here in town, so it's not that big a deal. Now, when I meet your parents, it will be a big deal."

"Might be sooner than you think. Apparently, Sandi told her mom about you. She called my mom and my mom called me, asking when they would meet you."

"Just let me know when, so I can brush up on my manners."

"I will. You're so crude you might need classes

from Miss Manners," she said, laughing.

After their iced tea arrived, Jack said, "There's something else I need to talk to you about, but it's not as pleasant, I'm afraid."

"Oh?"

"Yes." He took a deep breath and saw her apprehension grow. "It's about the overnight stays."

"I'm over too much?" He could hear the worry.

"No, that's not it at all. It's just that, well, when I have court in the morning and you have work, it gets a little—crowded—in the bathroom."

She nodded. "Yeah, I kinda noticed that."

"I have an idea, though, but I don't want you thinking I don't want you over."

"What?"

"The guest bathroom is down the hall from the bedroom. I was wondering if you could sort of claim that one as yours and move all your stuff in there? I mean, most people would kill for a bathroom they can call their own when they stay the night with someone."

His eyebrows were raised as if to ask, "Don't you think that's a great idea?"

She smiled at him. "I completely understand. I was kind of thinking the same thing about getting in each other's way this morning. I was afraid you wouldn't want me to stay over anymore or something."

"I thought about making that change for when I have court or an appointment in the morning, but I wondered what we would do if we ever decided to move in together."

She smiled at him. "You're thinking about

that?"

"Well, I mean, it's crossed my mind that it might happen. It's sort of the natural progression of a relationship, isn't it? Haven't you thought about that?"

"I have. I just didn't know you had."

"Well, not seriously or anything. I'm just someone who is trained to consider all possibilities."

Jenny frowned at him, but he didn't notice. "There's a side of you that's hard to get to know."

"Oh? What side would that be?"

"I'm not sure, but you're not the easiest person to get to know."

"Maybe I make it hard to get to know me to find out who's willing to make the effort," Jack said before taking a sip of tea and watching her reaction. For Jack this was true. He'd thought about it before when another woman had told him the same thing. Usually, it was the part of his past that he himself didn't like remembering that he kept back, but he'd been more willing than usual to discuss that part of himself with Jenny. It was the first thing that had surprised him about his reactions to her. With Carmen, they'd not talked about their own pasts until weeks after they'd moved in together.

Jenny gave him a smile that was more sad than pleasant, and leaning toward him across the table, she said, "Jack Turner, I'm in it for the long haul."

The server brought their lunch, and Jack changed the subject. "You've not asked me about what happened in court today."

Jenny leaned back into her seat and said,

"You're right. So what did happen in court?"

They talked about that and other mundane topics until they finished their lunch. When Jack dropped Jenny back at work, he said, "We have to be at Mrs. Dawson's at six. Is that okay?"

"Sounds great. I'll go home and freshen up a bit and be at your place by 5:45. Is that good?"

"Great. I'll see you then."

He started to pull away but Jenny stopped him. "Jack?"

"Yes?"

"I love you."

He smiled. "I know. I love you, too."

Her smile brightened a little. "Then we have a chance."

Jack drove home wondering what was bothering Jenny. Something that happened at lunch had upset her, though not terribly so. It hadn't been the bathroom issue. She'd been fine with that. Something, though, had troubled her. She'd behaved as if she wondered if he loved her as much as she loved him. He ran the conversation over in his mind but came up with nothing. He knew he could be clumsy in the relationship dance, and the events at lunch had him wondering if something might be missing from his personality.

He stopped and picked up Brinkley, who seemed out of sorts for being left home that morning.

"I understand," Jack said. "I'm feeling out of sorts myself." Jack made it up to him by taking him to the dog park, where he tried again to figure out what had bothered Jenny, without success.

27

Jack greeted Jenny when she arrived that evening, and the first thing she did was move all of her toiletries into the guest bathroom. After that, she changed into something more casual for dinner at Mrs. Dawson's and freshened her makeup. She seemed more herself than she had at lunch and after, and Jack wondered if he might be over thinking what had happened. He forgot about it until he had no other choice.

"What are we having for dinner?" she asked.

"I've no idea, but she's a good cook, so it will be delicious. Anyway, this is more about her meeting you and vice versa."

"I know. I'm a little nervous. What if she doesn't like me?"

"She will like you just fine. I know her well enough to know that. She's not a judgmental person."

As Jack leashed Brinkley and loaded him in the backseat, Jenny said, "Brinkley gets to join us, too?"

"Are you kidding? I don't even know if she would let me in the door if Brinkley wasn't with me. The only time I go without him is if I stop by while running an errand he can't accompany me for, and those are always brief and have a particular reason for not being able to wait until later. If I go for a real visit, he has to come, too. He and her dog, Goose, like to play together."

Jenny laughed. "She has a dog she named Goose?"

"Yes, but not for the reason you think. The dog she had when I first met her was named Yogi."

"After the cartoon character?"

"No, for Yogi Berra. She's the world's most ardent Yankees fan. She can recite stats on all the players and everything."

"So, then, why 'Goose'?"

"Let me guess. You don't know much about the Yankees, right?"

"No. Sorry."

"Goose Gossage is a famous player for them now."

"Okay. So she names all the dogs after her favorite players, then?"

"Yep. It's as if she finds the ones with the most unusual names, like Yogi and Goose, to name her dogs."

"Wow, she is a fan."

"She defines the source of the word *fanatic*."

"My dad's a football nut, so I was raised with the Chicago Bears on TV whenever they were on. That was more frequent when they had that defense and won the Super Bowl. I've noticed you don't watch sports much."

"Nah. I enjoyed playing baseball as a kid, but now I prefer reading a book."

"You don't read much when I'm around."

"That's because you're more interesting."

"Aww, that's sweet."

"And true," he said, noting how she had changed her mood since lunch.

They were arriving at Mrs. Dawson's, and Brinkley bounded out of the car, running to the front door and barking.

"He knows where he is," Jenny said.

"Oh, yeah. He loves to come here. I'm not sure if it's because he can play with Goose or the treats Mrs. Dawson gives him."

The door opened, and Mrs. Dawson stood there grinning. "Hello, y'all! Come on in!" She looked at Jenny with her arms wide. "You must be Jenny! Give me a hug!"

Jenny looked surprised to be welcomed with a hug by someone she'd just met but hugged Mrs. Dawson anyway. She said, "I'd better be Jenny, or he has some explaining to do." She laughed and Mrs. Dawson joined in.

"Well, come on in and make yourselves comfortable. I have to check on my pot roast."

"It smells delicious," Jenny said.

"I hope it tastes delicious," Mrs. Dawson said as she left them in the small living room. The TV was tuned to an Atlanta Braves game.

When Mrs. Dawson returned from the kitchen to join them, Jack said, "What? No Yankees?"

"They don't play today," she said. "I watch the Braves when the Yankees aren't on the TV anyway, which is too often for my taste."

"Have you become a Braves fan?" he asked.

"Well, they're growing on me—I guess you

could say they're my National League team. They have some very good players." She began talking about the players in the field, especially Tom Glavine, who was pitching.

Finally, she looked at Jack and said, "Do you think they'll win the series this year?"

"Mrs. Dawson, you know I'm not a fan of the game. If you want to talk about my views on tort reform, I'd be happy to chime in."

She shook her head. "Nonsense. What would I know about stuff like that?"

"About as much as I know about Major League Baseball."

"I've never understood why you don't watch it. You played as a youngster."

"I enjoy participating instead of watching from the sidelines."

"Suit yourself," Mrs. Dawson said and turned the TV off.

"I do have some news, though, and it has nothing to do with tort reform."

"What is it?" she asked before suddenly looking at Jenny with a shocked smile. "Are you two—?"

"Oh, no! Nothing like that!" Jack said, noticing Jenny's look of shock as well.

Then Mrs. Dawson began to blush. "Oh, dear. I'm so sorry." She turned to Jenny. "I must have embarrassed you to death!"

"No, really. It's okay," Jenny said. "While we have no plans in that direction, it's possible it could happen one day. The future is still cloudy on that subject. We've only just started to date seriously."

"Well, I embarrassed myself," Mrs. Dawson said. "It's just that I've been hoping for years Jack would find someone to settle down with, and who better than a lovely lady like you?"

Jack spoke up, wanting to move on from that topic. "No, I may have a line on finding my brother, Rick."

"Really?!"

"Yes. It seems his last known residence is in Jacksonville, and he seems to have moved from there only very recently. I'm considering going there to talk to his landlord to find out if he left a forwarding address." He didn't mention the letter he'd written because he didn't want to have to explain one day if he never heard back. Mrs. Dawson's heart would feel bad for him, causing her emotional pain.

"When do you think you'll be going?" Mrs. Dawson asked.

"Well, I have a couple of cases here I have to see to first, but once that is either done or I can take a break from them, I'll probably head over that way to see what I can find out."

"That sounds wonderful. Do you think you will find him?" Mrs. Dawson asked.

"I think the chances are pretty good, unless he didn't leave a forwarding address or some other way to contact him. Then, despite getting close to finding him, I'll pretty well be back at square one."

The stove alarm that Jack recognized from his days as a boy sounded, and Mrs. Dawson stood up. "That's my roast. Let me cook my famous homemade yeast rolls, and we'll be ready to eat."

Jack asked, "You made yeast rolls?"

"Of course. It's not every day you bring a young lady by for me to meet."

Jenny laughed. "Well, I for one am glad to hear that."

This was the second comment that suggested some jealousy on Jenny's part, even if it was said lightheartedly, and Jack made a mental note to talk with her about it. If she was seriously jealous of other women, he wasn't sure how he would handle that. He himself was not a jealous person. Being with one would create problems. He'd seen his share of people doing awful things to their spouses and significant others over jealousy. Then he wondered if not telling Jenny the full story about Carmen might be because of that fear in him.

As they ate, they chatted about everything from dogs to cooking tips. When Jack and Jenny finally stood to leave, Jenny said, "Thank you so much for having us. Now I know why Jack is so complimentary of you."

"That's wonderful, though I'm not sure I deserve the accolades."

"You do, Mrs. Dawson," Jack said.

"Absolutely," said Jenny.

"Well, thank you both. I'm sure that Jack has found a wonderful young lady as well."

"Come here, Brinkley," Jack said and put the leash he'd brought in from the car on his collar. "He isn't as happy to leave here as he is to arrive, so a leash is necessary," he explained to Jenny.

As they rode back to Jack's he said, "Can I ask you something important?"

"Sure."

"Are you the type of woman who is jealous of other women?"

"Not particularly. Why?"

"Because, you mentioned something about other women tonight twice, and though it was in a lighthearted, almost joking way, I wanted to be sure you weren't like that."

"What did I say?"

"When we arrived, you said something about how you better be Jenny or I have some explaining to do, and later you said you were glad to hear I wasn't bringing young ladies over every day. Like I said, I know you were being funny, but I just want to make sure there wasn't a kernel of truth to that."

"No, Jack. There was no truth to it at all. I was just nervous and trying to make her think I had a sense of humor. Did it really bother you?"

"Not until the second comment, though I can't exactly say it bothered me. I was just wanting to be sure you weren't a jealous kind of person. I've seen some terrible outcomes arise from jealousy."

"Like what?"

"Do you really want to know? It's not a pleasant tale."

She took a deep breath as if composing herself. "Yes, I do."

"When I was in New Orleans, this man who lived in a little town west of the city set his house on fire with his wife in it because he suspected she was cheating on him."

"Was she?"

"Yes, but that's not the point. Even if she was

cheating on him with a dozen people, there was no cause for him to do that. He should have just divorced her."

"I didn't mean to suggest he was somehow justified. I just think it's all so sad. Were there any kids involved?"

"Two. Fortunately, he arranged for them to stay with his parents that night."

"Jack, you don't need to worry about anything like that. I have a healthy amount of jealousy, but nothing possessive or dangerous." She paused for a second. "What about you? Do I have to wonder if you'll burn me up if you see me talking to another man?"

"Of course not. Don't be ridiculous."

"Then maybe now you know how I feel being asked the same question."

"Sorry. I didn't mean to upset you. I just wanted to know now instead of later. That kind of thing can make for a difficult relationship."

"Jack?"

"Yes?"

"Do you love me?"

"Yes."

"Are you the type to run around on someone?"

"No."

"That's what I thought. For the record, neither am I. No one in my family is. We were taught better." She looked at him in the darkness of the car. "And because I know that Mrs. Dawson and Hank were more responsible for who you turned out to be than your parents were, I know you aren't like that either."

"Then why did you ask?"

"To make a point."

"What point would that be?"

"That I love you and when I love someone I am as committed to that person as you are. I'd only be jealous if someone made a serious attempt to take you from me. But then, my anger would be directed at the other woman, not you."

He nodded and remained silent until they arrived at his house. They continued sitting in the car until Jack asked, "Do you want to stay the night?"

"Do you want me to stay?"

"Very much."

She smiled. "Then I'll stay."

"Did we just have our first fight?"

"I wouldn't call it a fight. Just a coming to terms." She leaned over and kissed him lightly. "Did your parents fight a lot?"

"No. They were happy with their drinks of choice. Beer for my mom and cheap whiskey for my dad. As long as they had that, they were happy."

"That's sad."

"That they didn't fight?"

"No, silly, that they weren't happy with each other enough to know what a great kid they had."

"How do you know I was a great kid?"

"Easy. Because you're such a great adult."

They went inside and Jack fed Brinkley his evening meal. After watching some TV, they went to bed and held each other.

28

Work lasted longer than expected on Thursday of that week, and when Jack arrived home, a car he didn't recognize sat in his driveway along with Jenny's. The Texas plates didn't help him. The sudden thought that he'd been wrong about where Rick lived made him wonder if his brother hadn't sought him out instead, but he immediately dismissed that idea. Somehow, he doubted Rick would be able to afford the late-model Buick that sat in his driveway.

He wondered if another cousin might be visiting Jenny. None of her brothers lived in Texas, or he would have thought perhaps one of them had come to visit her. A sudden suspicion occurred to him and he prayed he was wrong.

As he walked to the door, he checked out the Buick. To his surprise, the front door opened as he was looking into the car. Jenny stood there, leaning against the door jamb. She did not look happy.

"What's up?" he asked, already guessing the answer.

"You have a visitor."

"Oh?"

"Yes. A friend from your past. Do you remember Carmen?"

His suspicions had been correct, making him want to hide. Suddenly, his old girlfriend from New Orleans was standing behind Jenny, smiling as if he would be thrilled to see her. Her demeanor was the exact opposite of Jenny's.

"Hi, Jack! How ya doin'?" she asked with her Texas drawl. It had been the first thing he'd been attracted to, as well as the last. She still possessed stunning beauty, but that was only physical.

Jack looked at Jenny and her eyes said it all. He had no idea how long the two had been together talking, but he could see she knew there had been more to Carmen's feelings than he'd told her. He could see Jenny was holding her emotions in.

Carmen continued as if nothing was wrong. "What's the matter? Cat got your tongue? I know you're surprised to see me."

"Shocked, actually," Jack said.

"We've been havin' quite a chat," Carmen said. "Jack, how is it she thought we were just 'friends with benefits'? Didn't you tell her how much we were in love?"

Carmen's voice dripped with good cheer, as if this entire episode was just a misunderstanding that they would all laugh about later that evening. But Jack remembered that tone. It may sound cheerful, but it dripped poison.

"And here I drove all the way from Houston just to say hi and find out what you've been up to."

Jack knew there was more to the visit than that as Carmen glanced toward Jenny as if wishing she'd disappear into oblivion and leave her alone with Jack so they could pick up their former relationship.

He looked from Carmen to Jenny and back. “How did you know where I live?”

“When I called our landlord in New Orleans, she was happy to give me your forwarding address. I had to tell a little fib and say I owed you money, but after that she was happy to give me the address where you live. That and a map of Denton was all I needed, Sugar!”

Jenny looked daggers at Carmen. “Would you give us a moment, please?”

Carmen must have thought Jenny needed the privacy to say her final goodbye. Otherwise, Jack knew she never would have said what she did. “Why, sure, Honey. Take your time.” She turned and walked back into the house.

As Jenny stepped outside and closed the door, Jack was certain she was indeed about to say her final goodbye. Approaching him, tears began to roll down her cheeks.

“I knew you were holding something back! I just knew it!”

“Jenny—”

“Why wouldn’t you tell me y’all were in love? Why would you go on about how you both were just being with each other because it was better than being alone?”

“I—”

“You lied to me, Jack! You lied!”

“I can explain,” he said.

“Oh, can you?!” She crossed her arms, daring him to try to explain his lie to her satisfaction as the tears of pain and anger spilled and formed small rivers along her cheeks. Jack was suddenly reminded of the small rapids that formed along the roadside during storms when he'd played his childish game of floating twigs.

"First, I never loved her, but yes, she did love me. The reason I didn't want to tell you the complete truth was I felt—" His own chest tightened. "I felt ashamed."

"Ashamed? Ashamed of what?"

"How I treated her. Took advantage of her. I knew she loved me, and I lied to her and told her I loved her. Finally, I couldn't continue the lie. I told her I didn't love her anymore and had her move out. She left town and I had no idea where she even went."

"You told her you didn't love her anymore? So she thinks you did love her but stopped?" Jenny was still angry, but the vehemence had calmed.

"Yes."

"Jack, you also never mentioned that this all ended just last November, which she was more than happy to tell me. She's still carrying a torch for you. She's thinking that just because she's back that you'll realize your mistake and love her—again, in her mind."

"But I don't."

"Are you sure, or is this another lie to make me feel better?"

"Of course, I'm sure. I'm sorry I lied to you, but I figured there was no harm in it. Who knew she'd come find me?"

"That's not the point, Jack. A lie is a lie. If we can't be honest with each other, we have no future. If we're going to make something of our relationship, you have to be honest with me, no matter how much you think the truth will hurt me. No matter how much you're ashamed of the truth." A small sob burst from her as she said, "I love you, Jack, and I don't want to lose you. To her or to dishonesty!"

Jack pulled her to him. At first she resisted but then gave in and held him tightly. "I'm sorry she came here," he said softly.

"That doesn't bother me, Jack. I'm not crying because I think you'll kick me out and let her move in. That's ridiculous. I'm crying because you lied to me. That's all. It hurt me a lot more for you to lie than anything the truth could have done."

"I am so sorry. I really didn't think it was that bad."

"It was," she said, her tears subsiding. "Do you love me?"

"With all my heart."

"Then maybe we should go inform Carmen of that. I think she believes she's won you back."

"Okay, let's tell her to leave."

"Jack?"

"Yes?"

"Was she always this crazy?"

"She was always this possessive. A very jealous woman."

"How could you have been with a woman like that? She's—evil."

"I don't know that she's evil. She always had to have her own way, though, and she would assume everyone would do whatever was necessary for her to get what she wanted."

"That's evil, Jack."

"No. Just spoiled."

"Okay I'll take that answer, but she's still crazy. Her parents were like yours? Alcoholics?"

"Yes, but there was one difference. Her parents were rich. Owned land with lots of oil wells on it, spoiled her to the core."

"How is it she let you leave her in the first place?"

"It wasn't easy. I could tell you all about it, but suffice it to say, it was ugly. Maybe as ugly as this will become."

"Is she the reason you wanted to make sure I wasn't the jealous type?"

"Yes."

"Well, I'm not really jealous of her. I just don't like her."

"Today's the last day you'll ever see her."

"Good." She thought a moment. "But that sounds like you're some mafia guy who's going to make her 'disappear' or something." She giggled against his chest, and to Jack the sound was the sweetest music ever.

From the corner of his eye, he noticed Carmen standing inside the house, watching them through a window.

As they walked to the front door, Jack said, "She thought you were going to leave me."

"She thought wrong."

As they entered, Carmen strolled up to them, seeming oblivious to the problems she caused.

"So, Jack, maybe we should talk about how you made a mistake in leaving me?" Carmen said.

"No, Carmen. I didn't make a mistake at all. I don't love you. In fact, I never did. I apologize, but I used you. It was selfish of me. So you see, you're trying to revive a love that never was there in the first place. I love Jenny." He looked at Jenny then back at Carmen. "Not you."

Carmen's expression shifted to dismay, then anger as he spoke. She looked at Jenny. "Fine! You can have him!" she snarled. "But don't be surprised when he lies to you, too!" She turned to Jack. "You two can have each other! She deserves a weasel like you!" She went to the living room and grabbed her purse. As she walked out the door, she shouted, "Jack, I'm leaving! Once I'm in my car and gone, don't ever try to find me! You don't deserve me!"

As she climbed into her car and started the engine, she paused, apparently giving Jack one last chance to choose her. Jack had to wonder what he ever saw in her in the first place. She was beautiful and her drawl could make men melt, but beyond that, she was empty. He prayed it was indeed the last time he would ever see her. This time had been one too many.

Tires screeched, leaving rubber on the driveway that they would see but say nothing about for a long time. Then, Jenny closed the door and turned to him.

"Jack?"

"Yes?"

"If you ever lie to me again, I'm not sure I can stay with you. I can put up with a lot of things, but dishonesty isn't one of them."

He took her in his arms and held her again.

This time, he let his tears fall. It was the first time he'd cried since Hank's funeral, and it occurred to him that this day could have ended with losing another person who was as dear to him as breathing.

"I swear I will never lie to you again, no matter the consequences."

She held him as he wept, and because she loved him, she wept because he did.

They never spoke of Carmen's visit again, as if it never happened. Mostly, they were happy she had stopped by to make their commitment to each other stronger, but they were even happier that she'd left.

29

The following Tuesday, Jack drove to Wharton to see what Van had managed to do to enhance the VHS tape. He was anxious to see if the tape revealed what the smudge on the robber's wrist was. If it was what he hoped, the tape would exonerate Tom and cast suspicion on someone else.

When he walked into Van's Video, Van was behind the counter talking to a customer who was purchasing a laser disc player, which was the latest video technology.

When he finished with the customer, Van said, "I think you'll like what I was able to do with your tape."

"Oh?"

"Yes. Come into the back," he said and walked through a swinging door that led to the back of the store.

Pulling up the enhanced video on a machine, Van pointed at the smudge. The area of the image had been enlarged, and Frank could see the clear image of a tattoo that looked like the point of a star—the kind of tattoo Lonnie had on the back of his wrist.

Jack smiled and said, "Great job!"

"Does this help your client?"

"Absolutely. This is someone he knows. This so-called friend has a tat sleeve that ends with five-pointed stars on the backs of both wrists."

"Well, if I were on the jury, I'd see this is clearly a tattoo. If your client doesn't have any on the back of his right wrist, I'd vote not guilty without hesitation."

"That's what I'm counting on," Jack said. "I might even be able to get the charges dropped altogether."

"Good luck, and if you need more of this kind of work done, let me know."

"Sure thing," Jack said and left with the original tape and a laser disc with the enhancement.

Arriving at his office, he prepared a motion to dismiss the charges against Tom Gordon, citing the enhanced video as evidence that Tom had not committed the robbery.

After stopping at the courthouse to file the motion and get a time for the hearing, Jack stopped by to say hello to Jenny before driving to Tom's to fill him in on what had transpired.

Knocking on the door to Tom's trailer, Jack stepped in when Tom answered the door. He wore cutoff jeans and a t-shirt that advertised a local bar.

"You've not been drinking, have you?" Jack asked, indicating the shirt.

"Nope. Clean and sober since last seeing you. I bought this shirt last summer. Don't wear it often so it isn't worn out."

"Great. I have good news for you, possibly great news."

"What is it? I could use some great news."

"I filed a motion to dismiss the charges."

Tom seemed to freeze, staring as if he couldn't believe what he'd heard. "What? How?"

"That video of the robbery shows a man who is clearly not you."

"How do you know that?"

"Hold out your arms so I can see the backs of your wrists." Tom complied. "You don't have any tattoos there."

"You mean there's a tattoo on the robber?"

Jack just nodded with a sly smile.

Tom began to dance around the small trailer, whooping and raising his fists in the air. "Yes!"

"We're not out of the woods yet, but I think when ADA Herndon sees the enhanced video, he will have little choice but to drop the charges and arrest someone else."

"Who? You mean you can tell who it is from the video?"

"I think so, yes. The tattoo looks an awful lot like the point of a five-pointed star."

Tom's mouth dropped open. "Lonnie?"

"Yep. Apparently, that night you mentioned he came by and told you he'd buy the beer if you went for it, he either found the gun or already knew where it was and took it, knowing you wouldn't report the theft of a stolen gun."

"I never even knew it was missing."

"Did Lonnie ever come back to your place after the robbery?"

"I don't remember exactly, but I would think so. He would usually stop by a couple of times a week."

"Do you recall any particular time recently when he was alone in the trailer for any length of time. He wouldn't need more than a minute to replace the gun."

"Shoot. You know what happens when you drink beer. Lots of time in the bathroom. He coulda done it when I was in there or even if he went back to use the bathroom. It's not like I paid attention to how long he was in the head."

"Then I think we have him."

Tom's face clouded, and Jack could see what he was thinking. "Let the law do its job, Tom. You go trying to take revenge, and we might as well let you serve time for the robbery. He could file a complaint, and you'd be charged with assault and battery."

"But he set me up! You told me before it looked like the robber shot the gun off on purpose. It was probably to make it so they could find the slug and nail me for doin' it."

"Use your head, Tom. You need to stop doing the first thing you think of doing when you're angry. That's almost never a good idea. When we're angry, we typically don't think straight, and we often make bad decisions at those times. Give yourself a cooling off period. I promise you that if you wait until tomorrow, this won't seem like something you have to rush out and get revenge for. He'll likely be in jail by the end of the week. The hearing's Thursday morning, so just hang loose, okay?"

Tom looked at him, squinting as if trying to figure something out. "What do you care? I'm just that guy who bullied you when we were kids. I was the furthest thing from a best friend. You act like I never did anything bad to you. I just can't figure that out. Why would you care if I went to jail or not?"

"It's simple. I don't think you should go to jail for something you didn't do, even if you've gotten away with things you deserve to spend time in jail for. I think everyone is redeemable. Even you. If I can stop you from committing a crime and help you get your life together and headed in the right direction, a lot of people will be happier for it, you most of all. There won't be any more victims of Tom Gordon's poorly thought-out plans, and you will actually like yourself a lot more."

"I like myself fine!" Tom nearly shouted.

"Really? You're happy with the person who spent time in Raiford? You think he's some kind of hero?"

Tom's jaw set, and for a moment Jack thought Tom might take a swing at him. Instead, the firm jaw relaxed, and Jack saw a vulnerable man for the first time when looking at Tom.

"If you're life's so great, convince me," Jack said.

"It ain't great. It stinks, in fact."

"Okay, then tell me how it stinks."

"I'd rather not."

"Believe me, you'll feel a lot better if you do."

Tom appeared to lose all strength in his legs and sat down in a chair in the tiny living room. Jack sat on the sofa, a cloud of dust rising when he sat.

"Talk to me, Tom. What's bad in your life?"

"When I was a little kid, like maybe seven or eight, I got in a fight with another kid. The other kid beat me, mostly because I tried to fight fair, and he would do anything he could—bite me, kick me. Anything. When I got home, my dad asked me who won the fight. I said the other kid did—I don't even remember his name now 'cause he moved away not too long after that. Anyway, when I told my dad the other guy won, he beat the tar outa me. Told me if I ever lost a fight again not to come home." Tom fixed teary eyes on Jack. "I was only a little kid."

Wiping his eyes, he continued. "After that, I decided I would kill someone before losing a fight. Never did, but it also made it so I would pick fights with people littler than me. I was a bully. Mostly it was because I was afraid to go home if I lost a fight."

"I'm sorry to hear that."

"Ain't your fault. You were just one of the littler kids I chose to pick on. Back then, Carl would push it, too. It was his idea we go take the rods and reels that time when you were alone in the store. If it was my idea, I'd tell you, but it wasn't. I was happy to go along with the idea, though. It made me feel like I had power over somethin'. Gettin' drunk was just another way to deal with it all."

"Do you like it when you're drunk?" Jack asked.

"Not really." He looked at Jack. The tears had stopped, possibly by sheer will power, but he still looked sad. "You know that time when you came by and took all my booze?"

"Yes."

"After you left, I knew you'd missed some in a cabinet near my bed. It was whiskey, and I went back to pour me a shot or five. That's when it hit me. Here I was the worst enemy you had as a kid, and you were doing what you could to help me. Nobody ever did that before, and I mean nobody. I started thinking about that and I thought that if you were willin' to do that for me, the least I could do was not drink. It wasn't easy, but I knew I could do it 'cause I didn't have anything to drink while I was in the jail."

Taking another deep breath, he continued, "I have a little girl. Did you know that?"

Jack was shocked at this news. "No, I didn't."

"Yep. Her name's Lynda, with a 'y'. She's the greatest."

"How old is she?"

"Seven."

"How often do you see her?"

"That's just it. Basically, I don't, unless her mom's there with us. Sadie's afraid I might get drunk if she left Lynda alone with me."

"Would you?"

"No. But that don't stop Sadie. She's just thinkin' the way she does 'cause I always drank when we were together. Every day."

"Why do you think you wouldn't drink with Lynda around?"

"I'm happy when she's around, so I don't have to drink to get happy. She's like some kind of drug or something."

"Do you think Sadie would believe you'd sobered up and won't drink again if you quit?"

"Good question."

"Where do they live?"

"In Wharton. I only see Lynda when Sadie brings her. They never stay long, though. Maybe thirty minutes."

"Sounds to me like you have to try at least. You can become a good person. Like I said, everybody can be redeemed. You just have to be smarter about how you live your life."

"I talked to my boss the other day, and I don't have a job anymore. He says he needs someone more dependable. What am I gonna do for a job? If the boat captains won't hire me, who will?"

"I don't know, but we have to get the charges dropped first. That way at least you know you won't be going to prison instead of to a job."

"I know I said it before, but I'm really sorry I bullied you when we were kids. You didn't deserve it any more than I deserve what you've done for me."

"So far, all I've done is try. Let's wait to find out what happens with the motion to dismiss before making more plans, okay? I have something in mind for you as far as work goes. I'd actually been thinking about it for the past week or so."

"What kind of job is it?"

"I'll tell you when the charges are dismissed, because if they aren't, there won't be a job."

"Okay. Thanks, man." He paused a second, thinking and chuckling. "Life's weird, ain't it? Who'd have thought you would turn out to be the best friend I got?

"Yeah, weird," Jack said without pointing out

that Tom was not his best friend. “It’s no problem. I’m going to get you to turn your life around, Tom. We’ll both be happier for it. You’ll even be healthier.”

“Thanks.”

“I want you in court on Thursday when I present the motion to dismiss the charges. I want everyone to see you don’t have any tattoos on the back of your right wrist.”

“Will you be picking me up?”

“Yes.”

“Okay. What time?”

“Be ready at seven. I’ll take you for a good breakfast and then we’ll go to court.”

“Breakfast, huh? I usually only drink some coffee. That’ll be a treat.”

“Be ready by seven on Thursday. I’ll see you then. Stay out of trouble and we might get you through this mess.”

They said goodbye, and Jack went back to the courthouse annex to pick Jenny up for lunch.

He held off talking about Tom Gordon’s case until they were seated at Perry’s. “I think I may have gotten Tom Gordon off.”

“Really? How?” Her response reminded him of Tom’s reaction.

“You can’t say anything. Nothing is certain yet, but I have a motion to dismiss that will be heard Thursday. I’ll be going by to see Larry Herndon if he’s available after lunch to let him know what was found on the tape.”

“What if he drops the charges without the hearing?”

"He'll need to see the video, and I'll need to rent a laser disc player to show it in court. If he balks too much, I'll subpoena Van, the video guy, to be there to explain the veracity of the images."

After Jack dropped Jenny at her desk, he went to the DA's office and asked to see Larry Herndon for only two minutes. The receptionist knew him and said, "Sure, Mr. Turner. Let me find out if he can see you now."

She punched the buttons on her phone to connect to his office and said, "Hi, Blanche. Is Mr. Herndon available to see Jack Turner? He says it won't take a minute." She waited for a moment and said, "Fine, I'll send him back."

She hung up and said, "He can see you now, Mr. Turner, but he only has few a minutes to spare you."

"No problem. Thanks."

Blanche greeted him when he walked through the door. "Just go on back, Mr. Turner. He's expecting you."

When he entered ADA Herndon's office, Larry said, "Jack, I heard you filed a motion to dismiss."

"Yes. The tape was very revealing."

"Really? How so?"

"It clearly shows a tattoo on the back of the wrist of the man who robbed the store."

"You're sure it's a tattoo? It could be anything, couldn't it? Mud maybe? Or even dried blood from a small injury received while working the boats?"

"Nope. It's definitely a tattoo. Van at the video store said he'd acquit in a heartbeat with that kind of evidence."

"Well, Van isn't on the jury, nor will he be."

"Still, Larry, the evidence is overwhelming."

"I guess we'll have to see what the judge thinks on Thursday, eh, Jack? In the meantime, your guy will still be considered charged with armed robbery."

"I understand, Larry. I just wanted to give you the heads up because Judge Shelton told me to tell you immediately upon finding evidence of an exculpatory nature."

"Okay, you've done your job. Now, if you'll excuse me, Tom Gordon is not my only case."

"No problem. Later, Larry." Jack left the building and returned to his office, where an excited Brinkley waited to be taken for a walk.

"An extra long walk for you today, Brinkley," Jack said. "We'll consider it a doggy celebration."

30

At seven o'clock sharp, Jack pulled in at Tom's trailer. He didn't even have time to shut off the car before Tom opened his door and strode out, a smile on his face. He was wearing a long-sleeve shirt and tie, which surprised Jack. He'd never seen Tom in anything more than an old shirt and ragged shorts or jeans. He'd also shaved and had his hair cut. He could have been a guy working at an office supply store. The difference was striking.

"Wow. You clean up a lot better than I thought. You look like you're going on a job interview for a job as an office manager."

Tom grinned, and Jack saw that he would need dental work if he wanted such a job, but the outward appearance was definitely better.

"I even got a star tattooed on my wrist to celebrate!" Tom said.

Jack's eyes widened in shock and Tom burst into laughter. "Got ya!"

Jack smiled and backed the car out. "Yes, you did, Tom."

Arriving at a local diner, Jack told Tom to order whatever he wanted, that they had plenty of time since they didn't need to be in court for a while yet. Tom apparently took him at his word. He ordered steak and eggs, asking for two extra eggs, with both grits and hash browns, three pieces of toast, coffee, and a large orange juice. Jack ordered considerably less and marveled at Tom as he inhaled his food.

"For a man who only drinks coffee for breakfast, you can certainly put it away," Jack said, smiling.

"I said that's what I usually have, not what I want. I don't get a meal like this very often."

They finished and Jack paid the bill, leaving a generous tip. As they drove to the courthouse annex, Tom asked, "So what's this job you might have lined up for me?"

"I'll tell you once the charges are dropped. I don't want to add to your disappointment if we lose on the motion. This way, you'll be no worse off than you were if we lose. Otherwise, you'd know you also lost out on a job. Let's face one obstacle at a time, okay?"

Tom took a deep breath. "Okay, boss."

Jack jerked his head toward Tom, wondering where that moniker came from. Tom wasn't the type of guy to call anyone *boss*. At least he never had been from what Jack could tell.

Upon arriving at the courthouse, Jack opened his trunk and lifted a heavy case from inside.

"What's that?" Tom asked.

"A laser disc player to show the enhanced video of the robbery."

"Oh."

"Could you grab my briefcase? It's in the floor of the back seat."

"Sure thing," Tom said and followed Jack inside with the briefcase.

Because of the need to set up the disc player and monitor, Jack's motion would be the first one heard that day. They entered the courtroom and Jack saw Van seated in the front behind the defense table. Jack had hand delivered a subpoena to him the day before in case he needed him. Van hadn't been happy, but he understood. Van immediately stood and began setting up the laser disc player and connecting it to the TV monitor provided by the court.

"Thanks, Van."

"You can owe me," Van replied and took his seat once he'd finished setting up the disc player.

Jack and Tom sat at the defense table and waited. When Larry Herndon took his seat with his assistant, Tom stared daggers at him, as if considering ways to make him pay.

Jack noticed and said, "Tom, he's like me. He's just doing his job. You have to admit, the case looked fairly solid against you."

"Tell me something. Did you ever wonder how it was they came to see me about that robbery? I mean, who woulda told them I might have done it?"

"There aren't that many people with a prison record in Denton," Jack said. "Any crime like that will have them at your door whenever a surveillance video shows someone who looks like you."

Tom seemed taken aback by this news. "You mean, I might be dealing with being a suspect the rest of my life? They'll come find me every time a crime happens?"

"Not exactly, no. There has to be a probability that you committed the crime, first. I have to tell you, if I hadn't enhanced the video, I would have sworn it was you in it, especially considering the gun used was yours, whether the gun was legal or not. Especially since it was illegal, in fact."

"That ain't fair," Tom said and sat back.

"Life isn't fair, Tom. You'll be a lot happier once you accept that and decide to do your best with the cards you're dealt."

The bailiff entered from behind the bench and said, "All rise! This court is now in session. The Honorable Patricia Shelton presiding."

Trisha entered, took her seat at the bench, and said, "You may be seated." Everyone sat. "I see the first case is a motion to dismiss in the case of Florida versus Thomas Gordon." She looked at Jack. He could see the hint of a smile on her face. "Mr. Turner? Are you ready to proceed?"

"Yes, Your Honor."

"Mr. Herndon?"

"Ready, Your Honor."

"Okay. Mr. Turner, what do you have?"

"Your Honor, as you recall, the defense paid to have the original surveillance video of the crime enhanced to try to determine what evidence there was against my client, and to find if there was, as the defense suspected, visual evidence that the perpetrator was not my client."

"Yes," Trisha said.

"At this time, we would like to present the enhanced video and allow the court to draw its own conclusions."

"Very well," Trisha said.

"Your Honor, if I may," Jack said, "what you will see on the monitor is the digitized enhancement of the robbery."

"Of course," Trisha said.

Jack went to the player and inserted the disc. When the TV monitor came on, he pressed "play" and the scene progressed. When the video reached a point where the back of the wrist was visible, Jack stopped the video.

"As you can see, Your Honor, there is what appears to be a smudge of some kind on the back of the man's wrist." He waited a second so the judge could see what he was talking about. Jack pressed another button and the enlargement of the smudge came into view. It had the obvious shape of a point, as if the man wore a tattoo of a black triangle on the back of his wrist.

"Here is an enlargement of that smudge. As you can see, it is not a smudge at all but a tattoo. The lines of the obvious triangular shape have clear edges that are not a mere accident of the video or a place where the man committing the robbery got some dirt smudged on him. These lines were obviously drawn on by someone capable of drawing a straight line. In fact, this is a picture of a tattoo that is very similar to one worn by a friend of Mr. Gordon's—a friend who was frequently alone in Mr. Gordon's residence. Planting the gun there as evidence to frame my client would have been easy."

Larry Herndon stood. "Objection, Your Honor. The counsel for the defense is testifying."

"Sustained. Please keep your remarks to what

is already established, Mr. Turner," Trisha said and leaned forward to better see the image on the screen.

"Certainly, Your Honor. I would be happy to have my client sworn in for the sole purpose of establishing that a friend with such a tattoo was alone in the defendant's trailer and could have hidden the gun there."

"Mr. Herndon?" Trisha said, wanting to know if the ADA wished for that to happen.

"That won't be necessary," Herndon said.

Jack turned to look at Larry Herndon, who was now gaping at the video.

"Your Honor," Larry said, "it's entirely possible that Mr. Turner has somehow managed to make adjustments to this enhanced version to make it appear the subject has a tattoo. How do we know the video hasn't been tampered with in some way?"

Jack spoke up. "Your Honor, we have the expert who enhanced the original video in court today if you would like to hear from him."

"That would be helpful, Mr. Turner," Trisha said.

"Defense calls Mr. Van Harrison to the stand," Jack said.

Van rose and was sworn in. Sitting, he looked at Jack expectantly.

"Mr. Harrison, you were the person who enhanced the video of the robbery, is that right?"

"Yes."

"Did you do anything to the original or the enhanced version that would result in such a blemish on the end product?"

"Absolutely not. Adding such things would take more time than I have. Besides, I would never do such a thing, especially to evidence in a trial. I like my freedom, and altering evidence on a whim would endanger that."

"Have you enhanced video for a trial before, sir?" Jack asked.

"Yes. Many times."

"Have you ever enhanced video for the county's district attorney's office?"

"Again, yes. Many times."

"Did they ever question your integrity when you worked for them?"

Van laughed at the question. "No. I was trained by the FBI in video enhancement. I used to work for them."

Jack turned to Larry with a smile. "Your witness, Mr. Herndon." He couldn't help adding, "In fact, he's been your witness several times."

"No need for sarcasm, Jack," Judge Shelton interrupted, using his first name to make her remark more personal.

"Apologies, Your Honor."

As he sat, Jack recalled an important moment in Hank's trial when Trisha was Hank's co-counsel with her husband, Chuck. She had drawn an even stronger admonition from the judge back then when asking a witness a question that suggested some kind of collusion between the witness and Mr. Metz, the assistant DA in that case.

"Your apology to the court is accepted, Mr. Turner, but I won't speak for Mr. Herndon."

Larry smiled. "Same here, Your Honor."

"Okay, now that we've dispensed with that, do you wish to cross examine the witness, Mr. Herndon?"

Larry heaved a big sigh, apparently admitting defeat. Jack knew he would have to. To question the integrity of a man whom he'd used as a video expert and witness before would cast doubt on all the cases he had tried where Van had been their video expert. He was stuck and he knew it. Even the objection itself created a problem. Besides, Jack thought, it wasn't as if the truth was as clear as polished crystal.

"No questions, Your Honor."

"In that case, Mr. Turner, the court hereby rules that the video evidence is sufficient to grant your request for dismissal." Turning to Tom, she added, "You are free to go, Mr. Gordon, and I hope you manage to keep yourself out of my courtroom in the future as well."

"Thank you, Judge," Tom said. At the sound of the gavel's slam, dismissing this case and moving the court to the next one, Tom threw his arms around Jack and hugged him.

"Thank you, man! I will never forget this!"

Jack patted his back. "You're welcome." As Jack and Van packed up the laser disc player, the two chatted.

"If I ever need a criminal defense attorney, I'll know where to look," Van said. "I certainly don't think I ever will, but there's always that possibility."

"Thanks," Jack said and grabbed the handle of the large case that held the disc player.

As Larry Herndon started to leave, Jack asked him, "Are you going to arrest Lonnie Gilchrist? He's Mr. Gordon's 'friend' who has such a tattoo and the opportunity to plant the gun."

"Will your client testify to the opportunity?"

Tom said, "You bet I will."

Larry nodded as he left them. "Mr. Gilchrist will be arrested by lunchtime."

"Actually," Jack said, "he's a trucker and might not be back in town until Saturday. I guess it depends on if he has a run that took him out of town until then."

"We'll get him," Larry said and left the courtroom.

Jack grabbed the case with the disc player and asked Tom to grab his briefcase once again. They left the courtroom, and as they climbed into the car, Tom said, "So, what about that job you mentioned?"

"The truth is I need to hire you," said Jack. "I've been thinking about it, and I could use someone to do a little investigative work. Nothing that difficult and it won't require any knowledge of how to be an investigator or anything. Mostly, I need you to tail someone and report back to me for your first job. I'm willing to pay you enough each month to pay your rent and utilities and put some food on the table. Nothing drastic. Just, well, enough to make ends meet."

"You make enough taking on public defender jobs to pay me a living wage?"

"Not exactly. The truth is that Hank left me about ninety percent of his inheritance from his father. The other ten percent went to Mrs. Dawson. I will never be able to spend the money I have. It's invested and I'm able to live off the income it generates."

"You mean you're rich?"

"I guess you could say that. So, it won't be any financial burden on me to hire you. I've never been in it for the money anyway."

"Thanks, man. I really appreciate it."

"One thing, though, that is a requirement of working for me."

"What's that?"

"No drinking. No drugs. No crimes."

"You mean I can't even have a beer?"

"Do you want a relationship with your daughter?"

"Of course."

"Then it's up to you to clean up your life. Quit drinking. Everything that your daughter's mother could object to, get rid of it in your life. There is no other way. None."

"You're askin' a lot, man."

"I know. But I think you can do it."

"What happens if you find out I took a drink?"

"You're fired. Immediately."

"That's stiff, man. No warnings?"

"Nope. You understand the consequences, so if you choose to go off the wagon, you're making a choice to leave the job. Essentially, if you do what you've been told you can't do and I find out—and I will—then basically, you're quitting. You're firing yourself."

"What about some emotional support on that?"

"Go to AA meetings."

"Even the best of those people backslide."

"Yep. So you'll have to be better than they are. Look, when did you take your last drink?"

"That night you came over and took all my stuff."

"Shoot. You're half way there. That was, what? Two weeks ago? More? I've lost track. If you've been on the wagon this long, you just need to stay on it."

"Well, I was sorta hoping I could celebrate my freedom tonight."

"Figure out another way to celebrate it. Hey, you can celebrate your freedom, your job, and your commitment to sobriety all in one big event."

"Man, every 'event' in my life has been accompanied by alcohol or drugs."

"Well, there's a first for everything. Tell you what, come by my house tonight and we'll celebrate. I'll have people over and you can enjoy your new friends."

"Tonight?"

"Yeah."

"Okay. What time?"

"Be there at seven."

Jack dropped him at his trailer and said in parting, "Don't screw this up, Tom. It's the chance of a lifetime."

"I won't. In fact, I'm gonna call Sadie and let her know. Maybe I can talk her into coming to the party tonight. You okay with that?"

"Sure. And she can bring your daughter. I'd like to meet her. Assure Sadie there won't be any alcohol or drugs or anything else inappropriate for a seven-year-old."

"Thanks, man. I owe you big time."

"Just stay sober, Tom, and don't let me down."

"You got it."

As Jack drove off, he knew he'd been hard on Tom, but tough love was what he needed. He doubted Tom would be able to avoid falling off the wagon, and in truth he would still have a job if he did, but Jack needed to be sure Tom understood the seriousness of doing his best to remain sober and lawful. He'd do his best to be there to catch him whenever he fell off. It was odd to think he'd become a mentor to Tom when a month ago he wouldn't have given two cents to him, but that was how odd life could be.

Jack returned to his office and made some phone calls, the first to Chuck Shelton. Chuck said he would check with Trisha to see if she could be there, but added he would be there in any case. When Jack called Jenny and told her, she was skeptical that Tom would change but was fine with the party idea.

"We have to try," Jack said.

"I know. And I love you because you feel the need to do what you can for a guy who was your worst enemy when you were kids."

"Well, let's see if this pans out first. I might be tilting at windmills."

"At least it's a windmill worth tilting at," she said. "See you tonight."

"Okay. Bye."

After hanging up, he called the local office of

the DEA and asked the secretary who answered if he could speak to Clyde Harwood.

"Agent Harwood," Jack said when Harwood came on the line. "This is Jack Turner."

"Hi, Mr. Turner. What can I do for you?"

"I was wondering if you'd been able to tail Keith Breslin with any regularity lately?"

"I'm not at liberty to discuss that, especially over the phone."

"Okay, how's this? I have a man who can conduct sixteen hours a day of surveillance of Breslin. And I'll set it up at no cost to the DEA."

"Where can we meet in person?"

Jack gave Harwood the address of his office.

"I'll be there in an hour," Agent Harwood said and hung up.

While he waited, Jack phoned a local real estate company. He'd driven by the Breslin home after dropping Tom off after the trial and noticed a house across the street and a few houses west of where Breslin lived that was a vacation rental. The back of this house faced the Gulf. It was off season now, and Jack wanted to rent the place for a week or two to give Tom a base for watching Breslin's activities.

After making those arrangements, Jack fixed himself some coffee, petted Brinkley, and waited for Harwood.

31

July 15, 1989

Rick stood outside the home in Jacksonville that he had recently rented, considering his past and how his life had led to this moment. After his release from prison, he had reported to a halfway house in Jacksonville, where he was required to live for the first three months following his parole. While there, he managed to find a job as a construction laborer. He saved his money, stayed clean, and now would be settling into this small home while he kept his appointments with his parole officer.

When he was released from the halfway house, he used his savings to pay the first month's rent and security deposit on this two-bedroom home in an older section of the city.

At least, that was how the realtor had described the area. Rick would describe it as rundown. Some of the city's poorer residents lived in this neighborhood, and it showed.

As he looked up and down the block, he spotted Jasmine, who was Hammer's wife, as she checked her mailbox at the side of the road. Hammer had given Rick her address and phone number, and when Rick arrived in town, he'd called her. She had invited him to supper, where Rick had also met her brother, who lived there as well, and her two children. He and Jasmine had become friends, but nothing more. Rick couldn't do that to Hammer, who was as much responsible for his surviving his time in Raiford as anyone, not that Jasmine would do that to her husband either.

He waved to her and she returned the greeting before going back inside with her mail. As she was about to enter the house, she called to him, "Why don't you stop in for some coffee later? Roscoe wants to talk to you about something."

"I'll be down in a little while," Rick answered.

Rick stood there and wondered if he could get the landlord to let him work off some of the rent by fixing up the house a bit. It needed painting, as well as some repair to the gutters. There was more, of course, but he wasn't willing to do major repairs, which would be very expensive and take more time than he wanted to spend on the old house.

Rick was proud of his progress in regards to his problem, namely his dependence on opioids. He'd moved to Vicodin when he was still using because it was cheaper and easier to find. Now, however, he was clean, and he intended to stay that way.

It scared him every time he thought of this because almost immediately, a guilty fear rose in him with each promise he made himself. Addictive dependence was just one pill away.

"One day at a time," he reminded himself, striding inside and calling the realtor to see if some kind of exchange of repairs and rent could be worked out.

The realtor told him he would get in touch with the owners and let him know. When Rick hung up, he began his daily craving and decided it would be a good time to go see Jasmine and her brother, Roscoe, not to mention her two little ones, only eight and six.

After pouring himself a cup of coffee from the pot, Rick sat down and looked at Jasmine and Roscoe. "So, what is it you needed to see me about?" he asked Roscoe.

Roscoe wanted to know if Rick would like to go with him to see a man about a car. "I could use another set of eyes," he said, his gold tooth flashing in the sunlight pouring in through the sliding glass door near the table where they sat. "Besides, someone will have to drive my old car back if I get this one."

"I didn't know you had enough nickels to spend on a car, man!" Rick joked.

"Been saving up!" Roscoe said, laughing. "The wheels I'm driving now about to need some major work. I'd sooner spend the money on new wheels."

Rick had joined Roscoe and agreed that the car Roscoe was driving was on its last legs. After looking at the car he was considering buying, however, they both decided the purchase would only result in a lateral move rather than a move up.

As Roscoe's current car limped back home, Roscoe said, "So, you clean?"

"Yep," Rick asked.

Roscoe grinned. "Wanna get dirty?"

Although Roscoe's temptation made him angry, Rick kept calm. "No." He stared out his window before adding, "Well, I do, but I don't. I'd rather not get mixed up with that stuff anymore. It never leads anywhere good."

"Well, just askin'. I know where you can get some if you want it, so if you change your mind—"

"I won't change my mind," Rick said, interrupting. "In fact, could we talk about something else? The craving is always there, and talking about it makes me think about the need."

Roscoe held out a hand as if to calm Rick down. "Okay. Okay. I just didn't know if you was really off the stuff or still lookin' to get back on it."

Almost a year later, Jasmine moved away, taking a job at a convenience store in the town of Starke, which was near the prison. She wanted to be closer to the prison so she could visit more often. Roscoe stayed in the house down the street from Rick, but the friendship waned as Roscoe became more enmeshed in the world of illegal drugs. Rick was fine with the growing estrangement.

He still heard from Jasmine, and he would receive occasional mail from Hammer himself, who had told Rick that Roscoe was bad news the first time his brother-in-law had been mentioned.

Rick and Hammer were planning to go into business together when Hammer was released, fixing up and cleaning houses for real estate companies that handled the many rental houses in the Jacksonville area. Rental properties were always needing some kind of work, especially between tenants. Hammer still had another two years left in his sentence if he could get out early on good behavior. Three if he couldn't, but from all reports, he was doing well. In the meantime, Rick had more or less started the business on the side, having talked his own realtor into using him on occasion after the realtor saw what great work Rick had done on the house where he lived.

As he was sitting down to his supper one night, a frantic knock sounded at the door. He went to it and found Roscoe there, crying.

"What is it?!"

"Hammer! He's dead!"

Rick felt his body go numb and his knees start to buckle as tears welled.

"What?! How?!"

"He was exercising in the yard at the prison. His usual stuff—liftin' weights and all—and he had a heart attack. Just keeled over, they say!"

"Who told you? Jasmine?"

"Yeah." Roscoe stumbled to the sofa and seemed to crumple there. "He's dead, man! Dead!"

Rick made it to a chair before he collapsed, and the two men sobbed, sharing their grief.

To Rick, everything seemed useless. Life, work, sobriety—all of it suddenly had no meaning. Hammer would always be the best friend he'd ever had, and now he was gone in the blink of an eye.

After an hour of trying to console each other, Rick looked at Roscoe. He needed something to get him through this.

"Roscoe?"

"Yeah?"

"I think I need to get dirty."

Ten minutes later, Rick's sobriety died as quickly as Hammer had.

32

Tuesday, April 21, 1992

Agent Harwood sat in Jack's office and listened to Jack's plan, nodding throughout the conversation. He explained that with only one other agent working the case, their ability to tail Breslin was limited.

"I appreciate your offer," he said when Jack was finished. "Will your man take pictures? I can provide a camera and film."

"No problem there, and I have the camera. I don't even mind paying for the film if your office can handle the developing."

"Of course."

When Agent Harwood left, Jack took Brinkley home, stopping to buy some heavy hors d'oeuvres to serve as supper at the party to celebrate the charges against Tom being dropped. He also picked up some non-alcoholic sparkling cider, a poor substitute for champagne, but he couldn't serve a man alcohol after making him promise to stop drinking.

Arriving home, he cleaned the downstairs areas, including vacuuming and dusting. More than once, it occurred to him that had anyone told him he would be throwing a party for Tom Gordon one day, he would have laughed as if he'd been told the world's funniest joke.

When Jenny arrived, Jack greeted her at the door with a kiss.

"Well, someone's in a good mood," she said.

"The best."

"Are we having dinner?"

"Of a sort. I bought some heavy hors d'oeuvres and sparkling cider."

"Sounds good to me," she said. "I'm going to go shower and change."

"Okay."

Jack and Jenny were enjoying a glass of wine when Tom arrived promptly at seven. They put aside their glasses of wine and brought out the cider. Chuck Shelton arrived shortly after Tom.

"Trish couldn't make it?" Jack asked.

"Sorry. She felt it might not look right for her to attend a "get-out-of-jail" party for someone who was freed because she granted the motion to drop the charges."

"Wow. I guess she's right. I never thought about it that way."

"That's because you never looked at it as anything dishonest on either or your parts," Chuck said.

"Mr. Shelton?" Tom said when Jack entered the great room with Chuck.

"Yep. I know it might feel weird having me attend a party celebrating your win in court, and to be honest, I can't stay long, but I wanted you to know there are no hard feelings over something that happened over twenty years ago." Chuck extended his hand, and Tom shook it, a look of utter disbelief on his face.

When the doorbell rang again, Tom said, “That might be Sadie. She said she might come and bring Lynda.”

When Jack opened the door, a brunette woman about his age stood there, looking lost. “I’m sorry. I was given this address to meet someone at a party. Is this the right place?” Her face showed that she expected Jack to say she might be the victim of a practical joke.

“Are you Sadie?”

Her expression changed from doubt to shock. “Yes. Is Tom Gordon here?”

“Yes. In fact, this party is in his honor.”

Jack looked down and saw a pretty girl with dark bangs peeking from behind her mother’s thigh. “And you must be Lynda,” Jack said, extending his hand to shake hers.

She stared at the offered hand until her mother said, “Go ahead, honey. Shake his hand.”

The child took the hand shyly and Jack took the opportunity to escort her into the entry foyer.

Tom stepped into the foyer and said, “Hi, Sadie. I’m glad you came.”

“I thought you were playin’ some joke on me when I pulled up and saw this house.”

Jack said, “I’m Jack Turner. I defended Tom on the armed robbery charge.”

Tom said, “He’s the reason I’m out. He proved I couldn’t have done it.”

Lynda ignored the adults and stepped into the great room beyond the entryway.

"Don't touch anything," Sadie called after her.

"It's okay," Jack said. "She can't hurt anything, and I don't have anything expensive enough to worry about her breaking something."

Sadie looked relieved, and Tom ushered her into the great room, where he introduced her to Chuck and Jenny.

Later, when everyone else had left the small party, Jack turned to Tom and said, "I have a job for you."

"What is it, boss?"

Jack wasn't sure he could get used to being called 'boss,' even in what seemed a show of friendship, but he accepted it because it was better than most of the names Tom had used for him in the past.

"You remember me telling you about how I need you to follow someone?" Tom nodded. "Well, I need you to start tomorrow morning. You need to tail him without being noticed. You think you can do that?"

"No problem. I've done it before."

"This won't be someone you're just wanting to keep an eye on. You'll have to blend in and not allow him to even suspect you're watching him."

"I can do it. Don't worry."

"Do you know who Keith Breslin is?"

"Nope."

"He's a major dealer of illegal drugs. I'll need you to follow him and especially let me know if he uses a payphone."

"Okay. Do I drop the tail after he does that and find you right then or keep following him?"

"Keep following him, and write down everywhere he goes, no matter how trivial it may seem. We'll meet every night when you knock off at eleven. Come straight to my house afterwards and fill me in."

"What if I don't see anything that day?"

"Report to me anyway."

"Okay. I knock off at eleven at night. What time do I start?"

"At seven tomorrow morning."

"Wow. That's a long day."

"Don't worry. I'll pay you eight dollars an hour, with time-and-a-half for every hour after forty in a week. All you have to do is watch this guy, take a few pictures if he does something suspicious, and don't be seen doing it. That's more than minimum wage. Hopefully, you won't need to tail him more than a couple of days."

"What'll I do for food?"

"I have walkie-talkies. Let me know where you are at noon and six every day. I'll bring you something to eat and drink. Keep a cooler in the car with iced down soft drinks and water in case you end up having to sit for a while. Just don't let him see you."

"What'll he do if he does? Kill me?"

"I don't know, but I don't want to find out."

"What about a bathroom? I can't exactly go in a coffee can all the time or something."

"I've rented a vacation house across the street and a few doors down from his house. The rear faces the Gulf, so it won't appear strange your car is always in the driveway. Even something like that could raise Breslin's suspicions." He took out a key and told him the rental's address. "Here's the key. Do you have any suitcases?"

"Yeah."

"Are they nice or beat up?"

"Fairly nice, I guess. I mean you wouldn't look at them and think they were going to fall apart any second, or anything."

"Okay. I doubt they'll see you moving in anyway, but we can't be sure. Pack some clothes and essentials and plan to stay there for the next few days, at least."

"Does it have a TV?"

"I'm sure it does, but you can't be watching it. If Breslin leaves while you're watching a program, you'll miss him."

"So all I do is sit and stare out a window until he leaves and follow him?"

"Yep. You'll get paid eight dollars an hour to do just that, twelve when you reach forty hours."

"What if I'm in the can and he leaves?"

"That's a chance we'll have to take."

Jack gave Tom the address for where Breslin lived. "If he leaves, there's only one way out to the highway, so you can wait until he turns a corner to get in your car and follow him, and never be the car directly behind him once you're out of the neighborhood. You also shouldn't allow yourself to be behind him at a stop sign in the neighborhood. Be sure to keep as much distance as you can between you and his car. Waiting at the stop sign at the road that leads to the highway to see which direction he turns on the highway would be a great idea, too. It would be best if you can avoid being seen at all. What kind of car do you drive?"

"An '84 Chevy Impala. Why?"

"Is it in good shape?"

"Hey, I keep that thing sharp."

"Good. It's not some wild color, is it?"

"No. A light gray. Looks brand new. I wax it twice a month."

"That's great. It will fit in. Just don't let him notice you. Try to stay at least a block behind him. If he goes out on the highway, keep a few cars between you and him."

"I know, man. I've watched cop shows before."

Jack was nervous about doing this, but he had to keep an eye on Breslin from early in the day until late in the evening to find out where he was getting his drugs. He would take a shift of watching him, but he might have Danielle Wolford or Tiffany with him, and if they saw him, their surveillance would end.

Jack gave Tom the camera, which was already loaded with film, and a walkie-talkie. He instructed him how to use each and wished him luck.

At seven o'clock the next morning, Jack lifted the walkie-talkie from its charger and keyed the mic.

"Tom, this is Jack. Are you there?" he said.

"Sittin' here in this rather nice house waiting for the guy to come out."

"Good. Keep me posted."

"Roger that."

At five minutes before noon, Tom checked in. "Base, this is Tom Terrific. Do you copy?"

Jack lifted the small handheld and keyed the mic. “Don’t get cute, Tom. Just use our names.”

“Yeah, well, Tom is gettin’ kinda hungry. The subject just went into Captain’s Dock. He’s been inside for ten minutes, so I figure he’s gettin’ some grub.”

“Okay, I’ll be there in twenty minutes. Burger and fries sound okay?”

“Sure. My staple diet,” Tom said.

“Anything suspicious happen yet?”

“Not that I can tell. He ain’t been to a payphone. Mostly, he’s not done much of nothing. Left the house to come here. That’s about it. Boring job, you got here.”

“I can’t help that. As I said, you’re being paid just to sit watch someone. Did you write down the time he left the house and where he went?”

“Yep. That’s what you told me to do, isn’t it?”

“Just making sure. If something goes down, you could be called to testify in court about what you saw, and having exact notes will help you in your testimony if that happens.”

“Hey, you never said nothin’ about testifying in court.”

“It’s part of the job, Tom. Take it or leave it. Remember, you’re one of the good guys now.”

After only a short hesitation and a deep sigh, Tom said, “Okay, no problem. I’ll take it.”

“Good. I’ll be there in twenty with your lunch.”

That evening at six, Jack brought Tom his supper, some KFC, and shortly after eleven, Jack answered the doorbell, letting Tom in.

“What happened today?”

"A whole lot of nothin'. The guy doesn't even have a job. Just sits at home and goes to lunch. The rest of the day he was home."

"Did he go in or come out with anyone at lunch?"

"Nope."

"What about visitors? Did he have any?"

"None. The only other people to go in or out was the woman and girl you described to me. The girl left for school and returned this afternoon. The woman left around 7:30 and returned around 5:30. I guess she has a job."

"Okay, maybe we'll have better luck tomorrow," Jack said. "Did you write down the times when the woman and girl left and arrived back home?"

"Is that important?"

"Everything's important in a surveillance operation, Tom."

"I don't remember the exact times they left and came back, but I can guess pretty close. I thought I only had to do that with the guy."

"Nope. Everyone, Tom. Write it all down as it happens. Note the times, and if someone else shows up, be sure to get their picture."

"Will do, boss."

"You know, you don't have to call me 'boss,' Tom. 'Jack' will do."

"I know, but I always called the boat captains, 'captain.' You ain't a captain, so I figured I'd just call you 'boss,' because that's what you are. My boss."

"Okay, if you prefer that, it's fine."

"I do have a question, though."

"What's that?"

"You think I could get some snacks to munch on during the day? Maybe some stuff for a sandwich in case he doesn't go out? I coulda saved you the trip tonight if I'd had something to fix to eat."

"No problem. I'll have you something tomorrow night when you come by. In the meantime, I've got a few things you can take with you tonight to last until then."

Jack and Tom packed a few items that Tom found in Jack's pantry and refrigerator in a grocery sack, and Tom thanked him again for the job.

"You know, you're the first person to ever give me a second chance," Tom said.

"I'm sure I'm not the first. You just didn't notice it before."

Tom looked at Jack, his expression serious. "No. Never. The fact that of all people I know, you have done that means a lot to me. Don't make light of it."

As Tom held his gaze, Jack nodded. "Okay, I won't."

The next morning at seven, Tom checked in.

"Hey, boss. This is Tom, starin' out the window. Nothing's shakin' right now, though. Too early." His words were cut off momentarily with a yawn. "For everyone, I think."

"Okay. Keep me posted," Jack said.

Jack again brought Tom his lunch and supper, praying nobody at Breslin's noticed. When he'd brought Tom his supper, Tom said, "I hope this doesn't last into spring and summer. I'm gonna go crazy just sittin' here if it does."

"It won't last that long, Tom. My guess is we'll know something no later than Monday."

"I have to do this over the weekend, too?"

"If that's what it takes. I could take over for a bit if it does, but that'll be risky. I could be recognized."

"What have you been doin' while I'm out here dying of boredom?"

"Getting new clients through the Public Defender's Office."

"Oh?"

"Yep. By the way, they arrested Lonnie for the robbery. I heard when he saw the enhanced video with the tattoos, he said lots of people have tattoos on their wrists."

"He's probably right. I'm just glad I never got one there."

"Yes, but how many people with tattoos on their wrists also had access to your home?"

"Good question. The answer would be one."

"Bingo," Jack said. "My guess is he'll end up taking a plea deal within a week."

"I'm sorry he did that. I trusted him."

"Yeah," Jack said. Then a thought occurred to him that he'd wanted to ask Tom about.

"Tom, Lonnie's girlfriend—what kind of person is she?"

"Elyse?" He shrugged. "She's nice enough, I guess. Why?"

"When I was there talking to Lonnie, she came out in an almost transparent bra and short shorts."

Tom laughed. “She did?” He stood there, shaking his head. “Well, let’s just say neither one of ‘em care if she’s faithful or not. She was seeing if you were interested.” He paused. “Were you?”

“No. I was mostly embarrassed she would come out dressed like that. How do you know this?”

Tom winked. “I wasn’t embarrassed.”

“Does Lonnie know about this?”

“Of course. Man, she usually charges for her services. You didn’t know?”

“No,” Jack said, shaking his head in disbelief.

As he drove home, Jack thought about the ugly underbelly of society and felt sad that some people felt they were only good for selling their bodies.

At a quarter past ten, the walkie-talkie squawked and Tom said, “Boss? Boss? You there? This is Tom. Something’s happening.”

“I’m here,” Jack said. He could hear the excitement in Tom’s voice. “What’s going on?”

“He left the house and turned toward the highway. I followed, of course, and he stopped at the 7-11. At first he went inside and bought some smokes and I figured that was all the trip was about. But when he came back out, he used the payphone. He’s still on it, in fact.”

“Are you in the parking lot of the 7-11?”

“No. I’m parked in the lot of the Chevron station across the street.”

“Okay, Tom. That’s great. Be sure to stay with him when he leaves there, but again don’t be—”

“Yeah, don’t be seen. I got it,” Tom said, interrupting. Then he said, “Okay, he’s off the phone and he’s getting in his car.”

"Okay. Stay with him."

After a few seconds, Tom voice came from the walkie-talkie again. "Boss? This is weird. He's just going back home. He just turned onto the street that leads into his neighborhood."

Jack thought about this for a moment. "Okay, it's possible the call wasn't related to his dealing." He was silent again before adding, "Or the phone call is a set up for a place and time to meet someone for the buy. He didn't go directly there when Tiffany was with him when he made a call once."

"He's going back inside the house. He just shut off the porch light. I think he's in for the night."

"Okay. Go to the rental and watch for another fifteen to make sure he's not going out again. Then come here."

"Will do, boss."

Jack wasn't sure what the payphone call was about, but he hoped it was a call to set up a time and place for the drug buy. If it was, they would have the information they needed soon.

33

Jack phoned Tom the next morning at 6:30 and told him that he felt they were getting close to the end of this situation. Tom's relief was evident. He was obviously tired of surveillance. Jack knew he had gone into this thinking it would be as exciting as the action in a TV cop show, but he was finding out the reality. Almost all of surveillance was nothing more than waiting for something to happen, and until it did, it was like watching grass grow.

Jack spent his day studying the files of his next two Public Defender cases, but he saw little prospect of keeping his defendants out of jail. Then he realized he'd thought the same thing about Tom's case, possibly due to some prejudice on his part. He was still surprised to find he was actually becoming friends with his childhood nemesis, a person who had tried to poison his dog and had committed perjury to attempt to convict the best friend he ever had of a heinous crime. Jack thought about how people never know what life will bring. Enemies become friends, and friends become enemies. Jack had too much experience with the latter, but none with the former until Tom became a friend.

He wondered what Hank would think of this curveball from life and decided he would likely find it humorous. This made him wonder what Mrs. Dawson would think, and he felt that while she would accept it, she probably would never be able to trust Tom, and in a way, Jack couldn't blame her. There was still a small part of Jack that had trouble trusting him, but that was more from habit than anything Tom had said or done recently to make him suspicious.

Chuckling at the thought of telling Mrs. Dawson, he lifted the receiver of his phone and dialed her number. When she picked up, he said, "Good morning, Mrs. Dawson. I bet you'll never be able to guess who my new best friend is." Describing Tom as a best friend was overstating it, but he was going for drama, not accuracy.

"Oh! You got another dog?" she asked.

"Um, no. Not exactly. It's a human friend."

"Oh, Jack, you know I don't like these enigmatic games you play. It makes you sound too much like an attorney trying to entrap a hostile witness."

"I am an attorney."

"But I'm not a hostile witness," she said. "Now, are you going to tell me about your new best friend, or shall I hang up?"

Jack laughed. "Don't hang up. 'Best' is overstating it, but this new friend's identity will shock you."

"Fine. I'll sit down, then—okay, I'm sitting," she said, her matter-of-fact, get-on-with-it tone so familiar to Jack.

"Tommy Gordon," he said, knowing she might not recognize the name if he used his adult version of *Tom*.

Silence was her initial reaction. Finally, she said, "You mean *that* Tommy Gordon? Are you pulling my leg, Jack Turner?"

"Yes, that Tommy Gordon, though he goes by Tom now. I told you I was defending him."

"Yes, I remember you told me that, but I never expected you two to become fast friends."

"It wasn't exactly fast, but he realized I was on his side and would do anything legal to get him acquitted. I managed to get the charges dismissed by proving it wasn't him who robbed the store."

"How on earth did you do that?"

Jack explained about the videotape of the robbery and the tattoo that was evident once he had the tape enhanced. Mrs. Dawson was amazed at this turn of events, expressing her amazement freely.

"You are a great attorney, Jack. I've told you that before."

"Yes, but you had no evidence, just your feelings about me to base your opinion of my legal skills on. Now, you have evidence, though having a video enhanced isn't exactly performing legal miracles."

"What case are you working on now?"

"A complicated one. In fact, I really should get back to work. I just called because I couldn't wait to hear your reaction to Tom Gordon becoming an actual friend. It happened several days ago, but I hadn't thought of telling you until just now."

"Well, you've told me, but I don't want the two

of you going out and getting drunk together or anything. You work to bring him up to your level. Don't sink to his."

"I'm already in the process of doing that. Don't worry about me in that regard. I never was one for going out and getting drunk with anyone. You know that."

"Yes, I do, but people can change, and it's still my place to express my thoughts."

They said their goodbyes and Jack returned to his work.

That evening while he and Jenny were having an after-dinner wine, the walkie-talkie squawked and Jack heard Tom.

"Boss?! Boss?! I think he's doing the buy! Boss!"

Jack keyed the mic. "What's happening?"

"I think he's making the buy, and you won't believe where he is now."

"Where?"

"At the police station!"

Jack considered this for a moment. The police station? Then suddenly, everything fell into place.

"Tom, be sure to get pictures of him as he comes out. Did you get them of him going in?"

"Yeah, but it's just his back. I was so shocked he came here that I almost forgot."

"He could be just going in to see someone about something," Jack said.

"He was carrying a midsize gym bag that he picked up at a condo out on Sugar Isle. It obviously had something in it. Probably cash. Even if it was empty, why take an empty gym bag inside?"

"Wait. He went to a condo on Sugar Isle?"

"Yeah, just before coming here."

"How long was he inside the condo?"

"Not that long, barely five minutes."

"Did you see him with anyone?"

"No, it was on the third floor of Seaview Condos. I watched from the parking lot to see which one he went to. I expected him to knock or something, but he had a key. He let himself in and a few minutes later, he came out. The lights were off when he opened the door, and he turned them off when he left, so I don't think anyone else was in there."

"Do you know the number of the condo?"

"No, but I counted how many doors he passed from the elevator. He went in the fifth door when you take a left turn off the central elevator."

"Great work, Tom! Be sure you get his picture when he comes out of the police station."

Jack was about to click off when Tom nearly shouted, "He just came out! And he's carrying another gym bag, but it's not the same one."

"How do you know?"

"This one's smaller for one thing, and I don't think it's the same color, but I can't really tell."

"Get a picture of him with the bag!"

"Okay." A moment passed and Tom said, "I got it! I took like five pictures of him walking from the door to his car with the bag. Do you think it has the drugs in it?"

"Probably. We'll have to wait and see."

"You think his connection is in the police station? A cop?"

"That's my guess."

"But wouldn't that take some kind of, I don't know, coordination or something? I mean, you just don't waltz into the police station with a bag of money and walk out with a bag of drugs unless more than one person knows what's going on. And wouldn't Chief Hicks know something like this was going on and put a stop to it?"

"Not if Chief Hicks is the supplier," Jack said.

"What? You mean he might be the one supplying the drugs?"

"Think about it, Tom. Where else can you hide cocaine and not expect to be busted for possession? There's someone who oversees the evidence room, which is under lock and key and constant camera surveillance. A cop is stationed at the entrance to that locked room at all times to check confiscated evidence in as well as make sure nobody goes in and takes something out without having a good reason and signing the proper forms."

"They're selling the drugs they have for evidence?"

"Maybe, but I doubt it. Those are weighed going in and coming out, and later discrepancies are reported to the state, which would result in an immediate investigation. No, I think someone's buying the drugs from a supplier, bringing them into the evidence room of the police department, and selling to dealers down the line from there. If the Chief is behind this, there would be no record of these drugs coming in or going out. It's the perfect place to hide illegal drugs you've bought to sell to local dealers."

Tom swore under his breath. "Then we have quite a case going on here, don't we?" Tom said.

"Yes, we do."

"But couldn't someone inside the station be doing the selling, not necessarily from the vault?"

"Think about it. What's the one place nobody would be surprised to find bags of drugs? The evidence vault. It makes perfect sense."

"That's true."

Jack asked, "Are you following him?"

"Yeah. He's heading back to Sugar Isle. Probably to Seaview Condos again. My guess is he'll stash the drugs there now."

"Okay, you follow him. When he gets home, stay in the rental until I get there." Jack was considering something and needed to get some information if he could. He would have to go to the jail to find out, and if his suspicions proved true, he knew exactly how this whole affair was being handled at the station level.

"Will do, boss. Man, am I glad something finally happened. I was getting so bored."

"I understand. And I know I say this to you a lot, but be careful. At this stage, there's no telling what Breslin might do if he caught you."

"Don't worry about me," Tom said.

Jack drove to the police station and sat outside, planning his next moves. He needed to find out who was in charge of the evidence vault and who was working it tonight.

Getting out of his car, he walked to the front entrance and stepped inside.

Very little was happening that night from what

Jack could tell. He approached the man commonly referred to as the desk sergeant, though this officer had not attained that rank. He appeared to be old enough to have been on the job for about a year, maybe two. Jack felt the glow of luck.

"Excuse me, my name is Jack Turner. I'm an attorney. Is there some way I can speak to the officer in charge of the evidence vault?"

"Do you mean Captain Hicks or Corporal Landers?"

"Captain Hicks mans the vault?"

"No, but he's in charge of the vault. Corporal Landers is manning the vault tonight."

"Does Landers man it every Friday night?"

"No, but he's on the rotation. Tonight just happens to be one of his nights on duty there."

"And Captain Hicks makes the schedule, I guess?"

"Yeah. Listen, what's the deal? Do you need to see someone about some evidence? We don't do that during the night shift. Only during the day. And you need a court order to inspect anything."

"Yes, I'll do that. Thanks for your help," Jack said.

He left the station and sat in his car, piecing the puzzle together. Even Tom recognized that Chief Hicks would be aware of any shenanigans dealing with the evidence vault. Now, Jack had another piece to the puzzle. His younger brother, Carl Hicks, was in charge of the evidence vault. He wrote up the schedule for those who watched over the evidence in the vault, and tonight a particular officer was holding down that duty.

What if Carl Hicks, Corporal Landers, and Chief Hicks were working together to use the vault as a place to store illegal drugs obtained by one or all three of them? Jack wondered. He figured that Keith Breslin would call either Chief Hicks or his younger brother, Carl Hicks, one of Jack's former tormentors. In that call, they would set up a time when Landers was the evidence vault watchman for Breslin to come by and pick up the drugs being stored there with the other evidence. It was a perfect setup. The vault was a place where it would be ridiculous to use a drug sniffing dog to search. Chief Hicks and his brother were in charge of monitoring the inventory, so bringing in extra drugs purchased from large organizations, such as a drug cartel, would be easy. Either of the Hicks brothers could bring the drugs in for "storage as evidence" when Landers was on duty. It would never be inventoried as evidence, making it available to sell to dealers. It would even be possible to skim drugs from a bust before weighing and placing it in evidence.

Jack drove to the rental house and entered with his own key.

"All quiet on the eastern front?" Jack joked.

"Huh?"

"Nothing. Did he go back to the same condo?"

"Yep."

"And then straight back here?"

"Good guess."

"I do my best," Jack said.

"So do I."

"Let's go to my place and talk."

"Okay. I'll meet you there."

When they had settled in the great room with a beer for Jack and a glass of orange juice for Tom, Jack said, "I think we have them." He explained his theory about how the drugs were being held and delivered for cash payments from people like Breslin. Jack only mentioned the Hicks brothers, leaving out Landers for now since the chief and Carl appeared to be the masterminds of the whole operation. "I'm thinking Breslin isn't their only dealer. Too many people around willing to sell drugs for quick cash."

"Whose condo you think it is?"

"No idea, but my guess is it's either a rental they've managed to get a key to that they know will stay empty most of the year, or it's owned by one of them. Maybe even Breslin."

"Aren't there records for that kind of thing?"

"Yeah. Probably take about ten minutes to find out who owns it." Jack changed the subject, curious about something else regarding Tom's past.

"Hey, Tom, you still friends with Carl Hicks?"

"Are you crazy? Nah. We had a fallin' out years ago."

"What happened?"

"He was a rookie cop and needed a bust to help move up the ranks. He knew I had received some stolen property, and he busted me for it. Shoot, he'd even set me up with the guy I got the stolen property from."

"So, that ended the relationship?"

"Wouldn't it end it for you?"

"Yeah, I guess it would, but I doubt I would

have set myself up with trying to fence stolen property."

"Yeah, I ended up being charged with the theft, even though Carl knew I hadn't done the job."

"Do you know the name of the guy you got the stolen merchandise from?"

Tom said, "You're not gonna believe it. He ended up joining the police force about six months later. Name's Sam Landers."

With that information, Jack knew he was right about the setup for selling drugs out of the police evidence vault. Now, they just needed to prove it. First, they would need more information about the condo.

34

Jack and Tom drove to Seaview Condominiums to get the condo number that Breslin used for stashing money and drugs. Then Jack drove to his office, dropping Tom at the rental to get his own car so he could follow. He knew he needed to talk to the DA now, as well as Agent Harwood. He thought about where he might get Zeke Ward's home number and knew Chuck probably had it.

"Chuck, this is Jack," he said when Chuck answered his phone.

"You have any idea what time it is?" Chuck asked. "It's after midnight. I thought maybe one of the kids had an emergency. Give me a second to let my heart stop pounding."

"Sorry for calling so late, but it's necessary. Do you know Zeke Ward's home phone number? I have to speak to him right away."

"What about? You sound worked up."

"It's the Breslin case. It's about to pop wide open."

"Oh?"

"Yes. I had Tom tail him and we think we know where he's getting his drugs, who his supplier is, and where he keeps the drugs and the money."

"Holy cow!"

"I need to speak to Zeke right away, and I hope he has an after-hours number for Agent Harwood. We're going to need some search warrants right away. The drugs might not be where he left them if we wait too long."

"Zeke has caller ID. I doubt he'd answer a call from you because your number would come over as an unknown number in all likelihood. If I call him, he'll answer. Let me talk to him, and he'll call you."

"Okay, no problem. You think Trisha will sign some search warrants? We can even cover searching the jail for bugs with this."

"The jail? How does that fit in?"

"That's where Breslin's getting his drugs."

"Oh, my God," Chuck said, so shocked by this news his voice was nearly a whisper.

"Will you call Zeke as soon as we hang up?"

"Of course, and I think Trisha would sign the search warrants."

When Jack hung up, Tom said, "You think they'll do the searches tonight?"

"I think they'd better. I doubt Breslin keeps the drugs or anything else incriminating in that condo for long. Maybe some of the money, but almost certainly not the drugs."

"Will they search the jail, too?"

"Yes. They'll be looking for the gym bag of money. I think Trisha could sign a separate warrant to search for bugs in the interview room where we met. They were holding off on that to let the state bureau go in, but now I think we have them red-handed on the drugs, so that would be an easy thing to add on to the investigation of the department."

"This is going to blow it all up, isn't it?"

"I hope so." Jack sat for a moment thinking. There wasn't much else to do but wait for the call from Zeke now. "I better call Jenny and let her know I won't be home for a while."

"She's nice."

"I know."

"You thinkin' of takin' the plunge?"

"You mean marry her?"

"Yeah."

"I haven't thought that far down the road."

"Do you love her?"

"Yes."

"I wish Sadie and I coulda worked it out. She's a nice lady, too."

"Maybe you will."

Tom laughed. "That ain't likely."

"Is she seeing someone else?"

"Not right now. At least not that I know of."

"You never know, Tom. That's the wild thing about life. It's like being on a roller coaster with only the first few feet of track visible because everything else around you is total darkness. It can take some crazy turns."

"That's true. Look at us. If a month ago someone had said we'd be friends, I'd have laughed in their face."

"So, that makes your chances with Sadie all the more possible. I mean if we could end up burying the hatchet, why not you two? After all, you already have a history with her. You have a child together. There's a past life that you enjoyed together. Maybe you could capture that magic again."

"Well, don't hold your breath because I sure won't be."

"I won't hold my breath, but I'll help any way I can. Now, I need to phone Jenny."

He dialed his house and Jenny answered after only two rings, sounding completely awake. After explaining what he could of what they'd seen and what would be happening now, he said, "I know it's late, but you can do what you want—either stay there or at your place for the night."

"I'll stay here and keep Brinkley company," she said. "Besides, I like your place better than my cramped sardine can."

"Suit yourself," he said adding, "I love you" at the end of the call.

"I love you, too. Just do me a favor, okay?"

"What?"

"Let the DEA handle the police work. Don't start trying to be a hero if things go south, okay?"

"No problem there," Jack said. At that moment, he heard the beep announcing an incoming call.

"I have a call coming in. Probably from Zeke Ward. I'll talk to you later."

"Okay. Good luck."

Pressing the button to hang up and releasing it, Jack said, "Jack Turner."

"Jack, it's Zeke Ward. Chuck tells me the Breslin case is blowing wide open. Is that right?"

"Yes," Jack said, and filled him in on what they'd done and seen that night.

"Whoa!" Zeke said when Jack had finished. "I'll call Harwood. Chuck tells me Trisha will sign some search warrants."

"Yes, but there's another search warrant that needs to be served as well."

"What's that?" Zeke asked.

"I have reason to believe that Chief Hicks is eavesdropping on private conversations between attorneys and their clients. We need to search the interview rooms used for attorney-client meetings."

"What makes you think that?"

Jack explained what had happened with Tom. "There's no way they could have known that without being able to listen to our conversation."

"Okay, I'll get the search warrants. Do you know which condo he entered at Seaview?"

"3-K."

"Okay, Jack, we'll take it from here."

"I want to be there when this goes down," Jack said. "I'll stay out of the way, but I want to be there. It will provide a witness in case someone wants to claim something wasn't done properly."

After hesitating a moment to consider, Zeke said, "Okay, but only you."

"When will you be serving the warrant?"

"We should be able to go in first thing in the morning."

"It needs to be early, like around the time the sun comes up."

"I know how to do my job, Jack. Let me get the warrants together and signed. That should take about ninety minutes to two hours. We can meet at the condo at three o'clock with a no-knock warrant in case someone is in there that you don't know about."

Jack thought that was overkill, but he didn't

argue since there was a slight possibility Zeke was right.

"See you at three," Jack said.

When he hung up, he told Tom he could go back to the rental and get some sleep. "I'll come by in the morning after everything goes down," he said.

After Tom left, Jack went home to get a cup or two of coffee while he waited. When he entered, Brinkley met him at the door, his tail wagging. "Well, you wouldn't be much good against a burglar, would you?" Jack asked, reaching down and rubbing Brinkley's head and ears.

"Wow, you're earlier than I thought you would be," Jenny said, coming from the bedroom.

"I came by to drink some coffee. It's going to be a late night—or rather an early morning. I doubt I'll be home again until after the sun comes up. I didn't think you'd still be up."

"Having trouble getting to sleep for some reason," she said, smiling and kissing him. "Whew! You could use a shower."

"Good idea. It would help me stay awake."

"I'll make the coffee. You do something about that B.O."

He chuckled as he walked toward his bedroom. Twenty minutes later, he came into the kitchen to the smell of coffee, along with the aroma of cinnamon rolls baking in the oven.

"Mmm. That smells good."

"I know. It was supposed to be our breakfast after a romantic evening and some well-earned sleep. Since you won't be here for breakfast, and the romance will have to wait, too, I figured I'd just fix this now and we could enjoy it together."

"Good thinking," he said, wrapping his arms around her waist from behind. "I love you. You know that, right?"

"Yes." She turned to kiss him. "I love you, too."

After the middle-of-the-night coffee and cinnamon rolls, Jack left for the Seaview Condominiums in time to arrive before three o'clock. Pulling into the parking lot, he saw no activity and waited. About ten minutes later, he noticed several cars pulling into the area. As they parked, he saw Zeke Ward and Agent Harwood climbing out of one car. He approached the men.

"Good work, Jack," Zeke said, chuckling. "It's unusual for a defense attorney to work to put people *in* jail."

"I'm working to keep my client out of jail," Jack said. "And putting truly bad people behind bars is just a bonus."

Jack followed the line of men as they went up to the third floor. Except for the two men carrying the battering ram to bust the door down, they used the stairs instead of the elevator. One of the other men was a deputy sheriff with sergeant stripes.

When they stood in front of unit 3-K, Harwood held up his hand with three fingers up. He curled one finger at a time into his fist until he reached zero, when he pumped his fist. The men with the battering ram slammed it into the door, knocking it back and splintering the wood of the door jamb.

The men rushed in, announcing themselves, but

nobody else was there. Going through the condo, the agents found the bag of drugs sitting in plain sight on the floor of a closet when they opened it. Breslin was apparently not worried about anyone finding his secret location.

Upon inspecting its contents, they found eight bags of white powder, which they assumed was cocaine. Harwood pulled out a testing kit and after setting it up, he added some chemicals to a few grains of the powder. The reaction confirmed that this was cocaine. Weighing the bags showed that each weighed four ounces, making two pounds of cocaine with a street value of over $100,000.

"Now, we need to head to the jail and find the money," Zeke said. "You say it was delivered in a gym bag similar to this one?"

"That's what my investigator said," Jack replied. "I'm thinking you might locate it in the evidence vault."

"Do you think the chief is in on it?" Harwood asked.

"He'd almost have to be. He runs that place with a firm hand. Nobody does anything unless he knows about it."

"Well, then, let's go search the police station," Zeke said.

"Do you have the warrant to search for bugs in the interview rooms?"

"Yep."

"Great."

Agent Harwood had the two men with the battering ram stay behind to cordon off the condo and prevent anyone from entering. Then he sent two of the other men to Breslin's residence to arrest him. The rest of them climbed into their cars to drive to the police station.

When they entered the station, there was no activity, which was typical for the middle of the night. The same young officer was behind the desk.

"Can I help you?" the officer asked. He looked almost shocked that anyone other than another policeman had entered the station at this time of night, seeming to know instinctively that their presence signaled something bad.

Zeke presented the warrants. The deputy sheriff who had accompanied them carried a device for finding hidden listening equipment.

"I don't know about this," the desk officer said. "I think you'll need to get permission from the chief before you search anything here."

Zeke hardened his voice. "Young man, do you know what a search warrant is?"

"Yes, sir."

"I am the district attorney, Zeke Ward. These are legally obtained search warrants. We don't need anyone else's permission to search the jail for the stated items in the warrant. Are we clear on that?"

The officer nodded.

"You can call the chief and get him here. In fact, I must insist that you do that. However, we will begin our legal search immediately."

"Okay," the officer said, blushing. "I'll call the chief now."

As he lifted the receiver on his phone, Zeke said, "Could you get two officers to accompany us and show us where certain areas are located?"

"Uh, yeah." He turned to a door that was standing open behind him and called out, "Rushing?" Another officer stepped to the door. He looked tired and in need of some sleep.

"Yeah?"

"Would you and Blaisdell go with these men and show them what they want to be shown?"

"Sure." The young officer looked over his shoulder and said, "Hey, Frank, let's go." Another sleepy-eyed officer stepped out of the room behind the desk and the two men maneuvered around the massive desk to join Agent Harwood and the others. "What are you looking for?"

"One of you take this deputy to the lawyer-client interview rooms. The other one can take us to the evidence vault."

With the mention of the evidence vault, the desk officer looked at Jack, obviously remembering that he had asked about it earlier that evening. "Is this what your visit earlier was about?" he asked. Jack ignored the question.

The deputy went with the officer named Blaisdell and Rushing led the others to the evidence vault.

Jack noticed the concern in the face of the man guarding the vault. Looking at the officer's name badge, he saw that this was Corporal Sam Landers.

Zeke presented the search warrant.

"You guys can't search stuff in the evidence vault!" Landers said.

"Just watch," Zeke said.

At that moment Harwood's two-way radio crackled. "Harwood?"

Agent Harwood keyed his mic. “Yeah?”

“This is Collins in research. The condo you asked about is registered to an LLC called Witches’ Brew. It’s listed as being owned by a woman named Barbara Landers, who is its only employee.”

Jack looked at Sam Landers and noticed the color drain from his face as Landers suddenly put two and two together. He may have had his suspicions before, but this verified them. These agents had the dope Breslin had purchased that day, and the money used to buy it was sitting in the evidence vault that he had been in control of all night.

Being a cop, he also knew that they probably had some kind of visual evidence. Now, Jack saw a man who was now fairly certain he was going to jail for a while—a long while.

“Thanks, Collins,” Agent Harwood said, looking at Corporal Landers. “Your timing was excellent,” he said into the mic.

Zeke looked at Landers. “Now, open the vault, Corporal Landers.”

When he did, Harwood found the gym bag with the money in less than ten seconds. He held it out to Jack. “Is this the bag Breslin walked in with?”

“I’ll have to look at the pictures my investigator took, but it matches the description he gave me.”

Harwood stared at Landers. “And you are the only one who’s been here all night, Corporal Landers? Suppose you try to explain why you accepted ‘evidence’ from a civilian whom the DEA has been investigating for drug trafficking?”

"It was all the chief's and his brother's idea," Landers said.

Jack smiled, not at all surprised. Landers was going to spill the beans on all of them to try to save his own hide. He'd seen it a hundred times from clients. He'd had one in New Orleans who was willing to share the secrets of a crime family there to have his charges reduced to manslaughter. Jack cringed at the memory because the man had not lived long enough to testify.

At that moment, the deputy came up to where they stood and said, "This whole place is swarming with bugs." He wasn't talking about roaches.

Jack offered to be present as Landers' attorney while he confessed, and Landers accepted. Jack asked Zeke if Landers could get consideration for testifying against Chief Hicks and his brother. Zeke agreed, possibly more as a favor for the work Jack had done on the case. Jack knew that despite his own involvement in the case, what he had obtained for Landers would be the most any attorney could get for him, so the Florida Bar would have few questions, if any.

Corporal Sam Landers was in the process of making his statement when they received word the chief had arrived. Based on what they had from Landers and the evidence on the listening devices, they arrested Chief Hicks. As he was being handcuffed, he looked at Jack and said, "What do you have to do with this?"

Jack smiled. "Practically everything."

Later, Jack heard that Breslin was willing to talk, too, but since they already had Landers' statement, they really didn't need his testimony.

When they were finished and the sun had come up on a beautiful Sunday morning, Jack said to Zeke, "When can we get the paperwork on the plea deal with my client, Tiffany Wolford?"

Zeke smiled. "I think we can get that to you by Monday afternoon."

Jack stopped off at the home where Tiffany now lived with only her mother, who was surprisingly happy that Breslin had been arrested. Jack took her reaction to mean she was in on it all and wanted to appear innocent.

Jack told Tiffany, "It's official. I should receive the paperwork on the plea deal to get you probation on your charges tomorrow. Your file will be sealed."

"I really won't go to jail?"

"No jail. Probation, but you could end up in jail if you do anything else."

"Thank you," she said, though things would not turn out as well for her as Jack thought.

A short while later, Jack drove home. He needed some sleep. Jenny greeted him with a kiss and Jack decided he was as happy as he ever had been. The knowledge of his happiness made him wonder if there might be more to their future, and for the first time, he did not feel frightened of that possibility.

35

April 9, 1992

On the same day Carmen had arrived to attempt rekindling her romance with Jack, Rick Turner looked at the letter in his hand as if it had come from Jupiter. The front of the envelope showed his forwarding address, the letter originally having been addressed to the house in Jacksonville that he'd left recently after living there since his release from prison. He'd finally reached the point where he could no longer pay the rent and still feed his habit. He'd taken in roommates to help with the expense, but none of them stayed for more than a few months. He had gradually become aware that he was mostly working to buy the pills he needed. Sometimes he craved the needle, but the pills were easier to get and he didn't have to worry about dirty needles.

He had finally asked Jasmine a few weeks ago if he could move in with her and pay some rent each week. He wondered if he would become like his former roommates and disappear after finding it too hard to remain. Being the tenant was definitely different from being the leaseholder. Tenancy had a certain sense of freedom because the monthly rent obligation wasn't in his name. He felt free, as if leaving on any given day would cause no problems.

Jasmine had moved from Starke to the community of Lutz outside of Tampa. Rick had caught a bus to Tampa and she had picked him up there. He had only been there a few weeks.

Now, though, his past was about to find him. His brother had written. He'd talked about wanting to see him and thinking of him every day. Rick had thought of Jack, too, but whenever he did, he decided Jack was better off without him. Jack didn't need an addict brother around. It would be too much like their parents. Jack had mentioned their parents' deaths in a car accident, but Rick had already heard that from Tom Gordon in prison. Rick's only regret was not being there for Jack when he'd become an orphan.

Rick now began wondering how Jack had found him. He figured it had to be a long process. He'd not stayed put anywhere for long, his most recent quartering in Jacksonville being by far the longest stint yet in any one place.

Maybe the end of his transience had something to do with it. Finding what was essentially a ghost couldn't be easy, but Jack had apparently wanted to find him badly enough to stick to the task. He admired his younger brother for that.

Jasmine walked into the small living room of the house she shared with Rick. They'd become lovers almost reluctantly, having succumbed to their intermittent flares of desire as if they were just giving in to another habit that beckoned. Rick felt comfortable in the relationship, and apparently Jasmine felt the same.

When she came into the room, Jasmine found

Rick staring at a piece of paper and crying. "What's wrong?"

Rick could barely make out her frightened expression through the blur of tears that now surprised him. How long had he been standing there, crying?

Instead of answering, he held out the letter. It would explain everything.

She took it and read through it quickly.

"Your brother?"

"Yes."

"I didn't even know you had a brother."

"I haven't seen him since I joined the Marines."

She glanced back at the letter and then looked at Rick again. "He wants to see you."

"I know."

"Are you going to contact him?"

"I don't think so."

"Why not? He wants to see you!"

Rick looked at her and held his hands out as if putting himself on display for her to consider. "Look at me, Jaz. Why would I burden him with what I am now? Both of our parents were drunks. We both had miserable childhoods because of that. Why would I want to make his adult life just as bad? He once talked about running away one day. Now, we're adults. He wouldn't have to run away. He could just tell me to go. I'm not sure I could take that if I went through the pain of seeing him again."

"Rick, he says he doesn't care about what you've done or who you've become. He loves you."

Rick left the room, saying, "I won't go back. Let him think the letter never reached me."

Jasmine watched him step down the short hallway and enter his bedroom. Despite their sexual relationship, he usually slept in his own bed in his own bedroom.

Rick lay on his bed, fully clothed, and wept. He cried for who and what he was. He cried for how his choices had forged a trap he would never escape. It was a trap that prevented him from ever being a part of his family again, possibly not a part of any family. He and Jaz were just there for the other's convenience. He wallowed in self-pity until he fell asleep, even though the sun had not gone down yet.

36

Jack sat in his office planning a trip to Jacksonville and possibly other locations to search for his brother. He had put his law practice on hold for now—certainly not for longer than two weeks at the most—and would be leaving by car the next morning to either find Rick or discover where to look next. He was excited about what the next few days held in store and hoped he might be mere days from seeing his brother again.

Excitement had been the mood of the entire town over the past few days. News of the arrest of the police chief and his brother had spread within hours of the arrest, and everyone in Denton seemed to be talking about it, most with an "it's about time" attitude, not that anyone knew what had been going on. The Hicks brothers were simply that unpopular.

Jack had walked into the grocery store to buy coffee for the office that morning and had been nearly held hostage to tell what he could about what had happened. Because he was not either of the brothers' attorney, he could speak freely of the charges, though he shied away from going into much detail since he was also an officer of the court, and basically the investigation was ongoing, at least for a little while.

Jack had seen the interest in the eyes of the

people who had gathered in the coffee aisle to hear what he had to say, as if he were being interviewed by the press. He'd been more or less waylaid with questions by the grocery store's manager when she had seen him walking toward the coffee, and as they talked, the small crowd had formed.

He'd had a few calls from the local newspapers and TV stations, but he'd declined to be interviewed until after the trial.

Jack returned to the work on his desk and thought of Jenny. She had not stayed over last night, and that was bothering him, in addition to worrying whether or not his brother wanted to be found. It wasn't that she had suggested she stay at her tiny apartment instead. In fact, he had suggested it. He needed to prepare for his trip and wanted to eliminate any possible distractions. He recalled the hurt look in her eyes and now regretted the decision. He'd ended up not sleeping well as a result. He awoke around three that morning and considered calling her but decided against it. She would likely be sound asleep and not wish to be awakened in the middle of the night.

He phoned her now at work. He would be leaving for Jacksonville tomorrow and didn't want to sleep alone again tonight.

When she answered, he said, "Hey, it's me."

"Hi, me."

"I just wanted to tell you that I regret asking you to sleep at your place last night. I woke up around three and almost called you, but I figured I shouldn't wake you, so I talked myself out of it."

"You should have called." She sounded sad.

"You need your sleep, even if I can't get mine."

"Who says I was asleep?"

He paused. "Were you?"

"No. I woke up around 2:30 and didn't get back to sleep until almost four. I even considered calling you, but I thought better of it since you'd made your decision and I wouldn't be able to make you change your mind."

"You're wrong there. You should have called."

"Well, it's not like we can turn the clocks back or anything. What do we do now?"

"Will you come over tonight?"

"To stay over?"

"Yes."

"I'll think about it." He could hear the smile in her voice.

"Well, don't think for too long. Brinkley wants to know if he'll be sleeping in his bed or ours."

"Don't you mean *yours*?"

"No, as a matter of fact, I don't."

"If it's my bed, too, why am I sleeping in that cramped closet of an apartment?"

"I don't know. Why are you?"

"I'm not the one who suggested I sleep there last night, you know."

"Yeah, I guess you're right. So…what should we do about that?"

"We keep asking each other what we should do. One of us should come up with a plan."

"Jenny?"

"Yes?"

"I think we should talk tonight. Serious talk."

"Okay."

"See you after work?"

"Want to have lunch?" she asked.

"I do, but I'm tying up a few loose ends here at work before I head for Jacksonville and possible points unknown."

"I understand." He heard her sigh then suddenly become animated. "Oh! Did you hear about the Hicks brothers?"

"No, not yet. What happened?"

"It turns out they had quite the illegal racket going. Prostitution, drugs, fencing stolen property. You really helped make a major bust. The state bureau is involved now, too. They're going away for a while."

"Good," Jack said. "They deserve it."

"I agree."

"Well, let me get back to work or I'll not be home in time for supper."

"Okay," she said. "I love you."

"I love you, too," he said.

That evening when he arrived home, she had a small rib roast in the oven. "Dinner will be ready at seven," she said as he walked into the kitchen.

"Smells delicious."

"It better be," she said and stepped over to him to kiss him. The kiss was light but held a thousand promises.

"Do you have time to talk now?"

"Not really. Over dinner would be better. I have vegetables to chop, potatoes to boil for homemade mashed potatoes. That kind of thing."

"Okay, but let's hold off until after we've eaten."

"Jack?"

"Yes?"

"Will I think this is good news or bad?"

"It depends on you, I suppose."

She frowned but went back to preparing the meal.

After they'd eaten, they took a glass of wine into the living room and sat on the sofa beside each other.

Jack took a deep breath and said, "We talked about what we were going to do," he began.

"Actually, we asked that. We haven't talked about it yet."

"Good point. I think we should talk about it."

"Okay, what are your ideas?"

"Understand that if you don't agree, I can live with it," he said.

"Just tell me," she said. "I know you can live with whatever happens."

"I've thought a lot about it, and I'd like for you to move out of that closet of an apartment and move in here with me."

"Really?"

"Yes, really."

"Are you sure? I mean, you're not going to get me in here and decide maybe it was a mistake?"

"I think if you don't move in, it would be a mistake."

Jenny lunged for him and their lips met. "Of course, I will! My lease is up next week, and I was debating whether to sign a new one or not. I didn't want to sign a new lease and then have you ask me to move in."

They spent the evening making plans for her move. She would get some of her friends to help her move her things into the house, and she would put her furniture in storage until a decision could be made regarding what to do with it.

"Can you and your friends handle moving the furniture?"

"That's awfully sexist! Of course, we can. We're not a bunch of eighty-year-olds."

He laughed. "I would never suggest you were."

"We can handle it fine."

"In fact, I think even if you were eighty, you could handle it, okay?"

"That's better," she said and smiled.

They talked into the evening about a variety of topics: the Hicks brothers and Breslin, Tom, and Rick, including his plans for this trip. When he'd mentioned that he would be taking Brinkley with him and staying in pet-friendly motels, she had begged him to leave the dog behind.

"He'll keep me company in the evenings. After all, who's going to keep your side of the bed warm at night?"

"Where would he go during the day?"

"I'll bet Mrs. Dawson would keep him."

He smiled. "Good point."

When he rose in the morning after a much better night's sleep, he shared breakfast with Jenny, kissed her goodbye, grabbed his suitcase, and left. The drive to Jacksonville would take several hours. He plugged in a smooth jazz CD and headed toward Panama City and Highway 231, which would take him to Interstate 10. From there, it was a clear shot to Jacksonville. He would arrive in the early afternoon, taking brief stops and lunch into account.

As he drove, he thought about Rick. He'd certainly had time to get the letter, assuming he had left a forwarding address. Now, Jack wondered if perhaps Chuck had been right when he suggested Rick might not want to be found.

As he drove, he worried that perhaps the letter had caused Rick to leave wherever he had landed after Jacksonville. If his brother was on the run again, seeking somewhere he couldn't be found, Jack would have a lot of trouble finding him. He'd been lucky this time—extremely lucky, in fact. If Tom had not served time with Rick in Raiford, Jack doubted he would have been able to find him. Now that Rick was no longer under the watch of a parole officer, he might never be found.

Sudden regret filled him as he wished he had never sent the letter. He could have waited to do what he was doing now—driving to where he knew Rick had last been. That wouldn't have warned him that his brother was looking for him.

Deciding what was done was done and nothing could change that now, he pushed the thought from his head. If his letter had served as a warning rather than good news, he would have to give up his search. If Rick didn't want to be found badly enough to keep running instead of being with his brother, Jack would have to accept that.

He stopped at Lake City and ate lunch at Shirley's Restaurant, a local diner there that served Southern style meals. He had eaten there once with Hank when they'd taken a vacation after he'd moved in with him, and he remembered that he had loved the food there. Once he tasted his lunch, he decided his memory was correct.

After leaving Shirley's, he drove the rest of the way to Jacksonville. Using a city map he'd brought with him, he located the house where Rick had lived until a short time ago.

It stood in a fairly run-down neighborhood, which didn't surprise Jack at all. He doubted Rick had any money to spare.

Stopping in front of the house, he saw it was now occupied. An old Ford sat in the driveway, where patches of paint on the body were having a losing battle with rust. He climbed out of his car and debated what to do next. He could see that a TV was on in the front room of the house, so he figured whoever owned the Ford was inside. He finally decided to go knock and see if the person inside was at least willing to identify who the landlord was, either the owner or the realtor who handled the rental of the property for the owner.

As he stepped through the yard that was more sand and weeds than grass, the door opened, and a man came out.

He was about Jack's age, maybe a little older. His brown skin showed the effects of long hours in the sun over his lifetime.

"Can I help you?" the man asked, obviously not used to people stopping in front of his house and standing near the street staring at his home.

"I hope so," Jack said, approaching.

"Jus' stand right there," the man said. "We can talk from a distance."

Jack stopped. The man was looking at him with an odd expression. “Certainly.”

“So, what can I do for you?”

“My name is Jack Turner, I’m looking for my brother, and he used to live here.”

The man’s expression changed to one of surprise. “Turner?”

“Yes, my brother’s name was Rick Turner.”

Suddenly the man began to laugh. “He never said he had a brother.”

“You know him?” Jack felt a wave of confidence rush through him.

“Yeah, I know him. You’re his brother?”

“Yes. I’ve been trying to find him. I’ve not seen him since I was twelve.”

“Oh my! I thought you looked familiar. He looks like an older version of you, just a lot thinner.” He laughed. “Not that you’re fat or anything.”

Jack had figured he would probably be thin from the drugs.

“Do you know where he is?”

“As a matter of fact, I do.” The man made a “come with me” gesture with his hand. “Come on in. We can talk inside. Too hot out here.”

Jack followed the man inside and sat on the worn sofa that the man indicated when he said, “Have a seat.”

The man sat in an equally worn recliner next to the sofa and stuck out his hand to shake. “I’m Roscoe Jefferson. I used to live down the street until my sister moved to Raiford to be near her husband who was in prison there. Then a few months ago, I moved in here with Rick to share expenses and try to save a few bucks."

"And you had the phone taken out," Jack said.

"Huh? Oh, yeah. I couldn't afford it on what I make since losing the roommate raised my rent, so to speak."

"When did you last see Rick?"

"About a month ago."

"And you know where to find him?"

"Sure do."

The man sat still in his chair, staring and seeming to wait for something. Finally, it dawned on Jack what Roscoe was waiting for. He took out his wallet and withdrew two twenties.

"I'd be willing to pay you for the information."

"Thanks. A man could always use a little bit extra, you know?" He reached out his hand for the money. Jack gave him one of the twenties.

"That's to thank you for the hospitality. The other is for after you tell me where I can find Rick."

Tucking the twenty into his shirt pocket, Roscoe said, "He's livin' with my sister now. They ain't in love or nothin' like that. It's more a convenience for both of them."

"Where do they live?"

"Down near Tampa." Roscoe held out his hand for the other twenty.

"Tampa's a big area. What's the address?"

Roscoe's eyes took on a sly look. "You didn't say you'd pay for the address, just where he was. And that's in a community outside Tampa."

"How much for the address?" Jack asked.

"Oh, I'd say two more of ones like those?"

Roscoe said, pointing at the twenty in Jack's hand.

"How do I know you're telling me the truth?"

"I guess you don't, but you know where I live, and I could count on trouble I don't want if you find out I'm lyin'."

Reaching inside the wallet, Jack took out a twenty and two tens. That left him with only another eight dollars in cash. "That's all I have other than a few ones. Now, what's the address?"

Roscoe recited an address. Jack asked him to write it down, and Roscoe searched around for a pen and paper. When he'd found what he needed, he wrote down the address and held it out to Jack.

Handing the money to Roscoe, Jack looked at the paper. It was an address in Lutz, a place he'd never heard of. Roscoe had said it was outside Tampa, so he would drive there and find the small community called Lutz.

"Thank you," Jack said, tucking the paper into his pocket. "I must be going now."

"I understand. It was nice to meet you, Mr. Turner." He patted his pocket. "Very nice."

"Likewise," Jack said and left.

37

Jack decided to drive straight through to the town of Lutz. It would take about four hours to get there from western Jacksonville, including a stop for some dinner, which would be fast food this time. The drive ended up taking an hour longer because of a wreck on Interstate 75 between Ocala and the exit for Lutz.

By the time he was taking that exit, the sun had gone down. He needed to find a map of the Tampa area that included Lutz so he could find where Tom was living. He wanted to find him that night, but realized he would be fresher in the morning and more able to talk Rick into coming home with him if Rick balked, not to mention being able to have more time to plan his route. Besides, he'd waited this long, what was another day?

He stopped at a motel and checked in for the night, surprised at how tired he felt when he stopped. The motel had maps of the Tampa area, so he took one to his room. Once there, he found the street where Rick lived and mapped the drive to it.

He was keyed up but dropped off to sleep after phoning Jenny and filling her in on how his day had gone. When he told her he'd had to pay eighty dollars for the address, she was shocked.

"It was worth it," Jack had said. "I've been waiting for years to see him. I'd have paid a lot more."

The next morning, he rose early and checked out. He wanted to get to where Rick lived before he left for a job, assuming he had one.

It took him only twenty minutes to find the street. He drove down it until he arrived at the number Roscoe had given him. He prayed Roscoe hadn't been lying to him to get the money as he climbed out of the car.

Walking up to the door, he knocked after trying the doorbell but not hearing anything when it was pressed.

The door opened, and a startled black woman stood there, her mouth agape.

"You're Jack," she said, as if reminding him what his name was.

"Yes, I assume Rick is here?" His voice rose to make it a question.

She only nodded. "I'm Jasmine. My friends call me Jaz."

"Hello, Jaz. Is Rick at work or is he here?"

"He's here. Won't you come in?"

Jack stepped into the small house feeling dazed. He was within a few feet of his brother. The idea seemed foreign to him, as if he might be dreaming. He wondered if he would wake up at any moment in bed with Jenny—or worse, in bed alone and these past few months had all been a dream.

He and Jasmine stood there, saying nothing for a moment, and he wondered if she might be thinking this felt like a dream as well.

Jack was about to ask if she would tell Rick he was there when his brother appeared in the opening that led down a hall, presumably to the bedrooms.

Rick stood there gaping at Jack, his mouth literally hanging open. Jack became aware his own mouth was hanging open as well and shut it. Then suddenly, Rick was crying.

Jack went to him and wrapped welcoming arms around his brother, holding him tightly like a drowning man holds a life preserver. After a moment, Rick did the same, squeezing Jack hard and sobbing into his shoulder. Jack's own tears began and they did nothing but hold each other and cry for a full three minutes, Rick apologizing and Jack telling him it was alright.

When they finally parted, Jasmine was standing in the room weeping as well.

They finally went into the combination kitchen/dining room and sat while Jasmine made coffee. Jack noticed Rick's limp. Tom had mentioned it, but he felt it would be a good conversation starter.

"What's that about?" he asked.

"'Nam. Long story." He obviously didn't want to discuss it right then, so Jack dropped it.

"Would you like some breakfast?" she asked Jack. "It would be no trouble. We've not eaten either."

"Thank you, but I'll just have some buttered toast. I'm not that hungry right now," Jack replied.

"What do you want for breakfast, Rick?" Jasmine asked.

"I'll just have buttered toast, too."

"That's not much of a breakfast," Jasmine said and began preparing the toast. "Normally, I don't cook for Rick, but then his brother doesn't stop by every day either, so I'll play hostess for today."

"If it's a bother, please don't put yourself out for me. I can get something later," Jack said.

"I said it was no trouble, didn't I? I just didn't want you thinkin' I was his 'woman' or anything like that. I'm my own woman."

"That she is," Rick said and laughed.

Jack looked at Rick. He had aged more than the years they'd been apart. His face sagged and his hair was already going gray, even though he was only forty-two. The sagged appearance was especially startling considering he was rail-thin. To Jack, his brother didn't look healthy.

"So, what do you do now?" Rick asked.

"I'm an attorney."

"Oh, yeah. I heard about that."

"A lot has happened since you left to join the Marines."

"Long story?" Rick asked.

"Yes. Very."

"How long are you in town?"

Jack held his breath for a moment before stating his plans. "I was hoping to take you home with me."

"You mean for a visit? We can visit right here."

"No, Rick. I want to take you home to stay." He paused, glancing at Jasmine. "Jasmine's brother says you two are more like roommates than anything else."

"You saw my brother?" Jasmine asked.

"Yes. I went to Rick's last known address, and your brother was there. He told me where to find Rick."

"Well, if Rick leaves, that would be an inconvenience for me. I need someone to help out with the rent."

"I can help with that," Jack said.

Now it was Jasmine's turn to gape. Like Jack, she quickly shut her mouth when she realized it was open.

Jack considered offering to find Jasmine a job in Denton but decided against it. It might be better if Rick moved away from the influences he had around him now. He changed his mind about that later, though.

Rick said, "I can't just up and leave, Jack. Jasmine has helped me a lot."

Jack didn't want to talk about Jasmine with her standing right there, so he asked Rick to show him the house.

When they were in Rick's room, Jack said, "I'm sorry for springing this on you, but I'm not sure Jasmine is a good influence on you. You're looking rather strung out. Are you using?"

"No, not since I moved here with her. That's the deal. If I get high, I have to go."

"I want to put you in rehab to make sure it sticks. If you fall off the wagon, I don't know that you'll ever get back on without more help."

"I quit before, and only Hammer's death made me want to use again, Jack."

"Hammer?"

"He was Jasmine's husband. I met him in

prison. At Raiford. He's probably responsible for me even being alive right now."

"I'm sorry he died. How?"

"Heart attack, which was a shock. I figured he was the healthiest guy in Raiford."

"The heart's a funny animal. It'll move along just fine until one day, it doesn't. I'll bet yours could be healthier."

"A lot of me could be healthier, Jack."

Jack changed the subject. "Why didn't you come home when you got out of the Marines?"

"Actually, I did. I stopped by the high school and watched from the woods until you came out for P.E. I watched you."

"You did?" Jack felt the hair on the back of his neck prickle.

"Yeah. I wanted to hug you, but I couldn't. I knew you'd try to talk me into coming home, and I would've rather died than do that."

This made Jack realize just how much catching up they had to do. Part of him was angry his brother had watched him at school and said nothing. That he'd been selfish enough to abandon him for drugs and a transient's life.

"I'll make a deal with you. If you go into rehab down there for three months, you can come back here, and I'll continue to pay for rehab for you."

"I don't know, man."

"Rick, I need my brother."

"I know."

"And you need your brother. We can't go on like this."

Rick thought about it. "Rehab?"

"Do you want help getting clean?" Jack asked.

Rick thought about it. "Yes."

"It has to be your decision. If not, nothing that they try will stick."

"Are you sure it will help me?"

"Yes. It will help. Believe me."

"I don't know. What about Jasmine?"

"She seems stable. I would bet she will be here when you return. I'll pay your half of the rent while you're in rehab. If she's really helpful to you, then she can continue to help you when you get back, but you should continue the rehab."

"I don't know." Rick looked like a lost child, his eyes darted around as if looking for an answer to be written somewhere in the room.

"I just want to help you. I want my brother back."

"It won't be easy, though, will it?"

"You're most of the way there now. You've been clean already for a few weeks, haven't you?"

"Yes."

"Do you love Jasmine?"

"I don't know. Maybe. But I can't say that we're—in love—you know? Just, well, she's important to me." Rick stood still except for his trembling hands and arms. Jack wasn't sure if that was from his addiction or something else.

"Come home with me, Rick. It's where you need to be. If she's really the positive influence you say she is, she'll agree with my plan."

"Can we go ask her what I should do?"

"Sure, but as I said, it has to be your decision. Otherwise, it won't help. You have to want it," Jack said and led the way back to the kitchen table, where all three of them sat down with their coffee. Jasmine had fixed three cups of coffee and toast for them, adding a scrambled egg and a small slice of fried ham to her plate.

Jasmine said, “I called work and said something came up and I’d be about an hour late.” She looked at Jack. “I work at a twenty-four hour convenience store. The lady I relieve wasn’t happy, so I should do my best to get there earlier if I can.” Looking at Rick, she said, “Rick, you’ll have to call in for yourself.”

“Okay,” Rick said.

As they ate their breakfasts, Jack broached the subject that they needed to discuss.

“Jasmine, thank you for helping Rick get off the drugs. He tells me you keep him centered. I think that’s great.”

“It’s nothing,” she said. “He couldn’t stay if he got high. He knows that.”

“That’s what I want to talk to you about. As I said before, I want to take Rick back home with me and pay for inpatient rehab. It’ll be a three-month stint. I’ll give you his half of the rent and utilities while he’s away. I’m even willing to add another one-fifty a month to help out with other things he might help pay for. If he wants to, he can come back here when he’s done and continue outpatient rehab. How do you feel about that?”

She looked at Rick and Jack could see she loved him. Like Rick, he wasn’t sure she was *in love* with him in a romantic sense, but she cared deeply for Rick.

"If it helps Rick give up the drugs for life, I'm all for it." She sipped her coffee during the ensuing silence then continued. "You're a good person, Rick. One of the best. The only flaw in your character is your habit. I know you've kicked it for now, but what will happen if something goes wrong and you feel the need to get high to deal with it? Hammer would be proud of you for doing this."

Rick teared up. "He would?"

"Yes."

After a moment's thought, he turned to Jack. "Okay. I'll go. But I have to come back here when I'm totally clean and done with the inpatient stuff."

"It's a deal," Jack said. "I only have one other requirement."

"What?" Rick asked.

"When you come back here, we remain in touch. I never want to have to go searching for you again. Deal?"

Rick smiled. "Deal."

Jack turned to Jasmine, who was smiling. A tear spilled over her eyelid and rolled down her cheek. "I'll make sure he keeps in touch with you. Maybe we could come visit sometime."

Jack's own tears began to flow.

When they had all regained their composure, Jasmine said, "Rick, you better call in and tell them you're quitting. Explain why. Maybe they'll rehire you when you get back."

Rick stood and went to use the phone.

Jack hugged Jasmine, thanking her again.

An hour later, Jack and Rick were on the road to Denton. They would arrive in the late afternoon.

On the way, Jack told Rick about his first dog, Bones, as well as Hank and Mrs. Dawson. Rick remembered the man who lived in a broken down bus near the harbor and was surprised to learn that the man was actually very wealthy. He explained about Hank's trial and discussed how their parents died in a car accident coming home from a drunken party they had attended, filling in details Rick had never known. He told him how Hank took him in and raised him as if Jack were his own son. He ended his story by telling him about Hank's funeral and his inheritance.

When Jack told Rick about Jenny, he sat grinning at his younger brother.

"I can see you love her by the way your eyes light up when you talk about her," Rick said.

"Yeah. I miss her a lot just from these two days being away."

"You gonna marry her?"

"I don't know," he said before adding, "maybe."

It wasn't the first time the thought had occurred to him that he might marry Jenny one day, but it was the first time it started to seem more inevitable than not.

For his part, Rick did his best to explain where he'd been since being discharged from the Marines. He admitted there were gaps in his memory from the drugs. Jack was fascinated to learn the full details of the day Rick had spent watching Jack at P.E. and wished something unusual had happened that day in P.E. so he could recall the exact day.

Still, the event also angered him. He thought of

holding it in but figured it would be better if everything was out in the open.

"I gotta tell you, Rick, I'm angry you didn't come home. And I'm especially angry you sat and watched me at P.E. like some stalker."

"I'm sorry. I couldn't let myself be seen by you or anyone else."

"Why not? It's not like someone would shoot you or something!" he said, raising his voice despite telling himself not to.

"I just couldn't, that's all. I was a mess. Still am."

Jack stared at him for a moment. "Funny how I don't care about that. I don't care now, and I didn't care then. You're my brother, damn it! How could you just abandon me like that? No word from you at all. Nothing! I had to find out from a former fellow inmate of yours that you didn't die in Vietnam! I mean, why couldn't you at least write me a letter and tell me you survived? I lived all these years without knowing!"

"I'm sorry. It's all I can say. What do you want me to do? I can't take it all back. It's done! It's in the past now!"

"Think of the years we lost, Rick! Think of all the time we weren't able to be together!"

"I have, Jack! Every damn day!"

"Except when you were too high to even remember I was alive! Just like Mom and Dad! They were parents only when they weren't drunk! But what you did was worse! At least they were there when they were sober!"

They were both crying by now, and Jack had to

pull off the highway. He pulled into a gas station and parked away from the building.

"Why are you yelling at me about this now, Jack? Huh? Why? Like I said, it's not like we can change anything!"

"I never intended to get this angry, Rick. I didn't think I would, but suddenly everything just boiled over. I was alone in my life. If it hadn't been for Hank and Mrs. Dawson, I'd probably have ended up in prison alongside you. I was so fortunate to meet them when I did. But every second, I wished you were around to help me deal with things. We could have held each other up."

"You seem to have done fine, Jack. You're an attorney. Lots of money. A woman you love. I'm the one who needed propping up. I'm the one who screwed his life up royally and needs rehab to even have a chance at living a halfway normal life for the years I have left."

"Maybe if you'd come home instead of running away like a kid, you could have been a success, too."

"I was in no shape to come home, Jack. That's what you don't understand. If I'd come home, I probably would have dragged you down with me. Instead, you have a good life. I hate that I did it, but I wouldn't go back and pull you down into the gutter with me, because that's what would have happened."

"How do you know that?! How do you know?!"

"Because," Rick said. "Because you looked up to me. Before I left, you would copy anything I did.

You would have jumped off a mountain if I did it. Well, that's what I ended up doing. I jumped off a mountain into addiction. If I'd come home, you would be right there with me."

Jack stared into his brother's eyes, numbed by the words he'd spoken.

"So, you see, little brother. It's not that I didn't come back because I didn't love you enough. I didn't come back because I did love you. I still do."

Jack was speechless for a moment. Although he might be mistaken as to what path Jack would have followed if he'd returned, there was enough truth to the possibility that Jack understood Rick's reasoning. He had to accept his brother's beliefs.

"Okay," Jack said. "Okay. I get it now. I never thought of it that way. Welcome home, Rick."

"Well, better late than never," Rick said.

They filled up at the gas station, and Jack used a pay phone to call Jenny at work. He told her that Rick was coming home with him, and she sounded delighted. Her happiness that his drug-addicted brother was coming home with him made him love her all the more.

When they finally arrived at Jack's home in Denton, Rick sat in the car staring at the large house for at least a full minute.

"You live *here*?"

"Yep. And so do you until I can arrange for inpatient rehab."

"Wow." It was all he could say, apparently.

Jenny drove up as they were unloading the car, and Jack introduced her to Rick, who hugged her without warning.

Later, when Jack was in the bathroom, Rick smiled at Jenny and said, "My brother loves you a lot."

She grinned back at him. "The feelings are mutual."

"You gonna marry him?"

She laughed. "He has to ask me first."

"Would you say yes?"

She shrugged. "Probably. It's been a whirlwind romance if ever there was one." She paused for a second, considering. "But I love him more than I've ever loved anyone in my life, so yes, I would." She glared at Rick. "Don't tell him that, though. It wouldn't be fair and might make him feel obligated to ask."

"Don't be surprised if he asks you. I've been away a long time, but I can tell he has some very deep feelings for you. His eyes light up when he talks about you."

Jenny laughed. "My cousin said the same thing about me when I talk about him."

They celebrated that night by going to dinner at Giuseppe's in Wharton, one of the nicest restaurants in the county. When they arrived back home, Rick went immediately to bed, and Brinkley had joined Rick by going to his own bed as well, something Jack and Jenny had laughed about since he almost never went to bed until after they did. Once alone, Jack and Jenny sat up talking about his trip.

They finally went to bed around midnight, but tomorrow was Saturday, so they could sleep in.

That all changed around three o'clock that morning.

38

Earlier that day while Jenny was at work and Jack and Rick were on the road, a man had come to the house to disable the alarm system. This was a man well-versed in how alarms operated, and in less than fifteen minutes, he had rendered the device inoperative.

Wearing cloth booties over his shoes, he entered the house using a burglar's tool on the back door's lock, and within five minutes of beginning that part of the illegal entry, he was standing in the back mudroom where the dog food was located. He sprayed the dry food with an odorless chemical that would render the dog unconscious within an hour of his evening feeding time. The man had no problem killing a person because they did things that made their deaths necessary, but dogs were a different story. He would only kill one of them to save himself.

That done, he walked through the house to learn the layout before exiting and relocking the door. He would return late that night.

Now that the middle of the night had arrived, he used the same burglar's tool at the back door. He made fast work of the door's lock. As he passed the dog's kennel, he saw that the dog had not awakened. He would sleep off the drug and wake the next day as if nothing had happened, though likely not feeling his best.

The man had received the first call concerning this job earlier that week. A second call confirming the job had come that morning. After that call, he had come to the secluded house and disabled the alarm and spiked the dog's food.

He had been told to leave nobody alive in the house, but he didn't count the dog in that unless it woke up during his visit. He had arrived at the house near 11:30 that evening and could peer through a window to see Jack Turner and his girlfriend chatting on the sofa. He had watched and waited. At 2:57, he began his work to enter the house and kill the two people inside.

It would be an easy $25,000.

He always liked to look into the eyes of the people he killed—there'd been dozens—and this job would be no different. He intended to wake the couple and chat with them so they would know why this job was necessary before ending their lives. Then he would exit the way he'd come in, go home, and get some sleep.

He tiptoed into the hallway outside the master bedroom and crept to the door. Silently turning the doorknob, he opened the door to find the two sleeping beneath the covers.

He stepped to the foot of the bed and with a gentleness that was the height of irony, he grasped one foot that lay beneath the covers and shook it slightly.

The man groaned slightly in protest, so the

hired killer shook the foot again, this time with a bit more force.

"Hmm?" the man mumbled before shooting into a sitting position.

"Who are you?! What do you want?!" he said, which woke the woman.

The killer moved the hand that held the gun with a silencer to draw attention to it.

"Jack Turner?" the killer asked.

"Yes. What do you want?"

The woman sat still. The killer knew she was looking for an avenue of escape, but there was none without walking through him.

"Everyone calm down. I was sent by a friend of yours."

"Who?" said the woman.

"Keith Breslin."

"He's not a friend," the man said.

"Okay, maybe a little exaggeration on my part."

"Why did he send you?" the man asked, though the killer could plainly see he didn't need to ask the question. He already knew the answer.

"I believe you know the answer, which I guess doesn't surprise me. I always heard a lawyer never asks a question he doesn't know the answer to already."

Suddenly, the woman screamed, "Get out!"

The killer looked at her and indicated the hand with the gun. "Careful, there. You could have startled me and made this go off before I want it to."

Rick snapped awake at the sound of Jenny's

shout. He realized what she'd said, and just as quickly realized she had yelled to wake him up. Someone was in the house, and they were in danger.

He rose from the bed silently and eased himself to the door. Pressing his ear against it, he could hear faint voices, but not what they were saying. He could tell that one of the voices was male and did not belong to Jack.

Rick squinted, wondering where Brinkley was. Surely the dog had heard the intruder. Was it someone Jack knew? Could that have been the reason Brinkley didn't mind that he had come into the house?

Rick eased the door open and moved through the opening with a grace borne of his time in the Marines. He noticed how at ease he was, despite the danger, and realized the saying "Once a Marine, always a Marine" must be truer than he'd thought.

He moved silently into the hall and could now hear what was being said through the open door of Jack and Jenny's bedroom. The intruder was saying something about how someone named Breslin or Bresden had hired him to kill them both.

"Next stop will be Traitor Tom's place. I've been told to make his death a lot slower."

The man said to Jenny, "Sorry I have to kill you, too, but now that you're here…well, there's not much I can do about it."

Jack was the first to notice Rick in the hallway. His brother was standing still at the half-open door, listening but still moving very slowly into the bedroom, as silent as the moon. Part of Jack didn't want Rick to get involved. This man who'd broken in to kill them obviously knew nothing about Rick. He wasn't sure Rick had the strength to take on the stranger, and doing so might get Rick killed as well.

Jack said, "Don't do it." The killer thought Jack was talking to him, but his eyes were focused on the shadow behind him.

Rick knew Jack was telling him not to attack, but he also knew he had no choice. It was either save his brother and Jenny or die, whether from the killer's gun or the drugs he would take in abundance after Jack's death. Since there was no choice but death or saving Jack and Jenny, he knew what he had to do.

He thought back to his days in boot camp at Parris Island. He knew how to disarm a man, even if that man was aware of his opponent. This should be easier since the man standing in Jack and Jenny's bedroom obviously had no idea Rick was there. He had the added element of surprise on his side.

Without warning, Rick launched himself at the man, grabbed his wrist, and twisted with all his adrenalin-fueled strength. A muted shot burst from the gun, the bullet burying itself in the wall above Jack's head. Rick heard something in the man' wrist snap and the man yelled in pain, dropping the gun.

Rick's movements from beginning to end lasted no more than three seconds. He held the damaged wrist while Jack jumped out of bed and grabbed the gun from the floor.

Jenny grabbed the bedside phone and managed to dial 9-1-1 with her trembling fingers. When the operator answered, she said, "A man just tried to kill us."

Because the local police might have some officers who were still loyal to the Hicks brothers, she adamantly demanded that the sheriff's office respond instead of the Denton Police, telling the dispatcher that the situation was being handled and they were no longer in danger.

They brought the man into the living room, and Jack checked on Brinkley. He was relieved to find the dog in a deep sleep. Turning to the man who minutes before had meant to kill them, he asked, "What did you do to my dog?"

"Nothing."

Rick, holding the broken wrist, twisted it slightly.

"Aaahh! Okay! Okay! I just gave him a sedative. I sprayed it on top of the dry food this afternoon. He'll be fine in the morning."

"You came in this afternoon, too? Why?"

"To take care of the dog and learn my way around. Now, I'm not saying anything else."

Fifteen minutes later, the first deputy arrived, followed by two more ten minutes later.

By the time they left with the killer, who had only given a first name of Mark, the sun was beginning to come up.

Jack chuckled.

"What's so funny?" Rick asked. "I could use a laugh."

"Nothing really. It's just Jenny and I thought we'd be able to sleep in since it's Saturday."

39

Wednesday, June 17, 1992

When Jack's office phone rang, he almost let it go to his answering machine. He had decided to hire a secretary so he would no longer be required to answer the phone if nothing else, and when this call arrived, he was poring over the applications and placing them into two piles—interview and don't bother.

Deciding to set aside this task to answer, he lifted the receiver. "Jack Turner, Attorney-at-law."

A voice he recognized but couldn't place replied. "Mr. Turner?"

"Yes?"

"This is Danielle Wolford."

The wish he'd allowed the machine to answer seemed to double, but he feigned happiness to hear from her anyway. "Good morning, Ms. Wolford. How are you?"

"Not good. Tiffany's been arrested again."

He felt his heart sink. "I'm sorry to hear that."

"She needs a lawyer—again." The anger in her voice seemed to ooze from the earpiece like something alive.

"What has she been arrested for?"

"What else? Drugs. Cocaine again, but that's not all. She was high and did a snatch and grab at

Franklin Jewelers in Wharton. Ran off with a stupid gold chain necklace with a diamond. I guess she planned to hock it for drug money."

Jack hung his head. She had promised she would clean up her life. Of course, Tiffany was young and not the best at making decisions, but it was painful watching her make the worst decisions.

"Is she out on bail?"

"No. I told her to rot in there."

Jack wanted to explain that such a response was not helpful but knew his words would be ignored.

Ms. Wolford continued. "Since Keith's gone, money ain't exactly plentiful around here."

"How much was the bail?"

"Ten-thousand. Might as well be ten million."

He knew Tiffany had turned eighteen recently and would no longer be subject to the benefits of being a minor in the justice system. She would be interacting with older women who could be a further bad influence. He had the money to pay a bail bondsman, but he wasn't sure he should. It was entirely possible that her mother didn't want her home, so she'd basically be out on the streets, probably committing more crimes to survive.

"I'm not cheap either, Ms. Wolford," he said.

"Yeah, well, I was hopin' you'd sort of do it for old times' sake."

"You want me to take the case *pro bono*?

"What does that mean?"

"It means I take the case and don't charge you anything."

"Yeah, that's what I was hopin'."

He thought about it for a moment and made a decision.

"I'll represent her for a hundred dollars, but I won't go to court. She's going to have to plead. I can get her the best deal I can, but it won't be easy since she's on probation for the other charge."

"Whatever. Just tell her she can't come here if they let her out. I won't have her staying here to bring coke into the house and put me in jeopardy of getting arrested. She's eighteen now, so she can take care of herself."

Jack didn't point out the fact she'd been dating a man who was dealing cocaine and had even supplied her daughter with a couple of grams as payment for selling it. Nor did he mention that Tiffany had been doing a terrible job of taking care of herself.

Instead, he asked, "She's in jail in Wharton?"

"Yeah."

"Can you come by to sign the paperwork and pay me the hundred?"

Ms. Wolford heaved a sigh as if coming by was the biggest inconvenience of the past month. "Okay, but I can't be there until 5:30. I'm at work. We have to make it fast, so could you have the papers ready when I get there? I need to grab a bite before going to my evening job. I had to take another job as a cocktail waitress at The Blue Whale."

Jack recognized the name of a seedy bar that had opened a year ago on Sugar Isle.

"I'll have the papers ready for you to sign. Just bring a hundred dollars in cash with you." He wanted to avoid the possible bounced check.

"Cash? I'll have to stop at the bank for that!"

"Sorry, but that's what you'll have to do."

"Jeez. Fine. I'll see you at 5:40 then."

"Thank you. See you then." He hung up, happy to end the call.

Ms. Wolford arrived like a tidal wave at 5:47. "The bank took longer than I thought. I'll need to grab fast food now," she complained.

After signing the papers and handing over the cash, she left, calling over her shoulder, "Be sure to tell Tiffany she's gotta take care of herself now."

As she walked out, it occurred to Jack that she was actually a worse mother than his own had been. His mother was an alcoholic, so her disease prevented her from being a good mother to him. Once he'd reached puberty, she had more or less barely interacted with him. It hadn't been a willful abandonment, but one created by the need to get intoxicated. Perhaps she had recognized that just being in the house was all she could do for him.

Ms. Wolford, however, was like a poison to her daughter. Her selfish desires were more from her own narcissism than from a physical need for something that kept her from being a good mother. Jack's mother had never been willfully cruel. He couldn't say that about Danielle Wolford.

He called home to let Jenny know he was going to talk to a new client in Wharton and would be home late, probably around eight that evening.

"That's fine. Get home when you can. I'll keep your dinner warm."

Hanging up, he left to visit Tiffany in jail.

When he arrived at the jail in Wharton, he was

checked in and settled into a chair in one of the interview rooms. Tiffany entered moments later and was handcuffed to the table there. She had lost weight—weight she couldn't afford to lose in the first place. Her appearance reminded him of the day he found Bones, though she certainly was not as thin as he'd been.

"What are you doing here?" she asked, as if she was at a friend's house instead of in need of an attorney.

"Your mother hired me to represent you."

"She's actually spending money on me?"

"I take it your relationship with her is not going well?" he asked, feeling like a lawyer for asking a question he already knew the answer to.

"You could say that. The one and only time she visited me here was to tell me she wouldn't be visiting me anymore."

"Tiffany, I'd prefer we talk about your case. It doesn't look good for you, what with being on probation for possession already."

"Yeah, sorry about that," she said. "It's just that being high is better than being around the woman who gave me birth."

"Why didn't you call me? Perhaps I could have done something."

"You'd done enough already. More than she ever did for me."

Again, Jack tried to steer the conversation away from Tiffany's home life.

"I think we should try to get a plea deal."

"Yeah, whatever. Plea deals seem to be what my life was meant for."

He stared at her for a moment, realizing they had to talk about her life situation whether he wanted to or not.

"Tiffany?"

"Yeah?"

"There's something I never asked you, mostly because I felt it wasn't any of my business."

"What's that?"

"Where's your father?"

"How do I know? He got my mom pregnant and disappeared. I don't even know his name."

"Your mother never even told you that?"

"How could she? She didn't know it either. She got drunk at some party and ended up getting knocked up by one of the guys that had sex with her that night. She blamed me for looking like her and making it where she couldn't even figure out who my dad was from my looks."

"I'm sorry."

"Why? You're not my dad."

"No, I'm sorry that happened to you." He couldn't help adding, "She should have been a better mother to you."

"Yeah, well, she wasn't. Any other questions?"

He leaned forward and made sure she was looking into his eyes. When she was, he said, "You deserve better."

Tears welled and slid onto her cheeks. She leaned her head down to her shoulder and wiped her eyes on her sleeve. Finally, she said, "Maybe, but it didn't work out that way, did it?"

"I tried to save you from yourself and your situation. I had hoped that keeping you out of prison would allow you to get a new start in life."

"Yeah, well—you can't save everyone."

"Doesn't stop me from trying."

Leaving the jail, he went home for a dinner that should have been delicious but wasn't.

"What's wrong?" Jenny asked.

"Tiffany Wolford was arrested again. Cocaine possession and a snatch and grab at a jewelry store. She's going to prison after all."

She pulled him to her and held him while he cried.

The next day, he stopped in at the DA's office in Wharton and spoke to Zeke Ward. When he'd left, he'd talked Zeke into a ten month sentence in a minimum security prison for women, which was far better than he'd hoped she would receive.

Zeke ended the conversation with, "This is the last time, though. You've used up the goodwill built from helping get Keith Breslin off the streets."

Jack smiled and said, "What about ending the drug ring operated out of the Denton Police Station?"

"I guess we'll have to see about that one. I can't keep giving your clients less than they deserve."

"She's just a kid, Zeke. She's eighteen, but her emotional maturity has been stifled by her mother. Her life has been a living Hell."

Zeke shook his hand in parting and said, "That pretty well sums up most of the people in prison, Jack. She needs to find a path out of Hell, I guess, but don't hold your breath. Most people living in Hell stay there."

"Why do you think they do that?"

Zeke shrugged. "Because it's the only place they know."

He vowed to Tiffany when he saw her that he would still be her friend and would visit her, which he could do as her attorney. She gave him a hug before being led off to prison and said, "Thank you."

As she was led away, he wondered if she would ever find her way out of Hell.

He had told her about his brother and how he was getting his life together by going to rehab in the hopes it would inspire her to do the same. He had tried to assure her that all was not lost and never was as long as she didn't give up. She just had to realize she did indeed deserve better.

Several months later, on November 3, he heard Tiffany Wolford had hanged herself in her cell the night before. He had visited her on August 1 to check on her, which he tried to do on the first day of each month. She had seemed happier, less depressed. He had wondered before that visit if she might try to kill herself, but after she seemed happier, he felt maybe she had turned a corner in her despondency. Now he realized that the corner she had turned was that she had made a decision about ending her life. Her death was an unexpected punch in the stomach but harder to get over. The news was as sudden as lightning and reminded him how often people make this choice without warning. It was one sentence that couldn't be overturned once it had been carried out. It was a decision that people so despondent as to take their own lives could never regret or rescind. The finality was its own horror.

Her suicide reminded Jack of the daughter of the man named Mitch. Mitch had once worked with his father at Kirby's, and the daughter had stabbed her father before hanging herself in her jail cell. Such a waste of life happening twice to people he knew was profane. He wondered what he could have done to change the outcome of Tiffany's life, but was at a loss as to what it might have been. Still, it troubled him, and would for years.

He attended Tiffany's funeral along with Jenny, Chuck, Trisha, and Tom. Nobody else was there, not even her mother, Danielle Wolford. Jack gave a eulogy, doing his best to paint her as a beautiful young lady who had suffered too greatly to realize how beautiful she was. Sadly, it was a eulogy that could have been given for millions of people. The entire time he spoke, he felt he was inadequate to speak for her life. Someone from her family should have been there to send her on.

When he spoke to Mrs. Dawson about this, she said, "For some people, their family is not what the world would think it should be. We are Tiffany's family now. It may not be right, but it will have to do."

This reminded him of his own childhood, and he wept bitterly that he should have been so fortunate as to have found his true family while Tiffany hadn't.

He considered how family was a fluid thing. Rick was his brother, but he went decades without seeing or hearing from him. Ms. Dawson, the Sheltons, and Hank had been much more his family than anyone else had. His dogs had been like brothers. That Tiffany had never found a true family to love her was a testament to the need for everyone to have someone love them. Life was too precious to be cast aside since the future could hold such tremendous beauty.

If he'd learned nothing else in life, he'd learned that he was the forger of his own destiny. He would teach his children that basic fact, that life is what we make it.

He wished he'd been able to teach that to Tiffany. It was too late for her, but for every Tiffany a thousand others suffered through life. Perhaps he could form a discussion group for teens, give them a place to be themselves and talk about their plans and how to achieve them. All they would need was a guide who understood their plight.

Regardless of his childhood, life had turned out well. He felt as if he were floating on the wide Gulf of Mexico and anything was possible, even love.

40

Saturday, September 19, 1993

Almost a year later, Jack stood at the altar of the church, dressed uncomfortably in a Carolina blue tuxedo. Rick stood beside him as best man, with Chuck and Tom to Rick's right. As he stood waiting for his bride to come down the aisle, several past incidents ran through his mind.

The first was his first encounter with the young bully Tommy Gordon at the docks when Jack was not yet thirteen. On that day and many since, Jack would have believed the craziest, most unlikely statement to ever be uttered would have been, "Tommy Gordon will be one of the groomsmen at your wedding." It ranked up there with "Pigs will sprout wings tomorrow and fly."

Yet here they all were. Tom Gordon was now one of his friends, having cleaned up his life, proving to Jack that even later in life, destiny could be shaped. Tom had changed who he was in almost every way. Now, he stood as proof that life was more unpredictable than anything else in the universe, and that any life could be changed with love. Redemption was always possible, even for what was once the worst people. Of course, some of the bullies from his childhood—namely the Hicks brothers—had turned out just as he thought they would, but Tom Gordon turned out to be a complete surprise, and Jack was thankful for that.

Jack was also pleased that Tom had started seeing Sadie again. He hoped this time it would all work out. Now, Tom looked to Jack as a mentor, seeking advice on living his life. Tom also attended church each Sunday, and the change in him was amazing. He had gone from Jack's worst enemy as a child to a caring friend.

These things reminded Jack once again that life is a strange path, like the road wash in his childhood where he floated twigs for fun. Like those sudden waterways, life was filled with debris that could alter life's course, and only the lucky ones made it to their dreams. Along the way, the paths would turn and twist, leading people to places they never thought they would be. It was up to him, as it was up to everyone, to fight against the debris that wanted to hold him back.

He thought of Chuck, who would make a great state legislator if he won the election, which he was expected to do since he led his competitor by nearly twenty points in all the polls. Chuck and Trisha had been people he looked up to in many ways, but especially regarding the jobs they held and how they could help people in that capacity. Trisha's becoming a judge suited her talents and personality perfectly. The two had shaped his life in ways they would never understand—in ways even he might never understand.

Mrs. Dawson and Jerry Moreland sat together in the front pew on the groom's side of the gathering, along with Trisha. Mrs. Dawson represented his mother, and Jerry was a stand-in for the man who would have represented Jack's father if he were alive. Jack missed Hank and wished he had lived long enough to be here. He knew Hank would have loved Jenny, and she would have returned that love.

Because Rick and Chuck were in the wedding party, Ms. Dawson, Jerry, and Trisha were the only ones seated in the honored "groom's family" section of the congregation, along with Brinkley, who was there because Jack had insisted.

Mrs. Dawson was already crying, but as she had told him a week before, it was her right to cry at weddings, especially his, so he shouldn't bother trying to keep her from expressing her happiness in that way. It was obvious that Trisha Shelton would be joining her very soon.

As his mind wandered in those seconds, he recalled his decision to propose to Jenny and how that had played out. He had chosen a day at the beach to ask her, July 10. It had been a Friday, and he'd talked her into taking the day off and going to the beach for a day of relaxation. Now, the scene played in his mind like a favorite TV show episode....

Jack looked over at Jenny, whose body glistened with sunscreen. She was lying on her back, getting some sun and obviously enjoying the day. They had gone by The Oyster Shack in Denton for lunch before coming across the Denton Bridge to have fun at the beach. She wore dark sunglasses, and he wondered if her eyes were open or closed.

He reached over and lifted the shades, exposing her closed eyes. She squinted up at him.

"What are you doing? That's too bright."

"Just wanted to see if you were asleep."

"Nope. At least, not yet."

"I have something to ask you," he said, trying for nonchalance and finding apprehension instead. Jenny seemed oblivious to either.

"What?"

"Sit up."

She looked at him and smiled. "What is this about?"

"Just sit up. I have a question. It concerns what you want to do for the rest of the day." Jack didn't mention it also had to do with the rest of their lives.

She sat up and brushed some sand from her arms, a difficult task given the sunscreen acted like a sticky sand magnet.

She turned to him and sat with her legs drawn under her.

"No, stand up a second."

"What?"

"I want to go for a walk on the beach. You can help me up."

"Okay," she said, standing and reaching out with her right hand.

"You may need both hands," he said.

"You're not an invalid," she said as she reached out with her left hand as well. Jack took it, rising to one knee.

He could see an understanding of what was happening slowly dawn on her. Her mouth dropped open and her eyes teared up. Her right hand, which he no longer held, went to her mouth. He wondered if her heart was pounding as hard as his was.

"Jenny, I'll never know what powers of the universe led us to meet, but I am immeasurably glad they did. Since our first lunch together at Perry's, my life has felt more complete than it ever did before. I cannot see my life without you, and I want to make that permanent. You are everything to me. Will you marry me?"

At first, she said nothing, only nodded vigorously before holding out her arms to him and shouting, "YES!" He stood and they enfolded each other in a mutual embrace of love and longing.

They had spent the rest of the day choosing a date and making plans. When they arrived home, they called everyone they knew. Jenny's parents were especially happy.

Waiting for Jenny to enter the church, Jack now considered his brother, Rick, who had been through a nearly constant beating at the hands of life. His addiction had basically been all he had to depend on. Now, he was clean and gaining weight for the first time in years.

He had completed his inpatient drug rehab program, but instead of moving back to Lutz, he had talked Jasmine into moving to Denton instead, telling Jack that staying there would probably be a healthier choice.

Rick now worked for Jerry Moreland, and Jack considered the circular nature of life since he himself had worked for Jerry as a young teenager. Jack had hired Jasmine as his secretary when the first one he hired, a military wife, quit when her husband was transferred. Jasmine could type, though not fast, but she was working on improving her speed and learning the job.

Word had spread that Jack Turner was one of the best defense attorneys in the area, and his client list had grown in the past few months. He still didn't need the money to pay his bills, but the work kept him busy, and he liked that. He was also able to do some *pro bono* work when the opportunity to help someone in need arose. He always did that in memory of Tiffany Wolford. He had even started a college scholarship in her name that year, The Tiffany Wolford Memorial Scholarship. He hoped it was a fitting tribute. The first recipient, a young lady who had come from a broken home, was attending Florida State as a freshman, and her future looked bright—or at least brighter than it had.

As the music changed to the song Jenny had chosen as her wedding march, Jack's attention was drawn to the far end of the nave. When he saw Jenny, his breathing stopped for a moment as time itself seemed to stand still.

She was naturally beautiful, but in her bridal gown, her beauty was stunning. He heard the small gasp from those in attendance, and he beamed at the woman who in a few moments would become his wife and an equal partner in his life.

He took his own role as her partner seriously. He knew he might disappoint her at times in the coming years, but he would do what he could to never totally let her down. It was a promise he made to himself that he would do everything in his power to keep.

Jenny's father was beside her, beaming as he strode down the aisle. Jack and his new in-laws had hit it off perfectly. Jenny's mother had hugged him when they first met, and her affection for what she now called "my fourth son" could light a house.

Jenny's father had hugged him the first time they'd met as well and more or less welcomed him to their family. They had sat up talking until late the night they'd met, and everyone felt at home with each other. Jenny's father was particularly happy to meet Rick since he had contributed to finding him.

Jack had also hit it off with his new brothers-in-law. One, Dustin, was Jack's age, and they had bonded over chess. Dustin was a master at the game, so he'd beaten Jack the few times they had a played, but Jack had learned a lot from losing to him, and their bond had grown strong.

As Jenny took her place beside him, Jack turned to face the minister conducting the service. When he began with the words, "Dearly beloved," Jack had a momentary understanding of the full import of that phrase. They were all dear to him and beloved. The aptness of the phrase had never occurred to him before. Now its meaning became clear.

As the ceremony continued to its final blessing, Jack knew the full extent of how lucky he was. Time had moved on, and despite its twists and turns, he had come out fine. The best part was everyone at the wedding had joined him on that journey like twigs floating past the debris in the road wash to float in the wide Gulf of Mexico.

ABOUT THE AUTHOR

Charles Tabb is an award-winning author whose short stories have appeared in various literary journals. His other literary novels, *Floating Twigs* and *Canaries' Song*, are available through Amazon. He lives with his wife, two horses, and two dogs near Richmond, Virginia. When he is not writing, he enjoys traveling, visiting with friends and family, and reading.

If you enjoyed this book, please write a short review on Amazon and/or Goodreads. They are greatly appreciated by the author and potential readers.

You may find more about Charles by going to his website, charlestabb.com, where you can sign up for his monthly newsletter or just enjoy browsing his website. An accomplished speaker, he is also available for speaking engagements, often at no charge, either in person or virtually. He can be reached by visiting his website at charlestabb.com and clicking "CONTACT" in the top banner.

Made in the USA
Monee, IL
11 November 2024

69839726R00236